To My Marine
Julio !

Semper Fi !

BLOOD
OF
BELVIDERE

A Grenada Novel

Semper Fi !

Dunbar Campbell

ISBN-13: 9781492999249
ISBN-10: 1492999245

ACKNOWLEDGEMENTS

I am thankful to many, whose ideas, suggestions, and inspiration contributed to this novel. However, I am especially grateful to my critiquing partners, Joan Upton Hall, Sylvia Dickey Smith, and Joy Nord for their many hours of generous discussions and thoughtful editing. It could not have gotten this far without you. Insightful conversations with Ashley Steele and valuable scholarly research by Dr. Curtis Jacobs helped shape this story. Ann Wilder's long distance encouragement is still appreciated. Thomas and Julieta von Schimonsky, those Saturday mornings with you at Central Market helped breathe life into the concept. David Martinez and Jessica Steele, your incessant questions about the story helped keep it on track. Jerry Hagins, those early discussions anchored the idea that the story was worth telling. Steve Nichols, Rob Smith, and Brad, your military knowledge and Grenada experience added new perspectives. Russell and others, despite the different uniforms we wore, friendships survived. I will always remember the people of Gouyave, friends and family, who made my earliest memories some of my most treasured. Finally, my deepest appreciation goes to my wife, Susie, and daughters Malia and Crystal for their boundless encouragement and patience, especially during the long hours I spent alone with my computer, 'Betsy'.

Life travels upward in spirals.
Those who take pains to search the shadows
of the past below us, then, can better judge the
tiny arc up which they climb,
more surely guess the dim
curves of the future above them.

—Rich Gibson

Inspired by historical events

PROLOGUE

Mount Qua Qua, Grenada
Quarter past six in the evening
The 19th Day of June in the Year of our Lord, 1796

General Archibald McDonald stood beside the flaming torch at the doorway, his shadow stretching across the mud floor to an untidy stack of blood-stained machetes. Behind him, urgent winds howled through towering mahogany trees. He marched into the windowless room, past the blades and rumpled flags of the French Revolutionary Army. Straight ahead, on a table in the middle of the room, a bottle of sugarcane rum awaited him. The rum burned its way down his throat, its fumes chasing away the stench of death that choked the room and soiled his breath. Less than an hour ago, his archenemy had stood in this very rat hole. A man he had never seen, but who had wreaked terror across the island for the past year.

A gust scattered hand-scrawled maps to the floor, reminding him of the dispatch he needed to write before nightfall. He pulled up a creaky chair, unfurled a blank sheet of paper from his red coat, and began to write with the pen and ink his colonel left on the table for him.

> "*Your Excellency,*
> *We are yet to capture the traitor Fédon, but it is with great satisfaction that I acquaint you with news of victory. We have crushed the rebellion that pained the King's colony of Grenada these past months. It will afford your Excellency no small measure of pride to behold the courage of the militia and their gallant officers, with their resolute determination to defeat the savagery of these misguided Negroes and their Free Coloured leaders. There is no Godly way for Fédon to escape. We have*

this peak completely surrounded with enough lead and powder to render his carcass unfit for animal consumption.

On reaching the camp an hour ago a most distressing spectacle awaited us: upwards of twenty prisoners, stripped, with their hands tied behind their backs, having but recently been murdered in the most barbarous manner. The wretches held prisoner on this summit tonight will suffer the same fate to send a clear message across this island.

Given at Mount Qua Qua this nineteenth day of June, in the year of our Lord one thousand seven hundred and ninety-six and in the thirty sixth year of Our Reign.

God save the King!

General Archibald McDonald.

Brigadier-General of the Twenty-Fifth Regiment."

"Colonel!" General McDonald called out.

"Yes, sir." A tall officer in red coat and white blood-spattered pantaloons stepped into the room.

"Colonel, assign our fastest rider to deliver this message to the governor in St. George's forthwith." He handed the sealed letter to the colonel. "He needs to know of our victory before he retires to bed. If we find Fédon after nightfall, we will inform the governor in the morning dispatch."

"Immediately, sir."

"Any sign of the captain and his search party yet?"

"They should return any time now, General."

"Make sure he reports to me as soon as he arrives."

"Yes, sir." The colonel stepped out, the letter clutched in his hand.

Almighty God works in mysterious ways. General McDonald reflected on his years of humble service to King George. The general expected that with the American colonies lost, he had also lost his chance to secure a place among the new landed aristocracy in the British Empire. The stinging humiliation at Yorktown inspired a deep hatred for the French and American Revolutionaries, but it did not shake his faith in King George.

The general continued in loyal service these past fifteen years and now he awaited his rewards with gleeful anticipation. In this one expedition, he had gotten his revenge against the French and secured a magnificent estate, lavish in its promise of colonial status and wealth. He accepted, with hearty appreciation, his Excellency's offer to take ownership of Fédon's Belvidere Estate. Like the Governor, he too believed that the permanent station of a King's General in the heart of this bountiful island, would remind the slave subjects that their loyalties belong to King George, rather than to the French Republicans. In his new role, the general would tolerate no more rebellions in Grenada. In the name of the King, he intended to extract absolute obedience from all subjects. He planned for swift punishment to follow every hint of disobedience.

If his troops did not find Fédon tonight, the general planned to add from his own purse, one hundred pounds to the reward on the rebel's head, whether dead or alive. Fédon's only escape might come from a death leap off the precipice to his cowardly end, like some of his savages had already done.

After tonight, all that remained for General McDonald to add the status of gentry to his rank of general was to have his wife and three younger sons in England join him on his Belvidere Estate. His eldest son was already here with him in Grenada, serving the King as a captain in the Twenty-Fifth Regiment.

Horses trotted to a halt outside the hut. The general turned at the approaching sounds of metallic clinks and boot steps. A captain snapped to attention at the doorway, sweat dripping off his face and onto his grubby red coat. The captain's youth glowed beneath his black round hat and kindled a sense of pride in the general. The young man's blue eyes held an intensity that only came when one exerted his energies in battle for the King.

"Search patrol reporting back, sir," the captain reported.

"Come in, Captain. Did you find Fédon?"

"No, sir. He is not with the dead we found at the foot of the cliffs. He must still be up here among the prisoners."

"Let us go find out." General McDonald stood and adjusted his red waistcoat, crossed at the chest with white leather belts. Gold epaulettes hung at the shoulders. His black top boots crunched on the dirt floor as he headed for the doorway. "Bring along one of those machetes. The sharpest you can find."

The captain hesitated.

"Make haste, Captain. This is not over until we find Fédon."

The captain picked up a machete and followed the general into the misty twilight. Steady winds moaned through the trees. Beneath a nearby tree, about thirty rebel prisoners lay huddled in a pile of human misery. Loyal Black Rangers, barefooted Africans in red coats and blue trousers, stood guard holding muskets fixed with bayonets.

"Bring me that boy." The general pointed at a young rebel prisoner, no more than sixteen, dressed in a tattered pair of trousers, his hands bound at his back. Dried blood caked one side of his head and his sweaty black skin glistened in the light of flaming torches.

An African ranger walked over and prodded the young prisoner with his bayonet.

The boy struggled to his feet in obvious pain and limped ahead of the guard towards the general. He lowered his head and fixed his gaze on the general's boots.

The general barked. "Where is Fédon?"

The boy held his slumped posture in silence.

"Tell me where your leader is hiding, boy, and you're all free to be slaves again."

The boy looked up slowly and nodded at the remaining prisoners. "They go too, *oui?*"

"Yes," the general shouted. "All of you can go. But speak before I change my mind."

The boy glanced at the general and the captain with a meek grin. "You look father and son."

"I am losing my patience, boy."

"I tell you, and you promise we free go?"

The general stomped his boot and hissed. "Yes, that is what I said."

"Winds." The boy stared up in wide-eyed wonder at the cluster of swaying trees. "Winds…winds take Fédon. Fédon fly in wind."

"What in the name of King George is this savage mumbling about?"

"Sir," said the captain. "They have all been saying that. Something about Fédon disappearing in the winds."

"What African superstitious rubbish. I have heard enough. Off with his head, Captain."

"But you said—"

"Just do as you are ordered."

"But sir, must I act contrary to my passions?"

"Your only passions are to King and Country, son."

The guard slammed the butt of his musket on young rebel's back and knocked him to his knees in front of the general.

Tears streamed down the boy's cheeks. "You lie. Fédon punish all of you."

The general moved back three paces. "Off with his head, Captain, or you will face a court martial."

The captain held the machete stiffly at his leg. "But Father, you—"

The boy stared up at the captain. "Fédon will pain you and all your kind many years. Winds come back with Fédon—"

"Captain," the general yelled. "This is your last chance. Off with his head, now!"

The captain stepped forward with a full swing of the machete. The boy's torso tumbled over in a spray of blood and the severed head rolled to a stop at the general's boots.

The captain's hands shook in their grip on the machete.

"Control your nerves, son. It is going to be a long night." The general turned to the colonel. "Pass this order down the ranks. By the powers granted me by His Excellency the Governor, anyone heard in superstitious utterances about Fédon and winds shall pay with the loss of their heads."

"Yes, sir." The colonel saluted and marched off.

General McDonald turned to the guard. "Bring me another prisoner!"

PART I

CHAPTER ONE

The coastal town of Gouyave
Grenada
26 July 1963

Eight-year-old Scott McDonald awoke in the middle of the night to the front door creaking open in his aunt's stuffy house, cramped with luggage that had accompanied his family on their flight from Aruba a week ago.

Daddy mumbled in the darkness. Probably returning home drunk with his sister, Aunty Bridgette, after visiting friends he hadn't seen during his long absence from Grenada.

The wooden floor groaned and Aunty Bridgette whispered. "Watch the suitcases. I'll get the lamp."

The strike of a match and the whiff of burning kerosene reminded Scott that the airplane had taken them far away from the oil refineries and electric lights of Aruba to the fishing boats and lamplights of Grenada's coastal countryside. He'd worried about what his new island home held in store but those concerns eased during the past few days.

After the flat cacti-covered dryness of Aruba, Grenada's mountainous greenery delighted him with its raw life. The Grenada people tantalized his imagination with bright smiles and musical words. Barefoot children played in dusty yards. Skinny dogs chased cars. Plumes of smoke danced from outdoor coal pots and seasoned the air with spicy flavors. Thick aromas of fruits sweetened his breath. Even the sea smelled delicious. Scott and his brother sprinted along white-sand beaches and climbed the bountiful trees to steal mangoes. The boys embellished the plunders, rubbing their full tummies and plucking mango strings from between their teeth to entertain their sisters.

Each day's stimulation made sleep easy by nightfall.

Awake now, Scott stared up at the yellow light seeping through the opening above the bedroom door.

Chairs scratched the wooden floor in the kitchen and Daddy slurred. "Pass me . . . the bottle."

"Just one more, you've had enough tonight," Aunty Bridgette said. "Finish telling me what happened in Belvidere."

"I didn't think he would..." The clink of glasses sliced his words, and opened the way for sighs that always followed his rum shots. "When . . . there was blood . . . everywhere."

The jumbled murmurs aroused Scott's curiosity. Risking painful welts across his backside if caught eavesdropping, he nestled against the bedroom wall and hugged his pillow as he waited for the conversation to resume.

Daddy's words became clearer. "He saw me holding the gun."

Scott pressed his ear against the wall.

"There was blood everywhere." Daddy moaned.

Scott smothered his gasp with the pillow.

"It's all in the past now," Aunty Bridgette said. "Twenty years ago."

Did Daddy murder someone twenty years ago? Tremors rumbled across Scott's mind.

"How's that boy . . . ?" Daddy's question dangled in the brief silence.

"You mean Junior? He's in Richmond Hill Prison. Almost chopped off a prostitute's hand with a cutlass, going for her head."

"Damn."

"That night on Belvidere Estate changed him. Drinking, fighting, in and out of jail since he was fifteen. They nicknamed him Planass."

"Planass?" Daddy asked.

"You've been away too long. Yes, from the French *plan asséner* for beating people with the flat side of his cutlass."

"Maybe I made . . . made a mistake by coming back."

"Don't give up yet," she said. "Just keep Scott and Rodney off the streets. When Planass gets out of prison, he might go after them too."

Daddy groaned. "Let's get some sleep."

The lamplight faded. Doors opened and shut.

The silent darkness blanketed Scott again, but this time the sound of his pounding heart kept him awake.

***

The next afternoon, Scott sat on Aunty Bridgette's garden wall with Rodney, his older brother by two years. Scott stared at the old green-roofed Anglican Church across the street, wishing for a sign telling him if he should say anything about the conversation he'd heard the night before.

"You're quiet," Rodney said, his narrow face and straight nose a boyish image of Daddy.

"Sleepy. A nightmare kept me awake last night."

Maybe last night's exchange between Daddy and Aunty Bridgette had been just that—a bad dream. Nothing to upset Rodney about, especially since he would be angry with Scott for being nosy.

But Rodney had said brothers never kept secrets from each other. Like the time he confided in Scott how much he hated it when people said he looked like Daddy. And Rodney shared more than secrets. Just a few days ago, as they approached Pearls Airport on the bumpy plane ride from Aruba, he shifted in his tattered window seat to let Scott view the lush mountains and valleys below. Rivers raced down deep ravines, and waterfalls gushed from steep mountainsides like water pouring from giant jugs. Clusters of metal-roofed houses looked like storybook hamlets glued to green hillsides, and belts of white sand stretched for miles along the blue sea.

At that moment, the sound of propellers roaring in his ears, Scott had looked forward to sharing Grenada moments with Rodney. But now, those wishes dimmed under last night's whispers.

Daddy might be a murderer.

Despair clawed at Scott's stomach, even in the presence of the church across the street. Looking for a distraction, he glanced up at the steeple that watched over Gouyave.

His parents had talked so much about Gouyave, which they pronounced like *guava* without the last letter, it seemed he'd been here all his life. An old proud town where hurricane lanterns lit the streets and kerosene lamps graced homes at night. Gouyave's pride balanced on having the most fishing boats on the island and spawning the strangest tales.

Scott's relief finally came with the thought that maybe what he'd heard last night was just another Gouyave story, so he turned his attention to the street traffic. Buses rumbled by, blaring horns and belching smoke, their wooden benches crowded with chattering passengers and overflowing burlap bags.

An old man smiled and waved as he rode past on a donkey.

Just then, a barefoot boy in khaki shorts and ragged Coca-Cola t-shirt swaggered up with a blade of grass hanging from his lips. His dimples brightened the grin on his dark face, and his words flowed in highs and lows like the island's mountains and valleys.

"Aruba you from, right?" he asked.

"Yeah," Scott said. "What's your name?"

"Martin."

"How did you know we're from Aruba?" Rodney asked.

Martin sat on the wall next to Scott. "You grandmother tell me."

Scott's grandmother, Ma, stout and dark with silver hair, had cried when she cuddled her Aruba grandchildren for the first time at the airport. He wondered how Ma's hugs and soft smiles could have mothered Aunty Bridgette, a stocky brown woman with stern glances and piercing green eyes.

Martin twirled the blade of grass in his mouth and spat in the street. "All you whitey like you cousins and them in Belvidere Estate, *oui.*"

The new mix of words, flowing almost in musical tones, fascinated Scott.

"We're not white," Rodney said.

Martin rolled his bright eyes and made a sucking sound with his chalk-white teeth. "Brown, red, white, all same damn thing, *oui.* You meet them yet?"

"Not yet," Scott said.

"They live up in the bush," Martin said. "Too far."

The long distance to Belvidere was probably why Daddy's brothers hadn't visited yet. Maybe they would attend the welcome party Ma planned to hold in a few days.

Martin scratched his curly head of hair and pointed at the church. "Anybody show you the graveyard?"

"No," Rodney said.

"Best place to play cowboys and Indians." Martin swung his feet, with dried mud caked between his toes, and pulled a slingshot from his back pocket. "Town people say slingshot. In Gouyave, we say catapult."

Scott studied the catapult, a rough Y-shaped tree branch hacked to hand size, with two strips of red tubing fastened to the tops and linked by a piece of old shoe-leather.

"Leh we go." Martin leaped from the wall.

Scott glanced back at the house, recalling Aunty Bridgette's warning, with her stubby fingers aimed at him, that if she found him or Rodney in the church-yard, they would be flogged.

"Don't worry," Rodney said. "She left with Daddy this morning and won't be back till bedtime."

They sprinted across the street after Martin. His t-shirt flapped in the wind, the catapult dangled from his torn back pocket, and skin showed through the holes on the seat of his khaki shorts. He led the way through the open gateway and up concrete steps to a courtyard sweetened by flower blossoms. The sunset painted a red glow on the church windows.

Martin dropped to one knee on a brick walkway at the main doorway. "You must make the sign of the cross, or God will punish you."

Scott paused at the doorway and followed Martin's instructions. The empty church held a silence flooded with the fragrance of burning incense. A man-size crucifix hung against the back wall, held by huge nails protruding from bloodstained palms.

"Hurry up." Rodney's voice echoed down the walkway.

Scott caught up with them along a row of tombstones.

"Resting place for dead people." Martin stopped in front of a white tomb and pulled out his catapult. "If you walk on a grave, make the sign of the cross, else you body go rot and—"

Heavy footsteps clapped on the walkway.

"*Bonjai*," Martin whispered. "Somebody coming."

They darted behind concrete slabs. Scott trembled, afraid that his shaking knees might awaken the person sleeping beneath his feet. He made a quick sign of the cross.

The footsteps came closer, moved off to the grass, and then faded.

He peeked past the stone to the far side of the walkway. A man and a woman stooped at a gravesite in the shadow of a tree. The woman hugged the man, her head against his. The man placed a bouquet of flowers on the grave. He clasped his head, and sobs drifted in the steady breeze.

A few minutes later the couple stood and turned to leave.

Daddy and Aunty Bridgette.

"That was Daddy and Aunty Bridgette," Scott blurted out after the adults left the churchyard and disappeared across the street.

He led Rodney and Martin to the grave with the fresh flowers.

They read the white engravings on the gray marble: "Ruby Ferguson, Born 21 May 1923, Died 14 December 1940. Her baby Maria, Born 14 December 1940, Died 14 December 1940. May they both have everlasting peace."

"A mother and a baby in one grave?" Scott asked.

"*Bonjai,*" Martin said. "Same day too, *oui.*"

Rodney drew numbers in the dirt with a stick. "Ruby was seventeen years old. And the baby died the same day she was born."

"You ever heard Daddy talk about Ruby?" Scott asked.

"No. That's his business, not ours."

Maybe not Rodney's, but after last night, everything about Daddy was now Scott's business. Had Daddy shot Ruby and her baby? Maybe the shooting was an accident. Why else would he cry at their grave?

Martin led the way out the back gate to avoid Daddy and Aunty Bridgette. They passed the streetlight man as he pumped a lantern into a white glow, securing it to a curbside lamppost for the approaching night. In the distance, a pelican flew alone over the sea, bathed red in the mist of the dying sunset. Martin pointed up at a flock of pigeons returning to roost in the market rafters, but Scott felt his thoughts being summoned back to the graveyard. It no longer seemed a peaceful resting-place for the dead.

The graveyard had become a gatekeeper of old secrets that made men cry.

***

Three afternoons later, Scott stood on Ma's verandah and awaited the arrival of the Belvidere family to the reunion. Rodney threw sticks for Ma's dog in the yard, across the field from the weather-beaten Anglican school they were to attend in a few weeks. Scott's oldest sister, Claudette, giggled in a game of hopscotch on the platform below with their younger sister, Alicia, shiny pigtails hanging past their shoulders.

Inside, Daddy sat at the dining room table in low conversation with Aunty Bridgette while Mommy prepared a dish in the kitchen. Scott glanced back at Ma. She sat alone on the couch, in a checkered blue dress and white shoes, gazing up at her living room wall. Black-and-white family photos plastered the wall, around a large portrait of Queen Elizabeth II.

Scott worried that asking Ma about Ruby would betray his graveyard visit, so he thought of another question and sat next to her.

"Ma, what does *bonjai* and *oui* mean?"

"That's *patois*," she said. "Creole French, from the days when Grenada was French. *Oui* means yes and *bonjai* means good-God. Like when something surprising happens."

"Why do people here say that so often?"

"Because Gouyave full of surprises, me boy." Ma's laughter shook her bosom.

"Do your pictures have surprises too?" He swallowed hard and waited.

"Let's see." She held his hand and led him across creaky floors to the rows of pictures.

He pointed at a photo of a newlywed couple, a tall white man and a petite black girl, in front of a church. "She looks like you."

Ma chuckled and her gaze softened. "Seems like only yesterday me and your Pa married, 1919. God bless he soul. The same Anglican Church lightning burned down in 1899."

"Lightning?"

"Yes, they rebuilt it, but people still blame Fédon."

"Who's Fédon?"

"There's many Fédons, me boy."

She rubbed his head, and he inhaled her medicinal scent, probably from the white antiperspirant powder that streaked across her moist neck.

"There's the Fédon that people 'fraid," she said. "Then there's one they hate, and another they like. But you still too young to worry 'bout that."

Ma was right. Gouyave held many surprises.

She squinted, and tapped her finger on a picture of eight children and two adults. "Belvidere Estate, 1935. That's me and Pa. Aunty Bridgette, your Daddy, and Uncle Malcolm."

She named other faces, but none was Ruby. The old pictures of children playing on the lawns of Belvidere Estate seemed to echo with laughter long since silenced in Daddy and Aunty Bridgette.

Scott was about to ask Ma how Pa had died, but the sound of cars grinding onto the gravel driveway drew them to the verandah. Three cars pulled up, raising dust and scattering chickens.

Daddy and Aunty Bridgette went down the steps to the yard. Strapping brown-skinned men, with wavy hair and moustaches like Daddy's, stepped out of the cars and greeted him with back-slapping embraces.

All except the one with unruly hair and bloodshot eyes.

He stumbled up to Daddy and they shook hands without looking at each other.

"That's your Uncle Malcolm," Ma whispered to Scott.

Women with babies and children exited the cars to join the procession up the steps into Ma's house.

A few minutes later, Daddy's younger sister from St. George's, Aunty Hyacinth, pulled into the driveway with her chubby son, Oliver. Aunty Hyacinth, a slender copy of Aunty Bridgette with bright red lipstick and every strand of her beehive hairdo in place, strutted in heels up the steps and floated into the living room on a breeze of perfume.

Scott stood by the door, absorbing the deafening confusion of adult conversations and the playful screams of children. While Aunties Bridgette and Hyacinth managed the kitchen, Ma relaxed on the couch surrounded by her daughters-in-law filling creaky wicker chairs. She told humorous stories about raising her children in Belvidere and the women responded with applause and laughter.

Mommy, as plain as Aunty Hyacinth was flashy, sat with her hands in her lap and her legs crossed at the ankles. Scott immediately decided that Mommy, her smooth skin unblemished by makeup and her soft smile lipstick-free, was a better choice for a mother.

Daddy sat at the dining table with his brothers, drinking and talking while the melodies of Harry Belafonte, Mighty Sparrow, and Nat King-Cole flowed from a battery-powered phonograph.

Uncle Malcolm sat at the head of the table, staring at the glass in his hand.

Scott's stomach grumbled eager approval at the spicy aroma coming from the kitchen, especially from a Grenada dish Ma had started earlier. Her pot of mouthwatering *oildown* simmered with coconut milk, salted pork, chicken, dumplings, and chunks of breadfruit, the green rough-skinned fruits that came from huge trees in Ma's backyard. She had explained that the dish earned the name *oildown* because the ingredients, flavored with herbs and spices, absorbed the coconut milk, leaving only coconut oil at the bottom of the pot.

When Aunties Hyacinth and Bridgette added pots of curried goat and fish broth, Scott could no longer bear the temptation to sneak a bite. He headed down the steps to the yard and paused to pick up a water gun sitting on Aunty Hyacinth's shiny blue car.

"That's not yours!" Oliver's round face flushed in the late afternoon heat. He ran up and snatched the gun from Scott.

"Sorry, I didn't . . ."

Oliver turned and ran off.

Just then, angry shouts punctured by the sound of shattering glass exploded upstairs. Scott raced up the steps and bolted toward the shouting in the kitchen. Daddy and Uncle Malcolm stood glaring at each other. Pieces of broken bottle lay scattered in puddles across the floor. The scent of rum drenched the air.

Uncle Malcolm's face reddened. "Nobody wants you back in Grenada."

"Just keep Ruby's name out of your drunken mouth." Daddy's veins bulged on his neck.

"Pa would roll in his grave if he knew you still carried his name, you lying sonofabitch."

Scott flinched as Daddy punched Uncle Malcolm in the face, sending him stumbling against the wall. Uncle Malcolm wiped blood from his lip and charged at Daddy.

Daddy's other brothers wrestled the two men apart.

Ma stomped into the kitchen, kicking away broken glass.

"*Bonjai,* not Fédon again." Ignoring the danger to her feet, she pulled off one of her shoes and swung at Uncle Malcolm. "For your children's sake, leave the past buried."

Uncle Malcolm stormed out of the house with his family, and drove off.

At sunset, a dark cloud seemed to invade the house, dulling even the glow of the kerosene lamps hanging from the ceiling. The children still played in the shadows outside, but the jovial chatter between the adults dimmed to whispers bridged by gloomy silence.

Scott held Mommy's hand and glanced back at Ma on his way out the door after dinner. Ma sat alone, staring at her new shoes and wringing her hands.

Why would someone named Fédon burn down her church and lead her sons to fight each other?

On the wall behind Ma pictures smiled with happier memories from a place called Belvidere Estate.

***

When Scott walked out of Aunty Bridgette's house with Rodney the following Saturday morning, Martin was already seated on the wall facing the church.

He handed Scott and Rodney a catapult each. "I make them for you. All Gouyave boys have one."

"Thanks," Scott said.

Martin led them through several unsuccessful practice shots at birds in the trees. "Good, you learn fast. Now you ready to see Gouyave."

Scott stuck his catapult in his back pocket and followed Martin and Rodney along the stone walkway toward the coastline where fishing boats bobbed off-shore under white sheets of yelling seagulls. The main road choked with people in the midmorning heat and the market overflowed with a carnival of shoppers in straw hats, hair curlers, shawls, and undershirts. The verbal tug-of-war around tables stacked with rainbow colors of fruits and vegetables took on such a screaming pitch that Scott expected a fight at any moment.

He asked Martin about a raw odor thickening the air.

"They kill cows and pigs here every Friday night," Martin explained. "Next week we come see."

Martin led them away from the market square, past crowded shops and little houses with louvered windows overlooking sidewalks. He showed them the white police station and courthouse building overlooking the sea, and halted at a red iron bridge that spanned a rushing river.

"Brickie Hill." He pointed up at a hill that hung dangerously over houses balanced on skinny pillars. "Best place to fly kites, but Mr. Welsh live on the trail with a bad dog. He little boy fall off and dead. He only let old boys pass, fifteen or older."

Rodney tapped his chin. "Maybe there's another way—"

"Boy stop you *stupidness*." Martin sucked at his teeth and strutted to the other end of the bridge that opened onto a straight road about a half-mile long, crowded on both sides with more houses and shops.

"This is the Lance, where I from. A lot of *badjohns* live here." He explained that *badjohns* were men who drank and fought every day. "So stay with me."

Scott refrained from asking Martin if Planass had been a Lance *badjohn*, to avoid having to explain how he'd overheard the cutlass conversation between Daddy and Aunty Bridgette.

They strolled past small shops blaring calypso and country music. Bareback men sat around little tables next to boats in sandy yards, slamming dominoes and exploding in laughter. Others mended fishing nets under coconut trees in a lightning-speed dance of hands, twine, and giant wooden needles. Martin approached a group of boys tossing marbles in a clearing on the side of the road where clotheslines of sunbaked fish flavored the air.

He introduced Scott and Rodney. "Me friends from Aruba."

"You fish in Aruba?" one of the boys asked Rodney.

"No."

"But he could catch sea crabs," Scott said.

The boy laughed. "Crab just bait."

Another one twirled a blade of grass in his mouth and spat in the street. "Every Gouyave boy must have rod and line." He stared down at Scott's polished black leather shoes. "Leave them things home if you want to fish with us."

"Time to go." Martin waved at his friends and marched off down the street. "Matinee time. Gladiator film playing today."

Scott hurried to catch up with him. "Are we going to the movies?"

"Only if you have money."

"I have some." Rodney pulled a few coins from his pocket.

"Aruba money, look like shillings." Martin studied the coins, scratching his head. "Casa won't know the difference."

"Who?" Scott asked.

"Him." He pointed at a big man on a stool guarding the doorway of a green building across the street. "One of the baddest *badjohns*."

Several barefoot boys in worn shorts with catapults dangling from their pockets shuffled in a line to the door. They each handed Casa a coin and entered the theater.

"Follow me." Martin led the way across the street.

He joined the line and dropped three of the Aruba coins in Casa's hand.

Casa grabbed Martin by the arm and jerked him off his feet as if he were a rag doll. "Where you get that money?" Casa snarled, his silver tooth glittering.

Scott trembled, expecting to see *badjohn* Casa snap Martin in two.

"Them . . . them is Aruba money," Martin said. "Better than Grenada money."

"I know what money it is," Casa yelled. "Who you thief it from?"

Rodney stepped up to Casa. "I gave it to him."

Martin grinned in relief, stretched out his free arm, and hugged Rodney. "Me friends . . . *my* friends from Aruba. Rodney and Scott McDonald."

Casa squinted at Rodney. "You father name Hector?"

"Yes," Rodney said.

"Boy, you look like you father, *oui*."

Rodney glanced away.

"He back in Gouyave?"

"Yes."

"*Bonjai*, he brave to step foot in Gouyave again, *oui*." Casa sighed. "Tell him come have a drink with me in me rum shop next door. Go watch the movie, but don't let this little ragamuffin get you in trouble."

"I not no raga-whatever," Martin said.

"And don't make me throw you out again for talking."

Scott settled down between Rodney and Martin in the musty theater. Their wooden bench vibrated from an outside generator powering the projector and the screen came alive with muscular gladiators chopping off limbs and heads.

But Scott paid little attention. Questions careened through his mind, like the confused bats crisscrossing the glare of the projector light.

Had Casa said that Daddy was brave for returning because Gouyave had so many badjohns? Like Planass who chopped a woman, and Fédon who burned down a church with lightning and made brothers fight?

Scott elbowed Martin. "Ever heard of Fédon?"

"Boy, Fédon is the biggest, baddest, and oldest of all badjohns," Martin said. "Two hundred years old. Me grandmother say he ride a white horse, like a ghost."

"How can he live so long?"

"He mother teach him African magic."

"Shhh." Rodney rubbed Scott's head. "Casa coming."

Casa hurried past and disappeared through a side door.

As the movie slashed on, Scott found comfort in one thought. Nothing— not even Fédon's African magic—would make him hate Rodney the way Daddy and Uncle Malcolm hated each other.

CHAPTER TWO

A few days later, chickens scattered across Ma's dusty yard as Scott sprinted with Rodney and Martin through the gates and up the steps to her front door.

"Hello, me boys." Ma greeted them with a smile, her silver hair in tight braids drawn to a bun at the back of her head and the front of her green dress wet with perspiration.

"Ma, you know Martin?" Scott asked.

"Everybody know Martin." She gave them each a hug and led them into the living room. "Let me get you something to drink." She disappeared into the kitchen, the wooden floors complaining beneath her bare feet.

Scott collapsed in a rocking chair and settled under the cool sound of the river rushing behind the house. He glanced through the doorway and across the pasture to slices of blue sea peeking between coconut palms that waved over a field of metal roofs. Unlike Aruba, everything in Gouyave seemed within touch, and would probably feel even closer when they eventually moved into the house that Daddy was having repaired on the seashore.

Scott could hardly wait for the first note of crowing roosters that awakened the town every morning. With each passing day, Gouyave felt more like home, and Aruba a vanishing memory. Gouyave was more than just a place. It was a feeling. A feeling that fed Martin's carefree spirit as he roamed the streets in his rags like there was no other time or place in which to live. Scott wanted to be like Martin, but the swarm of questions about Daddy's family troubled him.

"Let's look at the pictures on the wall," Scott said to Martin.

While Rodney played with Ma's dog, Scott gazed up at the photos that Ma had not gotten around to show him at the family reunion.

Martin pointed at a house with tall pillars and wide steps in the background of one the family pictures. "*Bonjai*, that house big, *oui*."

Ma returned with glasses of lime juice sweetened with brown sugar. Scott gulped his drink, struggling with the desire to ask Ma if any of the girls in the picture was named Ruby.

Martin pointed at Pa. "He look like a white man, *oui*."

"Yeah, Scottish," Ma said. "His great great-grandfather came here as a British general."

Martin elbowed Scott. "See, I told you, you was white."

"But I am his grandmother, African, with black skin like yours," Ma said. "So what does that make him?"

Martin frowned, sipping his juice and studying Ma with bright eyes.

"What matters is the inside color." Ma pinched Martin's cheek. "Not the outside color."

"When did Pa die?" Scott asked.

"Too soon." She shuffled around the living room, pointing out photos, recalling dates and naming faces, but still, none named Ruby.

It puzzled Scott that both Pa and Ruby's deaths brought sadness to the family, but only Pa's pictures hung on the wall. Something didn't feel right about the way the family lost the inside colors that once gave them happiness.

Maybe the answer hid on Belvidere Estate, where Daddy planned to take them the next day.

✳✳✳

"Mosquitoes and sand flies will eat you alive in Belvidere," Mommy shouted at Scott the following day. "Leave those sleeves buttoned."

Scott frowned at his reflection in the mirror. He chuckled at the thought of Martin running around in black socks and leather shoes, the tails of his plaid shirt tucked into gray pants, cuffs buttoned at the wrists, and a scented cloud of insect spray protecting him.

Scott unbuttoned the cuffs and raced down the stairs to the waiting car.

Claudette sat up front with Daddy, while Scott and Rodney took the window seats in the back with Alicia between them. She wore a pleated yellow dress, and white stockings that Mommy insisted would keep away the mosquitoes.

"Where's Aunty Bridgette?" Claudette asked Daddy.

"Already in Belvidere." He drove up hills past little houses with smoke drifting from outdoor coal pots. "And don't worry. No fights today."

Scott leaned his head out the window and inhaled the fragrances of spice and guava blowing on a breeze that grew cooler around every corner. They drove across narrow bridges where children leaped into rushing rivers while women scrubbed clothes on sun-bleached rocks. Women balanced cocoa baskets on their heads, men rode donkeys, and boys led goats. Rolling hills of banana trees sped by and fiery flowers waved from the roadsides. Scott's senses tingled with an excitement he'd never known.

Just as it began to feel like they would drive into the clouds, Daddy spun the car onto a gravel road lined with tall palms. He stopped in front of a white brick house on a hilltop of sprawling lawns and flower gardens.

Aunty Bridgette waited on the bottom of wide steps that led up to a wraparound balcony with pillars as big around as coconut trees.

Scott jumped out of the car into a light mist and gazed over dense greenery that climbed to the mountaintops. Several cousins raced to the car giggling while Oliver scowled from the verandah with a toy collection displayed on the banister.

A truck rumbled to a stop in the driveway and a muscular man in stained khakis and black water boots jumped from the driver's side. A girl remained in the passenger seat staring out of the window.

"Remember Vincent?" Aunty Bridgette asked Daddy. "He's going to take the children for a drive while we talk."

Daddy embraced Vincent. "Long time no see."

"Glad you back, man," Vincent said.

"Twenty years and four children later. You have children?"

"One girl, Gillian, in the truck. Me wife in hospital with TB."

"Sorry. I know her?"

"Don't think so. She from Grenville. I meet her after you leave Grenada."

"Daddy, what's TB?" Scott asked.

16

Daddy glared at him. "How many times I tell you don't interrupt?"

"We go talk later." Vincent hoisted the other children onto the back of the truck and turned to Scott. "Sit up front with me and Gillian."

Scott climbed into the front seat next to Gillian and slammed the door shut.

Gillian, with pigtails touching the shoulder straps of her fading polka dot dress, clasped her hands between her knees and smiled with flashy eyes and a missing front tooth. "You went to church?"

"No." He rolled up his cuffs another fold and saddled his arm on the door the way adults did.

Vincent stepped on the gas pedal and the truck bounced down the road in a metallic racket that sounded like a hundred pots crashing on to a kitchen floor.

Scott glanced back at the house. Arm in arm, Aunty Bridgette and Daddy climbed the steps to the balcony. Uncle Malcolm stepped out from the open doorway. Daddy walked up to him, and the men embraced like brothers.

At that moment, Scott recognized the house as the one in Ma's picture.

This must be where Ma's children came to be happy.

Far away from Fédon.

Scott savored the fruity aroma thickening the air as he watched Vincent snake the truck along grassy roads through banana and nutmeg fields, and past overloaded fruit trees. Vincent shifted gears and spun the wheel, his big arms stretching his sleeves and his neck looking like a chopping block of muscle and veins. His build reminded Scott of the gladiators in the movie, but the muscles seemed out of place with his cotton-soft gaze.

Scott cleared his throat. "Mr. Vincent, you said something about TB?"

Gillian giggled. "Mr. Vincent?"

"Just call me Vincent," he said. "Gillian, tell him what TB is."

"A sickness that make you cough blood," she said. "Mommy has it, but we will send her to Barbados hospital when we save enough money."

"I hope she gets well soon," Scott said.

The truck hit a pothole and laughter roared from the back. Scott glanced behind just as Rodney handed Oliver a toy car that must have fallen. Oliver grabbed it without looking at Rodney. Claudette sat giggling against the side rail with her arm around Alicia, their eyes wide with excitement.

Vincent pulled up in the shadow of a huge mango tree. He let everyone out, then plucked about a dozen of the ripe fruits with a bamboo pole and passed them out.

Scott stood next to the truck and stared at his mango. In Aruba, Mommy had always sliced his mangoes so he wouldn't make a mess. He eyed Oliver biting the skin off a mango, juice dripping between his fingers and splattering his shirt.

"Let me show you," Gillian said to Scott. She massaged her mango with her fingertips until it lost its firmness. She then bit a tiny hole off the narrow end and sucked on it. "When you get all the juice out, is easier to eat."

She smiled and ran off.

He followed Gillian's instructions, later tossing the worn seed into the bushes and licking his fingers. He glanced down at his clean shirt and slapped at a mosquito on his elbow.

Vincent led them on a brief trek to a clear spring. He pulled out his pen-knife, sliced off several wide *callaloo* leaves, and showed them how to fold the leaves into coned cups for drinking the cool water. When a sudden downpour surprised them, he sliced off several more *callaloo* leaves with their long stems intact and passed them out to use as umbrellas.

Scott stood next to Gillian, raindrops pattering on the leaves over their heads and a little flutter in his heart.

After the clouds floated away, Vincent stepped into the stream. "When I was a boy, you Daddy teach me to catch crayfish," he told Scott, cupping his hands beneath a rock in the running water and pulling out a struggling crayfish. Vincent severed the head and handed the meaty body to Scott. "Try it."

Scott hesitated, but not wanting to disappoint Vincent, and with Gillian's encouraging smile, he chewed the bland flesh and swallowed it. Rodney also joined in the snack while the cousins screamed and pretended to be sick.

"Okay, leh we go and see a monkey at my house." Vincent drove down another narrow, bumpy road that cut through banana fields and entered a clearing with low wooden houses. He pulled up in front of a small house with clothes lines stretched across one side of the yard.

Gillian led the way past squawking chickens to a cage nailed to a huge tree behind the house. She opened the cage door and a monkey poked its head out. "Her name is Lady."

Lady climbed up Vincent's arm and sat on his shoulder. Her white face with narrow eyes and high eyebrows made her look like an owl. Vincent explained that she was a Mona monkey, descendant from pets English settlers brought to the islands from Africa during slavery. Since Grenada's mountains shared much in common with the African jungles, the monkeys adapted well in their new island home.

Lady pulled a fingernail clipper from Vincent's pocket and attempted to cut her own nails.

The group applauded.

Oliver pushed his way to the front, his shirt soiled with mango drippings, spinning a toy gun in his hand.

Lady zeroed her sights on the gun. She stretched out and pulled it from Oliver. She sniffed it, hurled it to the ground, and bared her teeth at Oliver.

The children laughed.

Oliver growled at Scott. "What are you laughing at?" He snatched up his gun and fled back to the truck.

On the return drive to the estate house, Vincent glanced at Scott. "You like it here, little man?"

"Yes. You too?"

"It's all I know. Me parents, and their parents too. All the way back to slavery."

"What's slavery?"

"That's when the white man force people from Africa to work the fields."

"Did Pa take you from Africa?"

Vincent laughed. "No. Slavery was long before your grandfather. Everybody knew Mr. McDonald. The old people call him *bakra béké* in French patois. The white boss."

"How did he die?" Scott asked.

Gillian fidgeted.

Vincent frowned at the narrow road for a few silent moments. "Nobody know how he died. But I will never forget that day. December 15th, 1940."

Bonjai.

Pa had died the day after Ruby and her baby.

Later that afternoon, Scott stood with Claudette and a flock of cousins in front of the estate house and waved goodbye to Gillian and Vincent. Gillian waved from the truck window, her fingers fluttering like the wings of a butterfly.

After the truck rolled down the hill and disappeared into the greenery, Claudette tugged at Scott's sleeve. "I found something."

He followed her as she skipped off in her muddied white shoes along the back of the estate house. She took a narrow track down to a green enclosure of hanging vines. A small house sat back against the woods, almost buried in the dark vegetation. Vines crawled around the handrails that led up to a narrow verandah, watched by two windows and a door nailed shut with planks of wood.

"Stay away from there," Oliver shouted from the top of the trail. "That's where Pa died."

"Get lost." Scott stepped toward the verandah.

"You'll be sorry. Pa's ghost lives there."

A younger cousin ran toward the estate house screaming. "Pa's ghost! Pa's ghost!"

Uncle Malcolm shouted from the rear balcony. "Get away from there."

Oliver hurried up to him. "It was Claudette and Scott."

Uncle Malcolm turned to Daddy. "Hector, control your damn children."

"Come here." Daddy pulled aside Claudette and Scott.

"Is it true that Pa died there?" Scott asked.

"Yes." Daddy stared down the trail at the cottage and his eyes moistened.

Scott's next words came so fast, they surprised him. "Daddy, who is Ruby?"

Daddy's face reddened, his breath scented with rum. "Who told you about her?"

Scott pushed his shaking hands into his pockets and stared at his shoes. "You said her name when you and Uncle Malcolm were—"

"This is the last warning to all of you," Daddy shouted. "Stay out of big people business or else."

Rodney strolled up to them. "I didn't do anything."

Daddy grabbed him by his ear. "This goes for you too."

"It hurts."

"It'll hurt more if you don't keep your brother out of trouble." Daddy released him, and stomped back into the estate house.

Rodney cupped his ear and snapped at Scott. "It's your bloody fault!"

CHAPTER THREE

Scott accepted with disappointment that Belvidere Estate was no escape from the clouds that shadowed Daddy. Daddy's daily drinking continued after the estate visit, ending each night with him stumbling and grumbling his way into the house. At Mommy's insistence, he occasionally took them on drives along the coast, slowing down one day to point out a black-sand beach called Palmiste. He promised to take them swimming there, but as his devotion to the bottle grew, the chances of swimming at Palmiste trickled to a drop.

Daddy's burdens, whether about Planass' eventual release from jail or because of his sorrow over Ruby and Pa, seemed to be wearing him out. His tired eyes and drawn face reminded Scott of the tears at Ruby's gravesite.

One Saturday morning, while the church bell rang in the background, Daddy announced he was going to inspect the renovations on their house by the sea. The bell echoed with Daddy's sadness and melted Scott's fear.

"Daddy, can I come with you?"

Daddy stared at him. "Sure." He remained silent on the five-minute walk until they paused at the intersection, choked with shoppers and automobile traffic. "Always look before you cross."

Daddy glanced in both directions and they hurried across the intersection to a stone driveway that ran past a shop and ended at the shore. He pushed open a gate behind the shop and startled a pigeon feeding in the dusty yard. It flew off, releasing a feather that drifted over Scott's head.

Except for several brick columns, the first floor of the plain house looked like an open carport with a paved floor. On the left side, concrete steps led up to the second floor, a patchwork of rough bricks and old lumber. On the right, a shack nestled against the carport, its window of mismatched wood secured at the top by rusty hinges and propped open by a stick. The window held a clear view through the carport and past the backyard to flocks of seagulls bickering over the sea.

Scott followed Daddy up to the shack.

"Hey, Farrow, you home?" Daddy called out.

An old balding man leaned out of the window and shook Daddy's hand. "Morning, Hector." His voice boomed.

"This is Scott," Daddy said. "The other boy home with an earache."

"Ah, I think I see your boys before." Mr. Farrow squinted over high cheekbones.

"We saw you riding your donkey by the church," Scott said. "A week after we arrived from Aruba."

"Now I remember. Old Zebra finally died. Had him even before your daddy go Aruba." He stuck out his big hand and his smile cracked into a hundred wrinkles. "My name is Neil Jude Farrow, but everybody call me Farrow."

"Nice meeting you, Mr. Farrow."

Mr. Farrow's hand swallowed his in a warm handshake.

"I know your daddy since he was a baby."

"And soon we'll be neighbors," Daddy said.

"But if you keep building up this wall." Mr. Farrow pointed at a wall the length of the carport that was up to his windowsill. "My window won't open no more."

"Daddy—"

"Quiet, son," Daddy said.

"Give he a chance, man." Mr. Farrow turned to Scott. "Go ahead, me boy."

Scott beamed. "When Claudette makes doll houses from cardboard boxes, she cuts holes for windows. You could leave a hole in the wall for Mr. Farrow's window."

Mr. Farrow laughed. "That could work."

"I okay with that," Daddy said.

Mr. Farrow winked at Scott. "You just earn a sweet-drink. Hector, let we have a drink." He handed Scott a red bottled drink and poured rum into two tin cups. The men raised their cups in a toast and swallowed their drinks in quick gulps while Scott sipped his sugary beverage.

If Mr. Farrow knew Daddy this long, maybe he'd also known how Pa, Ruby and her baby died—two days apart.

***

Four months after their arrival in Grenada, Scott's family moved out of Aunty Bridgette's cramped house and into the house by the sea. Scott and Rodney's room had two windows, one overlooking the sea, and the other overlooking Mr. Farrow's metal-roofed shack and outhouse. Claudette and Alicia shared the larger room past the bathroom down the hall. Mommy and Daddy took the room across the living room, overlooking the front yard and shop.

Bursting with excitement, Scott pushed open his windows and inhaled the sea breeze as waves splashed the back wall. He dodged past boxes and suitcases in the living room and rushed down the stairs to throw pebbles into the sea, a vast water field of sun-lit ripples.

"Howdy, me boy." Mr. Farrow stood at the window that opened into the carport.

Scott entered the carport, shook Mr. Farrow's hand and gazed at the new brick wall. "Needs painting."

Alicia, five years old, strolled up with a dry paintbrush. "Daddy said I could paint it my favorite color."

Mr. Farrow laughed. "What color is that?"

"Yellow," she said proudly.

Scott dashed up the stairs after chatting with Mr. Farrow, feeling at home, and knowing for sure that the feeling would last forever.

A few nights later, Scott lay in bed staring out the window at the stars and listening to the waves as the breeze lifted the thin curtains toward the ceiling.

The front door swung open and slammed shut. Heavy footsteps drummed across the living room to the dining area.

He listened to the sound of Mommy's bare feet hurrying into the kitchen.

"Your supper is warming," she said.

Daddy cleared his throat. "*Gloria*, what the hell . . . you looking at?" He stressed Mommy's name only when he'd gathered enough acid for a bitter argument.

A plate slid across the table.

Daddy growled. "I don't want your damn food."

A crash against the kitchen wall. Shattered pieces of plate rained onto the floor.

Scott sat up in bed. Rodney rubbed his eyes and moaned.

"Don't . . . walk away from me," Daddy yelled. "I trying my damnedest for you and the children, and all I get from you is disrespect. I'm sick and tired."

"And I am sick and tired of you coming home every night drunk. Even your children asking why you always drunk."

"All you do . . . is complain. Telling people my . . . brothers work me like a fool in Belvidere and will never pay me more than a driver like Vincent."

"Somebody is lying to you."

"What you doing when I trying to bring home a dollar?"

"You spent all your money drinking in Aruba. A blooming dollar from your brothers can't buy shoes for the children."

He yelled. "Shut your blasted mouth."

Slaps and screams.

Scott jumped out of the bed and rushed after Rodney into the dining area. Claudette raced in from the girls' room.

Daddy and Mommy struggled in the kitchen, his hands around her neck. She clawed at him. He held on.

"No!" Claudette clenched her fists at her sides.

Mommy pulled away from Daddy and stumbled to the sink in a coughing fit.

Claudette bawled, tears flowing down her cheeks. "No more fighting. You hear me? No more fighting."

Alicia crawled into the living room and sat on the floor biting her fingernails.

"You see what you doing to the children?" Mommy hustled them back into bed.

Scott lay in bed believing for the first time that Daddy might have killed Ruby and her baby.

The next morning, Scott paused at the front door on his way to school. Daddy sat in undershirt and blue pants reading a newspaper and sipping a glass of orange juice. Mommy served him a plate stacked with scrambled eggs, tomato slices, and sardines. Red marks ringed her neck and dark puffs discolored one side of her face.

Worried about Mommy remaining at home alone with Daddy, Scott asked her if he could stay home.

She gave Scott a hug and whispered. "Don't worry. I'll be okay."

He headed off to school, his thoughts in turmoil.

If Fédon could burn down a church and make brothers hate each other, then maybe he had also turned Daddy into a murderer.

The following night, Claudette entered the bedroom and tugged Scott and Rodney by their sleeves. "Time for stories."

"I heard a new one in school today," Rodney said.

They rushed down the steps to where Alicia sat waiting under the star-drenched sky. Waves roared against the back wall and a breeze rustled through the coconut trees.

"Scott, you start," Claudette said.

He recalled a story Martin had told him about a bloodsucking creature called a *lougarou* that used magic to enter bedrooms through keyholes, leaving bruises on the victims' necks as the only evidence of its evil deed.

"Is that what happened to Mommy's neck?" Alicia asked.

"No," Claudette said. "This is just a story."

Rodney told a tale about a beautiful female figure called *la diablesse* who walked the streets of Gouyave at midnight, in a long dress and wide floppy hat looking for wayward drunks.

"Drunks like Daddy?" Alicia asked.

"Maybe," Rodney said. "Last year she took a man for a walk to the edge of a precipice by the sea. She lifted her dress. One foot was the hoof of a cow. Then she lifted her hat. Her face was a skull. The man got so scared he jumped off the precipice to his death in the sea."

"We should warn Daddy," Alicia said.

Rodney paused and stared into the carport. "Look, there's a *la diablesse* over there!"

Claudette and Alicia screamed.

"Okay." Scott held his waist between laughs. "Who's next?"

A heavy voice boomed from the carport. "Me next."

The girls shrieked and ran upstairs into the house.

"It's only me." Mr. Farrow leaned out his window, his shadow stretching across the carport floor. "Can I tell a story too?"

Claudette crept back down the steps, but Alicia refused to leave the house.

"I like your stories," Mr. Farrow said in the wavering light of his kerosene lamp when they got to his window. "I have some too."

Scott sat with Rodney and Claudette on paint cans. Mr. Farrow lit a pipe and sat back in a chair at his window. He told amusing stories about a clever half-man half-spider named *Anancy*. Then he told them about a boy who had traveled the world on big ships. One day, the boy became a soldier and lost a leg in a war while rescuing a friend from gunfire.

"Would you be friends with a one-legged boy?" Mr. Farrow asked.

"Yes," they shouted.

"Would you believe me if I tell you I was the boy who lost his leg?"

"No," Rodney said. "You had two legs when you were riding the donkey."

"But you were facing only one side."

"And you were just standing," Scott said.

"I could stand on one leg," Mr. Farrow said. "You can too. Show me."

Scott, Rodney, and Claudette stood, giggling as they each balanced on one leg.

"Look at me." Mr. Farrow stood at the window with his arms outstretched.

"You're standing straight." Scott laughed. "You must be on two legs."

"Come and see."

Scott tiptoed to the window and peeked in.

Mr. Farrow balanced on one leg, his foot in a crude sandal. His other knee, lifted waist high and crisscrossed with leather straps, held a wooden peg.

CHAPTER FOUR

Just before sunset a few days later, Farrow adjusted his glasses to his tired eyes and read the letter he'd just finished at his window table.

January 13, 1964

My Love Jasmine,

I can't believe it's now forty-two years since that day. I have more news after my last letter. Hector McDonald is back with his family. They are my new neighbors. The children are in danger. I don't know how to save them.

They visit my window every day to hear the stories. If I tell them everything, it will be more than they could bear. If anything happens, Fédon will be blamed again. People are whispering, as if they are afraid he will hear them. Even after two hundred years. If only they knew the truth.

Thinking of your smile still warms my soul.

Neil.

The light from his kerosene lamp danced shadows across the page. How different the humble lamp was from the dazzling electric lights that illuminated modern buildings in the capital city, St. George's. On his rare bus trips to the city, just twelve miles to the south, Farrow felt like a foreigner. Surely, American tourists stepping off a cruise ship in St. George's harbor felt more at home than Gouyave men stepping off a bus in the city. Farrow imagined that the elites of St. George's sat in extravagant living rooms with telephones and electric radios, sipping Red Rose tea, speaking the Queen's English with intellectual flair, and raving about progress under the Union Jack.

When Farrow's grandfather introduced him to Gouyave as a youngster, the little town had been so captivating he could never imagine another place to call home. The town pulsed with tales of bitter betrayals and sweet revenge, slave rebellions and superstitions, washed ashore from the deep blue all the way up to the green plantation hills of Belvidere. The sagas spawned love in the hearts of many, but sparked raging fires in the blood of others, leaving tragic mysteries to be handed down in guarded secrets from generation to generation.

The mournful sound of a fisherman's conch shell announcing the arrival of a fresh catch stirred Farrow's own melancholy mood. His attention floated across the bay to the coastal road, where the river met the sea in the final breath of the misty sunset. Here, women still climbed the riverbanks with baskets of laundry or buckets of water on steady heads just like their great great-grandmothers had done before. And just as it was back then, the only light on the street along the bay came from the soft glow of a lamp tied to a lamppost.

So stubborn had been the people's hold on their past, that even the British failed to have them change the town's name to Charlotte Town in honor of Queen Charlotte. Two hundred years after the French fled her shores, Gouyave continued to cling to its French-given name, and to its past of swashbuckling pirates, slave revolts—and mysteries.

While the city folks lived for the future, the country people lived in this distant past, still alive with unrevealed secrets.

Gouyave would always be Farrow's home, because his life was in the past too.

He lit his pipe and savored the mixture of smoke and sea-salt air that filled his lungs. The breeze cooled the bald crown of his head and the sound of the crashing surf washed over him like memory waves, crests of joy followed by troughs of pain. The sea must be for people like him who craved the past to endure the present.

Everything that had ever mattered to him was gone. Everything, it seemed...except his memories, his secrets, and his fears.

He shut the window facing the carport and added the letter to a stack he kept in an old cardboard box under the bed.

More than forty years of letters to Jasmine he would never mail.

He had no idea where she was or if she was still alive.

Farrow settled onto the coconut-fiber mattress, and closed his eyes. Waves of memories battered his tired heart. His exhausted mind dozed in and out, returning him to that day more than forty years past. He was only twenty-nine years old, but he remembered well the day that his frozen soul felt its first warm ray of hope after two years in the death trenches of World War I France and three years in a cold British prison. He'd been stripped down to such an embittered pile of mangled flesh, bones, and wood that even children's laughter throbbed his nerves like a toothache.

That day, he had gone to the pasture down the street to water his goat, the only living being in his life. Buried in his thoughts with his sights on the road, Farrow avoided people's questioning stares, and ignored the boy who called him a one-legged pirate. The cadence of his wooden leg on the stone sidewalk echoed in the narrow street, drumming up visions of battlefield carnage.

He crossed the street to the pasture and gazed around.

His goat was gone.

A girl's voice, musical and innocent, came from behind him. "You looking for you goat?"

A slender, coffee-toned girl in a thin dress strolled up to him, her bare feet sweeping through the grass. Her long black hair gleamed in the sunlight and her eyes smiled attention he'd long forgotten how to accept. His fingertips tingled with the desire to touch her paper-smooth skin.

"It must have gotten loose," he said.

"It sick. I took it by the river to pour water over he head."

He followed her down to the riverbank where the goat lay on a flat rock. Its tongue hung from its mouth, and the eyes were glazed.

"I saw mongoose bite he a few days ago," she said.

"Rabies." Yet again, the British had struck him. English settlers had first imported snakes to rid the island of rats that arrived on their cargo ships. Then they brought the reddish-brown ferret-like mongoose to rid the island of snakes. Their efforts failed. By 1921 rats, snakes, and mongooses roamed the island, the latter attacking livestock and pets with devastating rabies.

This time the British had punished him by folly rather than bigotry.

Farrow's goat made a feeble effort to move, then shook and lay still.

"Oh, so sad." The girl cupped her mouth in her hands.

He looked around, smothering the grief at losing the only life that had needed him in years. "I have to bury it before dogs show up."

"I have shovel home." She pointed up at the hill on the other side of the river.

"My name is Neil." He surprised himself when he stretched out his hand to her.

"Everybody in Gouyave know you." She dusted her hands against her hips, and shook his hand. "You was together in the war with Mr. McDonald from Belvidere Estate."

An icy memory gnawed his chest, but the warmth of her hand melted the torment.

"Me name is Jasmine. Wait for me." With the grace of a ballet dancer, Jasmine hopped from rock to rock across the stream and disappeared up a trail beneath thick greenery. She returned a few minutes later balancing on the rocks with a shovel in one hand, a jug and two plastic cups in the other. She sat next to him in the shade of a mango tree and poured him a cup of orange juice.

He emptied the cup in one drink.

"I'll dig," she said.

"I've had more practice." He grabbed the shovel, limped to the shade of a tree on higher ground, and began to dig.

She sat in the grass close by, covering her crossed legs with her dress and nibbling on a blade of grass.

He felt her studying him while he dug. Sweat rolled down his forehead and soaked his shirt. He buried the goat, rinsed the shovel in the stream, and sat on the riverbank to catch his breath.

Jasmine sat next to him. "War must be bad."

"There is no word to describe war."

"That's how . . . it happen?" She glanced at his wooden leg.

In the six months since his return, this was the first time anyone had asked him about his leg.

"You know me," he said, "but I know nothing about you."

Jasmine said her last name was Bhola, the granddaughter of Calcutta Indians, brought to the islands with thousands of indentured servants to replace freed slaves reluctant to return to plantation nightmares. Her father supervised field workers at Dougaldston Estate across the river, while her mother cooked for the owners, the Ferguson family.

"Me aunt in Trinidad pick husband for me," she said. "But I want to stay here."

"You want to be in love before you get married, right?"

She laughed. "You find love *after* you married. Not before."

He laughed too, relishing the music in her voice.

Just then, a woman shouted from the hill. "Jasmine, time to come home."

"Maybe I see you again." She danced her way on the rocks across the stream with the shovel and cups in her hands, and disappeared up the hill.

Later, Farrow hobbled back across the field to the bay. He leaned on his crutch and tossed pebbles at the waves. He'd lost his goat, but maybe he'd found a friend.

That was forty-two years ago.

Farrow finally fell asleep, recalling how he'd wondered that day why Jasmine would want to see a one-legged soldier again, part man, part wood, and part ice.

The next morning, the sound of urgent screams outside his window suddenly wrenched Farrow from dreams of Jasmine.

"Mr. Farrow. Open up!"

Farrow rolled out of the bed and pushed open the window.

Scott stood in the carport with tears streaming down his cheeks. He pointed to the shore. "A . . . a body."

"What you talking about, me boy?"

"There's a dead body in the rocks!"

"Where you parents?"

"Mommy took Rodney to Dr. Branch. I don't know where Daddy is."

"Come around." Farrow let Scott into the front door and sat him by the window. "Wait here."

Farrow slipped his good foot into his handmade tire sandal and fastened the straps of his wooden leg to his knee. He limped out the door and struggled over the rocks to the shore. He scanned the area behind the McDonald's seawall. Shadows dodged the morning sun over the rocks and sea, distorting his vision. He limped forward, his peg sinking in the wet sand.

Up ahead, a wave rolled a clothed bundle on to the shore and a hand flopped to the sand.

"That was old man Ivan who used to ring the Anglican Church bell," Farrow told Scott after the crowd that had gathered in the McDonalds' yard drifted back to the street, carrying Ivan's body on a stretcher. "Must'a fall in the sea last night. People say he was drinking in the police station."

"I heard an old woman say *la diablesse* push him in the sea." Scott fidgeted in the chair at the window and nibbled on his fingernails.

"That's just superstition, me boy." Farrow stuffed his pipe, a dugout stub of corncob attached to a skinny bamboo handle. He cupped a lit match over the tobacco and sucked on the pipe until it flared. Hoping to distract Scott from his morning encounter, Farrow pointed out the window. "This is why I like this view."

They stared at the sun-drenched sea, basking with silver ripples as far as the horizon. Under an umbrella of blue sky, white clouds puffed and gazed down on a boat trailing fishing nets. Seagulls quarreled with pelicans over trapped fish as the fishermen towed their laden nets north toward Lance Bay.

"Would you believe the French wanted to buy Grenada from the Carib Indians for a few knives and bottles of brandy?" Farrow chuckled. "No money could get me to give this away. This is my paradise."

"If this is paradise, why is Daddy always so angry?"

"You could have paradise out here." Farrow waved his hands in the air. "But if you don't have it in your head, then you never feel it."

"Is that what's wrong with Daddy, he doesn't have paradise inside?"

"You father is in pain. But drinking make it worse."

"How come you know so much, Mr. Farrow?"

Farrow puffed his pipe and squinted for a few moments. "Pain without drinking was my teacher."

"Maybe Daddy is hurting because of the girl in the Anglican Church cemetery."

"What girl?"

"Ruby Ferguson."

"When the time is right, you father go talk to you about he life." He rubbed Scott's head. "Have patience, me boy. If you eat green mango, it sour you mouth. Wait till it ripe, it nourish you body."

Later, after Scott left, Farrow noticed that the framed picture above his bed had been moved. Had Scott looked at it? Farrow hobbled to the bed, lifted the picture off the ledge, and through moistened eyes read the dingy note taped to the back of the frame.

CHAPTER FIVE

The following afternoon, Mommy hustled them all into bed and retreated into her bedroom for her regular Sunday afternoon nap. In bed next to Scott, Rodney slept deeply. The waves assured Scott some peace, especially since Daddy had been gone since morning to attend Mr. Ivan's funeral.

Mr. Farrow's words fluttered through Scott's mind. Pain and secrets, where one appeared, the other lurked nearby like inseparable twins. Scott wondered what pain awaited him, now that he too had begun a collection of secrets—secrets he hadn't shared with Rodney. The first was overhearing Daddy's midnight whispers. Yesterday he stumbled on another.

While Mr. Farrow was organizing help to recover Mr. Ivan's body, Scott crept onto Mr. Farrow's bed for a closer look at the picture on the ledge. He took it down and stared at a fading picture of a girl about fifteen years old, in school uniform, white blouse with pleated dark skirt. Thick braids, like Gillian's, hung to her shoulders.

He was about to return the picture when his fingers brushed something loose at the back. He turned the picture around, and read a handwritten note taped to the frame.

20 April 1938
To Mr. Farrow, a friend sent by God.
Love always,
Ruby

Scott decided it was easier to hold the secret than to risk another of Rodney's scolding. Gouyave must have had two girls named Ruby around 1938, maybe about the same age too. One Ruby on Mr. Farrow's ledge and the other buried with her baby. Mr. Farrow's Ruby probably died a long time ago too, or else she would have given him a more recent picture.

Scott hugged his pillow and let his eyelids grow heavy in the sea breeze. The waves rolled him into an uneasy sleep, where bodies floated in the sea and pictures blew in the wind. Pictures of two girls in school uniforms and thick braids, like twins.

One of the girls screamed. Then the other girl screamed too, jolting Scott awake.

More screams, from downstairs.

Rodney leaped out of bed. Scott raced after him down the steps and into the carport.

He froze in shock.

Alicia stood naked, painted yellow from head to toe, her eyes and mouth screaming from behind her painted face. Daddy stood over her in the dark suit he'd worn to Mr. Ivan's funeral, his face red, his hair an entangled mess. The paintbrush he held dripped yellow.

"Hector, you'll kill the child." Mommy rushed into the carport toward Alicia.

"Tell your damn children to leave . . . my stuff alone." Daddy held the paintbrush up to Mommy's face.

"You promised them," she yelled. "Get out of my way."

Mr. Farrow's window swung open. "Hector McDonald!"

Daddy stared at Mr. Farrow.

"Shame on you, man," Mr. Farrow shouted. "Let it go. It go kill you and you family!"

Daddy's head slumped and a defeated shadow paled his face. The paintbrush fell to the floor.

The uproar must have spilled out to the street. An old woman with a battered straw hat and a hairy chin mole shuffled into the yard with two men.

"*Bonjai.*" She planted her hands on her waist. "But look at me cross, nah."

"Them McDonalds have curse, *oui*," one of the men whispered.

"Fédon riding again," she said. "I feel winds blowing."

***

A few afternoons later, Scott gazed into the sea, his chin on the windowsill. Red snappers and bright blue fish darted above patches of black sea urchins. He should be on the seawall with a fishing pole baited with the rock crabs Martin had taught them to catch. But the thrill of fishing shied away from all that had changed in the last few days. Daddy had become a monster and Mommy a stranger.

He had always thought Mommy was prettier than Queen Elizabeth. He used to study the English monarch portrait hanging on Ma's living room wall, and think that Mommy's coffee toned skin and warm eyes emitted a glow of life that the stiff portrait lacked.

But no longer.

A gloom had stolen Mommy's beauty like weeds overtaking a flower garden. Gray rings circled her eyes and a deep frown etched into her forehead. She became bitter, even blaming Alicia for the paint incident. "Stay away from your father's things," she said.

As for Daddy, Scott now had little doubt. If Daddy had killed before, he still had enough pain and anger to do it again.

A door slammed downstairs. Mr. Farrow limped across his backyard toward the seashore.

"Hold on, me boy." Mr. Farrow's advice a couple days ago seemed as meaningless as a hook without bait. "Stay afloat and you never drown."

Scott dashed out of the bedroom, almost running into Rodney who was just entering.

"I'm going fishing," Rodney said. "Want to go?"

"You fish. I'll talk to Mr. Farrow."

They hurried down the steps.

"I hope you boys don't run like that in the streets," Mommy shouted from the kitchen.

Rodney grabbed his pole, and they raced across the backyard and over the wall to the shore.

Mr. Farrow sat on a rock beneath a coconut tree puffing on his pipe. "Howdy, me boys. *Sa ka fèt?*" he asked in the patois he'd been teaching Scott.

"*Mwe la.*" Scott hoped that just being okay would not worry Mr. Farrow.

"These legs are getting too old for rocks." Mr. Farrow shifted his weight on the rock.

"We could build a bench, like in Casa's cinema."

"A bench by the sea?" Rodney snickered and headed down the shore.

Scott faced Mr. Farrow. "Do you know the woman who was in the carport last Sunday?"

"Miss Kate. She's a sidewalk vendor. Why?"

"She said Fédon's winds blowing. What does that mean?"

Mr. Farrow crossed his arms across his big chest. "Maybe Fédon used to sit on this rock too, back in the days of slavery."

"Was he a slave?"

"His mother was the descendant of a slave. His father was a French plantation owner." Mr. Farrow explained that Julien Fédon had been a Freed-Colored who also owned slaves. But what drove him was his hatred for the British for mistreating the French Catholics. Fédon recruited his own slaves and started a rebellion that almost drove the British from the island. In 1795, he captured the governor and forty-nine other British people in Gouyave. When British soldiers killed his brother, Fédon executed the Governor and his officials. "He had a nasty temper. The fighting went on for a year. Then a British General defeated Fédon and hanged the leaders."

"Fédon too?"

"No. He disappeared."

"Is he still alive?"

"You still too young to know some things." Mr. Farrow puffed his pipe and squinted at Scott through a cloud of smoke.

"But I want to know now."

"Fédon is a man and a lesson, like a spirit you feel but can't see. If you like him, you believe he was fighting to free slaves. If you fear him, you believe he's a revenge spirit."

"Revenge?"

"To punish the British General for killing Fédon's men and thieving he estate."

"Which estate was Fédon's?"

Mr. Farrow tapped his pipe on the rock. "Belvidere Estate."

***

Rodney swung the fishing line, hooked with crab bait and weighted with a metal bolt, and watched it splash into the water beyond the waves. He gripped the fishing pole and waited.

He wished he could hear what Scott and Mr. Farrow were saying, but all he heard was the waves whispering. Their conversation was probably just another hammering of Scott's questions, followed by more of the old man's stories. There was a time when he might have heard them, but that was before he'd lost half his hearing.

It had happened in Aruba, a year before the move to Grenada. Pirates in books and movies fascinated him with their menacing hooks and swords, and the skull-and-bones earrings that dangled from their ears. So when Rodney discovered Mommy's open jewelry box, he imagined her tiny white beads to be earrings pirates used to wear. Balancing a loose pearl on the ledge above his earlobe, he tilted his head in front the mirror to study how well he measured up as a pirate. The pearl rolled into the opening of his ear. He poked his finger in his ear to retrieve the pearl, only to push it further into the narrow channel.

He tried using a toothpick, but the pain grew. In panic, he ran screaming to Mommy, just as Daddy stumbled into the house, drunk. Daddy pulled him by his ear down the street to the doctor— one of Daddy's drinking companions.

Rodney never forgot the doctor's shiny tools and the sickening odor of alcohol on the man's breath. Pain shot through Rodney's head, and a gush of warm blood filled his inner ear.

"Ah shit," the doctor had said.

A sharp jerk on Rodney's fishing line pulled his mind back to the shoreline. He yanked the line and the struggle began. He pulled in two snappers that afternoon without Mr. Farrow and Scott noticing.

"What stories did Mr. Farrow tell you?" Rodney asked Scott after they returned home. Rodney had no interest in Mr. Farrow's ramblings. He simply wanted to prove that Scott's time with the old man was a waste.

"He told me about Fédon," Scott said. "The man that started a slave rebellion from Belvidere Estate."

"You know why they teach us about Christopher Columbus in school, but not Fédon?"

"Why?"

"Columbus was real. Fédon was not. What else he told you?"

"People believe Fédon is still looking to punish the general's family for crushing his rebellion."

"For two hundred years?" Rodney laughed. "Don't repeat that. People will think you *stupidee*. I bet this general also has a name we don't hear in school."

"General Archibald McDonald."

***

Farrow shut his window and fingered his way through a stack of papers in the box beneath his bed. He stopped at page 37. He'd read it many times, but after the conversation with Scott today, he needed the reminder.

With one foot on the threshold of the prison door and the other out of it, a pistol in one hand and a dagger in the other, "I will," replied he, "and shall require no other weapons but these in my hands, to execute your orders."

Farrow too had orders to execute. If Scott was the one to face the darkness, then so be it.

***

When Rodney rushed into the house for lunch the next day, the aroma of spicy fish broth greeted him. Daddy sat at the table with his head buried in a newspaper. Rodney squeezed past Mommy to peek at the chunks of his red snappers simmering in the buttery soup with vegetables and corn-flour dumplings.

"Where's Scott?" Mommy asked.

"He was behind me when we left school." Rodney sat in front of a steaming bowl at the table. He burned the roof of his mouth with the first spoonful, but he didn't mind. It was his fish, his lunch, caught by his hands. If something bad ever happened to Daddy, Rodney would provide, especially since Scott was only interested in fairy tales.

Just then, the squeal of brakes, and a woman ran screaming into the yard. "Mr. McDonald. You little boy get hit by motor car!"

CHAPTER SIX

Scott gazed up at the confusion of faces hanging over him. His back burned on the hot road and his head throbbed. He wanted to move, but couldn't. The only comfort came from his wet shorts.

A big man kneeled next to him bellowing words that rolled in like distant thunder. "You okay, boy?"

Scott opened his mouth but could say nothing.

"It's me." A silver tooth flashed. "Casa."

He remembered Casa, the *badjohn* from the Lance.

"You Daddy coming soon." Casa helped Scott to sit up.

Scott lifted both arms and inspected his elbows, bruised and covered with fine gravel.

"He okay," Casa announced.

"Move." Daddy elbowed his way through the crowd.

"I sorry. . . Mr. McDonald," a man stuttered. "He just jump in front me car."

"How many times I tell you to look before you cross the street?" Daddy glared at Scott and tugged at his belt buckle. "I have a mind to belt you little tail."

"Hold a minute, Hector." Casa rose to his feet in front of Daddy. "I see you boy running on the sidewalk. He just trip and stumble."

"I still think I should cut his ass."

"No you won't." Mommy pushed her way toward Scott.

He stood and dusted off the wet seat of his pants.

A woman giggled. "*Bonjai*, look like he pee he pants, *oui*."

"Let's go home." Scott tugged at Mommy. "I want to change."

"No," Daddy said. "You going back to school in your wet pants. And no lunch."

Scott returned to school with Rodney. They strolled across the field and joined the line of students waiting at the main door to have their names checked off the attendance list. The bruises on Scott's elbows burned, yet he considered himself lucky that Daddy had not been drinking. He just hoped no one noticed his wet pants.

Martin rushed up to Scott. "I hear what happen. Man, you look mash up, *oui*."

"I'm okay."

"Remember me?" A familiar voice came from behind him.

He turned, recognizing the braids and the smile. "Gillian from Belvidere, right?"

"Yes."

"I didn't know you go to school here."

"Mammy still sick, so I staying with my aunt on Back Street. Today is my first day in your school." She stared at his elbows. "What happened?"

"Fell—"

"He damn lie." Martin snickered. "He get hit by motor car."

"It's okay." Scott showed her his bruises to distract her from his wet pants.

"I donno which worse," Martin whispered in Scott's ear. "Me mash-up pants or you pee pee pants."

Scott bit his lip to restrain his laughter.

"Your bruises could get infected." Gillian pulled a white handkerchief from her shirt pocket. "Let me clean it off."

Glad to keep her attention on his elbows, he let Gillian dab his bruises until the school bell rang a couple minutes later. "Thanks. It feels better."

She smiled and stuffed the handkerchief into her shirt pocket.

He followed Martin up to the doorway, gave his name to the teacher with the clipboard and entered the school. He glanced back in time to see Gillian wave her fluttering fingers as the noisy crowd swallowed her up. He grabbed a seat in the classroom between Martin and Rodney.

"You hear the news?" Martin asked.

"What?" Scott asked.

Martin spat a green stem onto the wooden floor. "Somebody see Fédon riding he white horse on the Lance last night."

***

Daddy's mood softened during the next week. He came home earlier at nights and less drunk. One night after supper, Scott lay in bed and listened to Daddy and Mommy at the dining room table, chatting about friends they had left in Aruba. They talked about Daddy's lodge meetings, beach parties, and the last Christmas party when Mommy's sister visited from Trinidad. Scott remembered her well, her sweet perfume, fresh bread, and of course her homemade ice cream.

"Would you go back to Aruba?" Mommy asked Daddy.

"Sometimes I wonder."

Maybe Daddy wanted to return to Aruba to get away from Fédon. Scott's fears about leaving Gouyave vanished the next day when Daddy announced plans to raise chickens. Daddy enclosed the big space beneath the steps with chicken wire and a walk-in door, and released eight little yellow chicks into the cage. "You'll have to take care of them," he told Scott and Rodney.

"Daddy, could pigeons and chickens live together?" Scott asked.

"What do you mean?"

"Martin said he could catch us some pigeons at the market if we have a cage."

"As long as they don't make a mess."

That Friday afternoon, Scott and Rodney followed Martin into the market square. Rodney held a cloth bag while Martin clutched a can with rice soaking in rum that Rodney had stolen from one of Daddy's bottles.

"Best way to catch pigeons." Martin scattered the rum-soaked rice in the shade of the huge tree in the middle of the market square and glanced up at pigeons perched on surrounding rooftops. He spat at his feet. "Give them time. Let's go watch cow get kill."

They climbed onto a concrete table and peeked over the wall into the killing room. Scott recalled the first time he'd witnessed the Friday afternoon slaughter of cows and pigs. The scent of blood, flesh, and animal waste almost made him puke. But after a few more visits, the lingering odor of death no longer disturbed him.

With a chain around its neck, two men struggled to pull a cow into the room while a third man whipped the animal on its rear. One of the men slipped the chain through an iron ring anchored in the concrete floor. They yanked the chain until the cow's head met the ring at the floor.

"Ready," one of the men shouted.

A policeman entered the room, cocked a pistol, and shot the cow in the head. It collapsed onto the floor with a force that shook the building. The men lassoed the cow's hind legs to a pulley on the ceiling and hoisted the animal. Scott watched the bloody slaughter, wondering about the thin slice of time that separated life from the horror of death.

Later, they bagged six pigeons, sluggish from the rum-soaked rice, and released them into the cage after Martin trimmed the pigeons' longest feathers with a pair of scissors.

"When the feathers grow back, free them," Martin said. "They always come back home."

The following week, a big brown pigeon began morning visits, scratching and feeding in the yard along the cage. They caught it and trimmed the feathers.

When Scott rolled the fluffy leg feathers, he noticed a shiny metal ring.

Rodney inspected the ring. "Letters and numbers. Let's see . . .TRIN and four numbers."

When they asked Mr. Farrow about the ring, he tapped his forehead. "TRIN? Maybe a homing pigeon that flew from Trinidad."

"Is Trinidad that close to Gouyave?" Rodney asked.

"Birds used to follow my ships from Port-of-Spain to St. George's," Mr. Farrow said. "You can call your pigeon *Trini*. That's what we call people from Trinidad."

They placed the homing pigeon in the cage and named it Trini.

The following days rolled into weeks and the weeks into months, ripening rumors of Planass' pending release like an over-ripe mango about to drop from a tree. Scott pretended that day would never come, marveling instead at how the pigeons' feathers grew and the yellow chickens turned into seven white hens, and a red rooster with a daily wake-up crow. During those weeks, Mr. Farrow surprised the family with a spotted puppy they named Rex. Rex chased them around the yard during the daytime and slept in their beds at night.

When the rooster and hens had fully grown, Scott and Rodney started releasing them in the morning and letting them back in at sunset. But the pigeons remained in the cage.

One morning before school, Scott ran down the steps with Rodney and Rex. To their surprise, the cage door was open and all seven pigeons gone.

Alicia sat sobbing on the carport floor. "I was just trying to feed them."

"That's okay," Scott said. "They'll come back before dark."

Just before sunset that day, Scott waited with Rodney and Alicia on the top of the steps as Trini glided overhead, with the flock following, and landed on the roof. They flew down to the yard and strutted into the cage. From that day, the gate remained open during the day, but shut at night to keep out prowling cats.

A few days later, Scott leaned at the carport window chatting with Mr. Farrow and watching him carve a new tire sandal with a blade. Heavy footsteps thundered across the kitchen floor above them and dishes shattered against a wall.

"Better go see," Mr. Farrow said.

Scott sprinted upstairs and into the kitchen. Plate fragments littered the floor and a small brown feather floated out the window where Daddy stood.

"What the hell you doing?" Mommy stomped toward Daddy.

Daddy pointed his finger at Scott. "You and Rodney . . . better keep those damn pigeons out of the kitchen. Look at the mess they make."

"You made the mess," Mommy yelled.

Later she pulled Scott aside. "Don't worry, when he's drunk, he's too slow to hurt the pigeons."

***

Scott had overheard Daddy say that the Canadian government was going to rebuild their school across from Ma's house. But Martin was the first to say that during the construction the students might move into a newly built fish market on the Lance seashore.

Sitting on the seawall, Scott looked at Martin in disbelief. "That sounds crazy."

"It still new, no fish smell yet." Martin pulled in his fishing line. "You wanna see?"

"Let's go!" Rodney handed Martin their catch of three snappers, and a blue fish.

"One more thing." Martin stared at their shoes. "We don't need those."

Scott's bare feet felt cool on the brick sidewalk as he followed Martin and Rodney past musty stores and noisy rum shops, a catapult hanging from his back pocket. Crowded buses rumbled by on the narrow street, blaring horns, rattling over potholes, and belching smoke.

An old woman squatted on a stool beneath a store window, fanning flames in a cast-iron coal pot. Scott paused to inhale the aroma of parched corn sizzling on the grill.

The woman glanced up. "You want something, sonny boy?"

Even under her straw hat, he recognized Miss Kate, the woman with the hairy mole who had warned about Fédon's winds.

"Planass soon out," she said. "Fédon sending him on a white horse to find you. So look out!" A shallow mocking laugh sprang from her mouth.

He bolted, catching up with Rodney and Martin in front of the police station. If Miss Kate was right, Fédon must have gotten too old and now hired Planass to do his deeds.

They waited for Martin to drop off the fish at his house and then continued up the shoreline to the fish market, the low building that would become their school.

Martin pointed at the wide windows. "If you jump out, you land on sand. Easy to run away and go fishing." He showed them a hiding space for their rods on a ledge beneath the floor.

They explored the grounds around their new school, and target-practiced their catapults at low-hanging coconuts until Martin spat at his feet. "Let we go see Brickie Hill."

They headed back the way they had come and turned up a steep road just before the bridge, past unpainted houses with dogs barking lazily, children skipping ropes, and coal pots smoking with fried fish.

Scott gazed back over Lance Bay, a storybook picture of metal rooftops, white sand and blue water facing a glimmering gold sunset.

They climbed until the road narrowed into a trail that led to a small house nestled below a menacing cliff.

"Mr. Welsh house." Martin pointed.

The trees on the cliff waved like handkerchiefs in howling winds. The winds must have drowned out the yells of the man stomping up the path behind them with a cutlass, until he was upon them.

"You will die!" The man, a full bag over his shoulder, swung the cutlass in the air and blocked the boys' way back down the hill.

Planass? Scott's knees shook. He wanted to run, but his feet felt like lead. He glanced at Rodney and Martin for some signal to run. Like him, they both looked anchored to the ground with fear.

A dog barked in Mr. Welsh's yard. They were now trapped.

The man looked older than Scott expected, but had rock-hard muscles bulging against tattered shirtsleeves. His nostrils flared like an angry bull in its final moments. He swung the crocus bag off his shoulder and dropped it with a heavy thud.

Daddy should have warned them that Planass was out.

"Mr. Welsh." Martin stuttered. "I was show . . .showing me . . . my friends Brickie Hill."

Mr. Welsh? Scott felt lightheaded from the relief.

"If you climb up there, you will die." Mr. Welsh pointed his cutlass at the hill and his eyes glistened in the dying sunlight. "The wind will blow you away. Me boy used to climb up there. Said he could see Trinidad from there. Wind blow him and he land on a rock."

"We . . .goin' home now," Martin said.

"I know you is Miss Nellie grandson, but you two look like McDonalds, *oui*. Which one is you father?"

"Hector," Scott said.

"I will tell him keep you from here. Don't come back."

They dashed down the hill and didn't stop until they reached the bridge.

"Can you really see Trinidad from Brickie?" Scott asked.

Rodney gazed back at the hill. "There's only one way to find out."

CHAPTER SEVEN

Gillian sat on her aunt's verandah on Back Street, holding a book and recalling the days spent roaming around Belvidere Estate with her daddy in the old truck. She missed the rich greenery, the fruity flavor in the air and, of course, her pet monkey, Lady. Gillian cuddled the book to her chest, and gazed at the girls playing hopscotch just down the road, their shadows stretching across the street. The girls used to ask her to play too, but no longer.

She'd always had an excuse for not joining them. One day it was because her aunt wouldn't let her. On another day, it was homework, or that she was tired. But she'd never told them the truth. Playing was the farthest thing from her mind.

The fear of losing her mammy dampened Gillian's every thought and sapped her joy. Mammy and Daddy were her world. Losing one could mean losing both.

"Is best you stay with me aunt in Gouyave," Daddy had said after Mammy left the hospital for the seventh time a couple of months earlier. The Grenada hospital could help no more. "Just till Mammy go to Barbados. We don't want you to get sick too."

"But why can't the Grenada hospital heal her?" Gillian asked.

Daddy rubbed his calloused hands. "Government big shots like big cars more than sick people." He complained about a man named Gabbard. "Long ago he was for poor people. But now he Chief Minister, he won't even fart on people who vote he in power."

The savings they hoped would get Mammy to Barbados was shrinking fast. Daddy was already working all he could, leaving home before sunrise, and returning exhausted at night.

Maybe it was up to Gillian.

"Dr. Pilgrim, can I borrow one of your books?" She'd asked Mammy's doctor after another hospital visit.

"Sure, my dear." The graying Dr. Pilgrim led her and Daddy back to his office. "In my eight years here, no one ever asked me for a book." He handed her a first-aid book from his bookshelf. "Maybe one day you'll help me here."

She took the book home and read it three times with a dictionary close by. One day she would heal sick people like Mammy, she promised herself. But until then, she would read Dr. Pilgrim's books and clean Daddy's chapped hands with mentholated alcohol after his long days in the fields.

But even as her yearning to care for her mother went unnourished, she still treasured that bright moment at school. It lifted her spirit, and created butterflies in her tummy with the realization that yes, she too could be a doctor. Scott had not flinched, standing still as patients do for doctors, letting her nurse his bruised elbows with her white handkerchief. She wished she could have taken him home to dab mentholated alcohol on his reddened skin and to cover them with band-aids, as Dr. Pilgrim's book instructed.

She had taken the bloodstained hanky home, falling asleep that night with the hanky in her hand, and every night that week until her aunt told her it was time for laundry. But despite her aunt's scrubbing, the white handkerchief remained stained.

When Gillian explained the stain, her aunt gave a disapproving look, and told her about the rebel Fédon who still rode his white horse at night, searching for McDonald's or those who got too close to them. "Get rid of that handkerchief. McDonald blood is bad luck."

But Gillian kept the handkerchief hidden deep in her pillowcase. Scott had made her feel like a doctor, and she would never forget it, despite her aunt's warnings.

In the meantime, there were many more books to read. She laid the book in her lap and waved at the girls heading home. She decided to finish the remaining pages under the kerosene lamp in bed that night. Daddy planned to stop by in the morning to get the book for Dr. Pilgrim, and a painting of a nun she'd made for Mammy. She gazed down the road at the streetlight man pumping the gas lamp and roping it on the lamp pole over the intersection.

The rich aroma of cocoa, '*cocoa-tea*' as everyone called it, aroused her appetite for her nightly supper of cocoa, flying fish, and buttered bread.

She headed for the door and glanced in the direction of a truck rattling down the street. It looked and sounded like the estate truck her daddy drove. But he wasn't coming by until tomorrow morning.

The truck stopped in front of the house. The engine sputtered and died.

Daddy struggled down from the driver's side. Even in the dim streetlight, his watery eyes and quivering lips told her that her worst nightmare had come true.

"Mammy!"

***

"Mr. Farrow told me what you boys did." Mommy raised Rodney's suspicions in flickering candle light when she paused next to his chair after supper.

"What did they do this time?" Daddy looked up from his plate.

Rodney nibbled his fingernails. These old men gave him an earache. First, Mr. Welsh had complained to Daddy about their encounter on Brickie Hill, which led to an argument between Mommy and Daddy about the brothers' knockabout behavior.

Now Mr. Farrow was sparking more trouble, probably because he had seen them yesterday when they jumped out of the fish market school window with Martin. They swam in the sea, and fished, cooking two snappers with salt, pepper, and butter in a can over a wood fire. They plucked hot chunks of fish from the broth until not one sliver of the spicy fish remained. Finally, they passed the can around and drank every drop of the peppery soup.

They swam again, this time naked to allow their shorts to dry on the hot rocks. Later, with their stomachs filled, they had dozed off in the shade of a coconut tree until it was time to slip into the parade of schoolchildren returning home in the afternoon.

But Mr. Farrow could not have known this. They'd been hidden from the street by trees lining the shore.

Maybe Mr. Farrow had complained that Rodney and Scott stole planks of wood from the rubble heap at the old school. It was only junk wood, probably a hundred years old.

"Mr. Farrow said the boys built him something," Mommy said.

"What?" Daddy leaned forward.

"A bench." Rodney wished everyone would just shut up and leave him alone.

"Now when he sits on the shore, his leg no longer hurts," Mommy said.

Daddy faced Rodney. "Time you teach your brother something."

Maybe it was time Daddy's swollen belly and flushed face get lost.

"I hope the wave don't take it away," Mommy said.

"We put it on the rocks and tied it with ropes to the trees," Scott said.

Daddy stood and burped. "I'll be back."

"Where you going?" Mommy asked. "You've already been gone all day."

Rodney relaxed in his chair, thankful for the change in conversation.

"To visit Constable Robinson," Daddy said.

"You going to drink in the police station? You want to drown like old man Ivan?"

He growled. "I'm not old man Ivan."

"Take the boys so they not running wild," Mommy said.

Scott slumped in his chair. "I don't want to go."

"That's not your decision," Daddy said.

"Can I bring Rex?" Rodney asked.

"As long as you're seen and not heard."

"Stay away from the sea." Mommy's voice followed them down the steps.

The wall clock hanging behind the desk showed seven o'clock when they entered the Gouyave police station that night. Constable Robinson, a big brown-skinned man with a thick handlebar mustache and hairy arms, was sitting at the desk in a black-and-white striped shirt with silver buttons. His white hat was on the desk between a bulky black telephone and a logbook, under a gas lamp roped to the ceiling.

He shook Daddy's hand and pulled out a bottle of rum and two glasses from his desk drawer. "Let's have a drink for Ivan. He drink with me that night, but he stop in every rum shop going home before he fall in the sea. He never knew how to manage he grog."

The men clinked glasses with several shots of rum.

Seated on the low window ledge next to Scott, with Rex dozing on the floor, Rodney watched as Constable Robinson leaned forward and lowered his voice. "I hear England bringing electricity to Gouyave. But Gabbard only want he union workers to get the work, so he could collect dues for he bank account."

"Maybe he need a new car," Daddy said.

"While people dying like flies in hospital."

"You hear Vincent's wife didn't make it?"

"Yeah. Had to send he little girl to Trinidad," Constable Robinson said.

Scott turned towards the men. "Daddy—"

"Shhh . . . " Rodney elbowed him.

"I have news 'bout Planass too." Constable Robinson clunked his elbows on the desk and stared at Daddy.

Scott leaned forward.

Constable Robinson twirled his moustache. "Maybe the boys should play while we talk." He pointed down the darkened hallway. "Go see the bicycles I have in the last cell."

Glad for the chance to escape the drunks, Rodney grabbed Scott by the arm. "Let's go."

They ran past an opened iron gate into the shadowy hallway with Rex at their heels. From padlocked doors on both sides of the hallway, small windows with steel bars stared at them.

"Did you know Gillian's mother died?" Scott whispered.

"No."

"When I no longer saw Gillian at school, I thought she went back to Belvidere," Scott said. "Why did they send her to Trinidad?"

Rodney hissed. "You ask too many questions."

They stopped at the open doorway of a cell at the end of the hallway. A mist of light from a street lamp filtered through a barred window and reflected off two bicycles parked against the cell wall. A bare mattress lay on a low wooden frame beneath the window.

Rodney marched through the doorway and grabbed one of the bicycles. Scott pulled the other one and they tailed each other around the room, imitating the sound of motorcycles.

"Put down me damn bike!" A voice screeched from across the hallway. "Or . . . I break you little necks."

They froze. Rex barked.

"I go wring you dog neck too." Two hands gripped the bars in the shut door facing them. From between the hands, two big eyes glared out.

Rodney screamed, dropped the bikes with a clatter on the concrete floor, and fled back up the hallway toward the lobby with Rex and Scott racing after him.

"I'm not going to warn you two again," Daddy yelled.

"There's a man," Rodney said.

"Ah, don't worry about he," Constable Robinson said. "Too drunk to ride home, but want to fight."

Constable Robinson led Scott and Rodney back down the hallway into the open cell, a heavy key chain jingling from his belt.

"Go back to sleep," he shouted at the face in the door. He helped Rodney and Scott stand the bicycles up and staggered out of the room. "Stay here until me and you Daddy finish talking, okay?"

Daddy whispered in Constable Robinson's ear.

"You sure you want to do that?" Constable Robinson asked.

Without answering, Daddy slammed the door shut in Rodney's face. The cell vibrated with the clanks of falling bicycles, slamming bolts, and screams.

Hours later, keys rattled the cell door open and awoke Rodney on the mattress beneath the window. He scratched at his shoulders, itchy from the prickly mattress and bedbugs.

"Time to go home." Daddy's words floated on alcohol breath.

"Where are we?" Scott sat up rubbing his eyes and scratching his arms.

"Let's . . . go home." Daddy stumbled out of the cell and down the darkened hallway to the front door.

On the way out the front door, Rodney glanced back at Constable Robinson. The policeman sat in his chair with his upper body sprawled over the desk and his arms out, as if he was on a cross facing down. He sniffled and his moustache almost touched his eyes. An empty bottle and two glasses stood watch over the receiver, off the hook. The clock showed five minutes after two.

At that moment, Rodney knew it was time to put an end to Daddy's shit.

***

"We'll need Daddy's cutlass." Rodney's tone worried Scott as they stood in the carport a week following the police station incident.

Rodney's attitude had taken on a sharp edge since that night. Even when they fished, he nibbled on his lips with his gaze fixed on the horizon as if he was trying to see past it.

Maybe that was how big brothers behaved when they made plans. Rodney had ridiculed Scott's idea to build Mr. Farrow a bench on the shore. Yet, two days after Mr. Farrow told them that the big pigeon, Trini, probably flew from Trinidad, Rodney changed his mind.

They raided the rubble by the old school and assembled the wood, nails, and rope, beneath the coconut trees. They sneaked Daddy's tools, and after two days of measuring, cutting, and hammering, they rewarded Mr. Farrow for his knowledge on Trinidad pigeons.

The bench looked like a rough tabletop, held by a frame of two-by-fours. They set it over two rocks and secured it with ropes to the trees behind it. Scott was so excited to work with his brother that when Rodney asked to help him roll two logs up behind the rocks, Scott hadn't asked why.

But when Rodney demanded that he steal Daddy's cutlass from the garage, Scott hesitated.

"We'll need it tomorrow to cut a new trail to Brickie Hill," Rodney said. "Just you, me, and Rex."

Thrilled, Scott awakened with Rodney early the next morning, Saturday, while everyone else in the house slept. Rodney packed bread and fruits in a paper bag and Scott dashed downstairs to free the chickens and pigeons for the day. Scott watched the pigeons flutter away with Trini in the lead.

He sneaked Daddy's cutlass from the garage and traded it with Rodney for a zipped-up cloth bag.

"Heavy," Scott said.

"Something to eat, and a couple of presents for Mr. Welsh."

Rodney explained that if Mr. Welsh hadn't told Daddy about their Brickie Hill trek, Mommy would not have insisted that they accompany Daddy to the police station. "And we wouldn't have gotten locked up. It's Mr. Welsh's fault."

Scott wasn't sure he agreed, but he didn't ask about the heavy presents Mr. Welsh earned for getting them in trouble. It had become just as easy to keep his opinions, as it was to keep secrets from Rodney. Scott lugged the bag while Rodney carried Daddy's short cutlass in the waist of his worn khaki pants.

With Rex at their heels and catapults dangling from their back pockets, they headed toward the Lance. They turned right before the bridge and followed a dirt road alongside the river.

Downstream from Ma's house, Rodney pointed up at the hillside on the opposite bank. Thick greenery patched with wooden homes overlooked Gouyave. "That should take us behind Brickie Hill instead of past Mr. Welsh's house."

They crossed the river, leaping from rock to rock. They followed trails that crisscrossed between houses. Roosters crowed from trees and dogs barked from dusty yards but kept their distance when Rex bared his teeth.

At the last house before the tree line, a big woman emptied a night pan out of her window, staining the morning breeze with a urine scent. She wobbled out of the house and headed toward a smoking coal pot beneath a laden mango tree that sheltered her backyard. She fanned the coal pot, a cigarette dangling from her lips and her huge breasts wiggling in her thin nightdress.

"You here to thief mango?" Her hands akimbo on bulging hips, she sucked on her cigarette and glared at Scott and Rodney.

"We have we own," Rodney said.

They walked past the woman and entered the tree line, flattening thin shrubs as they went.

"I watching you," she said. "Dese days little boys too damn thief."

When they could hear her no more, Scott and Rodney broke out in giggles.

"You too damn thief, little boy." Scott poked at Rodney's chest.

Rodney collapsed on the ground in laughter.

After they recovered, Rodney led the way, chopping through the underbrush of stinging nettles and three-inch long prickles. An hour later they stumbled out of the jungle unto a ledge that opened up the world before them.

Brickie Hill.

Scott gawked at the sea, trimmed by white sand and rocky coastline, stretching as far as he could see. Behind him, mountains hung from the sky. A howling wind flapped his sweaty shirt.

"Look." Rodney pointed at a shadow on the horizon and inched his way toward the edge of the hill.

"Be careful." Scott worried that the winds could be Fédon cloaked in treacherous gusts, galloping his horse in search of his enemies' children.

"Trinidad," Rodney said.

"You think Mr. Welsh's son really saw Trinidad from here?"

"I *know* he did."

"Mr. Farrow said that sailors long ago used to mistake clouds for islands."

"That's no cloud," Rodney said forcefully. "That's where Trini flew from. And if a pigeon can fly from there, we can row there."

They devoured a meal of bread and bananas in a tree shade and prepared to return home.

Rodney pulled out several hand-sized stones from the bag. "Presents for Mr. Welsh's big mouth. Get ready to run."

He took aim and threw the first stone over the hill.

Nothing.

He threw another. Still nothing.

"We have three left," Scott said.

"The house must be a little more this way." Rodney threw again.

A loud bang.

Rodney threw another in the same direction and Scott followed with the last one.

Both stones found their target. Scott bolted into the woods after Rodney as the hillside exploded in a bacchanal of screeching birds, barking dogs, and angry yells.

Even out of breath, Scott could not help wondering what Rodney meant when he pointed at the horizon and said "we can row there."

An hour later, they entered the big woman's yard. The house stood silent, the door and windows shut. They climbed the tree and filled the bag.

"Hmmm, Julie mangoes, my favorite." Scott smelled one.

"Claudette and Alicia will like these too."

They stripped on the riverbank and swam naked to wash away their dusty sweat. Scott drank the cool water from cupped hands and rinsed the mangoes. They dressed and trudged home under the midday sun, Scott dizzy from the Brickie Hill conquest.

They arrived home to shouts in the kitchen. Claudette was sobbing at the dining room table. Mommy stood in the kitchen yelling at Daddy where he stood by the window.

A wave of anguish crashed over Scott.

Fédon must have taken over Daddy's inside colors.

Daddy stood in a mess of shattered dishes and brown feathers. In his hand, Trini's limp body hung by its stretched neck.

CHAPTER EIGHT

The official announcement bell ringing from the intersection troubled Farrow. He strapped on his wooden leg and limped out of his house into an early morning darkened by thick clouds. A gust slammed the door shut behind him. It had been years since he'd heard the bell before seven o'clock.

Just last week, Millie Cockrobin, the town clerk, rang the bell to announce the upcoming elections and on another day to let the town's people know that water was going to be shut off for plumbing repairs. But those announcements usually came around mid-morning. Farrow's concerns drummed to the cadence of his wooden leg tapping the pavement as he limped toward the crowd facing Millie.

Clothed in loose clothes and a black hat, she rang the bell with a vigor that shook her lean frame. She lowered the bell and read aloud from a clipboard: "Warning! Hurricane coming!"

"Oh God." A woman wailed in the crowd. "Not another kiss-me-ass hurricane."

"Papa God punishing we again," another said.

Millie read on. "If you live on the shore, leave your house and seek shelter in the churches by six o'clock this evening. Warning! Hurricane coming!"

Farrow eyed Scott and Rodney squeezing their way through the crowd toward him. "Good morning, me boys. Look like excitement tonight, eh?"

"Excitement?" Scott glanced at Rodney and back at Farrow.

"Hurricane," Farrow said. "We south of hurricane belt, so we don't get them often. But Hurricane Janet hit in 1955. Killed over a hundred people."

Rodney jammed his knuckles against his cheek and nibbled on the inside of his lips while Scott buried his hands in his pocket and shuffled his feet.

They were not the same boys Farrow had met almost a year ago. Each time they collided with their father's bad temper, they rebounded with harder faces, more intense eyes, and less visits to Farrow's window. Scott didn't show up after yesterday's ruckus, even though Farrow had left his window open for him. Farrow hadn't learned of Trini's fate until later that afternoon on his way to shore, when he observed them in the backyard digging a hole. They told him about Trini as they buried the bird in a shoebox and placed a stick cross on the mound.

Farrow considered asking them if they were hiding other secrets from him, but with Millie's warnings, the timing seemed awkward. "Put the bench in the cage to protect your chickens and pigeons from the wind."

"We don't have pigeons no more." Rodney's voice was flat.

"What happened to them?"

"We gave them to Martin," Scott said.

Millie headed toward the Lance, and the crowd dispersed in the steady wind.

"We have a long night ahead. Go get ready." Farrow shifted on his crutch, watching the boys walk away.

Scott paused at the gate and waved at Farrow without smiling.

Farrow had seen those burdened signs on the faces of an earlier McDonald generation, and the results were deadly.

Later that afternoon, Farrow heaved his cardboard box onto his mattress. The box felt heavy, either because he had gotten older, or because the box contained nine more years of letters since the last hurricane. Just as he had done the morning Millie warned about Hurricane Janet, he emptied the wrapped papers and letters into a big plastic bag, and then placed it into a burlap bag.

He might have to ask for someone's help to get to the Anglican Church for shelter, but there was one more thing he needed.

He reached for Ruby's picture, just as low voices drifted in the wind past his shut window.

"It's today or never," Rodney said. "We can do it."

"Okay," Scott answered.

Heavy footsteps shuffled and Hector shouted. "What the hell you boys doing with rope and my cutlass?"

"Mr. Farrow wants us . . . to pull up the bench."

Gloria called out from upstairs. "Scott, Rodney, come inside. Let's get ready for the church."

Hector's footsteps stomped up the steps. "What's going on at the church?"

"Don't you know there's a storm coming?" she asked. "We're staying at the Anglican Church tonight."

"They getting people bothered for nothing. We're staying right here."

"You stay by your drunken self."

The door slammed shut, but shouting continued in the house.

Rodney spoke again outside Farrow's window. "Let's go."

Light footsteps raced across the carport.

Farrow pushed open his window against the howling wind.

The boys were gone.

"Mr. Farrow! Mr. Farrow!" Gloria's voice shrilled in the winds.

Farrow awakened with a jolt, Ruby's picture still clutched against his chest. In the lamplight the clock on his table said half-past-five. *Dammit.* He was late getting ready for the church.

"Just a minute." He hobbled to the window and pushed it open.

The wind tugged at Gloria's dress, and wide-eyed anxiety laced her voice. "Have you seen the boys?"

"They were putting the bench in the cage an hour ago. I must'a dozed off while they were doing that."

"The bench is not in the cage or on the shore. Hector is gone too. Nobody on the street saw him or the boys."

"Go get ready for the church. I'll be right back."

When Gloria disappeared up the steps, Farrow shut his window, tightened the straps on his leg, and limped out of his house into a haunting chorus of winds and waves. Dark clouds mushroomed over the choppy sea and the first raindrops pinged like pebbles on his roof.

Getting his papers to safety would have to wait.

The door slammed behind him. He pushed his way toward the shore, his wooden leg sinking into the wet sand. Blowing rain stung his face and sea mist salted his lips.

He squinted at the cluster of coconut trees and thick brush against the sea-wall. No sign of the boys. He looked back toward the Lance, at waves crashing against the rocky shoreline. A sheet of metal roof blew into the sea and a wave splashed him up to the knees.

His vision fogged by sea spray, he reached the first coconut tree. Strange, the rising tide had not yet reached their favorite rock, but the bench was already gone, with the ropes.

Missing too were two logs the boys had rolled up behind the rocks.

Cutlass, rope, logs. What had the boys been up too?

The answer hit him like the bullet that shattered his leg. "Oh God, no."

A dreaded familiarity boiled in his stomach with a revulsion that reminded him of a December night in 1940.

In spasms, he threw up on the sand.

✱✱✱

"I think I know what your boys did," Farrow said to Gloria in the open door-way upstairs, the wind slapping his drenched pants against his crutch.

"What?" Her eyes pleaded for good news.

"I have to come inside." He glanced down at his sand-covered shoe and peg.

"Come in, please."

Farrow hobbled into the house and Gloria shut the door behind him. Claudette and Alicia sat at the table in the wavering candlelight. Alicia tugged her hair in a blank stare. In recent months she had become so quiet that people called her the angel of the family.

"Please sit." Gloria showed him to a chair.

"Claudette, take Alicia to the room. I need to talk to your mother for a minute." Farrow sat, his wet clothes sloshing in the chair.

"Do as Mr. Farrow say," Gloria said to Claudette. "Finish packing your bag for the church."

The girls disappeared into their room.

He cleared his throat. "I believe Scott and Rodney—"

The door swung open. Hector stumbled into the living room holding a bottle of rum. A gust from behind him snuffed out one of the candles. A gash on his forehead masked his face in blood and soaked the front of his shirt red.

"Those bastards thought they could get me." He chuckled. "I might be drunk . . . but I'm not stupid."

CHAPTER NINE

G illian sat on the front steps of her aunt's Laventille Road house in Trinidad, under swollen clouds darkening the hillsides. Early Port-of-Spain city lights struggled in the distance and thunder rumbled over flood warnings on the radio. Aunty Josephine had warned about a storm heading to Grenada, and possibly Trinidad. On her way out the door that afternoon, she said the storm might force her to work all night in the hospital.

Gillian worried about Mammy's grave getting soaked in the Anglican Church cemetery. She thought about Daddy being alone, and hoped he remembered to bring her precious monkey into the house. A glancing image of Scott brightened her thoughts, but an immediate fear quickly overshadowed it.

If Aunty Josephine worked all night, Gillian would be alone with Uncle Bertrand.

The door opened and he filled the doorway. "Time to come in."

"It's not raining yet, Uncle Bertrand."

"Remember what I tell you about calling me uncle."

How could she forget the name he had demanded she call him? A week after Mammy died, Daddy had shipped Gillian to Trinidad to stay with Mammy's sister Aunty Josephine, whose husband was named Uncle Bertrand.

Aunty Josephine, slender with pencil-thin eyebrows and bright red finger-nails, embraced Gillian at the bustling Port-of-Spain harbor. She held Gillian's hand as the taxi drove them up the congested Laventille hills, to the small blue house with louvered shutters, glass paned doors, and see-through curtains blowing in the windows.

Uncle Bertrand lay on the living room couch sucking on a cigarette, his brown skin in a dingy match with a grimy blanket covering his legs and a sweat-soaked undershirt ballooning around his gut. He scratched his reddish unkempt hair, grabbed a walking cane, and struggled to his feet, kicking aside a messy pile of newspapers on the floor next to the couch.

"You smoking around newspapers again?" Aunty Josephine snapped her hands to her narrow waistline.

"Welcome to Trinidad." He barged past her and stuck out his hand to Gillian, the alcohol and cigarette on his breath souring the air.

Gillian dropped her suitcase and shook his clammy hand. "Nice meeting you, Uncle Bertrand."

"Your uncle got hurt working in the oilfields," Aunty Josephine said. "He's home all day and night, so you won't be alone when I work nights. Just don't let him fall asleep with his cigarette burning."

He exhaled cigarette smoke through his nostrils and mouth. "I hear you want to be doctor. Maybe you could fix these legs."

"Don't embarrass the child," Aunty Josephine said.

"You Aunty say she wanted to be doctor too." He winked at Gillian. "But after all them books, she still emptying bedpans in the hospital."

"You fool," Aunty Josephine said. "You drank and gambled all our money on racetracks. Now you're just a crippled good-for-nothing. If I didn't have you, I would be a doctor."

She showed Gillian around the house, and helped her settle into her bedroom, a small room with stacked bookshelves, and a window overlooking the city.

"Don't worry about him," she whispered. "His pain killers make him say *stupidness.*"

Later, Gillian ate a hefty plate of curried chicken and potatoes and watched Aunty Josephine massage Uncle Bertrand's legs. He lay on the couch with his eyes shut, smoking and smiling.

One night a week later, while Aunty Josephine was at work, Gillian was watching a comedy show on the small black and white TV in the corner of the living room. Uncle Bertrand dragged on his cigarette and flicked the butt out the window. He shut his eyes, and within minutes was asleep in snores that drowned out the show.

She eased off the chair and tiptoed across the wooden floor to turn up the volume control.

Uncle Bertrand mumbled and sat up, rubbing his face. "Bring me another rum and coke."

When she handed him the drink, he stared at her.

"You're a sweet girl."

"Thanks, Uncle Bertrand."

"I'll tell you a secret." He emptied the glass in one gulp. "I'm not really your uncle. And your Aunty is not your real aunt."

"I don't understand."

"Come let me show you something." He stood with much less effort than in Aunty Josephine's presence, and headed across the living room without his walking cane.

She followed him past the kitchen to the main bedroom at the end of the dark hallway. The room smelled like one of the fashion stores she'd once visited with Mammy in St. George's. A dresser with a large mirror lined most of one wall. A display of perfume bottles and powder puffs filled the polished surface of one side of the dresser, and on the other side, a clutter of medicine bottles, cigarette packs, and tobacco dust. The bed, covered in black sheets and fluffy pillows, took up most of the room.

Uncle Bertrand pulled a shoebox from under the bed. He fingered his way through a stack of pictures and handed one to her. "Ever seen this?"

She studied the old family portrait.

"That's your Aunty's family, long ago." He pointed at a girl in the portrait. "This is your mother, the only that look like Trinidad *coolies*."

She recognized Mammy, a teenager with long black braids. The other three girls, including Aunty Josephine, had shorter hair, and shared the rounder lighter facial features of the older couple sitting on wicker chairs.

"Your mother was adopted. Beautiful, like you." He brushed her face with his hand.

She flinched and stepped back.

"If you keep this secret," he said, "I'll have more for you."

"You're a liar."

Maybe Uncle Bertrand's pills made him say stupid things and tell lies, like he did about his pain so that Aunty Josephine would give him daily massages.

Gillian dashed out of the bedroom and bolted into her room, slamming the door shut behind her.

"I am not your damn uncle," Uncle Bertrand shouted at her door. "My name is Sticks, you hear me? Sticks."

That was two weeks ago, but his bangs on her door still drummed in her ears like the thunder in the distance. If she could sit out here under stormy skies, unafraid, then she could stand up to Uncle Bertrand.

The door opened again. "Girl, it's dark. Come inside now."

"Yes, Uncle Bertrand." She glanced back at the storm clouds rolling in over the city. She entered the house and shut the door behind her.

"Josephine just called." Uncle Bertrand stood by his couch dragging on a cigarette. "She working double shifts. Just you and me tonight."

She squeezed past him to her bedroom and shut her door. She collapsed on the bed and dozed off holding her stained handkerchief and wondering if she'd latched her door.

She awoke later to raindrops pinging the metal roof and winds rattling the windows. A yellow glow filled her room. Her bedroom door slammed.

She turned toward the door, and screamed.

Uncle Bertrand stood over her with a lamp, his face disfigured in its shadows. "I need you."

CHAPTER TEN

Hector wiped blood off his forehead and kicked the door shut against the winds. "Here, Farrow." He stumbled forward with the bottle. "Have a drink."

A time warp gripped Farrow. Hector looked and sounded like his father, the Grenadian officer they had called Captain McDonald in the trenches. The force that had transformed the captain into an animal with fire in his belly now drove Hector to stampede over his own flesh and blood. Just recently, when Scott slammed his thumb in a car door, Hector poured rum into the wound and frightened Nurse Branch into stitching it without a shot to numb the boy's pain.

Farrow chose his words carefully. "You'll destroy your family like your father destroyed his."

Hector straightened up and hardened his face. "Say that again, and . . . I'll kill you."

"Look what you've come to. Threatening women, children, and old men."

"You won't be saying that if you'd seen me fight them off . . . "

"Did you fight with the boys?" Gloria shouted.

"No, woman! I haven't seen the boys . . .all day. What the hell . . .are you talking about?"

"Who cut you?" Farrow asked.

"Flying roofs. I had a fight with roofs blowing in the wind . . . just up the street."

Farrow released a sigh. The boys had not attacked their father. He'd been cut by metal roofing. But there had to be more. "So where are your sons?"

"I don't know and I don't care. I was in battle with flying roofs . . . for my life and my bottle." Hector laughed. "Got it? Battle for my bottle?"

"Dammit!" Gloria snapped. "The boys are missing."

"Good." He shook his head, showering blood on the floor and Farrow's wooden leg. "Then let's have a drink."

Farrow grabbed the bottle with one hand, and, with the other, jabbed Hector in the chest with the crutch, pushing him into a chair. Farrow handed Gloria the bottle. "Pour this down the drain and get him a towel."

She returned with a towel and hurled it at Hector's face. "You can't find your sons in your state."

"I don't know where they are," Hector said. "I was with Constable Robinson."

"Claudette said there was no one at the police station."

"We were having a drink in the bicycle room."

"I'm taking the girls to the church," Gloria said. "You stay here and pray the boys come home before the storm."

Farrow cleared his throat. "I don't think Scott and Rodney are coming home tonight."

"What do you mean?" she asked.

"I think they . . . ran away."

"They need a good whipping," Hector said.

"It's your fault, man," Farrow said. "You can't live in the past no more. They're all gone. Your father, Ruby . . . baby, and now your sons, gone."

"Leave Ruby out of this!"

"You still trying to fix what done and over. If you live in the past, you lose what you have now."

"Blame Fédon. Isn't that him blowing out there?" Hector held a towel to his head and moaned.

Farrow had hoped the boys were safe with Hector. But Farrow's dreaded suspicions about their fate made sense now. It was no coincidence that Rodney had become excited to build the bench, after Farrow told them that a pigeon could fly from Trinidad.

He recalled a passage buried deep in his bag.

What was the fate of Fédon was never certainly known; but as a canoe, with a compass belonging to him nailed to the bottom of it, was found overset at some distance from the island, it was generally believed that he had drowned while endeavouring to make his escape.

Farrow should have guessed the plan all along.

That was no bench the boys had built. It was a raft.

They were probably in the raging seas trying to escape to Trinidad.

***

Scott lay forward across the bench in the darkness, clinging waist-deep in the angry water. Seawater burned the opened blisters on his hands and splinters needled his chest. Rolling swells lifted the raft and slammed it into troughs that followed. Jagged swords of lightning slashed the blackness and thunder drummed overhead.

Rodney had said that if they left Gouyave before the storm, they would land in Trinidad before darkness. But it now felt like forever since they had pushed off from shore with Rex. Within minutes the darkness swallowed up the last daylight and showered them with a downpour of doubt. One of the ropes snapped like a thread. The sea plucked one of the logs from beneath the bench and stole their paddles in the confusion. The wind screamed across the surface of the water.

"You see that?" Rodney's shout sounded a mile away. He gestured with his chin. "A light . . . over there."

A speck of light flickered in the distance, but soon disappeared.

The ropes holding the raft together groaned and loose wood banged on each other. Rex whimpered and licked Scott's face.

"It's okay, boy." The numbness crawled up Scott's arms. He clung to Mr. Farrow's words. *Just keep afloat and you'll never drown.*

Over the howling winds, the sound of crashing waves.

"We're close," Rodney hollered. "Look out for rocks."

Scott paddled with his bare feet and squinted in the darkness at a shape that looked like a hill.

The waves grew louder. A web of lightning lit up the night. Land rose ahead.

Movement to the side caught Scott's attention. A wall of white water accelerated toward them. "Lookout!"

The wave crashed over the raft, swallowing them up in a deafening roar of water and sand.

***

The storm roared, but Farrow remained calm with acceptance that the end was near. Rain poured in through a gaping hole in the roof and the wind ravaged the room. Plates blew off the shelves and shattered against the wall. Leaves floated in three inches of water around his bed. From outside came the sounds of tin roofs peeling off houses like pages being ripped from a book.

He sat on his bed against the headboard, next to his burlap bag and cigar can. On his nightstand, in the fading lamplight, a metal cup filled thick with a blend of water and rat poison.

He tapped a fountain pen against his wooden leg and began to scribble on a damp sheet of paper held to a book with his pen hand, and sheltered by a piece of cardboard in his other hand.

> *My love,*
>
> *This is my last letter. There is a storm tonight and the boys are lost to the sea. I am to blame. I ran out of time before I fulfilled my duty.*
>
> *If the boys drown, someone needs to be with them. Waves are beating the yard and their house is shaking. I have a special drink to help me on my way.*
>
> *People may never know the truth about Fédon, but I hope you will. I have everything in a waterproof bag, with your name and the Anglican Church address. If they find you, have someone you trust study the papers.*
>
> *I also have forty years of letters for you. Your love saved my life.*
>
> *Concrete is falling next door and the wind screaming for me. My time is here.*
>
> *I will always love you*
>
> *Neil.*

He moved with haste, placing the folded letter into the cigar can which he squeezed into the plastic bag. He tied off with firm knots, first the plastic and then the crocus bag, and fastened the bag with rope to the headboard, just in case everything floated away.

The storm blew in through the skeletal remains of his roof, showering him and his mattress. Water bashed the floorboards to the sounds of nature run amok, screeching wind, crashing trees, and shredding roofs. Waves pounded the side of his house like beasts crazed by the scent of impending death.

He leaned back on his pillow, held the cup in both hands, and smiled. A peace welled up in his chest, as he gripped the cup and lifted it to his lips.

The McDonald's house shook and Scott's wall trembled.

CHAPTER ELEVEN

Gillian stared up at Uncle Bertrand, his face distorted by shadows. She bit her lip to hold back another scream.

"I need a leg rub to help me sleep," he said.

"But . . . I don't know how." The thought turned her stomach.

"I'll show you."

"I'm sleepy." She held her pillow.

"You'll go to sleep soon." He grabbed her arm and dragged her to the living room. He placed the lamp on the coffee table. "We lost electricity a couple hours ago."

Rain splashed against the windows.

"You know how Josephine showed you to knead flour for baking? Just do that, from my knee down." He lay back on the couch and held her arm in his grimy hands.

"I can't."

"C'mon girl. Just help Sticks relax. Then we go to sleep."

She sat at the edge of the couch and gazed at the carnival calendar on the wall to avoid his stare. She touched his knee.

He sighed, and his breath made her want to puke.

Tears rolled down her cheeks.

"Harder." He lit a cigarette and shut his eyes. "You're learning fast."

She released her thoughts into the fiery parade of costumes on the calendar.

"Now do the next leg," he said a few minutes later.

She kneaded his other leg and returned to the imaginary carnival world of flaming costumes.

"I can't anymore," she said.

"Do better next time. You didn't come from Grenada just to read and sleep."

She stepped away from the couch.

"One more thing." He sat up. "Say 'Goodnight, Sticks.'"

"I will tell Aunty Josephine."

He leaped to his feet. "And I will tell her I found you snooping around her bedroom."

"You're a liar!"

"And you're a little brat." He shook her by the shoulders. "Now say 'Goodnight Sticks.'"

"I will tell Daddy."

"Who will he believe?" He spun her around and slapped her on her behind. "Say it."

"Let me go to sleep please, Uncle Bertrand."

"Say it!"

"Sticks."

"Everything."

"Goodnight . . . Sticks." Gillian made a silent wish that the calendar would erupt in flames and send Uncle Bertrand to hell.

CHAPTER TWELVE

Scott struggled to his knees in the wet darkness, his head throbbing and his nostrils oozing salty mucus. He spat sandy seaweed. Through clogged ears, a rushing wave sounded like a distant waterfall. The wave knocked him down and rolled him into brush. He grabbed on to the undergrowth until the water retreated, then leaped to his feet and peered into the night, the wind slapping his shirt against his back.

"Rodney? Rex?" His voice whispered in the wind.

A bark. Rex sprinted up to him, then turned and ran back along the shore, barking as he went.

Scott stumbled toward the barks just as another wave knocked him off his feet.

A yelp just ahead.

He crawled in the dark. "Rodney. Rex."

Another wave assaulted the beach, rolling him into bushes with his hands flailing. He felt clothes and flesh. "Rodney!"

A moan.

"Wake up!" He grabbed Rodney by the collar and shook him.

Another wave rushed up and shoved them further into the bushes.

Rodney coughed, and water gushed from his mouth and nose. He struggled to his feet, wiping his face with the back of his hand. "Let's go."

They slogged inland, barefoot in waist-high underbrush with the back of their shirts pulled forward over their heads to shield against flying leaves and twigs. Rex followed, his tail tucked between his legs.

Lightning lit up a building standing watch at the far end of the bay. Pillars on the roof, like leftovers of a second floor blown away in the wind, stood at attention against the pale night.

They stumbled into the partially enclosed first floor. Stacks of plastic-covered bundles stood against the walls. They kicked their way over burlap bags and banana leaves toward an elevated floor in the far corner of the building. They heaped leaves on the floor and covered them with layers of cloth bags.

Scott removed his wet clothes and crawled into a bag on the makeshift bed, his teeth chattering. Relief and fatigue soon overwhelmed him and he fell asleep with Rex at his feet.

Scott awoke to Rex's barks and the chirps of birds. Sunshine seeped in through cracks in the sidewall. Rodney slept against the wall, the side of his forehead disfigured by a bump. Leaves, twigs and sand lay scattered across the floor.

Scott pulled on his damp shorts and stepped outside, becoming aware of his back pain and bruised knees. The sunlight warmed his skin in a breeze drenched with the scent of fresh seaweed and sea salt.

Rodney shuffled out of the building, yawning and stretching.

"What you think?" Scott asked.

"This has to be Trinidad. Now we have to find Mommy's sister in Port-of-Spain."

"I hope she doesn't send us back." The first thing he would ask for is her ice cream. Maybe she might help Scott find Gillian too. He already missed his sisters, but Rodney assured him that they would return for them once they got settled.

They grabbed a few ripe bananas from the building and hiked down toward the water. The calm surface, like a glass tabletop, reflected gulls in loud squabbles overhead.

Scott leaped over a knee-high pile of entangled seaweed and debris that stretched the length of the bay. "Black sand like Palmiste."

They swam and ate bananas while their damp clothes dried in the sun. An hour later they dressed and headed back toward the building.

"Look." Scott pointed at their wrecked craft, a mess of rope and wood pushed up against a coconut tree. He felt a twinge of guilt for stealing Mr. Farrow's bench and hiding their plans from him. Scott already missed the old man and now would learn nothing more about the secrets and pain that connected Fédon, Planass, and Ruby to Daddy.

Scott untangled his bag from the wreck and tossed out waterlogged bread glued to soggy shoes. He stepped into his shoes and immediately thought of Martin. He kicked them off into the debris.

"What you doing?" Rodney stared at him.

"I don't need shoes no more."

Just then the sound of a truck rumbled over the bay.

"Must be a road behind the building. Let's go." Rodney slapped Scott on the back and raced off with a light spring in his steps, waving his hands in the air. "Yahooo!"

They dashed across the sand and leaped over fallen trees toward the sound of the truck. Just behind the building, they came upon a narrow road covered by broken branches and mud. They stared down to where the road disappeared around the corner.

"You think they'll give us a ride to Port-of-Spain?" Scott asked.

"Only if they see my handsome face." Rodney giggled. "Stand behind me."

Scott lifted his fist and gave Rodney a playful tap to the chin. They sparred barefoot on the muddy road until a truck rounded the corner, meandering to avoid debris on the street. It inched its way toward them. Brakes squeaked and the truck stopped.

The muscular driver leaned out of the window, on his shoulder, a monkey that looked like Gillian's pet, Lady.

"You boys kinda far from home, eh?" Vincent grinned.

Scott sat in the front seat between Vincent and Rodney and stared ahead at the debris-covered road leading back to Gouyave, longing to calm the embarrassment churning in his chest. Rex fidgeted on Rodney's lap next to the window, while Lady clung to Vincent's shirt collar, bobbing as the truck bounced along. The storm tides last night had taken them less than two miles down the coast. How foolish of them. The only relief Scott felt came from Vincent believing their story that they had gone fishing, and had lost their lines and fish in the storm.

"*Bonjai*, you boys something else, *oui*." Vincent shook his head. "Walking in a storm to fish in Palmiste Beach."

They should have recognized the black-sand beach, but the building had lost its roof, and fallen trees had disguised the terrain around the bay.

Scott swallowed hard and glanced out the truck window. The sea reflected silver ripples under the sun and seagulls drifted over the water. The truck turned a sharp corner and headed down Mabuya Hill. Church steeples, houses, and coconut trees shared Gouyave's welcoming skyline.

A lump rose in his throat and his eyes welled. Gouyave would always be home. This little town, with its old people and old beliefs, cemeteries and gas lamps, seagulls and pigeons, sunny seas by day and stars by night. With stories of Fédon, friends like Martin, and heroes like Mr. Farrow.

"How is Mr. Farrow?" Scott asked Vincent.

"He house mash up. Nobody find him."

"Maybe—"

Rodney, his good mood now evaporated like rain drops on a hot road, elbowed Scott in his ribs.

Vincent drove past the park, dodging tree limbs and roofing sheets on the road, and pulled up at the main intersection where a small crowd mingled.

Martin leaped onto the back of the truck and shoved his head through the rear window. "Where the hell you went?" he shouted. "Never go nowhere without me."

Mommy pushed her way to the truck. "Oh merciful Mother of God." She cried, laughed, and prayed. She hugged Rodney and Scott as they climbed out the truck.

"Time to go home." Daddy had no anger in his voice as he led Scott and Rodney into the driveway.

Horror overtook Scott. The kitchen was gone, and below the void a rubble hill of concrete, lumber and a battered stove flattened Mr. Farrow's house.

"Mr. Farrow!" Scott raced up to the collapsed house.

A man shouted. "He not there. We look awready."

Scott dropped to his knees and peered through the maze of twisted tin and broken lumber. He lifted a roofing sheet and crawled in.

"Son, get out of there," Daddy yelled.

Scott snaked his way toward the rear wall. Exposed nails and splinters needled his hands and knees, already blistered from last night. He peered into a darkness soaked with the scent of kerosene and sea salt. A pencil-thin ray of sunlight pierced the debris and landed on the corner of Mr. Farrow's mattress.

"Get out now." Daddy's voice rang hollow.

Scott tugged at another roofing sheet over the mattress, exposing the broken bed frame. A round piece of wood with a metal cap protruded from the rubble. *The wooden leg?*

He crawled toward the head of the bed. A girder, one end pressed into the mattress and the other end jammed against the carport wall, groaned under a load of concrete blocks. He pulled one of the blocks and it slid off the pile and unto the floor with a thud. The rafter trembled, sending a shower of loose masonry rattling down on metal.

"Hector." Mommy shrieked outside. "Don't just stand there."

"Why don't *you* get him?" Daddy said.

Scott twisted a corner of roofing sheet and a splinter of sunlight bounced off a tin cup dangling on a finger. He tapped the cup loose and held the big hand.

"Good morning, me boy." Mr. Farrow's whisper strained from the wreckage. "Your wall save me."

***

"Scott, Mr. Farrow wants you and Rodney to have lunch with him today." Daddy stood on the kitchen counter hammering a board. A bandage strip on his forehead covered the seven stitches for the cut he'd received during the storm.

In the days after the storm, repairs echoed around Gouyave. Daddy and a work crew restored the kitchen, and, with materials donated by the church and rescued from the ruins, rebuilt Mr. Farrow's house while he recovered in the Anglican Church Rectory.

Mr. Farrow, his crutch in one hand, and hugging a bulging crocus bag to his chest with the other, gazed around the house with moist eyes when Scott held the door for him few days later.

"Welcome home," Scott had said, elated that Mr. Farrow was back, and Gouyave was home again.

"Mr. Farrow is cooking fish broth," Daddy reminded Scott. "Don't miss it."

Scott found Rodney in the backyard, staring into the sinkhole left by the storm. Daddy and the men had refilled most of the hole with ruined lumber and bricks after rebuilding the seawall.

"Mr. Farrow made lunch for us," Scott said.

"I don't want to listen to old people stories." Rodney stuffed his hands in his pockets. "We almost drowned because of it."

"You blame Mr. Farrow?"

If Rodney was wrong about a raft getting them to Trinidad, he might also be wrong about Fédon being only in Mr. Farrow's imagination.

"I blame everybody. . . you too!" Rodney kicked a bottle into the hole and stomped off.

Scott watched him disappear out the gate, realizing for the first time that he no longer cared what Rodney thought or said.

"Go have a seat, me boy." Mr. Farrow turned from the boiling pot on the coal-pot fire in his front yard and pointed to the chair next to the window.

A spicy aroma followed Scott into the house, crowded with a new bed, two chairs, and a table donated by the church. Light blue paint brightened the wooden wall panels. New beams supported the roof, a patchwork of shiny tin sheets interspersed with rusty ones, their nail holes plugged with tar to prevent leaks. The sea breeze poured through the window and soothed the midday heat baking down from the metal roof.

Ruby's picture sat on the ledge above the bed, the framed glass cracked down the middle.

"Eat up." Mr. Farrow filled two large bowls of steaming buttery broth, with floating chunks of red snapper, green fig, tomatoes, and corn flour dumplings.

"Hmmmm. Good," Scott said after his first spoonful. "Did you learn to cook on the ships?"

"I learned from an Indian girl, many years ago."

Scott devoured the rest of his lunch in silence. He dropped his spoon into the empty bowl, leaned back in the chair and dropped his arms to his side. "Thank you, Mr. Farrow."

"I save some for Rodney. He coming too?"

"He's vex with the world."

"Maybe he wish he was in Trinidad."

If Mr. Farrow suspected what their plans had been the night of the storm, he gave no hint.

He released the straps of his wooden leg, and stood the peg against the wall. "Feels good when it off."

Pale strap marks crisscrossed his leg. The raised scar, with a hundred stitch lines bordering it, looked like a centipede stretched across the base of his stump.

"We'll make you a new bench," Scott said.

"If rocks was good enough for Fédon, then is good enough for me." He lit his pipe and puffed on it. "Does talk about Fédon scare you, me boy?"

"Sometimes."

"Some people say he drown trying to get to Trinidad in a canoe." Mr. Farrow puffed his pipe and squinted behind the smoke.

"So a little boat can get to Trinidad?"

"Maybe. But a bench, no." He slapped the table and rolled his head back, filling the house with laughter.

Scott laughed too, rocking in his chair and holding his stomach. So Mr. Farrow did know.

Mr. Farrow regained his calm. "There are many stories about Fédon. People say they hear him riding his white horse at night. Some say he escaped by swimming under the island from Grand Étang Lake in the middle of the island to Black Bay, just south of Palmiste. Slaves believed he used black magic from he African mother to turn himself into a tree in the Mount Qua Qua mountains. They believe his spirit travel with winds to get his enemies to kill each other."

"You believe those stories?"

"A lot of it is superstition, but—"

"Super . . . what?"

"Superstition. Lessons for life." He tapped his pipe on the table. "Since people couldn't read or write back then, they put lessons in stories to pass down to their children. They used to say, '*Sa key tan parlay lutte.*' Patois for 'who hear tell the others.' Sometimes people remember the stories but forget the lessons."

"What lessons?"

"Just as there's a seed for every fruit, there's a seed behind every fight, every rebellion, every war. Today's fruits come from yesterday's seeds."

"But some fruits are good."

"True. But something happened on Mount Qua Qua that planted a bitter seed in General McDonald's family the day he crushed the rebellion. And now every generation of his family must taste the bitter fruit."

"But that was so long ago."

"Time don't matter. It travel like a disease from generation to generation in anybody with the general's blood. It could make brothers and cousins kill each other."

Scott waited for Mr. Farrow's next words, fearing what they would be.

"You family carry the general's blood. Pa's great great-grandfather was General McDonald."

***

When Scott left just before sunset, Farrow pulled an old letter from his collection and read it under his kerosene lamp.

"Your Excellency,

We are yet to capture the traitor Fédon, but it is with great satisfaction that I acquaint you with news of victory. We have crushed the rebellion that pained the King's colony of Grenada these past months. It will afford your Excellency no small measure of pride to behold the courage of the militia and their gallant officers, with their resolute determination to defeat the savagery of these misguided Negroes and their Free Coloured leaders. There is no Godly way for Fédon to escape. We have this peak completely surrounded with enough lead and powder to render his carcass unfit for animal consumption."

***

The next week Scott watched Oliver struggle out of the back seat of his parent's car with an air-powered pellet rifle and recalled Mr. Farrow's warnings about McDonalds killing each other. Oliver's parents, Aunty Hyacinth with jingling earrings and her husband with flashy rings, had already climbed the steps to visit Mommy and Daddy upstairs.

"What are you looking at?" Oliver asked, holding the rifle in one hand and a toy car in the other.

"Nice car," Scott said.

Oliver hugged his toy car. "You're not going to play with it."

"I mean you father car."

"It's not *you* father car. It's *your* father's car." Oliver rolled his eyes. "Country bookies just don't know how to talk."

"You understood what I said. So you a country bookie too?"

Oliver stared at Scott. "You could at least put on shoes and a shirt."

"I dress how I want. This is my yard, not yours." Scott returned to the fishing line tied to a stake in the backyard, now covered with dirt and grass. He pulled in the line, replaced the bait, double-checked the metal washer he used for weight, and tossed his hooked bait back into the sea.

Oliver strutted up to the wall with his pellet rifle and three empty bottles. He lined the bottles on the wall and stepped back a few paces.

"You can't shoot bottles here," Scott said.

"Watch me."

"No you won't," Scott yelled.

Rodney poked his head out of the upstairs bedroom window. "What going on down there?"

"He wants to shoot bottles on our wall."

Rodney disappeared from the window.

Scott moved over and stood in front of the bottles.

"I'll shoot you." Oliver cocked the rifle.

Scott rushed him, yanked the rifle by the muzzle and with a full swing, cracked the rifle stock across Oliver's shoulder.

Oliver screamed and dropped to his knees.

Scott heaved the rifle into the sea just as Rodney ran into the backyard. Daddy raced down the steps with Mommy and Oliver's parents behind him.

"What the hell's going on?" Daddy shouted.

Oliver pointed at Scott. "He hit me! And threw my gun in the sea."

Mr. Farrow pushed open his window and called out, but Oliver's shrieks swallowed up his words. The last thing Scott remembered before Daddy's belt ripped across his bare back was the pain in Mr. Farrow's eyes.

CHAPTER THIRTEEN

From where he stood on the gas station wall, Scott gazed over the mass of people waiting in the fading sunlight for the flip of the switch that would bring electricity to Gouyave. He'd noticed the progress over the past few months: workmen planting tall tar-scented poles in the ground, steadying them with cables, and stretching lines from pole to pole over the sidewalks from Gouyave to the Lance.

A new wooden pole with a shiny light holder towered above an old lamp-post in front of the nutmeg processing building across the street, just down from Lance Bridge. An unlit lamp dangled by rope from the old lamppost, as it probably had each evening since the days of Fédon.

Scott had seen similar lampposts in pirate movies at Casa Theatre. Maybe pirates once roamed these streets too, guzzling rum, torching buildings, and dragging away women. But Gouyave was Fédon's favorite town, Mr. Farrow has said. The rebel spared Gouyave the violence his men inflicted on Grenville where many died that first night, from cutlasses and fire under the full moon. Some killed in bed. Others beheaded in the streets. A gas lamp might have been the last thing many had seen before losing their heads to Fédon's temper.

Gouyave was also about to see its gas lamps for the last time tonight, but judging from the high mood of the hundreds crowded in front of a speakers' platform, Scott expected no deaths here. Even Mr. Farrow's warnings, about McDonalds killing each other, seemed farfetched.

Weeks had gone by since the fight with Oliver, but Rodney still fumed at Scott for the belting they received. Aunt Hyacinth and her husband had jumped into the car with Oliver sobbing in the back seat. As Oliver's father slammed the car door, Scott overheard him say to Oliver: "Don't worry son. They'll end up like their father."

What had he meant by that?

A slow-moving police motorcycle revved and backfired on the bridge. Rex barked from where he lay next to the wall.

"It's okay, boy," Rodney said, seated next to Martin.

A murmur swept through the crowd. People tiptoed. A shiny black car rolled across the bridge and followed the motorcycle toward the crowd. A woman shrieked and the crowd began to sing. "We go fight, fight, fight, for we leader."

The car pulled up beside the platform. A burly man stepped out from behind the wheel and opened the back door.

"That's Rabid," Martin said. "He fight like a mongoose with rabies."

A slender dark man in a white suit and hat emerged, waving a cane and flashing a toothy smile at the singing crowd.

"Chief Minister Gabbard," Martin said.

Scott watched intently, spellbound by the magic of Gabbard's presence.

People surged toward Gabbard. The burly man and several policemen surrounded him and led him up to the platform. Men in suits shook his hand. Gabbard turned to the crowd and waved his cane, triggering a screaming frenzy.

A priest said a prayer at the microphone and other men made brief speeches that made no sense to Scott. But when Gabbard took the microphone, Scott felt like he'd been seized by a power he could feel but not see. He wanted to sing with the crowd but did not know the words. He wanted to shake Gabbard's hand, but could not move.

Gabbard waved his cane and the crowd hushed. He barked words in an accent Scott had heard only during the BBC radio news. "Today is a Divine day. I'm protected by the spirit of my ancestor Fédon and anointed by the Supreme Being to bring you a brighter future. In 1951, I promised you freedom from plantation shackles. With God on my left and Fédon on my right, I delivered."

The crowd broke into wild cheers.

Scott nibbled his fingernails. If Gabbard was a Fédon, and believed in his spirit, then surely there must be some truth to the superstitions. Maybe Fédon had given Gabbard the African powers he was now using on the crowd.

"When I asked for your vote a year ago," Gabbard continued, "I promised you light. Once again, with God and Fédon at my side, I am here to deliver."

More applause.

Gabbard's energy grew as nightfall overran the town. He became a white suit in the darkness, swaying the crowd one direction and then the next, like fish helplessly hooked.

"Let there be light!" Gabbard flipped a switch and the streets lit up like a Christmas tree in Aruba.

The crowd roared and dogs barked. Bottles of rum and cans of corned beef circulated among the crowd. Cooking smoke spiced the air. People danced in the streets to calypso music as if it were a carnival.

Two hours later, Scott and Rodney said goodnight to Martin and headed home under the electric sunlight, past crammed rum shops vibrating with music and laughter. People staggered across the street, paying little heed to speeding cars.

Rex stared down a walkway at a man slumped against a wall.

Scott hurried up to him. "Daddy, you okay?"

Daddy heaved, and vomit splattered at his feet. He wiped his nose and spat. "Go . . . go home, son."

Rex squeezed past Scott's legs and sniffed at the watery pile.

Daddy stomped his feet. "Mash dog!"

Rex yelped and dashed into the street. Squealing tires and a nauseating bang shattered the night.

Scott sprinted across the street and dropped to his knees where Rex lay twitching in the drain. "Rex!" He pillowed the dog's head in his lap.

Rex looked up with a daze. Blood dripped from his mouth.

"Rex, please don't die." Scott's pain felt like he'd been hit by the car.

A shiny black car pulled to the curb ahead, with rolled-up windows.

Rabid struggled out of the driver's side. He tapped the front bumper with a nightstick and sprinkled broken glass onto the street. He glared at Scott, and then leaned into the open door. "Just a broken light, Boss."

Rabid squeezed in behind the wheel, slammed the door shut, and sped off toward St. George's. From the back seat, Gabbard waved his white hat at the people crowding the sidewalk, his windows still up.

CHAPTER FOURTEEN

Seated in the back seat of his official car as it raced south, Chief Minister Gabbard rested his white hat on his knee. He gripped his cane and gazed past Rabid's thick neck into the spray of headlights leading them. Except for that stupid dog getting killed, the Gouyave electric-light ceremony was a magnificent success. He reduced the accident to a speck of memory dust, and blew it away in the winds of excitement stirring in his gut.

Tonight was another solid step closer to his prize: Governor-General for life.

Surely, Fédon would smile on the day that a little black boy calculated his climb from a mud-floor plantation shack to the governor's mansion overlooking St. George's. Gabbard had vowed never to surrender his hands to manual labor, as his father had. The old man used to stumble home at night, pungent with sweat, and fall asleep on the dirt floor. His toes and fingers caked with mud, his khaki rags stained with banana drippings, he died with two shillings in his pocket.

But he had left young Gabbard an indelible lesson: those who used their minds would always exercise power over those who used labor. The accumulation of power became Gabbard's guiding compass. He would not rest until he reached the pinnacle.

He recalled his beginnings as a union leader, before the British allowed the elections that elevated him into political office. On strike for a two-percent pay raise, his people had turned the nightly skies red from blazing plantation hills. And when the riots spilled blood onto the streets, the British crawled to him, begging that he control his workers. Gabbard's radio broadcasts restored order in two days, with the help of his musclemen who cracked a few skulls to get the attention of the hard-of-hearing.

He'd never had a shortage of men for the finishing touches of his plans. Men like Rabid.

He tapped Rabid on the shoulder with his cane. "How's your friend in Richmond Hill Prison?"

"Planass?"

"Yes."

"He doing awright, Boss."

Yes, Fédon would admire Gabbard's style. Gabbard's great-grandmother had acquainted him with Fédon through her stories. Arthritic and toothless from old age, her mind was sharper than a cutlass. She liked saying *'sa key tan parlay lutte,'* who hear tell the others. And tell she did, until her last breath. She'd held Gabbard spellbound in the candlelight shadows of her musty shack, whispering Fédon back to life with tales of his cunning. He had outsmarted the British by reversing the shoes on his horses.

She walked Gabbard's imagination back down the agonizing centuries, and sailed him across the unforgiving Atlantic slave passages to where it all began on the West Coast of Africa. There, Fédon's Yoruba grandmother and her twin sister mastered the powers of manifest destiny from the ancestral spirits that resided in the sacred jungles. Before the gunshots, ropes, and long march in chains that ripped her away from her sister. But deep in the decomposing bowels of the slave ship, the Yoruba powers throbbed in her heart until Martinique's virgin streams, lakes and Silk Cotton trees welcomed them in ecstatic embrace.

When her master forced his lust on the young African girl, she mothered a daughter, to whom she passed along the ways of the ancestors. Now a *negresse libre creole*, the free daughter married a Frenchman and moved to Grenada, where she raised her family, including Julien Fédon, and made a home for her Yoruba traditions in the mountains around Grand Étang Lake.

Gabbard never forgot his first encounter with those powers at the lake, in the shadows of Mount Qua Qua. That full moon night he'd accompanied his great-grandmother on her long and final trek to a lakeshore landing decorated with colorful flags. She and other women danced and sang to drums and rattles. They danced faster and faster, harder and harder, until the spirits overtook their bodies in orgasmic spasms. Strange voices gushed from their mouths, and their eyes rolled white in the moonlight.

Young Gabbard learned that night that power one sees is no match for power one feels.

Gabbard's great-grandmother had said Fédon used that power to escape the British, swimming underneath the island from Grand Étang in the middle of the mountains to Black Bay seashores. He still roamed the minds of the people on his white horse, striking fear in all those who carried a single drop of his enemies' blood.

While absolute control over Grenada eluded Fédon, Gabbard intended to fulfill that destiny for them both. Gabbard would use swords and guns like Fédon had, but only when necessary. Gabbard had cleverer means of bending the British to his wishes and trapping the people's fears. He would control what people did, by controlling their fear.

Fédon would be Gabbard's weapon. Fear would be the ammunition.

Gabbard tapped Rabid on the shoulder again. "Tell Planass to pack his bags. I'll sign his early release papers tomorrow."

"That go make him glad, Boss."

"Tell him stay out of prison. I have work for him to do."

CHAPTER FIFTEEN

Daddy called out to Casa behind the bar. "Another round for everybody."

Scott wished he were home asleep tonight instead of in Casa's rumshop, sitting across the table from stone-faced Rodney. Casa hustled behind the bar in a sweat-soaked undershirt handing out drinks and making notes in his credit book. Cigarette smoke floated against the ceiling while a wooden radio with mesh-cloth speakers blasted calypso music next to a red Coca Cola icebox. Daddy stood at the far end of the bar with a group celebrating Armistice Day, November 11th, for Gouyave's last surviving World War I veterans: Mr. Farrow and Mr. Welsh.

Mr. Farrow had told Scott that the Great War ended on the eleventh hour of the eleventh day of the eleventh month in 1918. "The war that was supposed to end all wars but didn't."

Mr. Farrow and Mr. Welsh wore black open jackets and told war stories of days and nights in soggy trenches with dead and dying, and rats as big and brave as cats. But the biggest fear came from trench foot diseases that swelled men's feet, blue and twice their normal size.

"They couldn't even feel a bayonet stab," Mr. Welsh said. "Soldiers had missing flesh, eaten by rats when they sleep."

Daddy yelled out a joke and the men at the bar roared with laughter. He had other reasons to celebrate, with money he didn't have. He had staggered home that afternoon, saying he and his brothers were going to lease a gas station in St. George's.

When Daddy explained the details, Mommy exploded. "What deal was that? You giving your house to your brothers and dragging us to a little rental in town?"

"The boys will be closer to their cousin Oliver. Maybe now they'll get along."

When Daddy emerged from his bedroom two hours later saying that he was going to Casa's rumshop, Mommy demanded that he take Scott and Rodney with him.

Scott propped his elbows on the window table and gazed into the street. Female sidewalk vendors, in shawls and hair curlers, squatted behind coal pots sizzling with parched corn, fried fish, and blood sausages. His empty stomach grumbled at the mouthwatering aromas. He turned his attention to the over-loaded buses, tooting cars, and earsplitting motorcycles racing past under blazing streetlights, which intensified the ache in his chest.

He missed Rex.

He had asked Mr. Farrow if the accident three weeks ago might be Fédon's revenge, but Mr. Farrow dismissed Scott's concerns, and Gabbard's claim to be related to Fédon.

His comforting smile surrendered to a troubled look. "Politicians say any-thing to grab power."

The only power Scott understood and worried about was the electric lights that made him long for the gas lamp days. The intruding glare chased away the night magic, faded the sky's glitter, and dulled the storytelling that Scott had enjoyed on the steps with Rodney and their sisters. Just last night, Scott retreated from the bright intersection to his dark room. His thoughts drifted out his window and over the moonlit sea until the waves and sea breeze put him to sleep. He preferred his room any day, or night, over a rumshop.

Constable Robinson led the men around the bar in a toast with cheers of *Hep Hep Huray!* They gulped down rum shots and slammed glasses on the bar. The glow from the kerosene lamp erected a shadow performance of heads and arms on the dingy brick walls. Three weeks after electricity came to Gouyave, lamps still graced most homes and shops. Daddy had promised to hook electricity to the house, but now that promise would take a back seat to any plans to move to town.

What would life be like without Gouyave? Surely Scott would miss dive-bombing his thoughts with seagulls around fishing boats and dreaming of glid-ing over rooftops with pigeons. Would he again run through Belvidere Estate, sloshing mud between his toes and licking mango juice off his lips? He would always treasure the thrills of running away from school to go fishing with Martin. Even though Martin lacked in clothes and toys, Scott would miss his generous friendship.

It was too soon to leave Gouyave, with so many unanswered questions. What could possibly tie Fédon from two hundred years ago to events, people, and pain today? Only Mr. Farrow seemed to hold the answers. And Scott might never learn them if the family moved to town.

Whatever happened, Gouyave would always be home, even in a rum shop embracing memories of Rex, watching Daddy get drunk, and avoiding Rodney's glares.

Just then, a skinny, cocoa-brown man stumbled through the doorway and pulled up a stool at the vacant end of the bar. Casa served him a drink. The man gulped it and stared at the empty glass in his hand, tugging on a ram-goat beard and dangling a cigarette from his lips. He downed a second drink, and then a quick third. He slammed a few rumpled dollar bills on the counter and staggered toward the door. He glanced at Rodney, and slithered toward their table, twisting his beard and flashing his gaze back and forth between Scott and Rodney.

"McDonalds, eh?" His voice crackled. "Which one is you father?"

Constable Robinson bellowed from the bar. "Stay away from them boys, Planass!"

CHAPTER SIXTEEN

Planass looked nothing like the muscle-packed badjohn Scott expected. This bone-thin man confirmed Martin's claim that Richmond Hill prisoners were fed only bread and water, and had no barbers. A part down the middle of the man's head separated the front of his hair like menacing cow horns.

"Where you father?" Planass sputtered a nauseating vapor of rum and sweat.

Scott grabbed the table to steady his hands.

Daddy rushed up. "Long time, Junior."

Planass poked Daddy in the chest with stubby fingers. "Only me mother call me Junior."

"How is she?"

"Not you fucking business." He stared Daddy up and down, their noses almost touching. "And me name is Planass."

"So I hear."

"Rabid tell me you come back. I tell he, you not that stupid. Even if is two hundred years, I never forget." A dry chuckle stalled at his throat.

"Sorry." Daddy glanced away.

"Sorry don't mean shit." Planass pointed at Scott. "He look same age, eh?"

Mr. Farrow limped up, and almost knocked over a chair with his wooden leg. "It's over, man. Twenty years. You don't want to go back in prison."

"Prison is home." Planass grinned with gaps of missing teeth. "That's where I go dead."

"Time to leave." Constable Robinson grabbed Planass by his arm and led him to the door.

Planass stumbled out into the busy street.

Mr. Welsh drifted up on unsteady legs and sat next to Scott. "That . . . that Planass scary, eh?"

Scott nodded. Scary and confusing. What did Scott's age have to do with the anger that fired Planass? And why did Daddy apologize about something that happened twenty years ago? Aunty Bridgette had warned Daddy that Scott and Rodney would be in danger from Planass. But why?

When Daddy and Mr. Farrow headed back to the bar, Mr. Welsh sat next to Scott and rolled two stones across the table. "Found these on me roof a few weeks ago."

Rodney stared at Mr. Welsh with a straight face.

"Don't worry," Mr. Welsh said with words as sleepy as his eyes. "Farrow told me you boys in enough hot water. Just don't do it again."

"How did you know?" Scott couldn't resist.

"I know everything . . . in Gouyave." He took a swig from his glass, lowered his voice, and leaned forward with a sly wink. "Miss Mildred was by me for a . . . . a morning visit. She tell me about two McDonald boys that passed her house."

The big woman with the mango tree. Scott wondered if the stones had landed on the roof while the big-breasted woman was in bed with Mr. Welsh, naked.

Scott muffled a laugh, and Rodney's glare melted into a smile.

Mr. Welsh tapped his fingers on the table. "Yep. I know . . . *everything.*"

"Are you a war hero?" Scott studied the two medals on Mr. Welsh's jacket.

"No, but Neil Farrow is," Mr. Welsh whispered. "He saved you grandfather's life."

Scott dragged his chair closer to Mr. Welsh.

Mr. Welsh tapped the stones together. "I'll keep these a secret if you promise not to say nothing to Neil."

"Okay," Scott said.

"Me and Neil went to the war with you grandfather. First British West Indian Regiment, 3rd Grenada Contingent, 1915. You pa was an officer, a captain."

"Were you a captain too?" Rodney asked.

"In those days in the West Indian Regiment, soldiers were black and officers were white." He took a drink. "One night you pa . . . got lost in No Man's Land. Cold mud, barbed wire . . . German bullets like rain. Without permission, Neil went looking for Captain McDonald. Found him shot, but alive.

A German bullet shattered Neil's leg, but he never gave up. Took him three hours to drag you grandfather back."

"Then Mr. Farrow *is* a war hero," Scott said.

"For me and you, yes. But for the British, never. Even after they cut off his leg, they put him in jail for disobeying orders. Trying to start a mutiny, they say. He didn't come back to Gouyave until 1921, three years after the war."

"Couldn't he just tell them he went to save Pa?"

"We was only supposed to dig trenches. They didn't want black men shooting white Germans. No guns for us for a long time. So Neil crawled out there with knife in he mouth. You pa couldn't defend Neil in court, because the British didn't want nobody saying a black man save a white man. It really eat up you pa. He came back from the war a drunk."

"You know a lot."

"There's other things about Neil you don't know."

Scott waited.

"You know why he know so much about Fédon—"

Mr. Farrow limped up to the table, kicked out a chair with his wooden leg, and sat. "What stories he telling you boys?"

Mr. Welsh winked at Scott. "We talking about war."

"No more talk about war." Mr. Farrow glanced at his watch. "Time for one more —"

The front door flung open. Planass stormed through the doorway and rushed up to the table. He hurled aside a chair and roped an arm around Scott's neck. "Where's Hector?"

Scott gasped for air and grabbed at the arm choking him. *Somebody help me.* The words stayed trapped at his throat.

"That's my brother!" Rodney pulled and bit at the arm around Scótt's neck.

A fist swung past Scott's face. A thud. Rodney collapsed to the floor.

Daddy rushed up. "He's just a boy, Planass. Let him go."

"I was just a boy too, remember?" Planass sneered and reached under his shirt. "Twenty years I wait for you ass."

"He have a gun!" someone shouted.

Cold metal pressed on Scott's temple. He caught his breath and heard his own scream.

Mr. Farrow braced himself to stand.

"Stay right there old man, or you dead." Planass aimed the gun at Mr. Farrow.

Somebody help me. The thought screamed in Scott's brain.

Daddy stepped closer. "Take me instead."

Mr. Farrow struggled up from his chair.

"Stand back," Planass said. "Both of you."

"Let's talk." Mr. Farrow stepped forward. His peg leg caught between the table and his chair. He lost his balance and tripped toward Planass.

The gun exploded at Scott's ear and Mr. Farrow crashed onto the table. Smoke burned Scott's eyes.

Another explosion. Mr. Welsh tumbled to the floor like a bag filled with breadfruit.

Daddy shouted. "Shoot me instead, you coward!"

Another explosion.

Then darkness.

PART II

CHAPTER SEVENTEEN

Seven Years Later
Port-of-Spain, Trinidad

"Letter from Grenada." Gillian's friend, Sonia, handed her an envelope before class at the St. Francois Girls High School.

"It's from Daddy." When Gillian suspected a few years ago that Sticks was opening her mail and pocketing her money, she asked her father to mail his letters to Sonia's address instead.

"By the way," Sonia said. "Mom said you can start working tomorrow night."

"I can't wait." Gillian now had a sanctuary for the nights Aunt Josephine worked at the hospital, but shame still burdened her heart for acting too late.

Sonia must have read her mind. "Don't worry, I didn't tell her about Sticks. I just want you to get you away from that sicko."

"I know."

"Are you going to the movies with that cute boy?"

"He's not my type," Gillian said.

"You could be anybody's type if you expose a little of what God gave you." Sonia released the top button of Gillian's white shirt and adjusted her collar.

"When I find the right person."

"When? You're seventeen, and you still never had a boyfriend."

"I'd better read the letter before class." Gillian embraced Sonia and headed to a shady bench. She pulled a fifty-dollar money order from the envelope and read the letter.

Dear Gillian,

Here's a little something to put in the bank. I don't work for the McDonalds in Belvidere Estate any longer. I move to a small house in town to work the whiskey business. I will send you more money, when I find more business friends. I sometimes work at the port too, close to the McDonalds gas station. They still live on Marryshow Lane in St. Georges since the shooting in Gouyave.

I can't believe you in Trinidad more than seven years already. No one in Grenada would know you if they see you today. Every time I see Scott at the gas station, he ask me about you. Send me a wallet picture so I can show him how much you change.

With love,

Daddy.

Gillian held the letter to her bosom and a blush warmed her face.

Scott still remembered her.

That afternoon, Gillian opened the door to the Laventille Road house. As she expected, Sticks was on the couch snoring under his cloud of body odors. She tiptoed past his newspaper mess lying on the floor next to the couch, entered her bedroom, and locked the door. She fell back on her bed with the letter on her chest, shutting her eyes and allowing the memories of happier times to wash over her; Mammy's gentle hands shampooing her hair in the basin outside, driving with Daddy in the big truck through the lush fields of Belvidere Estate, and the side-splitting moments with her long-buried pet monkey, Lady.

But the memories did little to pluck the shame she harbored like a thorn in her heart. She recalled the day she tearfully recounted to Aunty Josephine how Sticks forced her awake to massage his legs during the storm.

Aunty Josephine had brushed it off with a laugh.

Maybe Gillian should have written to Daddy instead. But she had not, and her secret grew into a monster that smothered her life. As the days dragged into months, Sticks began to demand more than leg massages. As the months dragged into years, his zipper came down. He forced her hands from his legs to his ugly manhood, until his sick pleasure discharged on his shorts and collapsed him on the couch in disgusting groans.

She should have told Daddy then, but had not.

And it was her fault.

It was her fault that the hands that cleaned Scott's bruises had become pleasure tools for a pervert.

She scrubbed her hands so raw, that the medicated cream Aunty Josephine brought her from the hospital burned like hot coals.

That was when she decided to return the pain to its rightful owner.

The next time Sticks forced her hands on him the cream set his groin on fire. He screamed and wreathed around on the floor. She thought he'd gotten a heart attack.

But he lived, and she continued to wish he would die.

She was around thirteen when she told him that if he touched her again, she would kill him. So his abuse switched to verbal floggings that ripped her soul, especially when he called her a whore.

She dreaded the day she would tell Daddy what had become of his little girl. Her dream to make him proud was suffocating.

But through it all, she kept the stained handkerchief to remind her that she didn't have to lose her dream, still nourished with the memory of the day she'd treated Scott's bruises in Gouyave. So long ago.

She squeezed the handkerchief in the pillowcase and dozed off knowing that Sticks would never hurt her again.

CHAPTER EIGHTEEN

Scott gazed out the back of the crowded bus as it rumbled northward, meandering on the narrow potholed road between lush hills and sea-washed coastlines. The bus, a flatbed truck fitted with wooden benches under a canopy of polished mahogany, hit a pothole. A pig squealed behind Scott. He stretched over a box of vegetables to check the noose around the pig's neck. Satisfied that the animal would not choke, he settled back on the padded bench.

Scott recalled the night when he too was being choked. A bony arm locked around his neck while explosions hammered in his ear. He slipped into a silent darkness, and then awakened on his back, staring at the ceiling in a daze, his neck throbbing, and his throat on fire. Shouts around him. He struggled to sit up. His hands slipped on a warm wetness on the floor, next to Rodney and two men. Red everywhere. Pain surged up from his neck to his head, just as darkness had rescued him again.

Even after seven years, the memory still pulsated in wicked glee at the brick-walled questions imprisoning him. Why him? Why the McDonalds? Why? He'd always known that only Gouyave had the answers to free him. It had taken him seven years, but he knew he would eventually return.

Gouyave would always be home.

Little of the countryside had changed since the family's arrival from Aruba. The scenery flowed by as they had many years before. Wooden houses watched from thick greenery as sheep and goats grazed on hillsides sliced by rushing streams. Students in uniforms shared the roadsides with women balancing baskets of cocoa on their heads, pausing to watch the bus rumble by. Coal pot smoke danced in the air, still competing with the delicious scent of mango and guava as it did so long ago.

One thing had changed though.

Planass was back in Richmond Hill Prison, twenty years for murder. Just long enough for Scott to grow up and for Planass to grow old. The killer's shouts in the courtroom still echoed in Scott's ears. "You go see me again!"

"Drop one," a passenger called out. The bus screeched to a stop, letting off two people in front of a shop plastered with beer and milk posters. The teenage conductor, half-sitting with one leg planted on the outside step, collected the fares and emptied the coins into a jingling leather pouch hanging from his neck.

They drove past Palmiste Beach. The old building that had sheltered Scott and Rodney during the storm still overlooked the calm bay. But while peace had returned to Palmiste, it was yet to find a home between Scott and Rodney. They had not once discussed the night at Casa's rumshop, and little else since.

The bond that once held Scott and Rodney as brothers had floated away on memories poisoned with secrets and pain.

The bus crested the hill and Gouyave loomed before him. Church steeples commanded the skyline and coconut trees waved at the late afternoon sun. A lump rose in his throat.

The bus rolled down the hill and pulled up in front of the market.

He paid the conductor and jumped out. He doubted anyone could recognize his skinny frame in Daddy's blue oversized oil-stained shirt and the frayed jeans with the burnt hole big enough to pass an orange. They used to be Rodney's jeans, burnt when Rodney was smoking a marijuana joint and the lit tip fell into the folded pant cuff.

Scott wriggled his toes on the piece of cardboard he'd slid into his shoes to cover the holes in the worn soles, hoping that his jeans were long enough to cover the scuff marks and tattered stitching.

Certainly, no one would know him with his jutting cheekbones and wild Afro. He was nine years old when he left. Now he was almost seventeen.

Confident in his anonymity, he crossed the street to stare at their old house, now signed over to Daddy's brothers in exchange for his gas station lease in St. George's. Mildew discolored the walls. Ragged curtains flapped behind broken windowpanes. And where Scott once stood on the elevated yard to fish, the back wall lay crumbled in the sea and waves crashed just feet from the back of the house.

He turned and headed toward the Lance. Faces passed in the brisk Friday afternoon, some familiar. No one acknowledged him as he crossed Lance Bridge. He gave Casa's rumshop a fleeting glance on his way to the fish market that used to house his school. Today, shoppers squeezed past tables inspecting the latest catch. He inhaled the sea breeze, savoring memories of Martin.

He hurried to his friend's house on Back Street, but Martin's grandmother said she hadn't seen him in days. She didn't know what he did for a living, only that he frequently stopped by to give her American money. Scott decided not to tell her that Rodney had seen Martin a few months ago, diving for coins tossed by cruise ship tourists in the St. George's harbor.

No longer able to postpone the real reason he had returned to Gouyave, Scott headed to the little house and knocked on the door.

"Come in," a voice called out.

Some things in Gouyave had not changed.

***

Rodney sensed something was wrong. He dashed across the busy street to Daddy's gas station, already dark at eight o'clock on a Friday night. The gas pumps should have been cranking, with buses filling up for their return to the countryside after movies at Regal and Empire cinemas. A British battleship was also in port, dislodging hundreds of sailors to roam the island, so why wasn't there a line of taxis waiting for gas? And why wasn't Scott pumping gas here instead of pumping information from old people in Gouyave?

Daddy always complained about not having money for rent, or school uniforms, or for Rodney's visit to an ear specialist, so why the hell was he shut for business tonight?

Rodney glanced over his shoulder at Chinatown, a hamlet of lunch counters and bars adjacent to the port, fired up with calypso rhythms, spicy food, and prostitutes. Those damn jezebels would earn more from sailors tonight than Daddy would from gas.

Rodney shook the front door. Locked. Scott should have been the one here tonight, trying to get money for supper. After all the crap they'd gone through, why was he still digging up the frigging past, in some library or kiss-me-ass history book?

It seemed the family depended on Rodney—and blamed him when things went wrong.

He'd had it with having his ear pulled. He'd had it with being blamed for being expelled from school. No one asked the teacher why he slapped Rodney and pulled his ears just for getting a wrong answer in class. That was Rodney's final ear-pulling. He'd broken off the back of his chair and chased the teacher out the school.

They could all kiss Rodney's ass.

Hell, he could make more money selling *ganja* joints than those fools who finished school and held bank jobs. Customers like Oliver ensured that Rodney always had a few dollars in his pocket, enough to buy bread and cocoa on the nights Daddy was broke, or missing.

He peered through the gas station window. Light seeped from beneath the office door. He turned and surveyed the parking lot. One car—Daddy's old green Austin Cambridge, still crippled on oiled-stained bricks six months after a blown head gasket. How could he run a gas station, but not have a car that ran?

Rodney slid along the back of the building, startling a cat on top of an overflowing trashcan. He kicked past discarded oilcans and rags. Daddy should get his lazy idiots to clean up this shit. They were probably the best Daddy could hire at ten dollars a day, a whole lot more than the measly fifty cents a day he paid Scott and Rodney for pumping gas during school holidays. But that was before Rodney learned about earning faster money.

In dim light outside the window, he parted the overgrowth and peeked in. Daddy sat in his metal chair, slumped over the desk, his head buried in a mess of papers. Rodney fought his way through the brush to the back door. He let himself into the dark hallway, squeezing past jumbled boxes. He stood next to the foul-smelling toilet and finger-tipped the office door open.

Daddy's snores vibrated the desk under a clutter of loose paper, rags, and grease pencils. Saliva dribbled from his open mouth, smearing the blue ink on a letter beneath his face. He clutched a glass next to an empty rum bottle. The office reeked of rum and gasoline.

Rodney's anger boiled.

Maybe the baby had been the lucky one. She was to be named Jackie. What kind of life would she have had, growing up with a father like this, in a crowded house with a leaky roof, uncertain meals, and ignored illnesses? Jackie had been stillborn at nine months, after weeks of arguments between Mommy and Daddy.

Rodney fought back the tears. He felt punished by his helplessness. Like a falling row of drunken dominoes, the family had stumbled from one crushing defeat to the next. Around every corner of fleeting happiness, another fall waited. Maybe tonight was the moment he'd waited for, to save his family from the next fall.

The idea had first come to him on the Christmas Eve afternoon they waited for Daddy to take them to Jackie's funeral. While Mommy lay grieving at the hospital, they sat around the bare kitchen table under mildewed ceilings listening to the radio blare jingling bells and banging drums in carols of empty Christmas promises.

It didn't matter that they had neither a Christmas tree nor gifts. It didn't matter they'd had nothing to eat since breakfast—buttered bread washed down with cocoa-tea that Daddy had mistakenly sweetened with salt. What really mattered was that they'd waited in vain to say goodbye to the sister they would never know.

Daddy finally showed up drunk, at midnight. "If y'all want to go see . . . her tomorrow, the grave . . . has a tire on it." He'd stumbled into his room and slammed the door.

Watered with his tears for Jackie, Rodney's plan took root in the gas station office.

He scanned the littered office until he saw the heavy wrench.

His mind buzzed. Wrap the wrench handle with a rag to avoid fingerprints. Daddy wouldn't feel a thing. Make it look like a robbery; take whatever money he found. Wash his hands. Go home as if everything was fine. Tell Mommy that Daddy had worked late, and would spend the night on his cot in the station. Let those idiots find him in the morning.

All of Rodney's years of hurting, hoping, and hurting again, slammed into one agonizing moment of decision.

He grabbed a rag off the desk, reached for the wrench, and stood over Daddy.

CHAPTER NINETEEN

"**H**ere's what I found in the library," Scott said after a couple of hours reminiscing with Mr. Farrow in the lamplight. Scott handed over a sheet of paper with handwritten notes, eager for Mr. Farrow's response.

Mr. Farrow put on his glasses and read the notes. He tapped his eyebrow scar left over from the gash he'd gotten when he tripped into Casa's rum shop table at the moment Planass fired the gun. The first two bullets missed Mr. Farrow but hit Mr. Welsh, killing him instantly. The third shot had drilled the floor when Casa smashed a chair over Planass.

Except for his husky voice and the expanded baldness that glistened in the lamplight, Mr. Farrow had not aged much in the last seven years.

"They won't let me borrow the newspaper," Scott said. "So I took notes. The Grenada Chronicle, December 21st 1940."

"It's nothing new." He passed the notes back to Scott. "The police believed Pa killed himself."

"They said the investigation would continue. But there's nothing more in the newspapers after 1940."

Mr. Farrow shifted in his chair. "So what's your question for me?"

"Was Daddy present when Pa died?"

"It doesn't matter."

"Why is everyone so evasive?" Scott slapped the paper on the table. "Aunty Bridgette puts the phone down when I call, and won't even let me talk to Ma."

"She's been through enough. You opening old wounds, me boy."

"My wounds still bleed. I need to know why Planass hates me and Rodney!"

"People and events today don't matter."

"What do you mean?"

"You family have a long river flowing through them. Find the birth of the river and you find the lessons."

"Is that it?" Scott's annoyance strained his voice. "I just want to know how all this started."

"It started with Fédon—"

"Why do we have to go back two hundred years?"

"Are you going to listen, or act like a bloody lawyer?"

"Go ahead."

"When General McDonald crushed the rebels on Mount Qua Qua, he sent a young officer to search for Fédon. He never found Fédon, but something else happen up there. After that, there was bad blood between the general and the officer. The young officer was the general's son."

"Pa's great-grandfather?"

"Yes. The general took over Fédon's estate. Drank a lot. The slaves heard lots of fighting between father and son in the big house. One day the general's horse came home alone. Two days later they find him dead on the rocks below a bridge."

"Fédon's revenge?" He chuckled, hoping Mr. Farrow would detect the sarcasm.

"That was only the beginning. Every generation get grief. The general's son hung himself, and Pa's grandfather shot himself after his wife ran off with an English merchant."

"The seeds planted in one generation bears fruit in the next?"

"So you remember." Mr. Farrow forced a smile.

"You keep bringing up Mount Qua Qua. But something bizarre must have also happened on Belvidere estate in 1940. Within two days, four people died suddenly. Ruby Ferguson and her baby, Pa, and I read of a man who hung himself from a tree on the estate, the night before Pa died. The man left a son."

"His son was Junior, before he became Planass."

"Maybe I should be talking to him instead."

"Me boy, stay away from Planass, even in jail."

"I can't forget." Scott rubbed his neck, recalling the murderer's bony arms choking him. "I need to know what happened."

"It's time I talk to you father." Mr. Farrow tightened the straps on his wooden peg. "He at the gas station tonight?"

"Yes."

"I'll call him from the shop next door. He knows everything." He limped toward the door. "Have some more cocoa-tea. I'll be right back."

"One more question. How did you and Pa get along after you rescued him in the war?"

Mr. Farrow narrowed his eyes. "Who told you?"

"You lost your leg saving Pa, but they imprisoned you for mutiny. No one was to know that you saved Pa's—"

"Enough!"

"It was Pa's fault you lost your leg, right?"

"It was my decision to crawl out there," Mr. Farrow shouted.

"Why didn't Pa testify to keep you out of jail?"

"We lived in different times, son. He couldn't, even if he'd wanted to."

"You hated Pa for that, didn't you?"

"Everybody hated him!" His voice shook. "Just ask you own father."

It had been a long day and fatigue was calling Scott to sleep, but he had one final question before he let Mr. Farrow call Daddy.

"So who shot Pa? Was it Daddy, or was it you?"

***

Rodney stood behind Daddy's chair, the heavy wrench in his hands. The drunken son-of-a-bitch looked so innocent when he slept. His scowl relaxed, his face recast, untroubled, his barks traded for snores that rattled from his gaping mouth. Rodney tightened his grip on the wrench.

The phone rang.

Shit.

Daddy moaned. Without lifting his head off the table, he released his glass and reached for the phone.

If Rodney hit him now and knocked the receiver over, the caller might be alerted.

It rang again.

Daddy sat up and fumbled with the phone. "Hel . . .lo."

Dammit. Rodney backed out of the office, tugging at the door but leaving it slightly ajar.

"What's . . . happening, Farrow?" Daddy listened a few moments. "I don't have a damn thing to tell Scott. While he's annoying you, I going bankrupt. His only concern . . . should be his next meal."

The call lasted another minute before Daddy slammed down the phone.

Rodney hid behind the boxes while Daddy turned off the lights, locked the front door behind him, and stumbled into the night.

Rodney crept back into the office and flipped on the light. He sat at the desk, shuffling through letters with official letterheads. Some warned about late payments. Others made threats in legal mumbo-jumbo about canceling his lease. The gas station was out of gasoline.

He grabbed a handwritten sheet inscribed *Money to Collect*, an untidy list of names and dollar amounts. The thieves who never paid for their gas. He recognized the name at the top of the list owing over a thousand dollars. Neville Snyder, the government crook with the chauffeur-driven limousine and big-ass house on the hill overlooking Marryshow Lane. Living like a king while Daddy was going broke.

Rodney copied some of the names and amounts on another sheet of paper, stuffed it in his pocket and let himself out of the back door.

It was time to even the score.

CHAPTER TWENTY

The next morning, Scott awoke to the scent of cocoa-tea and the sound of waves. After the move to St. George's, it had taken him two weeks of restless nights before he could enjoy a full night's sleep without the waves. He rubbed his eyes and sat up in bed.

Mr. Farrow was sitting at the window and holding a mug. "Slept well, me boy?"

"Best I've had in a long time. Where did you sleep?"

"Didn't. The body can only sleep when the mind is at rest."

"Sorry if I was rude last night," Scott said.

"It's okay." Mr. Farrow's disappointment deepened the lines on his forehead when he explained that Daddy had not been in a talking mood when Farrow called.

Daddy's secrets were eating him from the inside, leaving him like an empty chamber with nothing but echoes of a distressing past.

Maybe Scott's visit to Gouyave was a mistake. Probably all Mr. Farrow possessed was his past too, and exposing it meant losing it. After all, everything about him seemed so unchanged. He still used the old kerosene lamp that had been dented in the storm. And the old picture of Ruby still sat in the frame with the cracked glass.

Mr. Farrow must have seen him staring at the picture. "Get it."

Scott stretched across the bed for the picture and handed it to Mr. Farrow.

"The day you took it down, you didn't put it back the way it was," Mr. Farrow said. "I could always see her from the window. But not that day. That's how I know you would come back. You always wanted to know." He lit his pipe and blew smoke toward the ceiling. "Her name was Ruby Ferguson. She's buried in the Anglican Church cemetery."

"How did you know her?"

"She was my daughter."

Scott watched Mr. Farrow in stunned silence as the old man struggled away from the table and fumbled around his coal pot. He returned with two cups of steaming cocoa-tea and a plate of golden-brown fried bakes, balls of dough deep-fried into delicious bread.

Mr. Farrow told him how he met Ruby's mother, Jasmine, at the park many years ago when she found his goat dying of rabies.

"I was young, angry at the world. Jasmine heal my soul." Mr. Farrow sipped from his cup. "When she get pregnant, her parents keep her in the house until she deliver Ruby. When I try to visit, her father chased me with a cutlass. Said Indians and Blacks shouldn't mix. Later I find out the Fergusons adopt Ruby. Jasmine move to Trinidad and I never see her again."

"How did you find Ruby?"

"Her mother . . . Jasmine smile like nobody else. I see Ruby in the Anglican Church ten years later with Mrs. Ferguson. She smile and then I know. I ask Dr. Branch, he deliver all babies in Gouyave back then. He say, if my heart say so, then is so."

Mr. Farrow got a garden job with the Fergusons so he would see Ruby, but she died giving birth at age seventeen, never knowing Mr. Farrow was her father.

"Was Daddy the father of Ruby's baby?"

"Ask him youself." Mr. Farrow looked like he was in physical pain. "By the way, you talk all night in you sleep."

"Rodney complains about that."

"Be careful. One day the wrong person might hear you secrets."

Later, when Scott followed Mr. Farrow to catch the St. George's bus, the intersection overflowed with people. "What's going on?"

"Gouyave fishermen starting a union," Mr. Farrow said. "A lawyer taking them on a march."

"Here they come," someone shouted.

A cloth banner led the way, painted with a swordfish and stretched high across the street by hand-held poles. One man stood out among the fifty men in battered hats and frayed clothes. Tall and brown skinned with neat Afro and manicured beard, he walked arm-in-arm with anglers in the middle of the front row.

The marchers stopped at the intersection. The tall man, in dashiki, jeans, and rubber sandals, climbed on to the back of a parked truck with a microphone.

He stuck one hand in his dashiki pocket and scanned the crowd. "Gabbard says he built a fish market on the Lance for poor people. He pays you a dollar for your fish, but he sells the fish to hungry Grenadians for two dollars. Who's getting the other dollar?"

The crowd booed.

"The money buys Gabbard and his stooges big cars and big houses. Brothers and sisters, this is shameless exploitation. The only way to stop it is for us to unite."

The crowd cheered.

"He make sense," a man said to Mr. Farrow.

"They all make sense in the beginning," Mr. Farrow said.

The speaker on the truck continued. "Gabbard tells people he's a descendant of Fédon. But Fédon led a revolution to free the oppressed. Gabbard is for rich fat cats!"

More jeers.

"Who's the speaker?" Scott asked Mr. Farrow.

"Roger Duncan, just finish studying law in England. Gabbard say he's a communist who want to start a revolution like Cuba. Maybe one day your paths will cross."

"Why?"

"Years before the rebellion, more than thirty French plantation owners, including Fédon, made an oath to the British. When the rebellion started, all of them break the oath, except one. Duncan's family is descendants of that free colored Frenchman. Your bloodlines are both enemies of Fédon."

Scott wondered if Duncan might also be on Fédon's revenge list.

***

Anxious to be alone with his thoughts, Scott jumped off the bus in the St. George's market-square. The blaring horns and shouting vendors faded behind him as he headed up Market Hill for the twenty-minute walk home. He crested the hill, strolled past the traffic box housing the snappy, white-gloved policeman, and climbed the congested Lucas Street, past schools, tailor shops, and small grocery stores.

He turned on to Marryshow Lane and gazed out over the horseshoe shaped harbor, recalling from his geography class that it was carved by a volcanic explosion and filled in by the Caribbean Sea millions of years ago. This marriage of fire and water must have been planned with anticipation of more drama to come, given the amphitheater hillsides wrapping around the harbor. The first, and possibly the most enduring act was the creation of Grenada's beaches, black-sand beaches from volcanic lava-flows and white-sand beaches from the coral gardens that encircled the island. In the distance to the south, the pristine white sands of Grand Anse beach sparkled for two miles in the afternoon sun, its bay like welcoming arms to the blue sea.

The virgin sands of Grand Anse had welcomed their first human footprints around the time of Christ when the Arawak people fleeing tribal warfare in the Amazons had rowed their canoes into the bay. They enjoyed a thousand years of peace on the lush island before their aggressive cousins, the Carib Indians, invaded and dominated Grenada for another five hundred years.

Caribs hunting in these hills must have been in awe at the fluttering white sails that carried Columbus past Grenada in 1498. But when the first British landed on Grand Anse in 1609, the Caribs were not in a welcoming mood: only eight of the original two hundred settlers survived. By 1651 the French established a foothold just south of the harbor and pushed the Caribs northward with guns and swords. Rather than surrender, most of the Caribs leapt to their deaths off Leapers Hill in Sauteurs. Any surviving natives would have witnessed the first shipment of anguished African humanity led off in shackles, and the smoking booms of naval canons as the Europeans battled each other for the island's sugar wealth.

Scott glanced around at the monuments of Grenada's turbulent past; the stonewalled Fort George, started by the French and completed by the British, guarding the harbor entrance on the peninsular to the west; Fort Frederick watching from the highest point to the east and overlooking Richmond Hill Prison, the sweltering concrete oven with matchbox windows and barbed wire

fences, home to Planass; and on the ridge above Marryshow Lane, the sprawling Government House, the Governor's official mansion and former residence
of Governor Home, captured and executed with forty-seven officials by Fédon
on Belvidere Estate in 1795.

Scott had already seen how unexplained events of 1940 ricocheted in
Gouyave twenty-five years later. But could the Fédon events still ignite tempers
that inflict punishment on the McDonalds and possibly the Duncans?

Predicting the future seemed pointless. Unraveling Daddy's past was excru-
ciating enough. Something had happened in Belvidere that forced Daddy from
Grenada and planted twenty-five years of murderous hatred in Planass.

Had all this started with Pa's death? Everyone might have hated Pa, but Mr.
Farrow seemed the only one with reasons to kill. Daddy had a gun, so maybe
Mr. Farrow used a knife. A vicious stabbing would explain the *blood everywhere*
that Daddy had whispered to Aunty Bridgette about. Mr. Farrow had crawled
into enemy lines with a knife in his mouth, and Scott had seen the way he used
his blade with rapid hand movements to shape his tire sandals. But Daddy's
occasionally strained friendship with Mr. Farrow hardly hinted that they shared
a murder secret.

And what of Uncle Malcolm's flare-ups with Daddy? Ruby might be the
link between them all, but could a mother dying at childbirth at age seventeen
trigger this much hatred?

The more the past unraveled, the less Scott understood.

He hurried along Marryshow Lane and gazed up at Oliver's hillside neighborhood, large brick homes, wrapped by manicured lawns, flower gardens, and
white picket fences. Music blared from a new house, a monstrosity of concrete
and glass owned by a government man named Snyder. Shiny cars lined the
steep driveway in the late afternoon light. Men in suits led women in evening
dresses, past a policeman, to the verandah.

On the lower side of the road, clusters of tin-roofed houses cascaded down
to the waterfront road called the Carenage. The slick *Nordic Prince* cruise ship
crowded the harbor and taxis collecting passengers congested the Carenage.
Martin would probably be there, diving for American coins, and probably won't
care that nine years after they had read her name at the Anglican Church cemetery, Scott finally discovered that Ruby Ferguson was Mr. Farrow's daughter.

The dogs greeted Scott with wagging tails as he ran down the steps on the lower side of Marryshow Lane to the small red-roofed house. He pushed open the front door, rattling the cracked glass pane, and entered the sparse living room.

"Your turn to go find your father." Mommy was seated at her favorite window beneath the water-stained ceiling, staring up at the hillside. "We need money for supper."

"Where's Rodney?"

"Just left, vex as usual."

Scott entered the bedroom that he and Rodney shared with the girls, a riot of mattresses, clothes and books. Claudette sat reading while Alicia dozed on their bed under the open windows. The little black transistor radio, tuned to the American Top Forty, was playing an *O'Jays* song about smiling faces and back-stabbers.

"What's wrong with Rodney?" he asked Claudette.

"Said he's tired asking Daddy for money."

"It's okay. I'll go."

"Rodney left something." She handed him a folded paper. "He said those are the people you should be looking for, not Mr. Farrow. Mr. Snyder is on top of the list."

"Snyder is having a party at his new house."

"Maybe that's where Rodney—"

"Ah shit!" Scott bolted from the house and raced across Marryshow Lane to Mr. Snyder's house.

He climbed the road past cars lined along the fence toward Snyder's driveway. Jovial conversation and laughter blended with live music from the crowded semi-circular verandah fronting the house. Huge glass windows and sliding doors reflected the red sunset in a perfume-scented haze.

He avoided the suspicious glare of uniformed men standing at the gate and continued past the house. In the backyard, long tables decorated with white cloth, red roses and sculpted pineapples awaited the guests next to a large grill belching a smoky barbecue aroma. Two men exited the kitchen, carrying a container stacked with steaming lobsters.

Scott pushed his way into the wooded area behind the house.

"What the hell you doing here?" Rodney growled, seated against a tree with a pile of rocks at his feet.

"Wondering the same about you."

"Taking care of business the way Daddy should have."

"With rocks?"

"You see the roof?"

Scott peered back through the foliage. Slate tile covered the entire roof with the exception of the highest area, which was squared off with polished chrome and capped with a domed glass skylight.

"About twelve hundred dollars' worth of glass," Rodney said. "Just what he owes Daddy."

"Let me talk to Snyder first."

"You joking?" Rodney sneered.

"Did anyone see you come here?"

"No. I came down the trail from Government House."

"If he doesn't want to talk, everyone will see me walk back down the hill. No one would know who did it."

"You have ten minutes."

Scott hurried down the hill to a policeman standing at the gate with arms folded. "I have to talk to Mr. Snyder."

"What you want?"

"It's a private matter."

"Boy, get out'a here," the policeman barked.

A heavy man with flashy jewelry and greased hair stepped out of the kitchen and called out to the policeman. "I need a hand."

"Mr. Snyder, can I talk to you for a minute?" Scott called out.

Mr. Snyder huffed his way to the gate, glancing first at the policeman and then at Scott. "We have a problem?"

Scott held eye contact with Mr. Snyder, hoping the man did not see his shaking knees. "I'm here to collect the twelve hundred dollars you owe my father."

"Who the hell are you, boy?"

"Hector McDonald's son. You owe him gas credit and his children have nothing to eat tonight."

Mr. Snyder's face paled and his words hissed out between clenched teeth. "You better get your tail out of here fast." He turned and stomped off toward the house.

Just then the music ended.

"Mr. Snyder, you're a thief!" Scott's voice filled the vacant silence. "You steal people's money while their children go hungry."

A tall dark man in a white suit stood erect among the guests on the verandah and glared at Mr. Snyder.

Mr. Snyder spun around to the policeman. "Break his legs if you have to."

The policeman pulled a baton from his belt and charged at Scott.

Scott turned and sprinted down the hill. The policeman pursued and swung his baton. Scott darted through the narrow space between two parked cars. The baton slammed on one of the cars.

He raced down the path between the cars and the fence.

And ran into a bear hug.

Rabid's hairy arms and barrel chest squeezed the air from Scott's lungs.

The policeman slithered up to them with a one-sided grin, his baton raised. "Hold him there, Rabid —"

Just then, a crack pierced the hillside like a gunshot, triggering a downpour of shattering glass and screams.

***

The dogs barked as footsteps crossed the verandah to the front door. Probably police on another attempt to have Scott confess he'd seen Rodney throw the rocks that shattered the glass roof.

Scott lay in bed trying to read his history book, *From Columbus to Castro*. The move to St. George's was supposed to have improved their lives. Now even Mommy had begun to drop hints that they would leave Daddy and move in with her ailing mother in the city. It'd be cramped. But so was this rat hole.

Uncertain times lay ahead. Especially after the police arrested Scott and Rodney, and Mr. Snyder filed a lawsuit against Daddy. Daddy could not afford a lawyer, and even if he collected his outstanding receipts, it would be insufficient. The gas company gave Daddy an extension on his lease to catch up on his payments. But if he failed to do so, they offered to find him a job in St. Croix, so he could repay his debts with American money.

The barking dogs and knocks on the front door drew Mommy's shuffling footsteps over the wooden floor. Scott entered the living room as she opened the door.

"Sorry to disturb you." A tall bearded man stood on the porch, wearing a dashiki and holding a folder. He glanced nervously at the dogs.

Mommy clapped her hands to silence them. "My sons have nothing more to say."

"I'm a lawyer. I want to defend your boys, free."

Mr. Farrow had warned that Scott and Roger Duncan might one day cross paths.

It happened faster than Scott expected.

CHAPTER
TWENTY-ONE

Scott worried that Mommy might have a fit if she knew where he was. He sat with Daddy at the food counter in Chinatown, an enclave of ramshackle restaurants next to the port, just down the hill from Daddy's gas station. She'd complained that Chinatown had more prostitutes than Chinese food. But when Daddy offered him supper for helping out at the gas station, Scott gladly accepted.

He gazed around in the fading sunlight, soaking up reggae music from overhead speakers and spicy aromas from steaming pots. American tourists, in straw hats and bright calypso shirts, sampled local food and beer at the counters and mingled with shapely girls in miniskirts and high-heels.

A stocky woman called out from where she stirred a pot behind the counter. "Mr. Hector, what for you today, sah?"

"Hey Monica. Crab and *callaloo* for me. And whatever me boy want."

Monica swaggered up to them, a smile lighting her smooth dark face. "What for you, sonny boy?"

"The snapper plate, thanks." Any other day, Scott would have preferred crab with *callaloo*, but he'd already had the leafy spinach several times that week.

"You old enough for a Carib?"

Daddy chuckled. "They been stealing my rum since Gouyave. Yeah, bring two."

Scott downed the cold beer and watched Monica return with their plates balanced on her arm, disfigured with sunken flesh and ridges of stitched skin from wrist to elbow.

She must have noticed his attention on her arm. "Planass was going for me head," she said. "Gabbard free him early from prison when he attack all you in Gouyave."

So Monica was the prostitute Aunty Bridgette and Daddy had whispered about that night in Gouyave.

"Jealousy," Monica said. "I hope he rot in prison."

Daddy sighed. "I'll take another beer."

Monica popped open two more bottles.

Scott gobbled down the spicy fish and rice and followed it with the second beer. A girl in hot pants and heels strutted on the gravel road past the lunch counter, flaunting full breasts in a skimpy top. She winked at him, her perfume inflaming his senses. He wished the girls on Marryshow Lane had as much flair. Some of the girls he knew acted as if a kiss on the cheek required a confession at church. He watched until she disappeared around the corner.

Just then, Vincent joined them, shaking Daddy's hand and slapping Scott on the back. He sat next to Daddy and called out to Monica. "Hey, sexy."

She leaned over the counter in front of Vincent, her breasts threatening to pop out of her low cut dress. "What you want for supper, lover boy?"

"You."

She kissed him on the lips. "There's more, but you go have to pay for that." She laughed, her heaving bosom causing beads of sweat to roll into her cleavage. She headed toward the pots, her hips swaying.

Daddy turned to Vincent. "How's things?"

"I have another cargo next month." Vincent lowered his voice. "It could get you twenty to one."

"I don't do that, man."

Rodney had hinted to Scott that Vincent smuggled whiskey from Venezuela. The discussion between Daddy and Vincent worried Scott, particularly since the government recently announced tough sentences for people caught in the trade.

Vincent continued. "That could help you pay them court fines. I was like you once. Worked hard. Even had a little shop before Gabbard and he boys shut me down."

"Why?" Scott asked.

"They say I could only buy goods from Snyder. One day they find contraband in me back room, so they take everything. Next day, me shop burn down, just so."

Monica served Vincent a plate of fish, rice, and peas, and a bottle of Guinness Stout.

He stared at her as she walked back to her pots. "She keep me from losing me head after Gillian's mother died."

"How's Gillian?" Scott asked.

Vincent's eyes lit up and he pulled a picture from his wallet. "She sending me a new picture soon. This was five years ago. She seventeen now. Soon, straight to America to be doctor."

Scott gazed at the black and white picture of Vincent and a slim girl, about twelve years old, with thick black ponytails. Even after her brief attendance at his school in Gouyave, he almost didn't recognized her as the little girl that held a handkerchief to his bruised arm and waved butterfly fingers at him. Her face reflected a soft sadness, but not enough to extinguish the gleam in her eyes.

Scott handed the picture to Daddy.

Daddy stared at the picture and his hand shook.

"She look just like her mother," Vincent said.

Scott wondered about Daddy's nervous reaction to the picture. Maybe the beers had distorted their vision and triggered the same thought in Daddy's mind as in Scott's.

Gillian looked like Ruby, the girl in Mr. Farrow's cracked picture frame.

***

Scott's anxiety boiled at the defense table where he sat between Duncan and Rodney. The gaunt judge on the elevated bench, his shuffling of papers the only sound in the courtroom, looked comical in his white wig and black judicial robe. But fear, not laughter, occupied Scott's mind. This hearing would schedule their trial date, a step closer to conviction. And the closer they got to trial, the more bitter the arguments grew between Scott and Rodney.

On the way to court in Duncan's car Rodney had hissed at Scott. "This is your damn fault."

"You threw the frigging rock. Not me."

"If I didn't, Rabid would have squeezed out your bloody brains."

The judge glanced over thick bifocals at the defense and prosecution tables. "There are two issues before me today. One is to clarify the charges and the next is the concern the defense has with the witness list. Is that correct Mr. Belmar?"

A man, dressed like Duncan in a plain black gown and wig, shot up from his chair at the table to their right. "Yes, Your Honor."

"If the crown wishes to present an outline of the facts, you may proceed."

"Yes, Your Honor," Mr. Belmar said. "On behalf of the government, I will serve an amended case summary in the light of new evidence. In particular, that Rodney McDonald and Scott McDonald met in the woods before the attack, demonstrating conspiracy and deliberation to inflict grievous bodily harm."

The judge turned to Duncan. "Has counsel for the defense seen the amended charges?"

Duncan rose to his feet. "I have, Your Honor. My learned friend, Mr. Belmar, was kind enough to hand me a copy in chamber this morning. But I wish to make clear that the charges on these boys are very serious and I beg to remind the court that, even for juveniles, the onus of proving guilt rests with the crown. The standard of proof required is 'beyond reasonable doubt.' This is a very high standard—"

"Mr. Duncan," the judge said. "This is no time for speeches. You'll have ample time to present your arguments to the jury. What's your issue with the witness list?"

"At the last directions hearing, leading counsel on behalf of both the government and defense submitted a list of nine absolutely bound witnesses."

"I thought we reached agreement on that list."

"Yes, Your Honor," Duncan said. "But the defense has since discovered the existence of another credible witness that we wish to add."

Mr. Belmar leapt to his feet. "Your Honor, the defense is making a blatant attempt to politicize this case. It has nothing to do with the government."

"I am confused," the judge said. "Who is this witness?"

"Your Honor, Mr. Belmar confuses me too." Duncan spread his arms in feigned bewilderment. "This is the most credible witness we have. Premier Forbes Gabbard!"

CHAPTER
TWENTY-TWO

If Premier Forbes Gabbard were outside in the heat, he might explode. He had repeatedly cautioned Snyder to keep his business at arms-length from the government. Now the idiot's carelessness was about to drag three government ministers into court to testify on the McDonalds incident. Then to make things messier, Belmar called to say that he, Gabbard, the most powerful man in Grenada, might also be summoned as a hostile witness for the defense.

Roger Duncan was playing with fire.

To calm his anger, Gabbard settled into his leather chair in his air-conditioned office, propped his feet on the desk, and gazed out over his sweltering city. He studied his fingers, nails buffed clean and evenly cut. He played with his ring, a heavy gold band lined with diamond chips and crowned with a jade nugget. The ticking seconds from his large gold-plated wall clock reminded him how far his mind had taken him in his fifty-two years. While his mind brought him power, his body pleasured the wives and daughters of his enemies and friends. Friends like Snyder, whose incompetence taxed Gabbard's patience.

When Snyder's twenty-three-year-old daughter called from London to say she was returning on vacation from her studies, Gabbard had his secretary reserve a private evening of lobster and champagne at his official residence. His manhood warmed at the thought of the gratitude she would shower him for awarding her that university scholarship, despite her poor academic performance.

The phone rang and he picked it up. "Yes?"

"Mr. Belmar on the line, sir," Gabbard's secretary said.

"Put him through." He waited for the connecting click. "What's the word, Belmar?"

"The judge ruled that you must take the stand, sir. I am sorry. We tried."

"Obviously not hard enough. Didn't you pass the judge an envelope like I told you?"

"Too risky," Belmar said. "I don't trust these Jamaican judges. Their loyalty is for London, not the islands."

"Have trust in money." Gabbard paused. "What's next?"

"The trial is next month. You're admitted as a defense witness."

"You don't understand, dammit. That communist lawyer isn't going to make a fool of me in court."

"That leaves us one choice. Drop the charges."

"Then bloody well drop the charges!" Gabbard slammed down the phone.

Did he have to think of everything himself? He was tired of these over-educated idiots, waving their British and North American degrees to get his attention. Sure, they may have used their family money and privilege to travel abroad to absorb social graces and education. But they lacked the brute efficiency of simple men who understood their role to obey and please those of superior abilities.

Simple men like Rabid,

Gabbard picked up the phone. "Track down Rabid for me. Try Chinatown."

Ten minutes later, the phone rang. "Boss. Is me, Rabid."

"Get over here immediately," Gabbard said. "Enter through the Mongoose Control office. Duncan might have spies."

Gabbard needed more men like Rabid for his life-long plan. Five years earlier, the British had granted Gabbard statehood authority to run the island's internal affairs, elevating him from Chief Minister to Premier, a step closer to independence from Britain. Independence meant total power over the island as Prime Minister. And after twelve years, he'd appoint himself Governor-General for life, a victory for both Gabbard and Fédon.

Nothing confirmed his kinship with Fédon's more than the Duncan-McDonald alliance, a rebirth of Fédon's worst enemies. Gabbard had plans for them, but first he would sell his British masters on his ability to control a restive population.

Fifteen minutes later, Rabid barreled through the doorway, his eyes fiery and hair wild.

"Grab a seat," Gabbard said.

Rabid reeked of cigarettes and beer in the chair facing the desk.

"Snyder needs help paying his contributions and bills," Gabbard said. "We don't want another McDonald case."

"Just tell me what to do, Boss."

"Snyder's problem is with smugglers taking away his business with their cheap whisky. The inspectors found contraband bottles last week at a hotel on Grand Anse beach. We must find the smugglers and stop them."

"No problem."

"I hear there's a planned delivery at La Sagesse Bay this week by that Vincent fellow. Make it look like smugglers fighting each other. I'll take care of the newspapers and radio. Tell the boys the envelopes will be fat after this job."

"Don't worry, Boss." Rabid grinned.

"One more thing." Premier Gabbard clasped his hands. "I smell trouble ahead with Duncan. I'll need more of your friends as we get closer to independence."

"Yes, Boss." Rabid smiled. "But me best padnah still in prison. You help him seven years ago. He not done with them McDonalds."

"I am the government. Name him and he's free."

"Planass."

CHAPTER TWENTY-THREE

After the judge dismissed the charges, Duncan led Scott into his small office at the top of Market Hill. "Your case exposes this government as the most corrupt and brutal in the English-speaking Caribbean. Gabbard must go."

Scott glanced around at untidy rows of books that overflowed bookshelves along the walls. The windows behind the desk opened to a panoramic view of the city, blocks of two-storied buildings, red roofs and white roofs against the blue sea.

"Grab a chair." Duncan hung his attorney wig and gown on hooks next to a bookshelf. "I'm sorry Rodney couldn't come too."

"Didn't want to be late for his job at Regal Cinema." Scott pulled up a chair below a poster of the bearded Che Guevara wearing a black beret with a red star.

"One of my heroes." Duncan pointed at the poster. "Executed by the CIA in Bolivia in 1967. Who are your heroes?"

"I like Martin Luther King and Mahatma Gandhi, but the only true hero I know is an old man in Gouyave. He lost a leg saving my grandfather in World War I."

"Another victim of Western imperialism."

"Most people think of him as a senile old man," Scott said. "But he taught me a lot about our history."

"Julien Fédon is another Gouyave hero."

Scott leaned forward. "What do you know about him?"

"Grenada's first revolutionary, an inspiration to downtrodden people."

"Then why all the superstitions?"

"There are those like Gabbard who feed ignorance to the masses to control them."

"Some in Gouyave believe the McDonalds were cursed by Fédon."

"Both the Duncans and McDonalds can be traced back to Fédon. I have an English name, but my family carries the blood of a Frenchman who fought under General McDonald against Fédon." He stroked his beard. "Today was a good day, but it's only the beginning."

"Of what?"

"The end of Gabbard. His last victory came from rigging the electoral list with people who died ten years before the elections." He looked intently at Scott. "But we have other means."

"Like what?"

"We're talking about historical inevitability." For the next two hours, Duncan wove visions of victimized masses yearning for liberation from hunger and exploitation. Until, in a moment sparked by revolutionary inspiration they strike out in spontaneous rebellion against their oppressors. "Revolution is inevitable."

Enthralled by Duncan's certainty about Grenada's impending transformation, Scott realized that he had missed the signs of momentous changes bearing down on the island. He felt ashamed that his obsession with his family's misery blinded him to the suffering others endured – people trapped behind oppressive walls of ignorance and poverty, their silent screams drummed out by the hammering of his family's past. The McDonalds were descendants of slaves and slave owners, but some still perpetuated the very dehumanizing system Duncan cursed.

Scott had neither the material abundance nor the desire to be a pampered bourgeoisie like Oliver. In his heart, Scott's true allegiance was to the Mr. Farrows and Martins of Grenada, the have-nots. What they lacked outside, they more than compensated for on the inside with deep reservoirs of humanity, true friendship, and trust. If revolution was for them, then revolution was for him.

Duncan stroked his beard and his eyes gleamed as he wallowed in tales of intellectual giants turned revolutionaries. Vladimir Lenin, Fidel Castro, and

Patrice Lumumba. With intoxicating passion, he expounded on the need to build a vanguard of disciplined cadres that would spark revolution in Grenada. "By any means necessary."

Duncan handed him a red book titled *Fidel Castro Speaks*. "Return it when you're finished, and I'll lend you another. What you and Rodney did was one step on the march to glorious revolution. And in revolution, you're either with us or against us." He stood and shook Scott's hand. "You're only seventeen, but you're one of us."

Scott hurried along Marryshow Lane in the waning afternoon light clutching Duncan's book. It all made sense now. The pain Scott had struggled with had little to do with Daddy's past. It was part of a bigger picture, an exploitative economic system, pitting man against man, and family against family. Daddy was as much a victim as anyone else.

Scott wanted Duncan's clarity. He wanted to grapple with something bigger than the urgency of day-to-day hand-to-mouth existence. It made so much sense; everything he had endured had prepared him for the coming revolution. If just the thought of revolution could trigger such excitement in his bones, then Duncan was right. Scott was one of them.

"Look who's here." Oliver's voice intruded from the shadow of a tree where Aunty Hyacinth's driveway met the main road.

A few boys sat on the wall under the tree, next to a white Volkswagen. Scott recognized them as acquaintances from his school, the Grenada Boys' Secondary School, GBSS.

Marijuana smoke soured the air.

Oliver cycled up to Scott and stared at the book. "Fidel Castro, huh? You going to grow a beard and smoke cigars too?"

The boys laughed.

"You escaped jail today," Oliver said. "But you're still a disgrace to GBSS and your family. Go back to Gouyave. This is my neighborhood."

Scott faced Oliver. "You having fun?"

"You still speak and look like a Gouyaveman. When you wear my shirts, why don't you show some class? Tuck it in your pants and wear a belt like I do."

"This isn't your shirt."

"What do you think the OC on your pocket stands for, Obnoxious Communist?"

Laughter.

"It stands for Oliver Cunningham, you county bookie. Do you think your clothes been coming from Santa Claus?"

The boys laughed again.

"No wonder they're so baggy." Scott ripped off the shirt, and threw it over Oliver's face. "I don't need your damn clothes.'

Oliver tossed the shirt to the street. "You'll end up like your drunken father."

Scott hurried home with laughter fading behind him.

When he barged into the house, Mommy looked up from her chair by the window. "Where's your shirt?"

"Why didn't you tell me that Aunty Hyacinth was giving us Oliver's clothes?"

"It doesn't matter."

"It does to me." Scott stomped into the bedroom and slammed the door shut.

Later that night, when Scott felt his eyes too tired to read any longer at the dining room table, he turned off the light and crawled into bed with the red book on his chest. Sleep came quickly, and so did dreams of him and Che, revolutionary comrades in the hills of Grenada. They shot rifles into the air and waved victory flags from mountaintops. Masses of people came out of their shacks with hungry babies clinging to their necks and tears streaming down their cheeks.

"We're free," they shouted.

When Oliver ordered the people to return to their shacks, Scott put out a cigar in his face.

Daddy ran up with a gun. "There's blood everywhere."

The gun went off with a bang.

Another bang. Scott awoke in a sleepy stupor. A rock banged like gunshots across the galvanized tin roof.

A car sped off.

Alicia screamed from the bed across the room and Rodney groaned in the bed next to Scott.

Scott raced into the living room and pulled aside the curtains. Headlights sped along Marryshow Lane, slowing to turn up Aunty Hyacinth's driveway.

He dashed back into the bedroom and jumped into a pair of shorts.

Rodney murmured. "Where you going?"

"None of your damned business." Scott scribbled a note at the dining room table, grabbed a matchbox from the kitchen, and bolted out the door.

Parked in front of Aunty Hyacinth's house, the white Volkswagen looked silver in the moonlight. Scott crept up the driveway and touched the rear hood.

Hot.

That son-of-a-bitch.

He kneeled beside the back tire, removed the valve cap, and depressed the pin with a matchstick. After the fourth tire exhaled its final breath, he stuck the note between the wiper and windshield, and sprinted home.

Rodney sat up in bed. "You getting us in trouble again?"

"Left a message for your friend, Oliver."

"Message?"

"Never mess with a Gouyaveman."

***

The next night, seated next to Vincent at Monica's counter, Scott finished his beer and glanced around at the busy Chinatown night. The enclave bustled with tourists, drunks, and scantily dressed girls. Reggae, calypso, and steel drum music blended in a soup of delicious rhythms, spiced with the aroma of peppered food and perfumes.

Scott turned to Vincent. "Time for me to get some sleep."

"Have one more, man. No school Saturday."

"I have to help Daddy with paperwork in the morning."

"Don't tell nobody this," Vincent whispered. "You daddy—"

"Another beer?" Monica called out.

"Yeah," Vincent said. "Bring two."

Monica served them two beers and strutted toward another customer.

"You were saying something about Daddy," Scott reminded Vincent.

"Love is gold." Vincent pulled Gillian's picture from his shirt pocket and gazed at it. "But without money, you lose everything."

Vincent looked like he'd survived his storms better than Daddy had. He still had rock-solid arms and a thick neck. He didn't have Daddy's potbelly, and his hairline had retreated only a little. But the risk-laced edge to Vincent's voice worried Scott.

"If you daddy go bankrupt, is St. Croix he gone," Vincent said. "But don't worry, he put he money where he mouth is."

"What? He only has money left for gasoline."

"I is a business man. If I can't make money for me friends, I better off dead."

Scott gulped down his beer. Daddy was gambling his last dollar on Vincent's cargo. That was probably why Daddy had asked Scott to balance his sheets in the morning, expecting a high payoff.

"The best Venezuela Scotch," Vincent whispered. "In time for Christmas."

A car groaned to a halt on the gravel road behind them.

Rabid squeezed out from the driver's side, leaving three men lurking in the car. He marched up to the counter, crunching gravel under his boots.

Vincent peeked at his watch.

"Full moon tonight." Rabid spat at his feet and gazed up at the sky. "Everybody better behave."

"Rabid, a Carib beer?" Monica called out.

"Nah. I on duty." He squinted at Scott with reddish eyes. "You again?"

"Just showing him me girl." Vincent held up Gillian's picture to Rabid, and then returned it to his shirt pocket. "He going home now. Right Scott?"

"Yes."

Rabid marched to the car and drove off.

Scott finished his beer and hurried to the restroom. When he returned, Vincent was standing on the road in animated conversation with another man.

"Is ten o'clock," Vincent said. "Where he is?"

"I dunno," the man said.

"We need somebody to keep watch."

"I gone." Scott headed past Vincent. "Thanks for the beers."

"Juss a minute." Vincent placed his arm around Scott's shoulders. "I need you help."

Scott peered from Vincent's truck, wondering how in an hour he'd gone from having a beer in Chinatown to watching a darkened yacht bob into the moonlit La Sagesse Bay. The desolate bay, eight miles from Chinatown, sat at the dead-end of a gravel driveway that tunneled through thick brush and coconut trees half a mile off the main road. The nearest house was a vacant colonial mansion a hundred yards down the beach, surrounded by high fences and overgrown gardens.

Vincent had explained to the other man that the moon, glowing unopposed in the naked sky, made it easy for the yacht to find the bay.

"But moon go make it easy for police to find we too," the other man said.

"Nah man," Vincent said. "I only worry about thieves if nobody stay with the truck."

And that was why he needed Scott to warn them with the headlights if anyone approached the truck while the men returned to the shoreline for more boxes.

Scott fingered the light switch and listened to the steady rustle of wind through the trees. A flashlight on the yacht turned on and off several times. Another flashlight returned the signal from the beach where Vincent and his friend stood silhouetted against the glazed sea.

Two dark figures on the yacht lowered a smaller boat into the water and loaded it with boxes. They shoved off and rowed to the shore. The four men offloaded the boxes on the sand and the small boat returned to the yacht. After several loaded trips, Vincent handed the yachtsmen a bulging paper bag. They returned to the yacht, and within minutes the yacht slipped away into the night.

Vincent and his friend shouldered boxes and struggled back to the truck.

"How you doin' Padnah?" Vincent asked Scott.

"Quiet. I could carry some boxes."

"Nah. I need you at the light switch."

Scott felt more relaxed thirty minutes later, after the men had gotten most of the whiskey stored in the truck. The beers he'd had earlier filled his bladder again, but he decided to wait.

"One more trip." Vincent headed back down the beach with his friend.

When the men were almost back to the truck with their boxes, Scott jumped on to the driveway to urinate against a tree just outside the truck door.

The wind in the trees must have drowned out the sound of the approaching car.

It rounded the corner and lit up the beach with high beams.

Scott leaned past the tree for a better view of the car. If they were thieves, the lights had already warned Vincent. Maybe he had a gun to scare them off.

Shouts on the beach. Two men, with cutlasses glittering in the headlights, raced toward Vincent and his friend from the direction of the vacant mansion.

Vincent heaved his box at one of the attackers and missed.

A cutlass slashed through the air. Vincent's friend screamed and fell.

Two other men leaped from the car.

"Leave that one for me." The bigger man stampeded down the beach waving a cutlass.

"Rabid, no!" Vincent's hands went up.

"No more Rabid for you." Rabid swung his cutlass.

Vincent collapsed with a gurgling scream. "Gillian!"

***

Gillian climbed Laventille Road toward her aunt's house, squeezing the door key in her pocket, and glad for the full moon that lit the hillside. Sticks would be snoring on the couch by now, like on the other nights when she worked with Sonia at the bar down the hill. Gillian didn't like the hours at the smoky bar, a magnet for drunks and prostitutes, but it was her pass away from Sticks when Aunty Josephine worked the evening shift at the hospital.

When Gillian had announced her intention to work at the bar, Sticks had struggled off the couch with his sweat-stained undershirt stuck to his chest. "You going to be a whore?"

She bit her lower lip, her hatred for him raging from behind her temples.

Aunty Josephine jumped in. "Watch you mouth, Bertrand."

"You let a child work in place like that?"

"I am not a child," Gillian screamed. "I am almost seventeen. I just want to save some money to visit Grenada."

"You lying little bitch. You just want to open you legs for those drunks."

"Bertrand." Aunty Josephine stomped across the wooden living room floor toward him. "Maybe you should find a job too."

"Ah, shadup."

When Gillian returned home from her first night at the bar, Sticks was unresponsive to her relentless banging on the locked door. Sonia's brother, who walked her home, lifted Gillian up to her bedroom window and into the room. The following night Sticks locked the windows as well. Gillian sent Sonia's brother on his way and waited on the steps for Aunty Josephine to get home. Gillian was dozing when a car pulled up with her aunt and her male coworker.

Aunty Josephine scolded Sticks, and, later that day, gave Gillian a key to the front door.

Gillian pulled the key from her pocket as she entered the walkway in the moonlight. Had it been darker tonight, Gillian might have asked Sonia's brother to walk her home. Only fifteen, he was taller than most boys his age, but she was tired of his boyish attempts to kiss her goodnight.

Most of the houses along the street were already dark, their metal roofs aglow in moonlight. Television lights flickered in a few windows. Gillian preferred it when Sticks fell asleep with the television on. It allowed her to enter the house without awaking him. Then she would turn down the volume, soft step into her room, and lock her door.

Each night, wood smoke lingered in the air from leftover cooking fires. But tonight's smoke floated thicker, and a strange yellow glow in the house reflected on the windowpane.

Fire?

Panic rising in her chest, Gillian rushed to the door, unlocked it, and pulled it open. Hot smoke blasted her face and sucked her breath away.

"Fire!" She stumbled back down the steps. "Fire!"

Lights came on in neighboring houses and shouts filled the night.

She held her breath, hunched over and rushed through the smoke-filled doorway. Fire rose from newspapers beside the couch. A hand dangled in the flame. She reached over and pulled Sticks' hand out of the flames to his chest. She grabbed him by his undershirt. It shredded.

The smoke seared her throat. Her lungs screamed for air.

With her back to the door, she clutched the couch by the armrest and pulled, gliding it over the wooden floor. She reached the doorway, her lungs ablaze and her eyes burned shut. Her mind wobbled and shouts faded in the distance.

Her legs gave way and she tumbled down the steps.

Next morning, Gillian squinted at the shadowy figures standing around her bed. Her eyes felt as if they were coated with hot sand. She shut her eyes and inhaled the comforting medicinal odor that permeated the air. She tried to speak, but instead triggered a coughing fit.

"You'll be fine." A man in white leaned over her and squeezed liquid drops into her eyes. "Smoke inhalation."

"Oh baby." Aunty Josephine swam into view at the end of the bed. "I'm so sorry."

"Uncle Bertrand?" Gillian's words struggled out in a painful wheeze.

"Still unconscious, but they say he'll be okay. Burned his hand."

"The house?"

"The neighbors saved it, but the living room and couch gone."

"I have some savings," Gillian said. "Don't look so sad."

"It's not the house." Aunty Josephine choked back tears. "Bad news from Grenada. It's your father."

CHAPTER
TWENTY-FOUR

Daddy looked confident at the head of the breakfast table, scanning the newspaper and sipping his orange juice. But Scott knew the only thing that separated Daddy's brief taste of optimism from a shattered life was the morning radio news.

News about murder.

Murder.

The word seemed mournfully frail to describe the brutality Scott had witnessed last night. He'd stayed undetected in the trees until Rabid and his men had sped off with Vincent's truck. Scott crept over the sand toward the scent of death, like the market on slaughter night. Vincent's severed head lay next to his shoulder in the blood-soaked sand, his vacant eyes in a dead stare at the moon.

Scott plucked Gillian's picture from Vincent's bloodied shirt pocket and ran, crying and throwing up as he fled the bay. He ran, hiding in the bushes when cars approached, swinging sticks at attacking dogs. Running and crying.

He finally stumbled into the house at three o'clock in the morning, scared and sweaty, his feet blistered and legs sore.

He wanted to shower, to cleanse the night from his pores. But instead, he crawled into bed rather than awaken the household.

Rodney sat up. "Phew! You smell like a whore. Must be the one Oliver saw you talking to when he drove by Chinatown tonight."

"You and Oliver can kiss my ass!"

"Shhh." Claudette shifted in her bed. "You'll wake up Alicia."

The visions had swirled on his mind keeping him awake in bed as they now did at the breakfast table. If Scott told Daddy what had happened, Daddy would insist they go to the police. But one of the four attackers was in police uniform. And how would Scott explain his own presence in the bay?

Sadness flooded his thoughts when he imagined Gillian's grief at the news. He stretched his legs under the table and pushed away his breakfast plate, his egg and buttered bread untouched.

"You not eating?" Mommy asked from the other end of the table.

Rodney chuckled. "Too much Chinatown food last night."

"Mind your frigging business." Scott growled.

"Okay boys," Daddy said. "Watch your language."

"What's Chinatown?" Alicia asked.

"Scott's crab hole," Rodney said.

"You can catch diseases in that place." Mommy turned to Scott. "By the way, I need you to kill and pluck a chicken for lunch."

"I'm helping Daddy at the gas station."

She turned to Rodney.

"Don't look at me," Rodney said. "Scott never here to do anything."

"I'll take care of the chicken." Daddy glanced up from the newspaper. "Scott, you go to the gas station and start on the books."

Daddy still had no clue the shock that awaited him. He stretched to the old Zenith radio on the china closet and turned up the volume.

The radio crackled. "The time is eight o'clock. This is the Radio Grenada news. A fisherman found the bodies of two men at La Sagesse Bay less than two hours ago. Police say it was the result a clash between smuggling gangs. The chief medical examiner at the general Hospital, Dr. Pilgrim, said the men were beheaded in the worst violence he had seen in his ten years at the hospital. An empty truck belonging to one of the victims was found abandoned on the north shore. The victims were Mr. Vincent Calliste, stevedore from St. George's and —"

The blood drained from Daddy's face and he slammed his fist on the table.

***

A few weeks later, Scott checked off the last item on the inventory clipboard in the gas station and stepped into the office. Daddy sat at his desk staring out the window in a daze. His head of unruly white hair with patches of black capped a face of sagging skin, drawn from years of defeat. Maybe St. Croix, away from his past, would be kinder to him.

"It's all done, Daddy," Scott said.

Daddy jumped. "I didn't see you standing there." He took the clipboard and signed the sheets.

"I hope you like St. Croix."

"I can get you an American visa to visit."

Scott forced assurance in his voice. "We'll be okay here."

"Chinatown is not safe any longer."

"Monica warned me at the funeral." She'd also told him how the news of the murders devastated Gillian, but did not explain Gillian's absence from the funeral.

"What's that?" Daddy pointed at a folder Scott held.

"Found it in your filing cabinet." He handed the folder to Daddy. "There's a picture in there of Ruby, like the one Mr. Farrow has."

Daddy opened the folder and shifted in his chair. "Farrow didn't tell me until recently that Ruby was his daughter. She never knew either."

"You can talk. I can handle the truth now."

"I made y'all hate me." Daddy's lips trembled.

"You lived with a lot of pain."

"We were seventeen. She was pregnant. We were going to get married."

Scott pulled up a chair at the desk.

Grief burdened Daddy's voice and reddened his eyes. "Dr. Branch tried to save them. Before she died I told her it was my fault. Maybe she wanted to spare me the guilt. Or maybe the morphine made her talk. Ruby said it wasn't my fault, because the baby was not mine."

Scott waited.

"Pa was the baby's father."

***

Daddy's plane taxied with a mechanical wail down the runway at Pearls Airport. In the distance, hillsides of lush beauty reminded Scott of the day he had first stepped off the plane from Aruba and into Grenada's green embrace. While the island's hold had tightened around Scott, the distance in the family had grown. Rodney refused to come to the airport, and none of Daddy's Gouyave relatives came to see him off. Only Mommy and Claudette came along, standing next to Scott in the crowded airport.

Daddy spent his last weeks in Grenada filing bankruptcy papers and drinking away his guilt over Vincent's murder. He'd said nothing more about Ruby, just that *Pa forced himself* on her during one of his drunken episodes. Was that how they called rape in 1940?

Now it appeared that both Daddy and Mr. Farrow had reasons to kill Pa. Mr. Farrow had served time in a cold military prison for saving Pa's life, and Pa had returned the favor by raping Mr. Farrow's daughter, the girl Daddy was going to marry.

Maybe Mr. Farrow had gotten to Pa with a knife, before Daddy showed up with a gun. The police report said suicide, but strangely did not explain how. And where did Planass fit in? Was there some invisible enmity haunting the McDonalds since that bloody day on Mount Qua Qua in 1796?

The plane roared past the terminal and into the clouds, taking with it possibly Scott's best chance to learn the whole truth.

Maybe those were meant to be Daddy's secrets. He'd paid a heavy price for them.

With Daddy gone, Scott felt a burst of energy for other more pressing matters. His conversations with Duncan came rushing back. Scott's preoccupation with personal calamities was minuscule in the rising tide of a people's revolution.

He turned to Mommy and Claudette. "Go ahead and take a bus home."

"Where you going?" Claudette asked.

"The student council has a meeting in Grenville with Duncan."

"About what?" Mommy asked.

"Gabbard sold the La Sagesse mansion to a British Lord," he said. "The new owner gated off the access road and wants to turn the beach into his private playground."

"Isn't that where those smugglers killed Vincent?"

"You believe everything you hear on the radio?"

"Calm down," Claudette said. "Nobody believes that."

Mommy sighed. "If it's not Rodney and marijuana, it's you and politics."

"Don't worry about me," Scott said. "Just keep Rodney away from Oliver."

"Since you got elected to the GBSS student council, I smell trouble."

An hour later, Scott leaned back in his chair at the St. Andrew's Secondary School and watched Duncan step up to the podium.

"Comrades," Duncan said. "Gabbard has flatly refused to discuss the La Sagesse situation with us. So we will register as a legitimate political party and compete in the elections with La Sagesse as a cornerstone issue."

"What's the point?" Scott asked from among the group of about fifteen students. "Gabbard will steal the election again."

"He will campaign to deceive. We will campaign to win the hearts and minds of the people."

A student snickered. "That's a lot of rum and corned-beef we have to give away."

Laughter.

"That's Gabbard's game, not ours." Duncan glanced around the room. "La Sagesse is an opportunity to show that the New Grenada Movement, NGM, is a champion of oppressed people. We will hold a people's trial. Since government is of the people, for the people, and by the people, don't you think that the people should hold Gabbard accountable for blocking access to their beach?"

"Yes," the group shouted.

"A week from today, we will hold a public hearing for the La Sagesse people to testify on how the blocked road affects them. We will have a people's jury, just like a regular court. And if Gabbard and Lord Barrington are found guilty, we'll remove the gates."

Applause and cheers.

"Comrades." Duncan's resolve stiffened his posture. "Prepare for confrontation."

***

"This is your last warning!" The police inspector stood with a megaphone in front of his armed contingent and shouted at the crowd. "Return to the main road at once."

The policemen fidgeted with batons, tear-gas canisters, and rifles. Behind them, a chain-linked gate blocked the road that had taken Vincent and his friend to their deaths.

Apprehension drummed in Scott's chest. Back at La Sagesse for the first time since the murders six months ago, he stood in front of the crowd, arm in arm with Duncan and Beverly Johnson, Scott's GBSS English Literature teacher. The crowd of about three hundred people had attended the mock trial on the field a half-mile back, where the jury of La Sagesse residents voted unanimously to tear down the gates.

The crowd had marched down to the gate an hour ago, and the noon standoff had begun to generate sweat and boiling tempers.

"Break down the damn gate!" someone shouted.

The crowd roared and pressed forward.

Duncan's raised hand swept an edgy silence over the marchers.

"You have thirty seconds." The police inspector glanced over his shoulders at his men. "Stand by."

The hammering of rifle bolts echoed over the crowd.

Duncan stepped forward, his dashiki soaked to his skin. "Inspector, you know me. You have my word. We'll remain on the road and on the beach. Just as the people have done for decades. No one will invade Lord Barrington's privacy."

"I have my orders."

Duncan raised his voice. "Do you follow Gabbard's orders, or the people's orders?"

The crowd cheered.

"I can have you all arrested," the inspector hollered.

"Do you have enough room in your jails for all of us?"

The crowd applauded and began to sing *'We shall Overcome.'*

Silence descended once again.

Duncan addressed the inspector. "Your policemen know we're right. They won't shoot us. Some of them live here in La Sagesse. Right?"

A few policemen nodded.

"Some of them have friends and relatives in this crowd."

"They will follow my orders," the inspector said.

"Are you going to order them to shoot their own brothers and sisters?" Duncan turned to the crowd. "If you know any of these policemen, please come forward."

"That's me nephew." An old man pointed at a policeman who then smiled sheepishly.

A girl pointed at another. "He's my second cousin from town."

"I'm warning you," the inspector shouted.

A policeman lowered his rifle and stepped off the road. "This is damn *stupidness, oui.*"

Others followed. The crowd pushed forward, mingling with the policemen.

"Hold your positions," the inspector shouted at the disintegrating ranks.

Scott glanced ahead at the unprotected gates, held together by a padlocked chain. He waved at some of the students. "Let's do it."

They charged the gate poles and began to shake them. The concrete supports loosened in the dirt and the gates fell to the side of the road with a deafening clang. The crowd applauded and roared past the bewildered policemen.

Scott raced with the crowd through the dense coconut groves that hid him the night of the murders. He sprinted down to the shore, tearing off his t-shirt and kicking off his shoes. He dove into the sea and swam out for a view of the beach. To the right, the elegant English mansion stood back from the beachfront, nestled among blazing flower gardens, and shaded by coconut trees.

A man in a suit on the top balcony scanned the crowd with a pair of binoculars. A uniformed man walked up to him with his hat in his hand.

The crowd leapt and danced. Many dove into the sea fully dressed. Duncan strode along the beach, embracing admirers. Beverly ran up to him in shorts and a wet t-shirt that clung to her body. He held her and they kissed.

If this was just a taste of revolution, Scott could hardly wait for the big day. Revolution, to strip privileged bourgeois like Oliver of the artificial social elevations that they used to demean the oppressed. Revolution, to disgrace Gabbard, to punish Rabid and his roughnecks, and to grant Gillian the justice she must surely crave.

Revolution as envisioned by Marx, practiced by Castro and promised by Duncan seemed inevitable now.

CHAPTER
TWENTY-FIVE

From the safety of the hillside road, Scott watched the channel of light blazing through the darkness to the ghostly figure dressed in a white suit and hat in the middle of St. George's harbor. Premier Gabbard, probably on a floating platform, looked like he was standing on water. He barked into a microphone that sent his fake British accent thundering against the amphitheater hillsides. "These NGM Communists sing Black Power songs to scare away our English visitors. Is that a good message to send about our Isle of Spice?"

"No!" The crowd shouted their disapproval from the horseshoe shaped Carenage Road.

"We already have Black Power in Grenada," Gabbard said. "I am black as night, and I am the power."

Gabbard's supporters cheered. Around two thousand, they had been bussed in from the countryside. Things had changed. In the 1950s, when Gabbard enjoyed the crest of his popularity, hordes of his supporters walked ten miles to listen to him.

The sparse gathering around Scott on the hillside street looked on stone-faced.

"What the ass do he?" Laughter escaped from a house on the hill behind him, where people sat at their windows to listen to Gabbard.

A man close by spat on the road and grumbled.

Gabbard played his trump card. "Three months ago, our landslide election victory paved the way for the next giant stride in Grenada's history: Independence from Great Britain. And we will achieve it with Divine guidance from God and Fédon."

Applause.

Landslide victory?

Many of the people who were openly opposed to, or even suspected of opposing Gabbard, had been turned away from the polling stations. Mommy was told that she had already voted and shown a signature she did not recognize next to her name. The British ignored protests over the outcomes, validated the fraud, and handed Gabbard his independence ticket on a silver platter.

A ticket to dictatorship.

Gabbard's words echoed around the harbor. "Fédon's spirit is watching. Let this be a warning to our enemies who want to do Grenada harm. I have ordered my Chief of Police to create secret police squads, the meanest and baddest roughnecks. Let those Duncan dogs be warned. Their games are over."

"We will fight, fight, fight, for we leader!" The Carenage Road crowd broke out in singing.

Scott glanced around and noticed a girl standing alone in the hazy street-light across the road. In heels and tight jeans, with the tails of her white shirt tied around her narrow waist, she puffed a cigarette with an aura of cool detachment under the cap that obscured her face. She dropped the cigarette and stepped on it.

When she looked up, she caught his gaze for a moment. Then she turned and strutted off toward Chinatown.

He decided to head home, unscathed by Gabbard's threats. Duncan, the only hope for the island, had become Gabbard's archenemy. The other opposition party cowered from government intimidation while Duncan's public meetings attracted increasingly larger crowds. Meanwhile, plans for revolution began to coagulate in secret NGM meetings and study sessions on scientific socialism and guerrilla warfare.

Scott recalled the study groups he used to attend under the tutelage of a bearded heavyset Professor Armstrong from Trinidad—until Oliver started to show up.

At the last meeting, Professor Armstrong introduced Oliver to the group as his cousin on the Cunningham side of the family. Oliver had just returned from his school holidays in Trinidad with an Afro and struggling goatee. In farmer-brown overalls and a pair of tire-sandals, he delivered a presentation on class struggle and the distinguishing features of the bourgeois and proletarian classes.

Scott almost fell off his chair.

Oliver had become a packaged revolutionary, looking like the oppressed, and speaking the language of the poor.

Scott avoided him after the meeting, and headed home with a few of Armstrong's books. When Scott turned the corner to Marryshow Lane, a white Volkswagen pulled up and exhaled marijuana smoke.

"Want a ride, Comrade cousin?"

Scott glared at Oliver under the streetlight. "I see you gave up embroidered shirts."

"Times have changed."

"You bought your change with privilege and money. You're a phony. Go home to your bourgeois dwelling on the hill and push around your proletarian maids when no one is looking."

"We're now brothers in the struggle," Oliver said. "Armstrong wants you and me to—"

"I don't give a shit what Armstrong wants."

"Then give me back those books."

"I don't need to read about struggle." Scott dumped the books on Oliver's lap where he sat behind the wheel. "You do."

After that night, Scott devoted less time to study groups, and more on student council activities like printing the banned NGM newspapers in hiding places around town. The GBSS Cadet Corps, which he'd joined a few years earlier, also kept him busy with rifle training and platoon drills. Just last week, the cadet platoon hiked up Mount Qua Qua, Fédon's final holdout.

Scott had faced the wind on the peak with his rifle over his head, absorbing the excitement of coming revolution.

Revolution seemed even more certain as Scott left Gabbard's diatribe behind, and hurried along Tyrrell Street around the corner that overlooked Chinatown. Scott had not seen Monica since Vincent's funeral and, with Rabid most likely at the Carenage event, Scott decided to visit her.

He sat at the counter and studied her from behind as she filled a bowl of fish broth from her pot. The food smelled as peppery good as before, but

Monica had lost weight and moved slower. The surprise in her eyes when she saw him equaled Scott's dismay at how much she had aged. Worry lines puckered around her eyes and engraved her forehead.

"What you doing here?" She dried her hands on her apron and shuffled over to him. "Rabid could be here any time."

"He's at Gabbard's meeting. I'll just have a quick beer."

"How's you father?" She opened a Carib.

"Sent me a birthday card last month. He's applying for me to join him in St. Croix, after school."

"Good."

"Nah. I don't want to miss the Revo—"

"Don't talk that stupidness around here." She snapped. "I hope you not going in that march next week."

"We're protesting hospital conditions. I'm on the student council. It's my duty."

"Your poor mother." She turned away and called out to someone Scott could not see on the other side of the counter. "Hey Trini, wanna watch the counter for a few minutes?"

"Sure," a young female answered.

"Meet me at the backdoor." Monica removed her apron and entered a darkened room next to the stove.

After a brief exchange of muffled voices in the room, a dark-skinned girl with a cap and thick braids slipped through the doorway, tying the apron around her waist. She strutted over to him, hips swaying, and heels tapping the wooden floor to the Reggae beat of Bob Marley.

She smacked her full lips. "Want another beer, sir?"

He glanced at his empty bottle. "Good timing."

She popped open a beer before he finished counting the last of his change.

"Sorry, I don't have enough." Embarrassment coated his voice.

"I'll pay for it if you tell me why you were staring at me at the meeting." She leaned forward and caressed the bottleneck with long elegant fingers, her manicured nails gleaming in bright red. She was bra-less, her dark nipples firm against her white shirt. Perfume sweetened the air and a smile twinkled in her eyes.

"You looked familiar," he said.

"Is that the line you use to pick up girls?"

"I'm not trying to pick you up."

"You know how to hurt a girl's feelings." She fluttered her eyelashes over dark steady eyes.

"I didn't mean—"

"I know what you mean."

"Where're you from?" He tried to salvage the conversation.

"Trinidad," she said. "I moved here a few months ago. Everyone calls me Trini."

"I once had a pigeon named Trini. It flew from Trinidad to Grenada."

"I came by plane." She laughed, extending her hand to him. "You must be Scott."

He held her hand. "How do you know my name?"

"Monica knows everybody."

She was probably his age, seventeen, maybe eighteen. But her makeup and demeanor made her appear older. He suspected she was another Chinatown prostitute. Yet, he sensed a soothing familiarity about her.

"You're drifting away on me." Her face beamed with a perfect smile.

"Just thinking. Did you have family in Belvidere?"

Her smile vanished. "You're playing a dangerous game." She walked off just as Monica returned. Trini handed her the apron, and whispered in her ear before disappearing through the back room and into the night.

Monica hurried over to him. "Boy, I don't want nobody killed. She's Trini. And that's that."

"I understand."

Just then, a car rumbled by. Trini waved at Monica from the passenger seat, her fingers fluttering like the wings of a butterfly.

An old memory drifted across Scott's mind, of a little girl he'd only seen twice before. Almost ten years ago, they'd sat next to each other on a truck-drive through Belvidere, shared a callaloo-leaf umbrella in the rain, and she'd nursed his bruises after that car incident. Both times she waved goodbye with fluttering fingers.

No. It couldn't be her.

Even after ten years, he felt sure he would have recognized her immediately.

No. Trini couldn't be Gillian.

Gillian would not be driving through Chinatown with Rabid, the man who had murdered her father six months earlier.

***

Scott held the microphone and faced the five hundred students in white shirts and gray trousers overflowing the GBSS auditorium. "The Headmaster has agreed that we have the right to protest the disgraceful state of the hospital, as long as your participation is voluntary."

Applause.

"But first we'll march across the street and meet the Anglican High School girls—"

Applause.

"This is a protest march, my friends. Not a love-in."

Jeers and grumbles.

"Listen up." Scott waited until the noise subsided. "We'll also join students from the Presentation Boys College and the St. Joseph's Convent. We'll meet Duncan and the nurses on the Carenage and then march to the Health Department. After the speeches, we return by the same route. Any questions?"

A hand went up at the back. "How is this going to bring down Gabbard?"

"Oliver, we're marching to protest hospital conditions, not to bring down Gabbard."

"The Revo needs more than singing and sweating in the streets," Oliver shouted.

"You don't have to sweat over hospital conditions in Grenada. When you're sick, your parents send you to Trinidad."

Boos from the students. Oliver stomped out the back door.

"Anything else?" Scott waited. "Okay gentlemen. Let's do it."

The students applauded and headed for the exits.

A student council representative ran up to him. "Scott."

"What's up, Lennox?" Scott respected Lennox, a serious student from Grenville who boarded at the GBSS Hostel. Lennox prided himself in his well-kept Afro and his popularity with girls.

"Some girl wants to talk to you," Lennox said. "Said it's important."

"Where's she?"

"Behind the Chemistry lab . . . man, she's hot."

Oliver walked up. "I have another question."

Scott ignored Oliver and lowered his voice to Lennox. "Who's she?"

"Said her name is Trini."

Scott pushed past Oliver, and found Trini on the rear steps of the chemistry lab, wringing her hands.

She looked younger in a colorful tie-dyed t-shirt, jeans and white tennis shoes with her braids tucked through the back loop of her cap.

"Don't go on the march," she said. "There's going to be trouble."

"Did Rabid send you?"

She swung at his face.

He grabbed her hand, the rush of anger surprising him. "How much is he paying you?"

Her lips trembled. "You're walking into a trap." She turned and walked off.

CHAPTER TWENTY-SIX

The first tear-gas canister landed in the crowd five minutes into Duncan's speech. Scott was standing a few feet away from him on the second story balcony of the Health Department. Among the crowd that filled Melville Street, flocks of students in school uniforms, white shirts and striped ties blowing in the sea breeze. Claudette and Alicia were also somewhere out there. Probably Trini too, in her fiery tie-dyed t-shirt, planted by Rabid to stir confusion.

Scott dismissed her, and turned to Duncan's speech.

Duncan seemed larger than life surrounded by nurses, a bearded giant shoulder deep in a sea of white. "Brothers and Sisters," he shouted into the microphone. "We just delivered the nurses' petition to the Minister of Health."

He lowered the microphone, whispered to one of the nurses, and then faced the crowd as the tension built.

Why would Trini, a Chinatown prostitute for Gabbard's murderers care about Scott's safety? Before his downfall, Batista in Cuba had used similar scare tactics to keep students away from demonstrations.

Duncan continued. "We asked him to listen to some of our sisters' concerns. But he has refused them even that fundamental courtesy."

The crowd booed.

"They don't care about nurses, the hospital, the dying. They don't care that there are no bandages, no medicine, and no beds. They don't care that women deliver babies on cold concrete floors. Gabbard doesn't give a damn about us."

The crowd roared.

The electricity energized Scott, and his optimism resonated with the fervor of the people. He belonged here, on the frontline of a people's revolution.

First the La Sagesse demonstration and now the hospital protests, escalating confrontation in Duncan's strategy to educate, agitate, and mobilize the masses.

Duncan had promised in secret meetings that the students would have a Cuban-style revolution. But first, they had to strengthen the people's confidence with the passive resistance advocated by Martin Luther King.

"Let's send Gabbard a message," Duncan hollered. "We will block these roads until he meets the demands of our sister nurses."

"Road block! Road Block!"

"This occasion is historic. All facets of our society, students and teachers, farmers and fishermen, store clerks and bus drivers are here to tell Gabbard, act on our pleas, or else, he has to go."

"Gabbard must go! Gabbard must go!"

Scott nudged Lenox. "Something doesn't look right."

The windows overlooking the balcony slammed shut and footsteps rumbled in the building.

"Don't worry —"

A distant pop from the north, like a truck backfiring. A canister trailed white smoke across the sky and landed in the middle of the crowd.

Tear gas!

Screams.

Another pop from the south. Canisters rained down from both ends of the street. A wave of panic swept over the crowd. Trapped between building walls and bottlenecked side streets, the only avenue of escape seemed over the sea wall. Some jumped into the sea.

More screams from above. Rabid charged out of the ministry's door, tightening a gas mask over his face. A mob of masked men followed with batons and ax handles.

Rabid pointed at Scott and metallic barks shot out of his mouthpiece. "Get him too."

"Let's go!" Scott leaped over the rail into a stampede of people rushing toward Granby Street, already choked by parked cars.

A covered truck screeched into the intersection. Men in khakis and gas masks leaped from the back of the truck swinging ax handles. Like a retreating wave, people roared back into the gas cloud, some coughing violently. A school-girl disappeared under a forest of legs.

Scott's eyes burned. His lungs screamed for air. He grabbed his throat and crumbled to his knees. Lennox seized him around the shoulders and yanked him to his feet. Lennox pointed at the long row of buildings facing the ministry.

"They're shut." Gas poured down Scott's throat and burned the air out of his lungs. *Let's jump in the sea* he wanted to shout. Instead, he stumbled blindly after Lennox.

Lennox led the way between a car and the building with his shirt over his face.

Through teary eyes, Scott noticed a wooden padlocked door on the side of the building. He pulled a loose brick from the road and hammered the bolt. The screws holding the bolt loosened and clattered to the ground.

The door gave way to his shoulders and he tumbled into a dark warehouse with Lennox.

Scott sucked down the musty air, glad for the relief in his throat.

"Over here," he yelled to people running by.

Lennox led the way into the darkness, a rising surge of panicked footsteps behind them. At the far end of the warehouse, a slit of light peeked out the edge of a shut door.

Gunshots in the streets.

"Shit," Lennox muttered.

Scott pushed open the door into a courtyard.

A man pointed at an open gate. "The back of EveryBody's Store."

He sped after the man through the gate and down a hallway that opened into the grocery store. They raced down an aisle and out the door into the street facing the Market Square.

A stream of people poured through the store, coughing, and stumbling against shelves. A stack of cans crashed to the floor.

Tears flowed down Lennox's cheek and mucous dribbled from his nostrils. "Man, we got to get out of here."

"Let's split up."

More gunshots.

"Oh God," a woman bawled. "They coming with guns!"

People scattered.

"Good luck, man." Scott shook Lennox's hand, then sprinted across the Market Square to a side street, up a deserted alley, and climbed brick steps to Church Street. He paused to catch his breath, looking back at white gas hazing over the city.

A girl in tie-dyed t-shirt raced up the steps to him. "Come with me."

He snapped at Trini. "Get lost!"

"They got Duncan and the nurses. They're looking for student council members."

"How come you know so much?"

"Trust me."

His temple pulsed. "Your man just ambushed us and you want me to trust—"

"He's not my man." Her eyes welled up. "I warned you—" She flinched as gunshots echoed in the distance. "They'll recognize you. Please come with me."

Something in her voice, her tone, her conviction, made him follow her up the steps and across a stone path to the back of the Anglican Church.

"Take off your shirt." She pulled her t-shirt up over her head, her dark skin glistening under a film of sweat. Her full round breasts rose with heavy breathing.

He struggled into her t-shirt while she slipped on his shirt, tying the shirt-tails in a knot above her navel, and rolling up the sleeves. She pushed his hair back, slapped her cap backward over his head, and fitted her sunglasses over his eyes.

"Monica is waiting for you on the Carenage, across from the union building." She handed him a key. "She'll take you by boat across the lagoon and give you directions to my house."

"Where're you going?"

"We'll talk later." Just as quickly as she had appeared, Trini vanished.

Scott sprinted through back roads and alleyways under a wail of sirens. He spotted Monica pacing the water's edge.

"Almost didn't recognize you," she said. "We don't have much time." She hustled him into a rowboat tied off at the seawall. "This was Vincent's boat, his water taxi to earn extra money."

"I'll row." Scott settled onto the middle crossbench and grabbed the oars.

Monica released the rope and sat upfront facing him, the scars on her arms like dark lizards in the sunlight.

An ambulance screamed toward the city center as he rowed the boat past anchored yachts and schooners. He glided the boat into the shadow of the *Skyward* cruise ship, berthed on the pier. Overhead, passengers hugged the rails, fixated on the crying city, and deaf to the enthusiastic yells of money divers in the water.

"Hey." One of the divers waved at the passengers. "Throw a Yankee quarter, and I'll dive for it."

"*Bonjai*," a familiar voice hollered. "Rich American like you don't have one little quarter for a poor country boy?"

Scott recognized Martin's dimpled smile under the head of wet curly hair. And instantly, they were back in Gouyave under the sun, swimming, fishing, cooking red snapper in melted butter, and watching movies at Casa's.

Scott leaned forward to call out, but Monica lifted her finger to her lips. In that moment, he felt like he'd become a refugee in his own country.

A man on the ship jingled coins in his hand and flung them overboard. A dozen hands in the sea waved in a frantic water dance to catch the money. Coins sprinkled into the water and, with the swiftness of seagulls after a meal, the money divers disappeared beneath the surface.

Scott maneuvered the boat past the rear of the giant ship and aimed for the swampy Lagoon Road. He docked the boat across from Regal Cinema and jumped out.

Monica gave him directions to Trini's house. "Remember, she want you to stay away from the windows."

He watched her row back toward Chinatown, and then he hurried along Paddock Road for about a half-mile. Just past a barbershop on the right, he entered a trail in the shade of a huge breadfruit tree. As Monica instructed, he crept down a rocky path along high hedges to the backyard of the fourth house on the left, light blue, with a red low-cut dress drying on the clothesline.

The key unlocked the backdoor with ease. He slipped into the little house and locked the door, peering through the glass pane to make sure he'd not been followed.

He entered a plain living room with polished wooden floors, a couch, and stacked bookcase. Light curtains blew in windows overlooking the lagoon. On the wall next to the front door, a Trinidad and Tobago carnival calendar depicted a scantily dressed young woman with butterfly wings aflame in dazzling colors.

He checked the closets for assurance that no surprises awaited him. He entered the bedroom, glancing past a dresser and a nightstand with a clock, to a neatly made-up bed below the window. A row of clothes hung in a closet in the far corner, partially screened by a shower curtain hanging on a stretched rope. Perfume in the air reminded him of the night he met Trini.

Next door to the bedroom, he looked around the shower, a narrow concrete enclosure with a full-moon showerhead in the ceiling. Female underwear hung on a line strung across the walls. In the kitchen, a small refrigerator hummed next to a two-burner stove, and clean dishes sat in a drainer on the counter.

He collapsed on the couch and gazed out the window at the sun-washed yachts bobbing in the lagoon. So much had happened so fast, he needed time to think.

Only Monica and Trini knew where he was, and both knew Rabid.

Monica feared him. Trini kept his company. Something felt odd.

***

Claudette confirmed Rodney's suspicions.

She rushed through the front door with sweat dripping down her face. "They're coming!"

"Who?" Mommy asked

"The police, for Scott," she shouted. "There's shootings in town."

"Calm down. You're not making sense."

Before the march, on his way to an ear appointment at the hospital, Rodney had walked past the police station. Policemen were handing axe handles and gas masks to a ragtag group of men.

Just as Rodney had decided to race into town to alert Duncan's people, Oliver pulled up in his Volkswagen.

Rodney jumped in and explained what he'd just seen. "I'm on my way to warn the marchers."

"Forget them. I'll take you home."

"People could get hurt."

"Some people deserve it. They don't know how to fight a revolution. My cousin Armstrong is smarter than Duncan." Oliver turned the car away from town and toward Marryshow Lane. "By the way, I saw Scott with another Chinatown slut this morning, at school. No shame. Heard Lennox say her name was Trini."

The name Trini still rang in Rodney's ears two hours later. When Scott had mumbled the name in his sleep a couple nights ago, Rodney had dismissed it as dreams about their Gouyave pigeon.

But Rodney had more immediate concerns if police were headed to the house. While Claudette recounted the morning events to Mommy, he pulled a plastic bag of marijuana from an opening on the side of his mattress, and concealed it by the big tree across the yard.

He rushed back into the living room. "Where's Alicia?"

"She fainted when they pointed guns at us," Claudette said. "The nurses took her to the hospital."

"Oh God, the pressure." Mommy's flimsy discolored dress hung from her thin frame. "Let's go find—"

The dogs barked. Heavy footsteps invaded the verandah and fists banged the door, rattling the cracked glass. The door swung open and Rabid pushed his way in with his big hairy arms. He held an ax handle, and a pistol grip protruded from his waistband.

Several men crowded in behind him.

Rabid growled at Mommy. "Where you boy?"

"Get to hell out of my house." Her blackened front tooth threatened to spit out.

The men pushed past her with axe handles and rifles.

"I'll report you to the police," she shouted.

One man grinned at her. "We the police now."

"Search everywhere," Rabid ordered. "If dogs get in your way, shoot them." He poked Rodney in the shoulder with his ax handle. "Where you brother?"

"I don't know." Rodney pulled Claudette by her arm. "Let's tie the dogs."

"Good idea." Rabid snarled.

Rodney and Claudette grabbed the four dogs by their collars and used ropes to restrain them below the house.

"Scott should get on a damn plane and join Daddy," Rodney whispered to Claudette.

They returned to the living room and stood with Mommy while Rabid's men trampled through the house and yard.

One of the men handed Rabid a red book. "Look what I find."

"Communist stuff." Rabid flipped the pages, and a stained picture fell to the floor. He picked up the picture and frowned at it before sticking it in his pocket.

He turned to Mommy. "Tell you boy give up at the police station. I have a friend from Richmond Hill Prison that might shoot him in the back if he running."

Mommy glared at him.

The other men stomped out the door and up the steps ahead of Rabid. Just as he got to the first landing, one of the dogs pulled loose and charged after him.

Rabid pulled his pistol and fired twice.

Claudette screamed.

The dog tumbled backward and lay still.

He turned to his men. "Don't worry, Trini will lead us to the boy."

CHAPTER
TWENTY-SEVEN

A mounting suspicion told Scott that trusting Trini was a mistake. Doubt clogged his thoughts while he paced inside her house. Without a phone, the isolation boxed him in. Each time a car drove by, he'd peeked through the curtains, half-expecting to see someone giving Trini a ride home. But each time, the car had continued along the rough road. Dogs joined in howling choruses when sirens wailed in the distance. The radio repeated bulletins about an impending Gabbard speech, but gave no news of the downtown mayhem. It worried him that Trini enjoyed a cozy enough relationship with Rabid to know of the attack, in advance. Yet, she arranged to have Scott hide in her house.

Or had she just trapped him?

He searched the house again, wishing he would find something, anything, to dispel or prove his misgivings. Nothing alarmed him in the kitchen, living room, or bathroom. But in her bedroom, scented cologne bottles and neatly folded underwear in her dresser teamed up with a Bible in her nightstand to disarm his qualms. He retreated to the living room couch and watched the dying sun stain the lagoon red.

Still edgy, he reached for a book tucked between a vase of flowers and the radio on the end table. He flipped through *The 1973 Color Atlas of Venereology*, and stopped at a page folded at the corner, plastered with grotesque pictures of human flesh ravaged by venereal diseases. Bold handwriting in the white space beneath the pictures spelled out the name and clinic address of a Port-of-Spain doctor. In parentheses, a long word that read like a medicine followed by instructions to take three times a day.

In that instant, the fragments Scott held of Trini's life converged into a crushing disappointment, thwarting his hope that she might be Gillian. Her sensuous walk, inviting smile, and nights in Chinatown with Rabid meant one thing: Trini was a diseased prostitute engaged in a dangerous game.

A car rumbled along Lagoon Road, and then stopped near the foot of the path that led up to the front door.

Car doors opened. Low voices.

Scott crawled to the window and peered through the curtain slit. He swallowed hard when he realized why Trini wanted him to stay away from the windows.

She was leading Rabid up to the front door.

Another man stood watch at the car.

She pointed to a gun sticking out of Rabid's waistband. He shifted the gun to his side and covered it with his shirt.

That bitch!

Scott wiped sweat from his forehead and darted to the back window. Two men stood in the shadows of the breadfruit tree up the trail. He crawled to the kitchen, pulled a long knife from the drawer, and returned to the front window curtains.

Rabid stood at the door with his hairy arms folded across his chest, watching Trini pull her keys from her bag.

Scott gripped the knife in his sweating hand and slid across the floor to the door.

If Trini came in first, he would grab her with the knife to her throat and force Rabid to hand over his weapon.

But what if Rabid came in ahead of her? Plunge the knife into his back, and grab the gun. Then force Trini to call out to Rabid's goons to drop their guns. They wouldn't dare risk shooting his little slut.

Scott could take her hostage in the car, probably filled with more guns and ammunition in the trunk. He would head for Belvidere and vanish into the thick jungle as Fédon had in 1795, and wait for the revolution.

And Trini? She'd have a lot of explaining to do, if she survived the next few seconds.

The door lock sounded like a rifle bolt slamming home.

He braced himself, fearing Rabid could hear his pounding heartbeat.

The door creaked open.

"Thanks for the ride," Trini said.

"Let me know if them school boys show up in Chinatown," Rabid said.

"Okay, see you tomorrow." She leaned into the doorway. "Papa, I'm home."

Papa?

She waved at Rabid and shut the door.

From behind, Scott covered her mouth with one hand and stuck the knife-point to her throat with the other. "Shhh."

Trini trembled in his arms.

Rabid's footsteps faded down the path.

Scott waited until the car drove off before he released her. "What the hell's going on?"

"You were supposed to stay away from the damn windows." With tears trickling down her cheeks, she pushed him. "After what I did today, you still don't trust me?"

"You're dealing with murderers."

"I know that, dammit!" She turned and dashed into the bedroom.

He grabbed the medical book off the couch and rushed after her. He swung her around by her shoulder. She looked every bit the contagious whore he'd hoped she wasn't. The white shirt grubby, the knees on her jeans a dusty brown and her tennis shoes scuffed in black.

He shoved the book in her face. "Is this another secret?"

"You don't know a damn thing." She collapsed on the bed.

"Keep the shirt." He tossed the book next to her. "I'm gone."

"Where are you going?"

He peeled off her t-shirt and hurled it at her. "I don't know what your game is. But I'm safer sleeping on the beach than here." He headed for the back door.

She ran after him and grabbed his hand. "Please don't go. It's not safe out there."

"I don't even know who you are."

"Yes, you do. It's me, Gillian from Belvidere."

Scott watched Gillian turn on the lamp on her nightstand. The little girl with the missing tooth and thick braids had blossomed into a woman with full breasts and curvaceous hips.

She pulled the Bible from her nightstand drawer and opened it on the bed, spilling a few pictures. She handed him the clearer original of the picture he'd taken from Vincent's bloodied pocket. "Me and Daddy, five years ago."

"He showed us a copy in Chinatown."

"Monica said he always carried it, but it was missing from the night Daddy—"

"He really loved you."

If the conversation continued about that night, he might end up admitting that he'd witnessed her father's murder and that he had the bloodstained picture in one of Duncan's books at home. Revealing the nightmare now would change nothing for her.

"Rabid will pay," she said. "I know he did it."

"But does Rabid know you are —"

"Only Monica and Dr. Pilgrim know the truth. And now you."

He picked up the medical book. "What about this?"

She laughed with mild amusement in her voice. "If I could fool both an educated GBSS boy and an ignoramus like Rabid, I can outwit all of Grenada. I showed Rabid the book in his car. He believes I caught a disease in Trinidad that chews condoms. He thinks I'm in Grenada to recover."

"Living here with your grandfather?"

"Staying with 'Papa'. I never even knew my grandfather." She stared up at the ceiling. "This book saved me once before. My uncle . . .that drunken bastard."

"If it's too personal you don't have to —"

"Monica told me I could trust you. I want you to trust me too."

In tears, she told Scott everything that she had endured after she moved to Trinidad, especially the abuse by Sticks, her Uncle Bertrand. After the fire, and the news of her father's murder, the doctors refused to discharge Gillian from hospital to attend the funeral, so Monica took care of the burial.

Sticks recovered from his burns, but a few months later began new advances on Gillian. Since he'd already accused her of being a whore, she bought the book and showed him pictures of a disease she supposedly had.

"He stayed away after that," she said.

"What became of him?"

"My aunt left him for another man and I moved in with Sonia's family. He fell asleep with a cigarette again. The flames left nothing. Rabid will get his too."

"Yes, after the Revo."

"You really believe in revolution?" she asked.

"It's the only way. Conditions are deteriorating every day."

"The hospital is worse than when Mammy died. I was there all afternoon today."

He pointed at the red stains on the white shirt. "Is that where you got those?"

"Dr. Pilgrim needed my help after the riot."

She explained that most of the shooting was in the air, but a student from Grenville was shot in the back and drowned when he tried to swim away. Duncan, Beverly Johnson, Scott's English literature teacher, a few nurses and student leaders were arrested.

"My sisters were there too. I hope they're okay."

"Dr. Pilgrim said your mother and Claudette visited this afternoon. He told them you were safe."

"Why were they—"

Gillian held his hand. "It's Alicia. She suffered psychological trauma."

Later that night, Scott pushed forward his empty plate across the table from Gillian, with gratitude now filling the vacancy left by the suspicions he'd had earlier. She'd served him a plate overflowing with curried chicken and vegetables, and calmed his concerns over Alicia. Dr. Pilgrim had kept her overnight for observation, after she had sat in the hospital all afternoon, pulling her hair and biting her nails.

"I don't know how to thank you," Scott said.

"I should thank you," she said under the dim incandescent bulb. "Stay right here."

Tight shorts hugged her behind as firm legs glided her across the wooden floor toward her bedroom.

She returned with a discolored handkerchief and spread it out on the table. "Remember that day at school in Gouyave, when you had those bruises from the car accident?"

"You kept it all this time?"

"You made me feel like a doctor that day."

He remembered the stinging embarrassment of his wet pants and Daddy's anger ringing in his ears. But it never crossed his mind that allowing Gillian to nurse his elbows with her handkerchief could mean so much to her.

"It kept me afloat during some tough times." She rested her hand on his. "Thanks."

He stood and faced her, his senses enflamed by the whiff of her perfume and the melodic theme from A Summer Place playing on the radio. Her smooth dark face and soft twinkle in her eyes stirred his desires. His lips met hers in a moment of rising want. He held her in a tight embrace and pressed his body against hers, his excitement growing with the sound of her rising breath.

She pushed him away. "I can't." She raced into the bedroom and slammed the door behind her.

How foolish of him to have forgotten that Gillian was still struggling from the years with her uncle in Trinidad. He cursed under his breath. If he didn't do something soon, he'd put his fist through the wall for his stupidity.

He collected the dirty dishes, plunged them down in sudsy water, and scrubbed them till they shined.

He returned to the living room, turned the radio dial to Radio Grenada, and sank into the couch. Still, Gillian remained locked behind her bedroom door.

The announcer came on a few minutes later. "Ladies and Gentlemen, The Right Honorable Premier Forbes Gabbard has an important message for the Grenada people."

The bedroom door creaked open and Gillian shuffled out holding a tissue. She sat on the couch next to Scott.

He held her free hand. "Sorry."

She rested her head on his shoulder.

Gabbard's faked British accent reeked with deceit. "My fellow Grenadians, the peace of our island was broken today by a band of hooligans. They claim to support the sick, but they keep nurses away from the hospital. They claim to support education, yet they take students out of schools to sweat in the streets. They claim to support the hungry, yet they ransack grocery stores."

His voice echoed in the still house. "These radicals blocked streets. They shouted vulgar slogans that even priests in our sacred churches could hear. During the madness they created, people were hurt. A student drowned when he jumped into the sea to escape their riot."

"That's a lie," Gillian said.

"But have no fear," Premier Gabbard said. "Providence has led our brave auxiliary police to capture fifteen of the perpetrators, some of whom were injured while resisting arrest. Others are still on the loose, but will be caught. They will receive the harshest penalties under the law. No one will stop our march to Independence from Great Britain. We are guided by the hand of God and the spirit of Fédon."

If there was any truth to a vengeful Fédon, it appeared he had succeeded with the McDonalds: Daddy was bankrupt and gone, a river of distrust separated Scott and Rodney, Alicia was hospitalized, and now Scott was on the run from police thugs. Could all these, as well as Scott's tutelage with Duncan, another Fédon target, be just coincidental?

With serious charges facing Scott, he considered turning himself in so he could plan his legal defense with Duncan. Remaining in Gillian's house might only increase the danger for her. Whatever Scott's ultimate decision, he planned to first get a good night's sleep on her couch.

She turned off the radio. "I know what you're thinking. Don't do it."

"Rabid will eventually find out."

"He's my problem." She retrieved a sheet and a pillow from her bedroom. "Tomorrow I'll go by the court house to see what they have on you. In the meantime, don't leave this house."

He didn't want to argue. He decided to slip out the door early next morning while she slept. "Sleep well."

"I'll sleep well because you're here." She disappeared into her room.

He turned off the light and let the lagoon breeze settle him into the couch with sleep-time memories of Gouyave. He was just drifting away when a hand on his shoulder pulled him awake in the darkness.

Sadness doused Gillian's voice. "I want you to sleep with me."

Fully clothed, he held her in bed as she sobbed more pain and guilt than he ever imagined a human could carry.

He kissed her wet cheeks and whispered her to sleep with words he never imagined he had. Then he stayed awake with her in his arms, listening to her warm breath on his chest, knowing there was nothing he wouldn't do to protect her.

CHAPTER
TWENTY-EIGHT

Gillian cringed at the sight of the prisoners shuffling into the crowded courtroom. Three disheveled nurses sat next to a few students in tattered uniforms. One of the students looked like Lennox but his puffy face and swollen lips made it difficult to be certain. Beverly Johnson sat next to him, her ripped shirt exposing a bra strap on her bare shoulder.

Duncan stood under the squeaky ceiling fan, the left side of his forehead disfigured by a bulge the size of a tennis ball and his crudely shaved head a grotesque landscape of chopped hair and lacerated scalp. The rumor in Chinatown was that Rabid had beaten Duncan in his cell with an ax handle and then shaved his head with a broken bottle.

The judge, aloof in official white wig and black robe, gazed over his glasses at the defendants like a pelican spying its next meal. Gillian wondered if he was also on Gabbard's secret payroll, like the judge who recently dismissed an assault case against Rabid. Rabid had beaten a man unconscious after he referred to Gabbard as Lucifer. If this judge honored the government's sedition charges, Scott's charges would be more severe, for avoiding arrest.

The judge hammered his gavel and peered down at the defense table. "Mr. Duncan, have you or your defendants received medical attention since your arrest?"

Duncan's split lips expelled his words in sputtering gasps. "No, Your Honor."

The judge removed his glasses and turned to the prosecutor. "Mr. Belmar, is this true?"

Belmar stood and muttered a few inaudible words.

"Speak up, Mr. Belmar."

"Your Honor, to the best of my knowledge no one requested a doctor."

"This is preposterous!" The judged slammed his fist on the bench. "Any medical doctors here?"

In the front row, Dr. Pilgrim raised his hand.

"Dr. Pilgrim, please take a few minutes to examine these defendants. I will adjourn for thirty minutes. Mr. Belmar, report to my chamber immediately." He banged the gavel, and stomped down a short flight of steps into a backroom.

Mr. Belmar snatched a few loose pages off his table and scuttled toward the judge's chamber.

If Gillian was with Dr. Pilgrim examining the injured defendants, or at least taking his notes, some who recognized her from the galley might say she was just a prostitute trying to make herself a name. Or worse, that she was Rabid's slut trying to get information from the defendants.

Tears welled up, but she found it easier to manage them now that her emotional dam, pregnant with grief and anger, had burst with such abandonment over the past few nights. The ease with which she'd opened up to Scott had not surprised her. For ten years she'd nourished the seeds of their bond, since he sat next to her in the truck on Belvidere and allowed her to nurse his bruises.

Today, she relished another moment.

As she was about to leave for the courthouse earlier that morning, Scott had kissed her. "I'll miss you."

"I think I love you." Her words found no resistance in her soul.

But the contempt and fear she harbored for Rabid continued to cloud the flickering light in her heart. If he discovered her deception, Grenada would not be big enough to hide her and Scott. Her best hope was for a popular uprising to send Rabid to hell with a noose around his neck.

But before this could happen, Duncan had to win this case.

Duncan, the last of the defendants to see Dr. Pilgrim, limped back to the defendants' table.

Whispers swept across the courtroom when Belmar exited the judge's chamber, wringing his hands and slouching like a cat caught in rain.

The judge took his seat. "This is the most blatant case of police brutality I have seen in my thirty years in British Commonwealth courts."

Gillian closed her eyes and prayed for good news.

"It is alarming when victims of a crime are charged with perpetuating the very crimes for which they suffered. But it is equally alarming when a government conspires to deny citizens their rights to assembly and free speech. The court is grateful that Mr. Belmar has recognized the flaws in the charges brought before me today. Case dismissed!"

Gillian hurried along Church Street in the midday heat, away from the boisterous jubilation outside the courthouse and headed up the hill past Fort George toward the hospital. Her heart felt torn between the judge's decision to drop all charges and the regret that Scott no longer needed her to shelter him.

A car rumbled to a stop alongside her.

Rabid sat behind the wheel, his hairy arm hanging out the window. A pale man with wild hair sat in the passenger seat with a rifle across his lap.

"Where you going?" Rabid asked.

"To see Dr. Pilgrim for more medicine. I don't feel well."

"He better fix you fast." Rabid sucked on his teeth and grabbed her arm. "I tired waiting."

"Sorry. You've been real understanding." She feigned a smile, promising herself to scrub his grime off her arm when she got to the hospital. "I can see why Boss likes you."

"He vex them communists free. It not safe for you to be walking around."

"I feel safe having you as my friend." She wondered how much longer she could disguise her growing nausea.

"That McDonald boy show up yet in Chinatown?"

"No, but I'll let you know if I hear anything," she said.

"I found this in his house." He fished in his pocket and pulled out a stained picture. "Find out how he got it."

At the sight of the picture, she heaved. Vomit splattered over Rabid's car door, side mirror, and his arm.

***

Gillian rushed through the front door, slammed it shut, and glared at Scott on the couch. "What else are you not telling me?"

"What are you talking about?"

"Rabid found Daddy's picture in your house."

He slumped on the couch and stared at the floor.

"You said Daddy showed you the picture in Chinatown." She plopped down next to him. "How did you get it?"

"I took it from his pocket . . . in La Sagesse."

Her lips trembled. "You . . .you . . .were there?"

"Yes." He held her hands and told her everything that had happened that night. "There was nothing I could do. Maybe if I had a gun."

She had known all along that it was Rabid. But the final confirmation struck her like a dagger in her chest. "Why didn't you tell me?"

"I was trying to protect you."

"You can't protect me from the truth. But now Rabid knows you were there that night."

"He can only suspect."

"He would have recognized me if my face wasn't stained by Daddy's . . . " She buried her face in her hands and wept.

He held her. "You changed a lot since that picture. No one would know it's you."

She dried her eyes with her sleeve. "I'll tell him Monica gave it to you, that she found it in Daddy's pocket when she identified him in the hospital."

"And if he doesn't believe you?"

"I'll make him believe," she said. "By the way, he was with a man who was looking for you too. His name is Planass."

Scott looked like her words had jolted every nerve in his body. His jaws tightened and he rubbed his neck.

"Are you okay?" she asked.

He told her about the night Planass attacked them in Gouyave. "He was supposed to be in prison another ten years. Maybe we should get them before they get us. I need a weapon."

"Rabid is worried about my safety," she said. "He's getting me a gun."

CHAPTER TWENTY-NINE

Scott gazed out Duncan's office window at the blue-sky umbrella hanging over the city, a silent witness to the winds of change sweeping the island. Gabbard's poisoned breath had blown seeds of revolution from the pages of Castro and onto the streets of St. George's, taking root in minds made fertile by desperation. Since the police attack on the march two weeks ago, a clear battle line had been drawn between the people and government.

Revolution loomed red on the horizon.

Duncan leaned forward over his desk, one eye still swollen half shut, overshadowed by the bulge on his forehead he'd received from Rabid's boots. "How's Alicia?"

"Hasn't said a word since the riot."

Alicia's delicate world had suffered one too many shocks. Even Scott's coaching to get her to talk was met with blank stares. She had spent the last few days in the company of nuns at the Catholic Church.

"The nuns want to take her with a group of orphans to Trinidad by boat," Scott said.

"Let me know if I can help."

"Thanks. How're you doing?"

"Better every day. Independence is a week away. Let's keep the demonstrations going to change the British minds."

With Gabbard's legitimacy crumbling, and foreign reporters and British observers roaming the island, another attack on peaceful marchers might force a national referendum on independence. Gabbard had ordered his secret police off the streets to create a false atmosphere of civility. No one had seen Rabid or Planass in the past week.

Duncan continued. "Since the riots, we have the momentum to tip the scale in favor of a British reversal on the independence decision. Businesses and unions are calling for island-wide strikes and marches to demand Gabbard's immediate resignation."

"The student union voted last night to join the teachers' strike next Monday," Scott said.

"Great, just keep everything peaceful." Duncan cautioned. "Gabbard and his goons are the villains and we want to keep it that way. No violence from our side."

Realizing that Duncan was already overwhelmed, Scott decided not to tell him about Lennox's aborted plan to firebomb the Carenage Police Station last night.

Lennox had taken on a sharp edge since his arrest and beating the day of the riot. After the meeting at GBSS last night, he had convinced Scott to accompany him and another student down a trail to an abandoned shack. Lennox switched on a penlight and led the way across creaky floors to a couple of cardboard boxes with rows of gasoline-filled bottles, rags protruding from the tops. The smell of gasoline permeated the air.

The windows overlooked the fire station, a long red building shared by the police.

It had taken Scott two hours of whispered arguments to convince Lennox that firebombing a police station on the eve of a student march against police brutality was a dangerous idea.

"The students want more action," Scott told Duncan.

Duncan probably detected the desperation in Scott's voice. "What else is driving you?"

Scott finally recounted how he'd witnessed the murders at La Sagesse Bay.

Duncan listened attentively until Scott finished, and then he held Scott by his shoulders. "That's a heavy burden for you to carry, but keep this between us. We suspected Rabid all along. We'll need your testimony one day. In the meantime, patience."

"Can't we meet with the British observers, to present the students' case on independence?"

Duncan tugged at his beard. "How long would it take you to gather up a petition of all the students on the island?"

"Maybe two days."

"It's time you meet the British Counsel General, Lord Barrington, so he can thank you for tearing down his gate at La Sagesse."

***

"I have good news." Scott lifted a thick envelope in front of the group of about twenty members of the Union of Secondary Schools at the Sauteurs Macdonald College. "In the last two days, eighty percent of all our students signed the petition opposing independence under Gabbard."

The student union met regularly to coordinate antigovernment demonstrations and fund raisers for Grenada students in Trinidad after Gabbard suspended their tuition assistance. Scott and Lennox usually represented GBSS at the meetings, so Scott was surprised to see Oliver in the back row.

The students applauded Scott's announcement, but Oliver raised his hand. "What good is the petition?"

"If you'd read the flyers we circulated the last two days, you would know the answer."

"I did, but I don't understand how—"

"That's your problem," Scott said. "You don't understand much."

"Let's stop the bullshit," Lennox said.

Scott continued. "The Counsel General has agreed to accept the petition tomorrow night. We must decide who delivers it. The location is secret. Duncan will arrange the details. We don't want Rabid getting his bloody hands on the petition before it's delivered."

Oliver half-grinned. "Then stop hanging out with Rabid's whore."

Scott clenched his teeth and waited for the hot blood flooding his temples to slow. "I move that nonmembers leave before we vote on who meets the Counsel General."

A student seconded the motion and they agreed unanimously to have non-members leave.

"You're all fools." Oliver stomped out of the classroom and slammed the door shut.

After the laughter subsided, the students agreed that since Scott and Lennox lived in town, they should deliver the petition. To avoid the risk of carrying the large envelopes by bus to St. George's, the group decided to have a Sauteurs student keep the petitions overnight and to hand them to Scott at GBSS the next day.

Later, Scott wiped the sweat off his brow with his sleeve as he and Lennox headed toward the bus stop in the blazing mid-afternoon sun. Three pony-tailed girls in white shirts and blue skirts skipped along the street. They looked so young and full of promise, like Gillian had been at that age, blissfully unaware of tragic surprises that life might have in store for them. His own life with Gillian had become a tapestry of grief, danger, and desire.

He wished there was more he could do for her, like put a bullet in Rabid's head.

Just yesterday, Gillian showed Scott the .38 caliber revolver that Rabid had given her after a few target practices. She and Scott discussed how she could entice Rabid to take her on a night drive to the Fort Jeudy peninsula. Scott would lie in wait at the dead-end, and, while she distracted Rabid in the parked car, Scott would creep up and shoot Rabid. Then they would roll the car with him in it off the cliff and into the currents, never to be seen again.

Lennox broke the silence at the bus stop. "Your cousin is dangerous."

"I wouldn't worry about Oliver. He's just hot air, a phony bourgeoisie revolutionary."

They boarded a bus and chatted in cautious undertones, but Scott felt drawn to the sea view as they headed southward, the blue water reflecting sunlit slivers. In the distance, fishing boats dropped their nets in wide circles and seagulls fed off the catch in attack dives.

By the time the bus pulled up in front of the Gouyave market thirty minutes later, Scott was already bathed in a wave of nostalgia.

He turned to Lennox. "I need to make a couple of visits here. We still have time for the last bus to town."

They strolled up St. Peters Street and crossed Cornet's Walk to Ma's house. She was lying on the couch with a wet cloth across her forehead. Aunt Bridgette sat on an adjacent chair fanning Ma with a piece of cardboard and stirring up a strong aroma of the medicinal Limacol. At age ninety, Ma was fading, but was still strong enough to ask about the family. He decided to skip Alicia's condition, and instead told Ma about Daddy's last letter saying he was trying to get them visas to move to St. Croix.

"He's worried about you," Aunty Bridgette said.

"Don't worry," Lennox said. "I'll take care of him."

"Just keep him away from Planass," she said.

Scott didn't expect her to reveal anything new, so he avoided further discussions about Planass.

An hour later, saddened by Ma's condition, Scott said good-bye and headed to Mr. Farrow's house with Lennox.

Mr. Farrow greeted Scott with a bear hug. "Good to see you again, me boy. *Sa ka fètè?*"

"*Tres bien*," Scott said.

Mr. Farrow looked the same, but the passing years dragged on his voice as it did on Ma's. Ten years younger than Ma, he still had the light in his eyes that reflected the expectancy of a child receiving a long-awaited present.

Mr. Farrow shook Lennox's hand. "If you is Scott friend, you is me friend too."

They followed Mr. Farrow into the house and sat around the table taking shots of rum from tin cups. A steady breeze flowed through the house and the surf thundered against the shoreline. A rusty car crowded the carport next door, but the sea was still visible from the window.

Mr. Farrow turned to Scott. "You reading French at school?"

"Like he was born in Paris," Lennox said.

"Good. You must know French to know Grenada history." He lit his pipe and took a couple puffs. "All you giving Gabbard horrors. Revolution talk is enough to make Fédon come back."

"My great-grandmother used to talk about Fédon too," Lennox said. "But always in fear."

"People afraid what they don't know."

They drank another round and Lennox excused himself to use the outhouse.

"I hear Planass free again," Mr. Farrow said to Scott once they were alone. "The night before Pa died, Planass father and mother had a fight. Planass mother was thrown for dead down a ravine. After, the father hang himself from a tree in front his son. Planass was only eight years old. Anyway, his mother crawled up the bank by her fingernails, barely alive."

"What was the fight about?"

Mr. Farrow was about to answer when Lennox strolled up and glanced at his watch. "Time to go."

"Gabbard is like a trapped dog," Mr. Farrow said. "That's when he will bite the worst."

***

Farrow reached under his bed and dragged out his old cardboard box. Except for the cigar can in which he kept his letters to Jasmine, the rest of the contents were still wrapped in the black plastic bag he had used the night of the storm.

Scott had changed so much. He had mastered French and history. He looked so knowledgeable in his school uniform and facial hair, speaking in urgent tones about demonstrations, strikes, and revolution.

It was time for him to learn the truth.

Farrow had waited for fifty years to turn his papers over to someone he could trust. He limped to the shop across the street, handed the shopkeeper a coin, and dialed the phone.

"Hello." The voice sounded like Oliver.

"This is Mr. Farrow from Gouyave."

"Ah yes, Mr. Farrow from Gouyave. This is Oliver. How may I help you, Mr. Farrow from Gouyave?"

"Is Mrs. Cunningham home?"

"No one else is home, Mr. Farrow. But I'd be happy to take a message."

"When you see Scott, tell him to come visit me as soon as possible."

"Yes, I will tell Scott."

Farrow knew immediately he'd just made a mistake.

CHAPTER THIRTY

Scott stood with Lennox on the jetty, clutching the bulky envelopes and gazing down Grand Anse Beach. Flaming torches around the crowded Beach Boys Club licked at the moonlit night. Strobe lights inside open windows flashed to the beat of reggae music. The aroma of barbequed chicken and fried fish drifted over the beach, along with laughter from the outdoor deck. The possibility of prolonged strikes starting the next day and the absence of Gabbard's goons on the streets must have drawn people out for one last night of frolicking.

Scott would have loved to take Gillian there, to hold her, and dance with her. To whisper in her ear that everything would be okay. But lately, he'd been so distracted with the petition that he'd had little time to risk the trail down to her house. He'd done it enough times now that the fear was beginning to subside.

Lennox pointed out to the sea. "Is that them?"

Scott peered at a small motorboat racing toward the jetty. Under the glow of the moon, he read the watch Daddy had sent him. "Duncan said 10:00 PM sharp."

The boat pulled alongside the jetty and the lone man at the throttle, in a black naval uniform with a pistol holstered at his chest, called out in a crisp British accent. "You chaps the students?"

"Yes," Scott said.

The man climbed on to the jetty and frisked them. "Procedures, you understand. Hop aboard. The CG is awaiting you."

A few minutes later, they climbed up a stepladder onto a large yacht aglow in brilliant light. Another armed guard led them up a short flight of steps into a sky lounge behind the wheelhouse.

Scott gazed around in awe. The sitting area, larger than the living and dining rooms at home combined, lavished with sofas, a game table, a bar, bookcases, television and a ceiling mural. Chrome lighting along polished wooden walls emitted a sense of opulence that made him feel out of place in his baggy shirt and worn jeans.

"Wait here." The guard disappeared down a stairwell and returned a few minutes later preceding a balding man in a white sweater and dress slacks. The guard snapped to attention. "Counsel General, Lord Barrington."

"Have a seat, lads," Lord Barrington said, puffing on a pipe. "It's an honor to have such patriotic young men visit."

"Thanks for having us," Scott said.

They shook hands. Scott and Lennox sat on a sofa, while Lord Barrington settled into a big leather chair facing them. Scott recognized him from newspaper pictures. His thick reddish moustache contrasted starkly with slicked silver hair bordering the bald crown of his head. Pipe smoke, probably the reason for his stained moustache, drifted past his face and vanished into a ceiling vent.

Scott doubted that Lord Barrington, probably the man Scott had seen peering through binoculars from the mansion, would recognize him from among the hundreds who had stormed the La Sagesse gates.

Lord Barrington nodded at the guard, who then served them red wine in crystal glasses and exited the room.

"I was told to expect radical students who organize violent demonstrations and invade private property." The Englishman spoke with a hint of sarcasm behind the haze of pipe smoke. "But you gents hardly seem like the ruffians who demolished my gate and stampeded my gardens in the name of revolution."

Scott reigned in the temptation to debate the La Sagesse incident. He suspected the nobleman wanted to derail the purpose of their visit. So hoping that Lennox would also not succumb to the trap, Scott sipped his wine and counted the seconds.

The Lord spoke again. "You have a student petition for me to consider?"

Scott handed the envelopes to Lord Barrington. "Eighty percent oppose independence under Gabbard."

The Englishman slid the envelopes onto a glass coffee table and pointed his pipe at Scott. "Impressive work, but you jolly well know that if Her Majesty's government reneges on the promise to dismantle her colonies, it will be hell to pay at the United Nations."

"We're not opposed to independence," Lennox said. "What we're saying—"

"I know very well what you're saying, my friend. But the true crux of the matter is will the Non-Aligned bloc at the UN understand?"

Scott jumped in. "I'm sure the international community supports an orderly timetable that allows the Grenada people to voice their position."

"Lads," Lord Barrington said. "This is precisely what elections are about. Premier Gabbard won by a landslide."

Scott snapped. "He got a landslide of seats, by a small margin of fraudulent votes in each district. My own mother was turned away from voting."

"There are improprieties in every election. It's not a perfect system, but it's the best mankind has designed so far. Don't discard your house because of a few roof leaks."

Lennox spoke slowly, his words laden with anger. "If the ballot cannot assure us our freedom, then we will turn to the bullet."

"We are under intense pressure from your friends like Castro and Gadhafi to drop our colonies, ready or not. Post them a thank-you card for your predicament."

"They have nothing to do with this fight," Lennox said.

"My young friends, you understand so little. Every national struggle is on one side or the other of the Iron Curtain. Your fight has friends in far off places that believe in the historical inevitability of world socialism. The only historical inevitability I know of is that Grenada will be granted independence at midnight next Monday."

Two hours later, Scott stepped off the jetty with Lennox and onto the sands of Grand Anse beach. Struggling to tame his despair, Scott gazed out at the motorboat speeding away, leaving a white-water trail under the moon. Why should Lord Barrington, coddled in pompous luxury, exercise power over Grenada's oppressed people? At a stroke of his pen, the Englishman was about to hand over the people to a madman. Unless the British government changed their minds, Grenada was one night closer to revolution.

Scott dipped into his pocket and pulled out a few coins. "I need a beer after that meeting."

"Me too," Lennox said.

Nestled low on the beach, among coconut trees between the Grenada Beach Hotel and the Spice Island Inn, the Beach Boys Club, also called the BBC, was a social equalizer. American girls showed off tanned legs in tight miniskirts and gyrated on the dance floor with young Grenadian men sporting afros. Prostitutes hooked foreign businessmen with practiced interest over glasses of rum-punch, and hippies negotiated marijuana purchases from dreadlocked Rastafarians.

Scott had also heard of sightings of others who couldn't resist the BBC spell, such as Frank Sinatra, Princess Margaret, and Henry Kissinger.

Scott and Lennox made their way through the crowd toward the bar. Scott recognized a few faces in the fervor of flashing lights and loud music. But most seemed to be foreigners, probably British observers and reporters drawn by the rising tensions on the island.

He leaned over the bar and shouted his order for two beers. He handed one to Lennox, just as a tall Indian man in his mid-twenties squeezed his way up to them. He said a few words to Lennox and disappeared.

"Something's come up," Lennox said.

Scott watched Lennox shoulder his way toward the front door, hoping he remembered Duncan's message to avoid provoking the government.

Scott's concerns vanished when he recognized Gillian in the dim light at the end of the bar. She wore a tight-fitting black dress, with a single shoulder strap, exposing her right shoulder and upper back. Her hair flowed in curly waves to her shoulders.

His glance met hers and her face blossomed into a smile that sent a warm sensation over him. He raised his beer in a distant toast.

Just then, Oliver's voice behind him triggered his temper. "That whore is going to get you in hot water with Rabid."

Scott swung around and slammed his fist into Oliver's flabby gut, spilling his drink and shattering his glass on the floor.

"Hey!" A man shoved Scott away from Oliver. "What the hell's going on?"

"It's okay." Gillian pushed her way past the man and grabbed Scott's arm. "He was just about to dance."

She led him away from the bar and onto the dance floor. "What was that about?"

"That was my cousin, a real ass."

"He said something about me, didn't he?"

"No, about me." He wrapped his arms around her and they swayed to a slow song. She smiled in the whiff of sweet cologne and Scott's anger faded.

He kissed her.

"I've been waiting for you," she said.

"How did you know I was going to be here?"

"When Rabid found out that I was coming here to help Monica in the kitchen, he told me to look out for students meeting on the Counsel General's boat. I figured you'd be one of them. So I am dancing with you to get information for Rabid."

"Tell him we drank so much wine with the Counsel General, I don't remember a thing."

It was after two o'clock in the morning when Scott stepped out of the BBC club with Gillian, glad she had suggested they walk home rather than accept a ride with Monica. Offshore, yacht lights danced on the moon-glazed sea. Up the beach from the BBC, calypso music flowed from the poolside dance floor of the Grenada Beach Hotel, while flaming torches along the hotel fence waved in the breeze, casting long wavering shadows along the white sand. A lone security guard puffed on a cigarette at the gate.

Shoes in one hand, they held each other around the waist and headed north on the wet sand, leaving behind hotel lights and thoughts of Oliver, Rabid, and revolution. A gentle wave rolled over their feet. Gillian giggled and pulled up her dress to her hips, exposing her legs, and teasing his desire to see more.

Scott kissed her on the cheek. "Want to go swimming?"

"In this?" She glanced down at her dress.

"In nothing."

She laughed. "No one ever asked me to go skinny dipping before."

"There's a first time for everything."

In the shadows of a giant flamboyant tree, he pulled her toward him and kissed her. She dropped her shoes and held him. They kissed, their mouths hungry for each other. His hand found her breast and their breathing raced.

"I want you," he said.

"I can tell." She pulled her shoulder strap down her arm, letting her dress fall to the sand and exposing bare breasts. She stepped out of her panties and raced toward the water, her body silhouetted against the moonlit sea. "You can have me if you catch me."

He dropped his clothes next to hers and dove in after her in the surprisingly warm water. He followed her out to a small fishing boat anchored offshore.

He caught up to her on the anchor rope alongside the boat. "You're a good swimmer."

"I learned to swim in Trinidad, Las Quevas. Sonia's mother used to take us there every Sunday. I used to swim way out, pretending I was escaping from Sticks."

"You don't have to escape anymore."

He held her, her skin silky smooth against his, and kissed her.

They swam back to shore and held each other in waist-high water.

He led her to the shadows of the flamboyant tree, and they lay down on the clothes. Their mouths eagerly sought each other, and their hands caressed each other's wet bodies. He took her breast in his mouth, her wet skin flavored by sea salt. They became one, their dripping bodies in a blissful rhythm that carried them on a journey of naked lust.

CHAPTER THIRTY-ONE

Scott had just crawled into his bed on Marryshow Lane five o'clock that morning, with Gillian's kisses still on his mind, when the dogs that had escaped Rabid's bullets started to bark. He peeked out the window. Lennox stood on the road next to a red car in the dull streetlight.

Scott jumped into a pair of shorts and sprinted up to the road.

"Sorry to wake you up," Lennox said in a fatigued voice, still in the clothes he had worn to Lord Barrington's yacht, shirttail hanging out of his pants and his sleeves rolled up to his elbows.

"What's going on?"

The driver's door opened and the Indian man, with whom Lennox had left BBC last night, stepped out.

Lennox introduced him. "This is Indian."

"We ain't have much time." Indian opened the trunk and swept aside mangoes filling a box in the trunk, revealing stacks of pipes, each with a short cord protruding from the top end. He handed Scott a plastic bag and passed him four of the pipes.

The pipes felt cool in Scott's fingers, but handling the potent ingredients of revolution excited him. He filled a second bag.

Indian shut the trunk. "Don't get them hot or wet."

"What's the plan?" Scott asked.

"Lay low until after Independence." Indian smiled a half grin. "Let them think they win. Guns coming next. Revo 'round the corner."

Lennox and Indian sped off, leaving Scott standing on the side of the road holding two bags of pipe bombs.

"Who was that?" Rodney asked when Scott returned to the room.

"None of your damn business."

"I hope you hide those bags good."

Scott doubted that Rodney could have seen him trudge into the bushes on the other side of the house to cover up the bags with shrubs against one of the big breadfruit trees.

Rodney sat up in the bed. "You better don't have police coming here and shooting my frigging dogs again."

"They're my dogs too."

"Quiet," Claudette whispered from her bed.

Rodney laughed. "You should tell Scott be quiet when he's calling out woman name in his sleep."

Just after sunset, Scott headed down the deserted road toward Belmont. Most businesses had heeded the call to strike. Streetlights were still on, but restaurants, gas stations, and even Regal Cinema stood in darkness. In contrast to other Friday nights, few people walked the streets. The occasional car sped by, and the scent of charcoal smoke reminded Scott that he had promised Mommy to buy a bag of coal on the way home. Now that cooking gas was not available, enterprising people had begun to produce coal in smoky underground ovens.

He darted down the trail to Gillian's house and tapped on her backdoor. Soft footsteps hastened across the wooden floor. The door opened and Gillian stood barefoot in a loose t-shirt and tight shorts. He stepped in and kissed her, savoring the warmth of her lips and inhaling her sweet perfume. He pushed the door shut with his foot and kissed her all the way into her bedroom, collapsing on the bed in an embrace of desire that only ended after they lay naked and soaked with each other's sweat.

After a few minutes Gillian sighed. "Scott, I am worried about what could happen."

"We have the momentum," he said. "The strike is spreading. And the port is only allowing emergency ships to dock, like the *Federal Palm*. It's taking Alicia and the nuns to Trinidad on Monday night."

"Dr. Pilgrim asked me to go with them, since I know Trinidad. But I can't leave Grenada until Rabid gets what he deserves."

"He will soon," Scott said. "By Monday, we'll have the biggest demonstration yet. Gabbard's only choice will be to step down."

"Rabid and Planass stopped by Monica today. They have 300 men waiting for any disturbance. About 100 of them were convicts until yesterday, released by Gabbard to serve as secret police."

He decided against telling her about the pipe bombs and rumors that guns would soon be distributed to start the *Revo*. He didn't want to burden her with any more secrets.

She held his hands to her bosom. "Rabid complained that he knows me for six months and he hasn't met my grandfather yet."

Scott thought for a moment. "Maybe it's time."

"If independence goes through, he's going to pick me up here 10 o'clock Monday night to attend the independence function."

"Good. You'll be on a boat to Trinidad before they find his body."

***

"Mr. Duncan," a BBC reporter asked in Duncan's office the next morning. "How can Her Majesty's Government trust your calls for a referendum on independence when your supporters talk of the violent overthrow of an elected government?"

Scott and Lennox sat on a desk jammed against the back door, as three foreign reporters faced Beverly Johnson, NGM leaders, and Duncan across his desk.

"When we talk about revolution," Duncan said, "we mean the peaceful transformation of political power to create a just society. This country has been plagued by election fraud, political corruption, and police brutality." He pointed at the discolored swelling on his forehead. "We're the ones suffering from violence. Not Gabbard."

Scott admired how Duncan's mastery of words simplified, yet illuminated the Grenada reality.

Another reporter raised his hand. "Mr. Gabbard said that the national strikes violate the rights of people to travel and to eat. Do you agree with that?"

Duncan clasped his hands. "Strike is a spontaneous response by the people. Their instincts tell them that Gabbard is bad for their lives. If the people choose to strike and demonstrate in the streets, we will stand with them. I hope you come out on Monday morning to witness history."

The Monday demonstration was on Duncan's mind when Scott and Lennox stepped into the office before the reporters arrived that morning. Duncan and Beverly reminded them to exercise self-restraint on Sunday, and encourage massive numbers on Monday. He advised them to spend Sunday with students around town, calming them and encouraging them to show up on the Carenage in uniform by nine o'clock Monday morning.

Neither Duncan nor Beverly hinted that they knew about the pipe bombs and guns.

Were they clueless, or just cautious?

"We also need help to prepare the newspaper on Sunday night," Beverly said.

"No problem." Scott had been through the routine before. NGM operatives would meet him and other trusted students behind the Regal Cinema and drive them to safe houses around town to run the mimeograph machine and to staple the newspapers. Every few hours they would pack up and move to another house to throw off police.

Just last week, secret police attacked a student caught distributing the newspapers. Dr. Pilgrim told Gillian that the boy received a hundred and twenty stitches on his back from the cutlass assault.

Now it seemed it would take more than a cutlass to slash the tension in Duncan's office as the minutes inched toward Monday.

Scott glanced around the crowded office, and noticed something odd.

A poster of Martin Luther King had replaced the poster of Duncan's hero, Che Guevara.

Had Duncan made the switch just for the press conference?

If so, was Scott blinded to other deceptions that were not as apparent?

He'd read that the first step in revolution was deception. But it was an Aristotle quote that troubled him: *"Youth is easily deceived because it is quick to hope."*

***

Scott guessed the time to be around midnight. Even if his watch had not recently died, it would have been useless under the thick clouds that blacked out the moonlight. He quickened his pace, anxious to get some sleep after a busy Sunday preparing anti-Gabbard posters, briefing students, and printing NGM papers.

The city had buzzed with the expectation that Gabbard's last evil breath would soon be stifled by either a British-forced resignation, or revolution. Talk of revolution floated like steaming molasses in Scott's conversations with young men mingling by Regal Cinema, students at the Presentation Boy's College, and striking dockworkers.

"Remember," Scott had said repeatedly. "True political power will only come from the barrel of a gun. If the British fails us tomorrow, we will seize power by any means necessary."

The NGM newspapers they printed and stapled that night spoke of revolution with the certitude of sunrise. Yet few had guns, and fewer yet knew of the existence of pipe bombs in the hands of student union members.

The Grenada Revolution felt like a phantom plan that everyone believed in, but no one had seen.

Scott calmed his doubt with the notion that, in the interest of surprise, the plans were secure in the hands of select NGM members, like Indian.

Then again, Duncan had said that revolution was the spontaneous combustion of a population oppressed to the boiling point. On this last night before independence, the city was in a pressure cooker mood. And Scott hoped the excitement would not keep him awake.

He unlocked the door and stepped into the house.

Mommy slumped in candlelight at the dining table, gazing at a government newspaper.

"You boys are killing me." She pointed at a newspaper article. "Claudette found this in the bread shop up the road."

The article criticized the speech he had made a few days ago on the Anglican High School grounds, calling for a student strike.

Someone had circled his name in red.

"So?" He'd seen his name in the newspaper before, especially after his election to the national student union.

"Your name was circled in the shop. A few of Rabid's men were leaving when Claudette walked in. One looked like Planass." Mommy groaned. "Where's Rodney tonight?"

"I saw him this afternoon racing across the Careenage with Oliver in the Volkswagen."

"Marijuana again. He left here this afternoon with black plastic bags."

Panic seized Scott. He grabbed a flashlight and sprinted out of the backdoor to the breadfruit tree. He pushed past vines and shrubs and pointed the flashlight.

The pipe bombs were gone.

***

"I need the gun," Scott said to Gillian in her bedroom after waking her up by tossing pebbles against her window.

"I thought you said there won't be any violence tonight." Confusion stressed her face in the candlelight.

"Oliver and Rodney are about to blow tomorrow's demonstration." He told her about the missing pipe bombs. "The Volkswagen is gone. I have to find those idiots before they do something stupid."

"The pipe bombs would have been safer here, under the house." Her voice took on a solemn tone. "Scott, I want to fight this fight with you."

"I didn't want you to worry."

He'd also tried to protect her from the details of her father's death. But it struck him now that all along, her life had already prepared her for the harshest realities.

"Just trust me with the truth," she said. "I'll hold the gun. If we're stopped, they won't search me."

She tucked the gun into her waistband and covered it with her shirt. They slipped out of the back door and hugged the shadows on Paddock Road alongside the perfumed Botanical Gardens, alive with chirping insects and bellowing bullfrogs. Pillars at the open gateway hid them from a car that raced past and disappeared down Tanteen Road.

Maybe Oliver had heard of the aborted plot to firebomb the police station, and wanted to use the same plan to prove his revolutionary worthiness. Scott led Gillian up the steps to Lowther's Lane. They headed down a brushy trail that ended at the ramshackle house overlooking the police and fire station.

Scott raised his fingers to his lips and took the gun from Gillian. He crept into the house. The only thing left was the lingering smell of gasoline.

They headed a half-mile to the intersection that led to the Governor's House and Gabbard's official residence. From the shadows, Scott observed two cars blocking the road and several of Gabbard's secret police in casual conversation.

"Oliver's house is close by," he whispered. "Let's see if he's back."

To avoid police traffic, Scott took a back road overlooking the Tanteen valley. He regretted the decision a minute later.

"Halt!" A dark figure stumbled from behind a tree, fumbling to turn on a flashlight while holding a rifle.

Gillian squeezed Scott's arm, brushing his fingers against the pistol stuck in her waistband.

Reeking of alcohol, the man flashed the light at Scott. "Where the hell . . . you going?"

"Walking my girlfriend home." As he'd learned in the cadet corps, Scott shut one eye to protect half his night vision from the glare.

He jabbed Scott's shoulder with his rifle. "You look like . . . a communist. What you name?"

Scott considered his choices, telling the truth and getting arrested, or lying and facing deeper trouble if the man later recognized him as a McDonald. Just then, the flashlight reflected on the rifle bolt.

It was not in the firing position.

Given the man's awkward handling of the .303 rifle, he had probably never fired one before. If they ran, they might just have time.

"You hard of hearing?" the man growled. "What you name?"

"What's *your* name?" Gillian asked.

"None of you business."

"It will be if I tell Rabid you were drinking."

"Answer me or . . . somebody dead tonight." He fumbled with the flashlight and rifle, still pointed at Scott.

Just then, an explosion rocked the valley below.

Dogs howled.

The man turned in the direction of the explosions, his rifle pointing away from Scott. "What the—"

More explosions.

Scott saw his chance. Two quick steps and he slammed into the inebriated man, knocking him on to his back. The rifle and flashlight clattered across the dark road.

Scott pulled the pistol from Gillian and pointed at the man.

"Don't move." He turned to her. "Take the flashlight and see if you can find the rifle."

"We don't have time. Others could be here any minute."

Gillian was right.

Scott grabbed her arm. "Run!"

They were already halfway down a side trail to Marryshow Lane before a rifle shot whizzed through the trees way above their heads.

The man's words echoed against the hillside. "Next time, you dead."

***

Gabbard awoke to elbow jabs at his ribs.

"Did you hear that?" Snyder's daughter asked, lying naked in bed next to Gabbard.

"Hear what?" he asked, annoyed by her disregard for his sleep.

"Sounded like a bomb."

She always seemed driven by a wild imagination. Earlier that evening, after a dinner of lobster and champagne, she'd hinted that he should appoint her the first Grenada ambassador to the United Kingdom. A far cry from the office supervisor position he'd already reserved for her in his ministry. Her athletic body and insatiable appetite for his manhood would have more pleasurable use here in Grenada than in London —

An explosion in the distance ripped through his thoughts.

He grabbed the phone off the nightstand, and dialed his emergency number. "Answer the fucking phone!"

Another explosion.

She hugged her pillow. "Maybe—"

"Get dressed."

She rolled off the bed and headed to the bathroom.

Finally someone answered the phone.

"What the hell took you so long?" Gabbard shouted.

"The watchman in the Botanical Gardens was on the other phone, Boss. Somebody throw bombs in the buildings."

"Did he see anything?"

"Just a white car speeding away."

"Get me Rabid, now!"

CHAPTER THIRTY-TWO

"**T**hose sons of bitches." Scott led Gillian in the dark past Snyder's house on Marryshow Lane, their footsteps drowned out by howling dogs. The commotion had brought people in subdued conversations to open windows, fixated on the valley below.

"You can go home," she whispered. "I'll be okay."

"No way."

By now police cars would be racing to the bombings, Rabid and Planass among them. Anyone found on the street would be suspect. Even Gillian.

Maybe it was time Mommy met Scott's Chinatown friend.

They reached the steps to his house just as a Volkswagen squealed on to Marryshow Lane.

Scott pulled the gun and jumped into the street.

"No!" Gillian screamed.

The car accelerated, and then swerved away from him. He leaped to the side, but too late. The blow to his leg knocked him off his feet. Glass shattered. The gun flew out of his grasp. He landed hard and rolled to the side of the road.

The car skidded across the street and stalled.

Rodney jumped out the passenger side. "You fool."

"I could kill you!" Scott limped across the street and body-slammed Rodney into the car.

Rodney pushed him off. "You want *Revo*? Now you have *Revo*."

"You'll have school children blood on your hands tomorrow."

Scott shoved him aside and reached through the passenger window. He swung and connected with Oliver's shoulder.

Rodney grabbed Scott from behind and wrestled him away from the car. They fell in the street. Scott elbowed him in the mouth. Rolling across the street, they swung at each other. Rodney held Scott's throat with one hand and punched him in the mouth with the other.

Scott tasted blood. He turned to avoid Rodney's fist, in time to see Oliver pull a tire iron from the car.

In the headlight glare, Gillian grabbed the gun off the road and pointed it at Oliver. "Back off!"

"You'll regret that, whore." Oliver jumped into the car and sped off, his tires squealing.

Scott and Rodney continued to trade punches.

The commotion must have awakened the household. Mommy stomped up to them in her nightdress, swinging a shoe. "Stop it. Your father should see you now."

Claudette and Gillian helped Mommy separate Scott and Rodney.

A distinct familiarity in that moment made Scott feel like he was staring into a mirror of time.

This had happened before.

Daddy and Uncle Malcolm fighting in Gouyave. Ma in the middle of her sons, swinging her shoe and crying for her husband. Uncle Malcolm speeding off into the night.

The night Ma had cried out the name Fédon.

***

Farrow stood over his table gazing at the burlap bag in the yellow light of his kerosene lamp. Unease had awakened him, calling on him to act.

Today he would finally discharge the burden he had been carrying since his ailing father braved the Atlantic on a steamer to deliver the box to Farrow's dark cell. That cold February day in 1919 he assumed a purpose far greater than mourning the loss of his dignity, his freedom, and his leg.

People might say that Fédon was preparing to strike again. But this was more deadly than any ordinary curse. It hid in plain view. But the time had come to expose the Fédon truth. And there was just one person he could trust to do that.

Oliver obviously had not given Scott the message for him to visit Farrow. So Farrow would go to Scott.

He finished his breakfast of cocoa-tea and fried bakes, grabbed the bag, and shuffled into the dark to await the first bus to St. George's.

***

Scott grabbed his school uniform and led Gillian in the darkness through brushy trails to Tanteen, and over the GBSS hill to Lagoon Road. With the police and fire engines concentrated at the Botanical Gardens, they slipped past Regal Cinema to Gillian's house where she iced and wrapped his swollen leg. Unable to sleep with the pain, at dawn he showered and struggled into his uniform.

He patted a towel against his busted lip and rinsed out the blood from his mouth.

Gillian called out from the living room. "Gabbard is about to speak."

Scott collapsed next to her on the couch and turned up the radio.

"My Fellow Grenadians," Gabbard said, his fake British accent even more pronounced. "Early this morning, communist revolutionaries attacked government buildings in the Botanical Gardens with pipe bombs. The bombings were a signal for the people to start revolution and stop independence. It failed. No one came out. And no one will show up at their little meeting today. Except maybe a few sweaty students.

"My friends, we are on to them. Those who threw the bombs left fingerprints. Scotland Yard investigators who came here to celebrate our independence will identify the perpetrators and we will punish the guilty severely.

"I am meeting at my Mount Royal residence at nine o'clock this morning with hard working farmers who are scared that the port strikes will put them out of work. I am only inviting the strongest toughest men to attend. Dangerous NGM members may still be loose with bombs, so it is not safe for school children and women to leave their homes.

"My Fellow Grenadians, today we will be welcomed as a peace loving country into the family of independent nations. Neither bombs nor demonstrations could stop us. May God bless each and every one of you."

"I'd better leave." Scott kissed Gillian. "I have to meet Duncan at his office."

Worry dimmed her eyes. "Be careful."

"They'll be looking for idiots in a white car. Not students in uniform."

She kissed him at the back door. "I love you."

"I love you too. I'll be back after the march."

He limped down Paddock Road to the GBSS Hostel.

Lennox was waiting. "What happened to you?"

"Let's walk." Scott recounted the night's events as they crossed Tanteen field toward the Carenage.

"I never trusted your cousin," Lennox said.

"He'll pay." He glanced over his shoulder at the British battle ship, H.M.S. *Bacchante*, docked alongside the pier, its engines humming eerily on the calm water. The only other ship, at the far end of the pier, was the *Federal Palm*, the royal blue and white inter-island freight and passenger ship scheduled to take Alicia and the orphans to Trinidad tonight.

Across the street, at the police station entrance in the fire station building, a policeman passed out ax handles and rifles to men in plain clothes.

Lennox quickened his pace. "I have a bad feeling."

***

Premier Gabbard sat alone at the polished dining table sipping the last of his black coffee and basking in satisfaction that all was going well. The bombing appeared to be the amateur job of a few NGM zealots, but it handed him a tactical advantage. He wiped his lips with his napkin and smiled.

His opponents were about to learn a lesson they would never forget.

"Have your men come to my meeting like they're going to chop sugar cane," Gabbard had said when Rabid phoned in the news that one of the pipe bombs had not gone off and that the getaway car was a white Volkswagen.

"Planass rounding up the men now."

Gabbard had been assured by representatives from Her Majesty's Government that independence was a forgone conclusion. Some even hinted that firm police action was justified after the bombings. His coveted prize was within his grasp, but he wanted it crowned with the recognition by the people that he was the undisputed Boss of Grenada.

To wait until his first day as Prime Minister would be a mistake. He wanted to spend tomorrow surrounded by his worshippers, soaking in the glory of his milestone and reading congratulatory cables from world leaders.

Today, Grenada would know that he was through playing games. The bombings gave him just the closing hand he needed.

The maid, barely twenty years old, in a tight skirt and a bosom-spilling top, rushed across the spacious dining room to the table. "Sir, an urgent call on your private line."

He winked at her and patted her firm buttocks. "You're my only urgency today, sweetheart." He hurried into his study and picked up the phone.

Excitement laced Rabid's voice. He explained that the bombs had awakened one of his men, the shopkeeper who lived on the hill overlooking the McDonalds. The shopkeeper had witnessed a confrontation between the McDonald brothers, their Cunningham cousin, and a girl with a gun under the streetlight.

"All must not be well in the NGM nest," Gabbard said.

"The young McDonald just walked past the fire station, limping from the car hitting him. Must be he cousin Cunningham white car that was in the bombing."

Gabbard thought for a moment. "Don't touch young Cunningham. His father and I owe each other big favors."

"Yes?"

"Cunningham was eager to see his brother-in-law, Hector, leave Grenada for St. Croix. There's talk Hector killed his father when he was a boy. Cunningham is ashamed of him, so he gave us some papers to force his bankruptcy. With Hector gone, Cunningham hopes to increase his share of Belvidere Estate."

"Boss, I'll leave Cunningham boy alone, but Planass want some action on McDonalds."

"He'll get his action. First, I'll call Mr. Cunningham make him an offer he can't refuse."

Gabbard instructed Rabid on the plans for the morning. The day was still young. Like an alley cat with a mouse whose death was sealed, Gabbard intended to use his claws and killer instincts to wear down his opponents until they pleaded for their own demise. "And find the girl. I want to know who's supplying the guns and bombs."

"The shopkeeper say she sounded like she from Trinidad. Maybe my friend Trini could help us find her."

***

After Gabbard's third broadcast, Rodney turned off the radio and paced outside his bedroom door. Why the hell had Oliver and him not thought of fingerprints on the pipes? Rodney did not expect that when he sprinted up to the building with the last bomb, the fuse burning, that it would be a dud.

To make matters worse, Scott showed up in the middle of the damn road.

If Rodney had not grabbed the wheel and forced the right turn, Oliver would have run him over. Then that sonofabitch Oliver drove off, leaving him in a fight with Scott.

Scott changed so much since he met Rabid's girl, Trini. But then, after hiding out for days since the riot, his sleep talk had replaced Trini with another name.

Gillian.

"Maybe," Rodney had casually mentioned to Oliver, "Trini is Gillian from Belvidere."

Oliver had squinted at Rodney. "The little girl with the monkey. I remember the day we met her."

Rodney remembered that day too. The day Daddy pulled his ear because of Scott.

His rage began to simmer, but then Alicia's voice drew him into the bedroom.

She sat in bed, rocking with the pillow to her chest. "Boom! Bang!"

Claudette hugged her.

"When did she start speaking again?" he asked.

"Last night after the bombings."

"Boom," Alicia said.

Claudette handed her a pair of knitting pins and a roll of yarn, a new hobby that kept Alicia occupied in her own world.

"Bang!" Alicia began to knit.

A car braked on the street above and the dogs barked from where they were roped under the house.

Claudette pulled open the curtains. "Oh no. Rabid."

"Shit," Rodney said.

"Boom," Alicia said.

Footsteps charged down the steps. The barking grew desperate. A crash at the door sent a downpour of shattered glass.

Angry voices filled the living room. "McDonald boy, we here for you ass!"

Mommy screamed. "Get out."

Rodney stepped out of the bedroom. Rabid and two of his men faced him, each with a rifle.

"He's not here," Rodney said.

"We here for you." Rabid growled. "You brother tell us you have bombs."

He slammed the rifle butt into Rodney's stomach, shooting pain into every inch of his body. He collapsed to his knees and vomited his breakfast at Rabid's boots.

Mommy and Claudette tried to reach Rodney, but the other men pushed them to the floor.

Rabid barked. "Get up, boy!"

Rodney wanted to move, but his body remained curled over in agony that stabbed every nerve in his body. He coughed blood.

A boot slammed him in the head, tumbling him across the floor.

Mommy's screams filled his good ear.

"Boom! Bang!" Alicia ran into the living room, swinging her plastic knitting pin.

Rabid knocked her to the ground.

Another boot hammered Rodney's head. His world turned dark.

***

The previous night's events swirled a repertoire of rage and forebodings in Scott's mind.

"The bombing was my fault." He explained the night's events to Duncan and Lennox in the Market Hill office.

"Not so quickly," Duncan said. "Reporters are on their way here. Let me gather my thoughts. By the end of the day, things won't feel the way they do now."

Quickened footsteps entered the doorway and a reporter rushed in. "Rabid just pulled up."

"Hurry, this way." Duncan unlocked the backdoor while the others pulled aside the desk blocking it.

Scott and Lennox bolted down a flight of steps to the back alley. The door slammed behind them, followed by a drag on the floor as Duncan and the reporter shoved the desk back into place.

Scott peered up the alley leading to Church Street. A policeman stood watch with his back toward them.

Heavy footsteps stomped into the office upstairs.

"Good morning Rabid." Duncan's voice was calm. "Are you going to join our press—"

"Where McDonald boy?" Rabid shouted.

Scott glanced around. If they raced across the alley to the other side, either Rabid might spot them through the window, or the chickens scratching the dusty yard would scatter in panic and alert them. A rooster squeezed its way past loose chicken wire that enclosed the crawl space below the office steps.

Scott peeled back the wire and led the way under the steps and into the dark area below the office, foul with chicken droppings. He squatted next to Lennox, their heads against the floor,

"Look around," Duncan said upstairs.

Boot steps thundered around the office. The window opened and someone spat on the steps.

"Don't forget to look under the desk," Duncan said.

"Tell McDonald we know he have bombs," Rabid said. "He brother tell us everything."

That traitor, Rodney!

Another set of footsteps at the doorway, followed by a cheerful English accent. "What have we here? Can I get a picture of you with your rifle?"

"Take one picture and you dead," Rabid said.

Footsteps stormed out of the office and the door slammed shut.

Laughter erupted in Duncan's office.

At that moment, laughter sounded alien to Scott.

***

"Mr. Cunningham." Gabbard held the phone to his ear with one hand and admired his jade ring and buffed fingernails on the other. "Premier Gabbard speaking."

"Mr. Premier, what an honor," Cunningham said.

"It's my pleasure." Gabbard hated to converse with those high-society pretentious types who would have held their noses in his presence, had he not the political clamps with which to squeeze their balls. But he'd mastered their social graces to grin and skin, when it served him. He sipped tea from the fine Chinaware cup Snyder's daughter had brought him from England. "And how is the Madame today?"

"Just fine, thank you."

"The police received a disturbing bit of news this morning."

"Yes, I heard your broadcasts, Mr. Premier. Quite a despicable act of lawlessness."

"Indeed. But Scott McDonald is implicating your son, Oliver."

"Preposterous! That scoundrel is as worthless as his drunken father, keeping company with Chinatown prostitutes. The police should disregard his accusation as equally worthless."

"My sentiment exactly. Your son is a fine example for our youth." Gabbard sprinkled a little spice. "I can see him holding a diplomatic post in London after his studies."

"That's very kind of you."

"I promised the police to use the goodwill you and I have to assist the investigation."

"How can I remedy this matter?" Cunningham asked.

"If Oliver could tell us about Scott's activities, we will protect your son's reputation and close this case within the hour."

"Thank you, Mr. Premier. Oliver is in his bed asleep, like he was all night. I'll call you back right away."

Gabbard gave him the phone number and hung up.

The phone rang five minutes later.

"Mr. Premier," Cunningham said. "Oliver just assured me that Scott's information is false."

"I'm glad we arrived at this conclusion together."

"But Oliver did have something to pass along."

"Yes?" Gabbard smiled. Young Cunningham had learned well from his father.

"Rabid's girl, Trini, is not who he thinks she is."

An hour later Gabbard stood in a red shirt and tanned slacks on his verandah, facing the mob of three hundred men on the lawn of his Mount Royal residence. Without a microphone, he reached deep into his burning ambitions to fire his words.

"I am a giving and forgiving man," he said. "But I will never run away from a fight."

The men cheered.

"This morning, I served you the best cocoa-tea and the tastiest corned-beef. Even a little Rivers Rum to keep your spirits high. I gave you electric lights. But while I give, the NGM takes away with strikes. If we don't stop them, those communists will take away everything I give you."

The men, most in tattered dungarees and work boots, roared their disapproval. Some waved cutlasses. They reminded Gabbard of his father. He thought them flea-brained and unkempt, with no calculated motivations, except those drilled into their heads.

"I give you confiscated land from my Land for the Poor program to grow your bananas," Gabbard shouted. "Now the NGM want to spoil the fruits of your hard work by shutting down the port."

The men booed.

"I worked with Her Majesty's government to help you become a proud independent nation. But the NGM fools want to take away your independence too."

Laughter and boos.

"The NGM have their little march today. Well, it's your right to demonstrate against them for all the bad they did against you."

The men applauded.

"When you meet them on the streets, tell them you want your electricity returned, you want the port opened, and you want the shops opened so your children can eat."

"We will fight, fight, fight for our leader." The men sang and pranced around, slapping cutlasses against their boots to the beat of the union song that had thrilled Gabbard so many times since his labor-union days.

He could feel the fury building. "If they throw bombs, we will throw bombs too. If we bleed, they will bleed too. I promise you, as Almighty God is my witness, and with the spirit of Fédon behind us they will pay!"

Gabbard mingled with the crowd after the speech, shaking hands and joking with the men. Their sweaty odors and stained work clothes revived memories of his father, and fueled Gabbard's resolve to never surrender the power he'd fought for all his life.

Rabid and Planass squeezed their way toward him.

"Boss." Rabid's pistol protruded from one side of his waist and a cutlass hung on the other. "We ready."

"Be patient. Let the sun drain the communists of their energy. Make this a day they'll never forget." Gabbard turned to Planass. "If the McDonald boys haven't killed each other yet, you can have them."

Planass grinned.

Gabbard faced Rabid. "Cunningham boy had some valuable information. Your Trini friend is no Trinidadian. She's Grenadian, from Belvidere. The daughter of that dead smuggler, Vincent Calliste."

CHAPTER
THIRTY-THREE

Scott looked over the thousands overflowing the Carenage, packed solid as far as he could see in both directions, by far the largest crowd he'd ever seen in Grenada. Magnetized by the hope of a last-minute British reversal on independence, and adorned in the sunshine with umbrellas, work clothes and school uniforms, their *"We shall overcome"* verses drifted in the sea breeze.

A hush descended over the harbor as Duncan stepped up to the microphone on the second floor verandah of the union building.

"I smell victory," he shouted.

The crowd roared.

Maybe Duncan had been right all along. The momentum was now on their side. How could the British shut their eyes to such massive opposition?

"The bombings this morning were just another calculated Gabbard ploy," Duncan said. "Another desperate act to justify his despotic rule. This should be a warning to the British. Halt independence right now!"

Scott felt a pang of discomfort at the ease with which Duncan discarded the truth about the bombings. But discomfort quickly succumbed to the fury that engulfed him when he recalled that Rodney had sent Rabid to find him. He tempered the burn in his gut with the elation that by tomorrow, none of it would matter. The bombings, Rodney and Oliver's betrayal, and Scott's leg pain would dissolve in the euphoria of revolution.

Duncan's self-confidence must be fanned by a secret plan for a government takeover today.

Scott squeezed along the union building to find a place to rest his aching leg.

Without warning, someone grabbed him from behind and slammed him face first into the wall.

He twisted around and forced away the hands.

One eye glared at him from a battered face, the other wedged shut by a purple bulge.

"You're dead." Rodney slobbered through fat bloodied lips

"Rodney, what the hell happened to you?"

"You screwed up for the last time."

"Rabid got to you, didn't he?"

"Don't play stupid with me." Rodney grabbed him by the throat.

A man pushed them apart and stared at Rodney. "Man, who did that to you?"

"That sonofabitch." Rodney pointed at Scott.

"I didn't," Scott said. "He's my brother."

"You're no brother of mine."

Just then, a woman screamed. A roar went up from the crowd. People pointed up at the hill overlooking the Carenage.

Scott glanced up between the buildings. Fear flooded his chest. Heading down Lucas Street in a crazed carnival jog, hundreds of men waved cutlasses and ax handles in the air.

"Secret police!" A woman yelled.

The crowd began to scatter, sweeping Rodney away in the chaos.

Someone on the verandah upstairs shouted through the microphone. "Remain calm. Just let them through. Have the men move up front and place the women and children behind. Remain calm."

Trying to ignore his leg pain, Scott forced his way through the doorway of the union building and hobbled up the steps toward the verandah.

Duncan huddled in urgent conversation with a tight circle of supporters. He paused and glanced at Scott with eyes drained of their energy.

"Where are the guns?" Scott grabbed him by his arm.

Confusion muddled Duncan's face. "What guns? Get downstairs and keep the students calm."

Something was wrong. Where were the guns Indian promised?

A man barreled past Scott and shouted at Duncan. "We must get you out of here now."

Duncan and a few men scuttled down the stairs and out the back door, leaving the building thick with fear.

The reality hit Scott like a blow to his gut.

Duncan and the NGM had no plans. The crowd was at the mercy of Gabbard's thugs.

Scott pushed his way to the verandah.

Quiet descended over the crowd. People squeezed to the sides of the road, opening a path for Gabbard's men.

The gang shuffled onto the Carenage waving their weapons and singing "We will fight, fight, fight for we leader!"

For a moment, it appeared that the mob would continue on their way without confrontation. But just as the last man reached the front of the union building, another man stepped out from the crowd and slapped him on his side with a cutlass.

The men engaged in a playful scuffle.

As if by signal, the rear half of Gabbard's mob turned and charged into the crowd while the others raced toward a *Fanta* sweet-drink truck parked in front of the funeral home just up the street. They grabbed bottles off the truck and hurled them into the middle of the crowd.

The Carenage exploded in screams, stampeding feet, and bloodied uniforms.

"We have kerosene over here," someone shouted downstairs.

Scott raced down the stairs. Lennox waved him toward a stack of kerosene cans against the back wall.

"We need bottles," Scott yelled.

Lennox pointed to a storage closet. They grabbed several empty bottles off the shelves and began to fill them with kerosene. Other students joined in.

"Use your shirts for rags." Scott pulled off his school shirt and shredded it, stuffing pieces into the bottle and leaving a tail hanging out. Someone handed him a lighter. He lit two bottles and crouched outside the door.

Gabbard's men had retreated behind cars and the *Fanta* truck under a barrage of rocks and bottles from about thirty marchers. Most of the crowd fled up side streets and across the Carenage past the fire station.

One of Gabbard's men stood next to a car and aimed a rifle. A shot rang out, and a glass window shattered behind Scott.

"Shit!" He cussed himself for not taking Gillian's advice to keep the gun.

He charged forward and hurled the bottles in quick succession toward the cars shielding Gabbard's men. The bottles crashed onto the street with muffled explosions and flames that died as quickly as they rose.

Lennox and another student threw several more kerosene bottles with little effect on the attackers.

More gunshots.

They ducked back into the doorway just as a tear gas canister spewing white smoke landed on the street in front the doorway.

Scott wrapped his hand with rags from his pocket, grabbed the hot canister, and hurled it back toward the attackers.

He sprinted through the doorway just as bullets smashed into walls behind him. The remaining students rushed out the backdoor.

Only Lennox remained with him.

"Let's get out of here," Scott shouted.

"There're still students upstairs."

"Damn!" Scott bolted up the steps and pushed open the first door.

About twenty students, mainly girls, sat on the floor, clinging to each other and staring at him with teary eyes and quivering lips.

A gray-haired man sat with them, a cassette recorder in his lap.

"We must leave now," Scott pleaded.

"I tried," the man said in a calm voice. "I'll stay with them. I'm Roger Duncan's father."

"Thank you, sir." Scott shook Mr. Duncan's hand and looked at the girls. "Anybody wants to leave with me?"

One girl inched forward.

"Anyone else?"

Gunshots outside. The other students flinched but remained frozen on the floor.

He led the girl into the hallway as Duncan's father shut the door behind them.

Scott held her hand and raced down the steps with her. He pointed her out the back door and down a narrow walkway. "Run as fast as you can."

The girl had barely started down the walkway when she screamed.

He glanced in her direction. She stood with her hands over her head. Two of Gabbard's men ran up with rifles. One of the men knocked the girl to the ground with his rifle butt.

The other man raised his rifle and aimed at Scott.

Planass!

Scott ducked into the doorway just as a bullet slammed into the wall above his head, spraying concrete powder on his bare back.

"Run!" He yelled at Lennox and rushed out of the front door.

They turned left away from the main group of attackers.

A truck screeched to a halt across the road, blocking their way. About a dozen of Gabbard's men bailed out with ax handles. They cornered students against the union building, Lennox among them.

A man clubbed Lennox on his back. He howled and tumbled face first onto the glass-strewn road.

There was only one direction left for Scott to go.

He raced across the street, crunching shattered glass beneath his shoes. He leapt onto the sidewalk and dove into the sea, kicking off his shoes as his arms pulled him deep into the wet darkness.

Just as he felt his lungs would burst, he surfaced for a quick breath of air. Gunshots splattered in the water around him. He dove again working his arms and legs hard. If he could just make it past the boats ahead of him, he could hide alongside. Then swim to the tourist ship that had pulled into the harbor during the march.

He emerged again for air and glanced over his shoulder at the road.

Axe handles raised and fell. People crumbled to their knees. Others lay still on the street.

Planass leaned over the hood of a car and aimed his rifle.

Scott dove. Something punched him hard on his left shoulder.

Maybe a passing boat.

He tried to swim. Pain shot across his chest and back. He attempted to paddle with just his right arm, in pink water.

If he could get to that boat, just ahead.

His arms ignored his will. He rose for air.

Gunshots echoed in the distance, splattering around him like raindrops.

The pink water wrapped around him like a cool blanket. Salty water filled his lungs. His vision turned gray and a silent peace took away his pain.

CHAPTER
THIRTY-FOUR

Premier Gabbard paid scant attention to the black car meandering up the hill in the fading sunlight. Assured his men would obey his orders to turn away all visitors, he sank into the plush rattan chair under the flamboyant tree. He sipped his favorite afternoon drink: a light rum-punch on ice with a pinch of nutmeg and a wedge of pineapple biting the rim of his glass.

No one deserved this moment, and this place, more than he did.

Gabbard's official Mount Royal residence, carved from a stubborn jungle into a paradise of regularized lawns, hanging palms, and crashing water, nourished his desire for control. Maybe it was the only trait he'd inherited from his father. But while his father craved control like a desert thirsted for rain, and died never tasting a drop, Gabbard thrived on it. Today, raw power coursed lavishly through his veins.

He savored the drink, anticipating his crowning moment when, at midnight, the Union Jack would be lowered over his island for the last time. He would have achieved international status and supreme control as Prime Minister of his very own tri-island nation of Grenada, Carriacou, and Petite Martinique.

A security man cut short his solace. "Counsel General Barrington at the gate, sir. Say he won't leave till he speak to you."

"Dammit." Gabbard reflected for a moment. "Okay let him in, but take a long cigarette break before you return to the gate."

The British had kept Gabbard waiting for twenty years. Now he could return the pleasure with gusto. He watched the guard light a cigarette and stroll around the back of the residence, on the longer walk to the gate.

Ten minutes later, Lord Barrington, sweaty in his thick suit, marched across the lawn with two uniformed escorts at his sides.

Gabbard purposefully remained seated. "Care for a rum punch?"

Lord Barrington wasted no time. "With all due respect, Mr. Premier. Have you gone mad?"

"What are you talking about?"

Lord Barrington sat at the edge of the chair and leaned toward Gabbard. "Order your men off the streets. The hospital is overflowing, and your people are looting the capital to shreds."

"They want food."

"So why are they stealing radios and jewelry, while your men look on or loot as well?"

"There's a price for striking."

"Are you forgetting you also used strikes to get where you are today?"

Gabbard leaned flat-footed toward the Englishman. "I am not to be blamed. We had a clash between two legitimate demonstrations. But the NGM group that threw bombs at the Botanical Gardens started it by throwing kerosene bombs at the agricultural group."

"Agricultural group?" Lord Barrington chortled, and twirled his red moustache. "Was it your agricultural group that shot Roger Duncan's father in the back while he protected a room filled with school children?"

"It was an unfortunate accident."

"I can get you a cassette recording of the shooting if you like. Nothing that occurred today was accidental. Why haven't you ordered a search for the body of that McDonald boy?"

"He supplied the bombs last night and threw Molotov cocktails on the streets today."

"It matters not to you whether they're seventeen or seventy. I met that young man on my boat. He deserves a decent burial."

"We have many problems and I'll deal with them one at a time."

"Let me add a couple more. Your Governor has tendered her resignation to Her Majesty the Queen. The Duke landed in Barbados to attend your independence celebrations, but he's just boarded his plane to return to London instead. All Caribbean heads of state have cancelled their participation. The only one attending is that dictator from Haiti."

"Should I feel troubled?"

"My independence recommendation to Her Majesty's government was my worst career blunder. This is a sad day for the Grenadian people."

"We're all upset about today's events." Gabbard didn't want to prolong the Englishman's intrusion with any more arguments. "I'm sure a few relaxing days at La Sagesse would restore your confidence in my government."

"The La Sagesse Estate is for sale." The Counsel General leaned back in the chair. "I want no part of this island under you."

"You'll return, once I clear up this communist plot."

"I am afraid you've just opened the gates to communism in Grenada. You made Castro look like an angel today." Lord Barrington rose and stomped off with his men.

Gabbard recalled the need he once felt for the approval of those British bastards. How foolish. After tonight, his new friends would have names like Pinochet, Amin, and Papa Doc.

He glanced at his watch. By now, almost sunset, Rabid should be calling in his report.

Two minutes later, the maid hurried over to him with the phone, the lengthy line snaking behind her.

"All done, Boss," Rabid said on the phone. "Duncan and them up in Richmond Hill Prison. They going to be hurting for a few days. We questioned the Indian and his GBSS friend up in Grand Étang. Every time we hang one of them by their neck, we get more names and more pipe bombs."

"Good work. Tonight we celebrate. Tell the boys to expect fat envelopes. Where are you going now?"

"Lagoon Drive. If Cunningham boy right, Trini seeing her father in hell tonight."

"Make it clean, a celebration accident, maybe a drowning. We've had enough blood today."

***

Scott concentrated with all his might to make sense of his fragmented aware-ness. Far away, a conversation droned with strings of flat words void of mean-ing, some coated with an emotional female's voice.

"Is he going to be okay?" the girl asked.

"As long as the stitches hold," a man said.

The conversation rolled on, even after Scott turned his exhausted shut-eyed attention to other scattered pieces of his puzzle. He was lying on a bed. His left shoulder throbbed. A tight wrap restrained his left arm to his chest. A medicinal aroma soaked the air.

"Dr. Pilgrim, I don't know how to thank you," the girl said.

Gillian?

"You did the right thing coming to the hospital to get me," Dr. Pilgrim said. "He lost a lot of blood. But he should be okay for the boat ride to Trinidad."

Scott struggled to talk but every nerve in his body protested.

"I have to hurry back," Dr. Pilgrim said. "Clean up, in case you have unwel-come visitors."

Scott recognized Monica's voice too, in another conversation on the other side of the bed. "You strong in the water, boy."

A male answered. "Me, Scott and Rodney used to swim a lot in Gouyave, *oui*. That's how I end up diving for money."

Martin?

What could have brought these four to the same place at the same time?

Scott's memory gates swung open. The Carenage, gunshots, Lennox on his knees as ax handles slammed on his back.

Scott groaned. "Lennox."

"Dr. Pilgrim," Gillian called out. "He's awake."

Scott forced his eyes open. "Where's Lennox?"

"Don't move, sweetheart," she said. "Lennox is in the hospital, recovering."

The tall gray haired Dr. Pilgrim hurried to the bed. "You had a nasty shoul-der wound. No bone damage, but movement can rip the stitches apart."

Scott gazed up at the faces drifting around him and at the curtain hanging on the rope across Gillian's bedroom closet. "How did I get here?"

Martin placed his hand on Scott's right shoulder. "Boy, you head hard, *oui*. How many times I tell you don't go swimming without me?"

Martin's grin relaxed him. "You were there?"

"I was diving for money before the shootings." Martin explained that the tourists on the ship had turned their attention from tossing coins to taking pictures of the chaos on the waterfront road. When he saw the attackers shooting at someone in the water, Martin dove in after him and pulled him behind a yacht. "With all that hair you have, was'sen till Monica show up with the rowboat, I know was you."

"I must leave now." Dr. Pilgrim stood by the bed holding a leather satchel. "Things will be better once you get to Trinidad—"

"I'm not going," Scott said.

"Yes, we are, with Alicia," Gillian said. "It's too dangerous to stay."

"And you need serious medical attention," Dr. Pilgrim said.

"Then take me to the hospital," Scott said.

"They don't know you're alive." Gillian explained that the NGM leadership was in Richmond Hill prison and that independence would be official at midnight.

"Those mother—"

"You must rest," Dr. Pilgrim said. "It's getting dark. Martin, come with me. We'll make a stop in Marryshow Lane and get you and Mr. Farrow on a bus back to Gouyave."

Scott looked up at him. "Mr. Farrow?"

"Gillian will explain later."

Monica turned to Gillian. "I have to see the nuns to plan the trip, but I'll be back soon. You two will be here alone. Don't let anyone in until I come back."

"Rabid is not coming here until 10 o'clock tonight," Gillian said. "But we'll be gone before he shows up."

Scott sat propped up on a pillow, sipping the water Gillian held in a cup to his lips. He wished he could remove the worry that strained her face in the candlelight. He decided not to ask her about their plans for Rabid. Today's events had changed everything.

"You okay?" he asked.

She kissed him on his cheek. "I thought I'd lost you."

He reached for her hand, but the pain stopped him.

"The radio said you drowned." She told him how Rabid had taken Lennox and his Indian friend to Grand Étang for questioning. They were returned to the hospital alive, but with rope burns around their necks. "Duncan's father died, shot in the back."

"Murderers!" He gazed at the ceiling. "My mother must be losing her head tonight."

"Martin already told her you're okay. I gave him directions to your house this afternoon."

"So why are they going back to the house?"

"Mr. Farrow is visiting. Dr. Pilgrim will take them to the market to catch a bus back to Gouyave."

"Mr. Farrow never comes to town."

"He came to see you. He'd given Oliver a message a few days ago for you to visit him."

"That snake, Oliver. He didn't tell me shit."

"Mr. Farrow sent this." She handed him a piece of paper from her nightstand.

"My boy, we have to talk as soon as you are well. Stay alert. Fédon is dead, but Fédon is alive."

"Scott, get up. Rabid is here!"

Scott awoke in pale light with Gillian pulling at his right hand. The pain rose out of his left shoulder and shot across his upper body. The injection Dr. Pilgrim had given him was wearing out.

A loud car rumbled to a stop on the gravel road below.

"Where's the gun?" Scott asked.

"It's still light. Gunshots with Rabid's car outside will only attract more police." She grabbed a pillow and helped him out of the bed. "Hurry. Come with me."

Too weak to argue, he followed her out the back door. Every step sent pain drilling down his left side. She helped him down the edge of the house along a path lined on both sides with low shrubs. She parted a thin area of hedge bordering the house and he followed her into the dusty crouching space below her floor.

212

"Stay here." She placed the pillow on the dirt.

He eased back onto the pillow.

She pulled the gun out of her waist and handed it to him. "In case something goes wrong."

"No," he said. "You might need it."

But she was already gone.

He rested the gun on his chest and waited.

Heavy footsteps rushed the front door. A crash, and the door swung open upstairs.

"Rabid," Gillian shouted. "What the hell you doing?"

"Where you grandfather?"

"He's gone."

"No more games, bitch. I know who you is now."

A slap.

She screamed.

Scott gripped the pistol and struggled to his knees.

"I shoulda know you was Vincent daughter." Rabid growled. "Cunningham boy tell us everything."

That fucking Oliver!

Scott crawled toward the hedge, leaning on his right elbow and holding the gun in the same hand.

More slaps. More screams.

"You father deserve what I gave him," Rabid shouted. "Today was your McDonald friend last. Tonight is yours."

Gillian screamed again.

Scott tried to move, but pain paralyzed him where he knelt.

He fell on his shoulder wound, shocking every nerve in his body. His ears burned with a scream as unconsciousness swallowed him.

Scott awoke with his face in dirt and his hand around cold metal. His chest felt sticky. The silence upstairs jerked him back.

Gillian!

Unsure how long he'd been passed out, he used his right hand to lift himself to his knees in the darkness.

He crawled through the hedge onto the walkway, and staggered around the house to the backdoor, afraid of what he might find. He placed the pistol at his feet and turned the doorknob. He lifted the pistol and slowly pushed the door with his foot. The door squeaked open and he glided into the dark house.

His sight adjusted. A chair lay on its side in the hallway. Flowerpots littered the living room floor.

He tiptoed around the mess and peered through the living room window. If Rabid's car was still there, the darkness under the trees obscured it. Satisfied that no one was in the kitchen or living room, Scott turned to the bedroom.

He stood with his back against the wall next to the shut door.

"Gillian," he whispered.

No answer.

He raised his voice. "Gillian."

A moan.

He pushed open the bedroom door with his foot.

Starlight seeped through the thin curtains. Gillian lay on the bed, her hands and legs bound to the posts, and her mouth tied with a rag.

He crouched into the room, glancing from side to side, expecting at any moment to see Rabid jump out from the shadows. Gillian gave no warning, so he shuffled to the bed and got down on his knees. He laid the gun on the nightstand and pulled the rag from around her head and mouth.

She flinched when he touched the swells around her eyes and cheeks

"Quickly," she said. "He's going to be back anytime."

"What did he do?"

"Nothing. He said he's coming back to have me for his independence celebration." She struggled with the rope on one leg while he untied the other.

"Let's wait for him."

She touched his sling. "You're bleeding. We must get you on the boat."

"But Rabid—"

"We'll think of something later. We have to leave now."

A car squealed to a stop and a car door slammed shut.

"He's back," she said.

"Monica maybe?"

"No, she's coming through the backdoor from Belmont Road. Give me the gun."

"I'll do it. I can use my right hand." He tiptoed into the living room and peeked past the curtain.

Footsteps hurried up the walkway toward the house.

Scott braced himself next to the door and lifted the pistol.

***

Rodney zipped up his clothes bag under candlelight and glanced around the room one last time. The room felt as empty as the painful void in his chest. Tortured memories echoed from the dingy walls. He'd always wanted to know what it was like to have a real family, but maybe it was never meant to be. Daddy had been gone a year now. Alicia had already packed and left with Claudette in a church van. Scott's hardheadedness had gotten him shot, and in hiding. Now the only thing Rodney could do to protect Mommy, was to leave too.

He'd had enough, and needed time to regroup. He didn't know yet where he might go. What he needed most tonight was a good night's sleep. He might return one day to put the family back together, but without Scott and Daddy.

He took a lit candle into the bathroom and stared at his busted face in the cracked mirror.

Mommy walked up to the door behind him. "It's dangerous out there."

"It's not safe here either. Thanks to your son."

"He has a name."

"Not to me."

"For Christ's sakes, he was shot." Mommy wrung her hands. "I wish God would tell me what to do."

"The same God that took your baby, give you a drunken husband, and give me a traitor for a brother?"

"Stop it! I didn't like the way you talked to Mr. Farrow tonight either, especially in front of Dr. Pilgrim and Martin."

"Mr. Farrow believes in Fédon as you believe in God. Dragging around a bag of stupid papers. He deserved to hear the truth."

"Maybe he knows more about the truth than you do."

"Don't make me laugh. My face hurts." He grabbed his bag and headed for the front door. Then he turned, and held Mommy in a long embrace. "I'll be back."

***

Scott's hand trembled with the weight of the gun. He couldn't miss this close to the door, and with as big a target as Rabid.

The door squeaked open.

He tightened his finger on the trigger.

A head leaned in. "Gillian?" It was Monica.

Scott lowered the gun and sighed.

"We're here," Gillian called from the bedroom door. "Come in quickly. Why did you come in the front?"

"The police have roadblocks on Paddock Road," Monica said.

Gillian explained all that had transpired in the last couple of hours.

"My poor baby." Monica inspected Gillian's face. "Let's go. The nuns are waiting."

They piled into Monica's car. Scott lay on his right side on the back seat, covered with a blanket and stacks of Monica's restaurant towels.

They drove slowly through darkened streets, Monica apologizing for each pothole she hit.

Scott clenched his teeth to block the pain wracking his shoulder. Searching his mind for a distraction, he thought of Mr. Farrow's note.

Fédon is dead, but Fédon is alive.

How could anyone be alive after two hundred years, and still manipulate events today? Mr. Farrow probably carried solid reasons in his plastic bag to explain the connection between Fédon and the McDonalds' sufferings. Either that or Grenada's turmoil had finally pushed his sanity off a cliff.

Monica slammed on her brakes. "Police roadblock."

"Just stay down," Gillian whispered to Scott. "Don't worry. I have the gun."

A hand slapped the car, and a voice barked. "Where all you going?"

"Don't point no gun in me face, boy," Monica said. "I ain't one of them communist NGM people, you know."

"What you hiding under them towels?"

"Pots and pans. I cooking for independence fete, and you making me late."

Another voice spoke up. "Hey, she run a restaurant in Chinatown."

"Okay," the first voice said. "Go, but drive slow tonight so we know you not NGM on the run."

The nuns at the convent led Scott to a back room lit by candlelight. They served him fish broth and helped Gillian replace his bloody bandages. He bit his lip as she removed blood-soaked gauze with a pair of tweezers, rewrapped his arm, and supported it with a sling over his right shoulder. The nuns cut off his afro and shaved his face.

In light for the first time tonight, he stared at Gillian's swollen eyes and puffy cheeks. She gave no hint of pain or discomfort, but he hoped she didn't see his shame for not protecting her.

He thanked Sister Gertrude for their help.

Sister Gertrude, swathed in full-length blue habit and starched veil, had a no-nonsense voice and a crisp Irish accent. "Me lad, the only authority we recognize is God. This is his *woik*."

A door opened and Claudette walked in with Alicia. Claudette held his free hand, while Alicia stared at the floor.

"You look like one of me flock." Sister Gertrude adjusted a nun's habit over Scott's head and shoulder to hide his wound. She explained that the ship's manifest listed three nuns, Sister Gertrude, plus Scott and Gillian disguised as nuns. "We'll make three trips to the port. You'll go on the first."

"What about Gillian?" he asked.

"She and Claudette will help me with the toddlers on the last trip." She handed Gillian a plastic container with a syringe. "Dr. Pilgrim said you know how to do this."

Gillian held his right arm and inserted the needle. He must have looked surprised at the ease with which she delivered the dose of pain medicine. Probably thinking how silly he looked dressed like a nun, she smiled and glanced away.

The Anglican Church clock clanged in the distance.

"It's quarter past ten," Sister Gertrude said. "Time to go."

By now, Rabid would know that Gillian had escaped. The streets would be more dangerous. They exited the back door of the church and crossed the alley to the waiting van.

Gillian held Scott in a tender embrace and whispered in his ears. "I will always love you. Hold this, just in case." She slipped the handkerchief into the bag the nuns had packed for him.

"I'll be waiting for you." He kissed her puffed cheek and climbed into the van with several younger teenagers.

Sister Gertrude drove past groups of armed men on dark streets. No one attempted to stop them, probably because of the church insignia on the van doors, and Sister Gertrude's tough reputation around town.

On the Carenage, the headlights glittered on bottle fragments swept to the side of the road. A yacht sat low in the water with only its mast and wheelhouse above the surface. Bullets from the police attack that morning must have punctured the side and sprung leaks. Store windows looked like entrances into dark caves, from which looters emerged with boxes on their heads. The sea breeze blew in a whiff of smoke from one of the businesses, looted and burned to ashes.

Scott's thoughts simmered with a blend of anger and sadness.

They pulled up to the harbor gate topped with barbed wire.

An armed policeman approached Sister Gertrude. "Passports?"

"Listen lad, I still have two more trips of orphans," she said. "Once everyone is on board, I'll go over the list and passports with you."

"Just following orders." He swept his flashlight over the faces in the van, and then scribbled on a piece of paper. "Okay, let them through."

Sister Gertrude drove through the gates and down the pier past the British war ship. She pulled up alongside the ramp to the *Federal Palm*. A single hanging incandescent bulb lit the way onto the ship.

"Quickly. Grab your bags and get on board."

Scott rested on a crate in the belly of the ship, exhausted after his struggle up the poorly lit plank, across narrow hallways congested with luggage and sleeping passengers, and then down vertical stairwells. Despite the odor of diesel and stale seawater drenching the cabin, he was glad he could force himself on his right elbow to look out through the porthole. From here he would see Gillian and Alicia arrive on the last trip.

He pulled off the nun's habit and waited.

Sister Gertrude drove up thirty minutes later with the second group. Two nuns, dressed in school uniform to look like teenagers, headed up the ramp with a crying baby and a few infants.

Sister Gertrude sped off the pier to retrieve the last group.

By now, Rabid might have ordered his men to search all vehicles. Gunshots in the distance reminded Scott that Gillian still had the gun.

Forty agonizing minutes crept by.

The ship's horn bellowed its departure warning against the dark hillsides.

Dogs howled.

The horn blew again, yet no van. The minutes ticked by. Maybe they were being searched.

Headlights stopped at the gate. The ships' horn blew one extended blast as the van raced down the pier.

Sister Gertrude led Alicia and the other children up the ramp. Gillian followed, dressed as a nun. The van sped off the pier and out the gates.

Scott settled back on the crate as mechanical tremors awoke the ship and it began to pull away from the pier.

Gabbard and Rabid had won this round. But Scott knew he'd return. There were still too many wrongs to correct, secrets to uncover, and wounds to heal.

For now, he felt grateful he had Gillian on the ship with him, probably working her way down the ladders in her disguise to find him.

Footsteps clanged down the stairwell. A nun approached with a familiar stride.

"Where is Gillian?" Scott shouted.

"She's not coming." Rodney pulled off the nun's habit over his head. "Oliver—"

Hatred disgorged from Scott's gut with a savage growl. He charged off the crate. Something ripped on his shoulder and sprayed his face. He tasted blood, but felt no pain as his knuckles kept pounding Rodney's beaten face.

***

Gillian clung to the fence between the deserted Chinatown and the port. She watched as the *Federal Palm* reversed from the pier and followed the flashing yellow lights of the harbormaster's boat toward the outer harbor. Without the harbormaster's direction, ships were blind until they reached open water. One radio call from the shore, and the harbormaster could leave the *Federal Palm* stranded for the police.

Gillian shivered in the sea breeze.

The hilltop fort glowed in electric light, like an alien craft suspended against the dark sky. Military music from the independence formalities drifted over the island, still in darkness from the strikes.

A truck screeched to a halt at the harbor gate. Armed men jumped out.

"Stop that boat!" One of the men charged up to a police officer at the gate.

"But the nun say —"

"I don't care what the bitch say. Give me you damn radio."

Gillian unzipped her bag, just in case and hurried down the gravel road to the gate. Maybe Rabid, too humiliated to reveal that Trini had outsmarted him for six months, had not alerted his men about her.

She walked up to the man who had shouted at the police officer. "What going on, Planass?"

"Cunningham boy tell us McDonalds hiding on board." He pointed his rifle at the police officer. "Give me the damned radio now before I pump lead in your rass."

She had to get his attention, quickly. "It's true. I saw a McDonald get on the boat."

Planass stepped up to the police officer, his aggravation growing. "See what I tell you?"

"But only the sick girl." Gillian pointed to her head. "If you pull a crazy girl from the boat, people go laugh at you, man."

Planass eyed her suspiciously. "What you doing here?"

"Look." She grabbed the flashlight from the police officer and held it at her chin to exaggerate the swellings on her face.

"Who do you that?"

"The older McDonald boy. He say is my fault his brother drown." She pointed the flashlight at the gun in her bag. "Rabid gave me something for him. I've been watching all night. No McDonald boy got on the boat."

Planass lowered his rifle.

Just then, celebration fireworks lit the sky over the fort, exploding like bombs, and bathing the *Federal Palm* in red light as it steamed out the harbor with Scott, Rodney, and Alicia.

Dogs sent a howling chorus over the city.

Planass and his men fired their rifles into the air.

"When you see Rabid, tell him to meet me in Chinatown," Gillian shouted over the commotion. "I have some fireworks for him too."

Planass laughed.

Gillian sat in the sea breeze at Monica's darkened restaurant and watched the *Federal Palm's* lights disappear over the horizon. It dawned on her that she was sitting on her father's favorite bench. She had come to Grenada to seek justice for him, and tonight that meant one thing.

Rabid must die.

By now Planass would have told him where to find her. She pulled out the gun and marveled at the cold power in her hand.

The seconds felt like minutes. Another gust rattled the wooden buildings. A window slammed.

An occasional car sped by on the main street, casting headlights on a car parked at the Esso gas station overlooking Chinatown.

Maybe Rabid had parked at the gas station and crept into Chinatown.

She tightened her grip on the gun and stepped away from the bench.

Then she heard the car.

There was no mistaking its rumble. It crawled into Chinatown with just the park lights on, like yellow eyes of a wild animal stalking a prey.

Stalker would soon become prey.

The night's chill took flight. Her cleavage dampened and a bead of sweat rolled down her cheek.

She ran behind the restaurant.

The car stopped next to the bench. The motor died.

"You forget you bag on the bench." Rabid bellowed.

Dammit.

He might sit there all night waiting for her to move. She'd planned to catch him as he was driving slowly by, allowing her to run up to the driver's side and shoot him. With the car now silent, he would surely hear her shoes on the gravel. She decided against removing her shoes, remembering the broken bottles scattered around Chinatown.

"I know you there, bitch," he hollered.

It was time. She could wait no more.

She took a deep breath, stepped on to the road in front of the car and fired into the driver's side, shattering the windshield in a flash of glass. The high beam clicked on. She fired into the blinding light. The car door opened.

Maybe he'd fallen out.

She moved to the side to avoid the direct blast of the headlights and fired into the car door.

Out from behind the light, Rabid came roaring toward her.

She calmly pointed the gun at the face she hated most in the world, and pulled the trigger.

✳✳✳

Scott squinted at the lights blazing down at him in the white room. A nurse at his bedside checked his pulse.

"My name is Josephine DeFreitas," she said in a solemn tone. "I'm Grenadian too, from Grenville. I volunteered to work this ward when I heard we had wounded patients from Grenada."

"Nice meeting you, Josephine." Fatigue strained his voice.

"You almost bled to death. The nuns said you went crazy on your brother."

He wriggled the fingers on his right hand, and his knuckles ached. The first punch had landed on Rodney's face as he was trying to explain how Oliver had driven him to the church. Oliver's name triggered a frenzied blur of teeth, blood, and pain.

Those bastards must have wrangled their way with the nuns to leave Gillian behind.

Scott searched his thoughts for hope that the nuns had hidden her at the convent until the next boat for Trinidad. But that could be another week, if she didn't give in to the temptation to find Rabid first. Would she do that alone? Duncan was in prison and Lennox was in hospital. Neither Dr. Pilgrim nor the nuns would forsake their humanitarian professions for the ugly business of assassination.

Monica was the only one left for Gillian to trust with the plan to kill Rabid.

Josephine lifted the sheet off Scott's leg. "You got a nasty blow. Massage it every day for circulation."

He'd almost forgotten the sideswipe from Oliver's car.

"My husband Bertrand had a leg injury too." Josephine mumbled on, almost to herself. "I used to massage him, but he just wasted away on that damn couch."

Scott's mind was elsewhere. "Any news from Grenada?"

"Another death last night." She gazed out the window. "Radio Grenada called it an independence celebration drowning."

That did not surprise him. Gabbard now had absolute control over the island. No more public meetings, NGM newsletters, and BBC reporters to balance the lies.

"Who died?" he asked.

"The radio said Dr. Pilgrim identified her as a drunken prostitute from Trinidad. Bertrand used to call her a whore too, before the fire took him."

Bertrand? Leg injury? Fire?

Sticks!

A boiling wave of despair crashed over Scott.

"Only I know who she really was." Josephine wiped her eyes. "Poor Gillian."

CHAPTER
THIRTY-FIVE

St. Croix, U.S. Virgin Islands, one year later

Scott guzzled the beer, crushed the can in his hand, and popped open another one on the coffee table. He'd drink a damn six-pack, icy cold, and it didn't do shit to quench the night heat in Daddy's little apartment. Neither the squeaky ceiling fan nor the open windows stopped the sweat. He peeled off his soaked shirt and tossed it over the couch.

He couldn't fool himself any longer. The beers had nothing to do with fighting the heat. Just like Daddy, Scott had surrendered his faculties to alcohol rather than face the grief that clawed at him every waking moment. The worst occurred in the middle of the night, when the beers wore off and silence cloaked him. The flicker of a memory, maybe the light in her eyes, her laugh, or her kiss would blossom, and she was alive again. But soon the vacuum in his soul would remind him.

Gillian was gone. Gone forever.

It took at least a six-pack to numb the exposed nerves of his loss.

He recalled Mr. Farrow's warning that pain was a good teacher, but that drinking made it worse. Today, those words belonged to another time and place.

He popped open another beer in the sparsely furnished apartment, one of four adjoining units at the bottom of a hill that repelled the trade winds. The area, called Work and Rest, was a three-mile walk from the job he'd held at Amerada Hess Oil Refinery since the doctor released him to work eight months ago.

Even the name Work and Rest annoyed Scott. He worked his ass off in that noisy iron city, but never got enough rest.

He finished the beer and headed to the refrigerator.

"I'll take one." Daddy shuffled out of the bedroom with disheveled white hair and blue work pants.

Scott grabbed two beers and tossed one to Daddy. They sat on the couch and drank in front of the black-and-white television. *The Price is Right* show evoked fewer thrills than the blank living room walls. The silence between Scott and Daddy hung thick in the air. There was little to discuss. Even casual conversations remained strained by Daddy's stone-faced refusal to explain why Planass wanted to kill Scott.

Daddy spoke first. "Got a letter from your mother."

Scott took the letter from Daddy's outstretched hand.

Mommy wrote that she'd finally heard from Rodney. He had roomed with Mommy's sister in Trinidad, but moved out three months ago. His letter, with a Guyana stamp but no return address, said he was okay and no one should worry about him. Scott sure as hell wouldn't.

Meanwhile, Claudette worked as a bank teller, and Alicia, since returning from Trinidad with the nuns six months earlier, remained at home, disengaged from the world. Mommy also wrote that she had taken a bus trip to Gouyave, her first visit since Ma passed away in her sleep during the week of independence. Besides mentioning a brief chat with Mr. Farrow, Mommy seemed careful with her words, saying nothing about the government. People were minding their own business, she wrote.

The unspoken truth was that Gabbard had prevailed. His cunning and brutality had defeated the Grenada *Revo*.

Scott flipped to a second page, a blue Roman Catholic Church announcement. It invited worshippers to memorial services for "the lonely desolate souls without families" buried in the hospital cemetery.

Among the buried souls listed was a single name, Trini.

Hot anger filled Scott's head. He grabbed another beer and slammed the door on his way outside.

The *Revo* let Gillian die without her name.

The next morning, in his gray uniform, helmet and steel-toed boots, Scott made his rounds in the oil refinery promoted in company brochures as the largest in the western hemisphere. He checked gauges, recording temperatures and pressures in a world congested with fuel-stained air. Highways of hot pipes linked humming towers, clunking pumps, and screaming compressors. Satisfied that the measurements registered safe levels, he marched away from the bacchanal toward the less chaotic field of giant storage tanks that fed thirsty oil tankers at the refinery port.

The radio hanging from his belt crackled. "Come in, McDonald."

He recognized his superintendent's voice.

"McDonald here, over."

Scott had lost respect in the man for refusing to replace a contaminated water fountain. After workers in his area continued to experience stomachaches, Scott wrote letters to the union threatening to call a strike if they failed to act. Maybe the superintendent was calling about those letters, or to hound Scott again to get a haircut.

"What's your location, over?" the superintendent asked.

"Phase Three, tank farm, over."

"Keep your position. Maintenance team on the way, over."

"Ten-four."

Relieved, he remembered his scheduled tower inspection for the maintenance department. He recalled the first time he volunteered to crawl through the manhole on the ground level, snaking his way up the partitioned belly of the ten-story tower with a flashlight and logbook, searching for metal cracks and deformations. Two hours later, he emerged onto a grated platform a hundred feet up, covered in oily soot like he was playing *jab-jab* for carnival.

Despite having to breathe potentially toxic air, he looked forward to the next inspection. It guaranteed him privacy with his thoughts.

He was surprised to see Daddy behind the wheel of the blue maintenance truck parked along the drainage canal. The passenger, a man Scott had seen around the refinery, stepped out of the truck and lit a cigarette in the smoking area.

Scott crossed the wide concrete driveway. "I was expecting the tower crew."

Daddy wasted no time. "The union called me."

"Your friends finally took a golf break to read my letters?"

"You're asking to get fired."

"We'll strike if they don't protect the workers."

"It's not your business."

"I drink the water too."

"I don't know why I got you that Green Card." Daddy snapped. "You belong in Grenada."

"Planass would like that." Scott chuckled. "You still think he's not my business too?"

"This has nothing to do with him."

"What's the difference? Let's pretend there's no contaminated water, and there's no Planass."

"I never said that."

"That's the problem. You never say anything."

Daddy must have realized the futility of arguing further. He glanced over at his coworker, a solid man with tattooed forearms and the rigidity of a telephone pole.

"Rush, you ready?"

Rush put out his cigarette with his fingertips, stuck the filter in his pants pocket and stepped into the truck without taking his sights off Scott.

After work that day, Scott stretched over the pool table in the smoky *Junie's Bar* and hummed to Gladys Knight's *Midnight Train to Georgia* blaring from the jukebox. He aimed the cue stick and knocked the eight ball into the corner pocket.

"Good game." He shook hands with his opponent, a Puerto Rican friend from work.

"Easy for you to say, hombre."

Junie's Bay had become a daily stop on Scott's trek home since his physical therapist recommended stretching exercises to restore the full use of his left shoulder. His shoulder no longer protested the pool-table therapy, but the game added a protective layer of distraction around his sanity.

"I'll pay if you rack 'em." An American accent rolled on a smoker's gravelly voice.

Scott recognized Daddy's friend. "Rush, right?"

"Yep." His handshake vibrated up Scott's arm.

"Nice to meet you," Scott said.

Rush snapped quarters into the coin slots and the balls rolled out like rapid-fire cannons.

Scott racked the balls on the table. "All yours."

Rush chalked his cue. "Pool can teach a lot about life. First, you must be focused." He fired the cue ball into the stack with a violence that shot two balls into the pockets.

"You have stripes," Scott said.

"If you want to win the war of life, choose your battles. Fight them one at a time. Too many battles, and you'll lose the whole goddamn war."

Rush cued up and shot another striped ball into a side pocket. He kept talking about wars, battles, and focus until he hit all the striped balls into the pockets.

"And when you win, celebrate." He shot the eight ball into a far corner pocket. "Let's have a beer."

Scott gazed at the table, unable to remember if he'd ever lost a pool game without a shot.

They ordered beers at the bar.

"What do you want to do with your life, son?" From the shades of gray clustering in Rush's blond crew cut, he looked to be pushing forty.

"Haven't thought much about life lately," Scott said.

Rush swigged from a can of *Schlitz*. "That's your problem."

A flush of anger warmed Scott's head. "Did Daddy send you to talk to me?"

"Nope. I learned all about you from that conversation with your father today. You need a family."

"I already have one." Impatience scorched the edge of Scott's voice.

"Not that family. You need a brotherhood to calm that fire in you, or you'll self-destruct."

"I don't know what you're talking about."

"Yes you do, dammit. I was once like you."

Scott wanted to argue, but Rush was right. Scott had become a volcano, fed by molten vents of disillusionment, betrayal, and grief.

"By the way, you'll have a new water fountain tomorrow." Rush glanced at the watch on his tattooed wrist.

"Yeah?"

"A friend in town analyzed a sample of the water and found high levels of contamination. I told the superintendent my next stop was the newspapers."

Scott ordered two more beers for them and excused himself to use the men's room.

When he returned to the bar, Rush was gone.

The barman handed him a folded napkin. "Rush paid, but he left you this."

Scott opened the napkin. *Semper Fi.* "What is Semper Fi?"

"It's what Marines tell each other. Always Faithful."

"Merchant Marines?"

"Nah, military. U.S. Marines. Rush served two tours in Vietnam. He's only twenty-eight years old."

"Younger than I thought."

"He roughed up the superintendent today about a rusty water fountain," the barman said. "When they tried to fire him, he said he'd already resigned. He's on his way to the airport right now. Going back to his brothers, the Marines."

Daddy's anger spewed out on rum-saturated breath. "When you quit your job, you should bloody-well give a two-week notice . . . not a two minute phone call!"

Scott understood Daddy's disappointment, but it was too late. "Tell them count the month I waited for the water fountain."

"What does that have to do with quitting your job?"

Scott didn't know and didn't care.

"And where you going?" Daddy pointed at the bag Scott held.

"Catching a flight to an appointment in Puerto Rico."

"With who?"

"The Marines."

"You're crazy."

***

On a cool South Carolina morning three months later, Scott marched with his Marine Corps graduating battalion across the parade square on Parris Island. The reviewing stands hummed with thousands who had come to see their uniformed relatives, transformed into warriors by months of rigorous training.

It seemed an eternity ago that the midnight bus had delivered Scott and a group of unsuspecting recruits into the jaws of hell. At the gate, Drill Instructors greeted them with robotic precision and mechanical barks that changed lives forever. For the next ninety days, steel fists and iron bellows hammered relentless lessons of discipline, motivation, honor, and trust. Scott thought that pain and its cousin, fear, would never depart his body.

Thoughts of escaping Parris Island struggled against stories of runaway recruits being pulled out of the swamps, their eyes gouged out by flesh-eating crabs. The lucky ones were escorted back by shotgun-toting locals for a hundred dollars each. For some, suicide seemed the only escape. Scott recalled the night he discovered a private in blood-soaked sheets. Even then, the Drill Instructor, a Vietnam veteran who had shaken the hands of death, seized the moment to teach the platoon another lesson.

"You moron!" He jumped on the rack and grabbed Private Kupar by his t-shirt, slapping him back to awareness. "Next time ask me for a real blade, asshole."

By the third week, the fragments of Parris Island chaos began to solidify into an energized core within Scott.

He wondered if life in the islands had been a practice run for the tests of will he faced on Parris Island; the turbulent years in Grenada; his Cadet Corps training with British .303 rifles; his miles on St. Croix roads in steel-toed boots and knapsack.

Muscles bulged where once there was pain, fear gave birth to confidence, and his Drill Instructors promoted him to squad leader. By graduation day, a clear day bathed in cool sunshine and warm euphoria, Scott's platoon had been altered from a busload of scumbags into a disciplined fighting unit, a band of brothers.

The commanders addressed the new Marines with speeches about war and peace, and the virtues of the Marine Corps, an amphibious force in readiness to take on a troubled world.

In a moment stretched by thirteen weeks of anticipation, platoon commanders dismissed their Marines. Families and friends invaded the square with embraces, flowers, and cameras.

Scott imagined Gillian in jeans and his school shirt, the tails tied around her waist, rushing from the crowd, her smooth complexion aglow and her lips seeking his.

But the click of a nearby camera terminated his dream.

At that moment, he realized his chest would always be home for his grief, his earlier desire to escape it now replaced by new strength to embrace it. He would protect her memory, with her handkerchief safely buried in his sea bag. Her brief life had become his compass, his purpose for living, aflame with the promise that those responsible for her pain and death would pay.

In the jubilant sea of many, U.S. Marine McDonald stood alone, but not lonely.

Gillian would always be alive in him.

***

Rodney stared at Armstrong and Oliver, both sporting full beards, crumpled fatigues, and muddied tennis shoes. Oliver slapped at mosquitoes attacking his face. This was the first time Rodney had seen the two since they recruited him a year ago in Port-of-Spain to receive clandestine military training. Rodney wondered if they had come to join the group of twenty Grenadians being trained secretly by the Guyana Regiment deep in the Amazon jungle, or were just visiting to deliver a pep talk.

"Comrades, you're doing a brave thing," Armstrong said to the group gathered around him. "Gabbard won the first round because we didn't follow the strict principles of Marxist revolution. Lenin and Che would smile at what you're doing here."

The men, all in camouflaged uniforms and berets, applauded. Rodney felt a closer attachment to these men than to his own brother.

He returned his attention to Armstrong.

"Gabbard is trying to present a democratic image to the United Nations. We'll accommodate him. We'll run in the next elections. We'll play his game, but we'll prepare for revolution here. Real Marxist-Leninist revolution. Soon, Comrades, you'll be heroes of the Grenada Revolution."

Like Duncan's visit two weeks earlier, Armstrong's visit came like a sea breeze to the jungle-locked camp, rows of ramshackle wooden barracks furnished with hemp hammocks and home to nonstop guerilla training and political classes.

"We will throw Gabbard in jail," Armstrong said. "We will overthrow the capitalist system and build a *dictatorship of the proletariat* for the people."

The men cheered again.

"We must be alert for enemies within. Some will look and act like friends, but if we drop our guard, they will stab us in the back. We must crush counter revolutionaries before they strike."

Armstrong and Oliver spouted convincing words about liberation and freedom, but something bothered Rodney. They talked about Marx, Lenin and Castro, even Fédon and Che, but never about the leader of the New Grenada Movement, Roger Duncan.

After the speeches, Oliver signaled Rodney to follow them to the jeep. Rodney had hoped they would stay longer to share more news of Grenada, like Duncan had. Maybe the pungent lunch of stewed green figs, cassava, and wild game was too much for their delicate upbringing.

Armstrong pulled Rodney aside. "Comrade Oliver told me you're working hard for the revolution."

"We all do," Rodney said.

"There are more sacrifices ahead. I hear your brother is a Yankee Marine, a professional imperialist mercenary."

"I have no idea and I don't care."

"Then help us guarantee, after the Revolution, that he never returns to Grenada."

"Sure." Rodney spat disgust through the space where Scott had knocked out a tooth that night on the boat.

"And," Oliver chimed in, "if he does return, that he never leaves alive."

PART III

CHAPTER THIRTY-SIX

Kaneohe Bay
Hawaii, 1983

Scott kicked off the blanket and gazed up into the darkness. Sweat drenched his pillow for yet another sleepless night. The torture had accompanied him on his tours in the Carolinas, Virginia, and Japan, and now Hawaii as a Platoon Sergeant. Even as he barked loud orders to his platoon, his past remained silent to questions that flooded him since Gouyave.

How did these people and events, years gone and ten thousand miles away, still rupture his sleep? How could he live in a free country, yet be imprisoned by his past?

Even at twenty-seven, the boyhood torments hung on, visiting him more frequently during the last month than at any other time since Parris Island. Marine Corps rigor had cemented in him a protective dam against his anger. But in the stillness of the night, his guard down and his heart exposed, Gillian's loss trickled over the wall to soak him in sweat and provoke his rage.

Planass, Rabid, Oliver, Gabbard, Rodney. There had to be a common thread of deception linking these people.

Fédon is dead, but Fédon is alive.

Making sense of Mr. Farrow's note was like trying to squeeze beer from a rock. Mr. Farrow must have sensed Scott's frustration with the vague letters over the years. Sadly, the pages between them dwindled, and eventually stopped after the revolution.

So much had changed after the 1979 revolution, which eventually over-threw Gabbard, pushed Grenada into the Soviet orbit, and turned Scott into an enemy in American uniform.

An enemy of the revolution he'd risked his life for as a teenager.

Unable to sleep he rolled out of his rack, dressed only in his shorts, and headed down the darkened hallway into the TV room.

Lieutenant Baker, Scott's platoon commander and battalion Officer of the Day, stood in uniform at the duty desk scanning a thick green logbook. A former football player for Stanford University with an economics degree, the muscular square-jawed lieutenant had served two years in Jamaica with the Peace Corps before taking a commission with the Marines. His interest in the Caribbean drew him into regular conversations with Scott.

"G'morning, Staff Sergeant."

"Good morning, sir."

Lieutenant Baker glanced at his watch. "It's zero dark-thirty. Forgot the platoon has the day off?"

"Looking for something to bore me back to sleep."

"Then you might want to read this." Lieutenant Baker handed him a magazine off the desk.

The bearded Fidel Castro filled the *Time Magazine* cover in a jubilant bear hug with Roger Duncan.

"Thank you, sir."

"There's a section on the Grenada Revolution."

Scott recalled the elation he'd felt in 1979 when the television news reported that a popular revolution had finally toppled and imprisoned Gabbard, Rabid, and their secret police. Scott, a corporal then in North Carolina with three months left on his four-year enlistment, had written a letter to Duncan explaining his plans to return and contribute his military experience to the *Revo*.

But then the anonymous letters started. They accused Scott of being a counter revolutionary and warned that if he landed in Grenada, friends and family would also be suspects. He ignored the letters until Mommy wrote him that suspicions were rampant on the island and that the timing was not right for his return. He reenlisted for another four years and received orders for Japan, and eventually Hawaii.

Scott flipped the pages of the magazine. "There goes my sleep."

He returned to his room, collapsed on the rack, and switched on his reading lamp. The main article covered the threat of Soviet influence in Latin America, especially after the 1979 Grenada revolution.

"A big revolution in a small island," Fidel Castro called it.

Castro contrasted his failed 1953 attack on the Moncada Barracks to the successful 1979 attack on Gabbard's True Blue Barracks. He talked about the night Comrade Rodney McDonald, who had lost half his hearing at age nine but doubled his night vision, had led forty liberators up the hill overlooking the military camp. The men stormed the camp with 303 rifles and cutlasses, hurling Molotov cocktails through open windows.

Within twelve hours, the island had been liberated from Gabbard.

But, another article pointed out, the initial euphoria harnessed to build bridges and schools, and to jump-start an abused economy, had dissipated four years later. From behind the scenes, Armstrong directed more of the island's energy into geopolitical adventures with communist countries than in promoting the people's welfare. The glossy promises of revolution that Scott used to dream about took on a sinister cast. Headlines screamed of Soviet Bloc embassies, prison tortures, and newspaper shutdowns on the island.

Moreover, Duncan turned his back on the promise of free and fair elections, the very thing that angered Scott when Gabbard denied Mommy her vote.

The Americans also spread another layer of dark clouds over the island. The President warned that the new airport under construction in Grenada was for Soviet MIG fighters, a threat to vital shipping lanes and economic centers, including the Panama Canal and Venezuelan oilfields. American military exercises in the Caribbean looked like dry runs for a Grenada invasion.

The Cold War had entered a hard freeze, and Grenada was adrift in an icy sea of sharks.

Thriving upon the people's fears, and under Bulgarian counter-insurgency training, Comrade Oliver Cunningham had risen to Chief of Internal Security. Phone taps and letter openings became the tools of his trade.

Scott recalled how Oliver had mocked the revolutionary books Duncan loaned him. Today, Oliver masqueraded as a revolutionary on the backs of a hoodwinked population.

Now, even Gillian's murderers might go unpunished.

Gabbard, Rabid, and Planass lingered in prison without trial. Why?

If Duncan wanted Scott to testify on the La Sagesse murders, he would hop on the next plane. But the revolutionary dreams of justice that had so fired him in Grenada remained just that, dreams.

He'd also tried to call Dr. Pilgrim and Sister Gertrude to find out how Gillian had died. But he finally gave up. Maybe her murder had been too horrific for them to talk about. Dr. Pilgrim was always too busy to get on the phone. And Sister Gertrude's stern advice had been for Scott to move on with his life.

Sleepless nights like tonight helped him to dismiss her warnings. There was just one thing left for him to do to liberate his past: return to Grenada.

Even if this might be the worst time for a U.S. Marine to be snooping around the island asking questions.

Scott finally gave up on sleep just before dawn. Hoping to distance himself from his revolving thoughts, he returned the magazine to Lieutenant Baker, jumped into his Honda, and sped off toward Waikiki Beach for an early morning swim. The drive over the Koolau mountain range revived memories of the steep winding road past Grand Étang. By the time he sat on the beach, the misty sunrise over Diamond Head crater and the crashing waves had transported him back to Grenada.

He glanced down the beach for a break in the memory fog closing in around him.

That's when he saw her.

He desperately wanted it to be true. She'd long vanished from his life. Yet here she was, walking barefoot on the sands of Waikiki, just as she used to on Grand Anse beach. Her jeans rolled up to just below the knees and a white cotton shirt fluttered against her shapely body. She held a pair of blue sneakers in her hand.

How could this be possible?

In one frantic motion, he leaped to his feet and took off after her. He yelled out her name, but she continued her stroll, a Walkman in her hand and headphones covering her ears.

He rushed up behind her and grabbed her arm. "Gillian?"

She turned in surprise and dropped one of her shoes.

Like so many Hawaiian girls, this girl had a gorgeous blend of Polynesian features, an exotic Asian touch around her eyes, a deep bronze tan, and long black braids.

She removed her headphones. "Excuse me?"

"I'm sorry. I thought you were someone else."

How could he be so stupid? He picked up the shoe just as a small wave rolled over their feet.

She must have seen the dust storm of disappointment blow across his face. "It's okay."

He handed her the shoe and hurried up the beach to where he'd been sitting just seconds before.

The girl walked through the glimmer of the Hawaiian sunrise, and disappeared into the shadow of the majestic Diamond Head crater.

It was time to fill his cold empty space.

Time to go home to Grenada.

***

"Staff Sergeant McDonald." The duty NCO handed Scott a note. "Urgent message."

Scott hurried into the office and shut the door, recognizing Claudette's New York number. No one else called and letters were scanty. Just after the revolution, he'd received a letter from Lennox with assurance that in his capacity as deputy administrator in the ministry of health, he would do all he could for Alicia at the mental hospital. Scott's reply letter remained unanswered.

When Claudette answered the phone, they chatted briefly about her two young daughters, and about her husband, an engineer she'd met in St. Croix during her brief stay with Daddy.

It struck Scott that the McDonald family had now fragmented in four, thousands of miles apart.

Claudette's tone grew serious. "I spoke to Rodney last night. He's in Washington D.C. as a military attaché for Duncan."

"Shouldn't they be in Moscow instead?"

"Duncan is unhappy with the direction Grenada is taking and wants to patch things up with the United States."

"Armstrong and his gang will never go for it."

She paused. "This call isn't about Armstrong. It's about Rodney."

"Yeah?"

"Rodney said if you plan to visit Grenada like you said in the letter to Mommy, buy a one way ticket."

"Why?"

"Scott, don't go. If you land in Grenada you won't leave alive."

***

"Okay Leathernecks, listen up." Scott glanced over the eighteen faces of his platoon, their muddy sweat overpowering the smell of freshly cut grass along the barracks.

Griffin, a rugged scar-faced Corporal from the hills of Tennessee, raised his hand. "What's with the rumors, Staff Sergeant?"

"I'll tell you, just as soon as Jones shuts his trap."

Jones, from the Chicago ghettoes, had boyish looks that suggested he belonged more in a Boy Scout troupe than with a band of professional killers.

Griffin turned to Jones. "Shut your face, maggot."

"Your mama loves this handsome face," Jones said. "And don't forget it, son."

"You're so ugly, your mama tied pork chops around your neck to get dogs to play with you."

Jones grabbed his crotch. "Ask your mama about the bone I saved for her."

The Marines laughed.

"You going back home, Staff?" Jones asked. "I hear there's some bad shit goin' on down there. A Marine got wasted in El Salvador the other day, sitting in a café."

"Yeah, hombre," Santana from Puerto Rico said. "They gone communist in *Granada*, like Cuba."

Throughout his years in the Marines, Scott had to explain that despite his complexion and dark hair, he was not from Granada, Spain.

Jones laughed. "Granada is a city in Spain, dipshit. *Gre-nada* is an island in the Caribbean."

"Settle down." Sergeant Harris, Scott's second in command, glared at the troops. Tall and lean, the former Hells Angels biker from California had the energy of a racehorse. To him, every hill had to be climbed, and every doorway was a pull-up bar.

"Is your brother a communist, Staff?" Griffin asked.

"I ain't never seen a commie," Jones said. "But if I do, before he could say 'Lenin', he'd be one dead mother-f—"

"That's enough!" Harris snapped.

The Marines had come from every corner of American life, but with one common desire: to be the meanest, greenest killing machine in the Marine Corps. Although they tossed verbal hand grenades among themselves, Scott knew they would kill for each other. He'd grown accustomed to the friendly badgering that flavored Marine conversations, but he was not in the mood today.

"Marines, Aaten...hut!"

The platoon snapped to attention, heads locked to the front, rifles held firmly along their right legs.

"First things first," he said. "Colonel Blanchard was pleased with your combat readiness at Bellows Field today. If I go to war, I want every damn single one of you with me. Ooo-RAH!"

"Ooo-RAH!" The roar bounced down the narrow field between the two-storied barracks.

"I also want to clear up some of the bullshit I've been hearing." He glanced around at the men. "I'm going to Grenada next week, but it's not a one-man recon mission, it's not a CIA mission, and there's no invasion planned. That's cockamamie bullshit. Sergeant Harris will be in charge in my absence. Anything he says goes. If I hear of any belligerency while I'm gone, your ass is grass. Paaraade . . . rest!"

The men snapped to the parade-rest position, shifting their left feet to the left, thrusting their rifles forward, and popping their left hands against the small of their backs, in one swift motion.

"At ease!"

They relaxed.

He turned to Sergeant Harris. "Anything else?"

"ANZAC Day," Sergeant Harris said.

"That's right. I'll be selecting seven of you for an honor guard firing squad to commemorate the Australian and New Zealand military at Punchbowl National Cemetery this weekend. There'll be ladies there too. Time to look good. Dress Blues, gents."

"Now you talking," Jones said.

"Don't celebrate yet. If you plan on getting shit-faced at the enlisted club tonight, I got news for you. Reveille is at zero four forty-five. Ten miles in full combat gear, Marines."

Groans.

"One more question, Staff."

"What now, Jones?"

"You said you're going to Grenada, but you never said squat about coming back."

***

The bus rolled into the Punchbowl National Cemetery parking lot after dawn. The squad came to attention during the flag-raising, as gusts whipped the huge flag on its way up the pole, sending loud clapping echoes along the boulevard.

Lieutenant Baker pulled Scott aside. "The State Department issued a travel advisory for Grenada. It's getting dangerous."

Younger than Scott, Lieutenant Baker was well-read, well-traveled, and eager for conversation about Grenada. In one particularly open discussion over a few beers at the club, Scott had told him about his teenage beliefs in Marxist revolution.

The lieutenant listened attentively, and finally said, "Oppression leads to desperation. I would have believed the utopian promises too."

"It's not just believing. It's wanting to believe when you're left with no other choice."

"Purity in ideology is no match for man's arrogance. Marxism concentrates political power. Dictatorship of the proletariat is really dictatorship by a few, a recipe for totalitarianism. Grenada is heading down that path. Watch your back."

"I appreciate the concern, sir. I'll be okay."

Scott inspected the Marines, each with an M16 rifle. He carried a non-commissioned officer's sword, sheathed in a scabbard of black leather. "Look sharp and no eye-balling. Remember, snap and pop."

The sun rose over the collage of uniforms, suits, and aloha patterns. Women brightened the audience with rainbow colors of flowered leis and flowing muumuus. The sweet fragrance of Hawaiian flora drenched the air over the courtyard facing the solemn *Courts of the Missing*, huge walls of marble embedded with accounts of battles, victories, and sacrifice.

After somber music by the Marine band, and speeches by dignitaries about the honor of just wars, Scott marched his squad to a platform beneath the courts. His sword gleamed in the morning sunlight as he directed precision volleys of gunshots into the air, slicing the peace over Punchbowl. Jets from Hickam Air Force Base flew overhead in the missing-man formation, joining a moving chorus of booming cannons and martial music. The Marine band played the *Last Post* and the chaplain closed with prayer.

Later, Scott dismissed the squad and walked up the steps to the marble walls, studying the giant maps of Pacific battles.

A female voice interrupted him. "Do I still look like her?"

A girl stood at his side in heels and an alluring sleeveless dress that hugged every curve on her body. A wide pink hat and dark sunglasses shielded her eyes.

"Pardon me, ma'am?"

"My turn to surprise you, *oui*." She removed her sunglasses. Her eyes and soft accent struck a familiar chord.

"Of course. Waikiki Beach. Sorry about that. I was daydreaming that morning."

"Do you always daydream?"

"Only when I'm alone."

"Then don't be alone." She smiled. "I liked how you handled the sword today."

"Thank you, ma'am. It comes with lots of practice."

"Nice shine too."

"Stayed up all night polishing it."

"I hope that's not all you do with your nights. Can I hold it?"

"Not here. Military regulations."

The fragrance of the flowered lei around her neck sweetened the tease in her voice. "You won't break a rule for me?"

"If I know you better, ma'am."

"Call me *ma'am* one more time, and I'll never talk to you again."

"I wouldn't want that. But since I don't know your name . . . "

"Glad you asked." She extended her hand. "Danielle Lee."

"Scott McDonald." He shook her hand. "You sound French."

"It's my first language. My grandmother was French, and grandfather Chinese. I was born in Tahiti, French Polynesia."

"French was one of my better subjects in school, but I forgot most of it."

"I'll help you remember."

"Promise?"

"Only if I have your number."

He scribbled the number on a piece of paper she handed him. "Are you going to the reception in Waikiki this afternoon?"

"I'll let that be another surprise." She walked away, tucking the paper with his number in her bosom.

***

Later that afternoon, Scott changed into swim shorts and walked toward Waikiki Beach on a path that crossed the Hale Koa Hotel grounds of sprawling lawns and flower gardens shaded by tall palm trees. Crowds mingled around a huge white tent. Hawaiian *kalua* pig simmered in underground ovens and seasoned the air with a juicy smell. On the beach side, loud cheers accompanied a volleyball game between Australian soldiers and Scott's Marines.

Scott dove into the ocean and swam out to a platform thirty yards offshore. He lay on his back and dozed off in the sunshine to the gentle rolling of the platform.

He awoke to drops of water falling on his chest.

"Surprise!" Danielle stood over him in a skin-toned bikini, as bronze as her tan. She flicked her wet fingers at him, and twisted water out of her long, black hair. She sat next to him and slipped off her bikini top. "I hope you're not embarrassed."

"Just surprised . . . again."

"In Tahiti, wearing a top on the beach is prudish. I'm not a prude, am I?"

"Exciting, yes. Prude, no," he said. "What brought you here from Tahiti?"

"I attend the University of Hawaii. Doing graduate studies on the historical development of French-Creole linguistics."

He raised his eyebrow. "Do you mind saying that again, real slow?"

"Oh, be quiet." She laughed. "It's the study of how history influenced French Creole speech in places like Louisiana, French Polynesia, Africa, and the West Indies. The university has one of the top linguistic programs in the country."

He told her about Grenada's early years under the French, and the words that still sprinkled the language.

Danielle perked up when he told her about Mr. Farrow and Julien Fédon. "How did Mr. Farrow know so much about Fédon if there are no books or studies?"

"I've wondered about that for twenty years."

"You looked so sad that day you stopped me on the beach." She sighed and lay down next to him. "Who was she?"

In the nine years since leaving Grenada, no one had known him well enough to ask about Gillian. Even then, he might have been on guard about what he revealed. Had his grief finally reached a saturation point? Maybe his first encounter with Danielle, thinking she was Gillian, had cracked the combination lock to his dam. He shut his eyes from the sunlight and with the ease of water gushing from a tap, told Danielle everything.

"I am flying back in a couple of days," he said.

She walked her fingertips across his shoulder scar. "I'll be waiting for you when you get back."

CHAPTER
THIRTY-SEVEN

Scott gazed out the window at the rolling greenery below, twenty years since his first view of Grenada. From the plane, everything looked and felt the same.

Until they landed at Pearls Airport.

He crossed the tarmac, scanning the area in the noon glare. Air Cubana and Aeroflot planes sat in a parking area adjacent to the terminal. In a compound enclosed by barbed wire, three rows of barracks capable of housing approximately five officers and a hundred troops. Ten armed soldiers guarded key points of the airport terminal. The runway ended on the shores to the east, a likely insertion point for Zodiac inflatable rubber boats. He could position Santana and Jones, his sniper team, with their G3 SG-1 in the hills facing the terminal, while the main attack—

What the hell was he thinking? Maybe he needed this vacation.

He entered the terminal and presented his Grenada passport to an immigration officer sweating under a sluggish fan. A teenaged soldier in green fatigues stood next to the booth, tapping his fingers on the barrel of his AK-47 rifle.

The officer shuffled through the passport. "When did you leave Grenada?"

"Nine years ago, but I need to renew—"

"Just answer me questions. Why no departure stamp?"

"Long story."

"You getting ready to spend a long time in Richmond Hill Prison," the officer said.

"Call Comrade Cunningham. He knows what happened."

He squinted at Scott. "You Captain McDonald's brother?"

"Yes."

"Stay here." The officer grabbed the passport and disappeared into a back office. A few minutes later he returned empty handed. "You can go, but we keep your passport. See Comrade Cunningham for a new one."

Scott threw his bags into a taxi, and they headed toward St. George's. In just minutes, it looked like Rodney's threat was falling into place. Without a passport, leaving Grenada won't be as easy as it was nine years earlier.

***

Scott rented a car in St. George's and headed across the Carenage. The roads felt smoother and the schools looked less tarnished by rusted roofs and peeling paint than he remembered. While vehicular and pedestrian traffic still had a vibrant flow, the revolution had clearly taken Grenada into a new age. Armed soldiers drove by in a rumbling convoy of Bulgarian military trucks. A cargo ship at the pier bore the red hammer and sickle flag of the Soviet Union, and rows of gray warehouses stood where Chinatown once steamed with food and girls.

He wanted to go up to the hospital to visit Gillian's gravesite, but decided he needed Monica to accompany him. It seemed like just yesterday Daddy had taken his sister, Aunty Bridgette, to visit Ruby's grave in Gouyave. Scott recalled how Daddy shook in grief, twenty years after losing Ruby.

Scott had lost Gillian for half the time. He wasn't sure how he would react to a tombstone with the name Trini on it.

He turned off the main road and headed up toward Marryshow Lane.

Without knocking, he eased open the new door replacing the one Rabid had shattered.

Mommy, plump and healthy, rushed from the kitchen into his arms and wept.

She held his face as her lips trembled. "I want my children home."

"I'm home."

He inhaled the mouthwatering aroma coming from the kitchen and looked around. The living room felt more complete with a new dining table, couch, and a phone on the end table. Claudette had told him that Mommy received a phone a few weeks ago, but understandably, Claudette discouraged him from calling. The ceiling smiled down with a new coat of paint, and pictures adorned bright walls.

One picture showed Duncan embracing Fidel Castro. Another had Rodney in uniform, holding hands with a little girl.

"That was at his last promotion," Mommy said.

"Who's the pretty thing?"

"Dr. Pilgrim's daughter."

He thought it strange that Dr. Pilgrim, mid-sixties by now, still fathered babies.

"How come you never sent me pictures?" Mommy asked.

"Didn't take too many, but I brought some for you." He wondered if his reluctance to send pictures had anything to do with him knowing Oliver's fingerprints would be all over them.

He settled into the bedroom, transformed from the chaos he remembered into a comfortable room with one bed, and two nightstands with lamps. A new built-in closet displayed meticulous sets of People's Revolutionary Army uniforms with Captain Insignia, spit-shined shoes, and combat boots.

He suppressed a flicker of pride.

Mommy knocked and entered. "Rodney did the work, but the materials came from the money you and Claudette sent. Alicia stays here too, whenever Lennox gets her a weekend pass from the hospital."

He asked a few questions about the night he left Grenada, but it was obvious Mommy knew nothing about the fight on the boat, or about Gillian's death.

"How's Daddy?" he asked.

"His last visit was two years ago. Still drinks."

They chatted over a hefty lunch of fish, vegetables, and rice and peas, and then drove up the steep winding road to the Fort Frederick complex on Richmond Hill to visit Alicia. She'd spent a few months in Cuba for psychiatric observation, and according to Mommy, was showing improvements.

He glanced at Mommy as he drove, pleased at how healthy she looked, either because of Daddy's absence, or because of Rodney's efforts to bring home revolutionary benefits. Her round cheeks were smooth, and the discolored tooth that once smudged her smile was now repaired.

"May God bless Duncan and the *Revo*," Mommy said. "Free medical, education, and food for school children. But all we hear on the radio is that America wants to stop the *Revo* and put back Gabbard."

"As long as Duncan leads the *Revo*, Gabbard can't return."

"Nobody likes that you join the Marines."

"It's my career. It has nothing to do with Grenada. This will always be home."

"They call you a *counter*. Every week another counter-revolutionary get killed or arrested. *Heavy manners* they call it."

"Don't worry, I'm just visiting."

A guard waved them into the parking lot facing the Crazy House, a yellow and white two-storied building surrounded by eighteenth-century stone walls, and overlooking Richmond Hill Prison. A nurse led them down a hallway past mental patients idling in doorways. One man held a broomstick like a rifle, roaming the hallway and pretending to shoot at patients.

Alicia sat on her bed, her knees drawn up to her chest, staring at the floor with a pair of knitting needles and a roll of yarn next to her feet. She'd gained weight, and the white in her hair surprised him.

He leaned over the bed and touched her hand. "Alicia, it's me Scott."

She smiled, and pinched his cheeks. "It's about time, soldier boy. Looks like they feed you good, eh?"

"You too."

He handed Alicia the new knitting-set Claudette had asked him to buy, complete with patterns, yarn, glass beads, and stainless steel needles.

"Thanks." She giggled. "Stainless steel pins don't break."

He pointed to the yarn on her bed. "What are you making?"

"A sweater for Dawn's doll."

"Dawn?"

"Dr. Pilgrim's daughter," Mommy said.

"He's still having children?" Scott asked.

"No, Dawn is his granddaughter. His daughter is also a doctor."

Scott wondered what else he'd missed over the past nine years.

Alicia stared at him. "There's something dark about you. Do you go to church? Cuba has the best churches, but they're always empty. Like the people are afraid they will burn down."

When Scott and Mommy left the Crazy House around mid-afternoon, he slowed the car down the hill to inhale the view of the blue-watered horseshoe harbor. Red-roofed pastel colored houses nestled into the green coliseum hillsides and flamboyant trees blazed in red blossoms. A floral menu of delicious fragrances blew into the car and briefly satisfied his appetite for a memory called home.

Mommy pointed at a gray ship maneuvering into the harbor. "Cuban ship. When they're in port, we lose electricity at night."

"Why?"

"To offload things nobody should see. Just be home before dark."

"You're always looking out for us." He hugged her with his free arm.

When they returned home, he changed into shorts and jogging shoes, and drove to the Point Salines Airport construction site.

In a recent press conference, President Reagan had presented a map of the new airport and quoted Armstrong as saying that Grenada did not need American permission to accommodate Soviet MIG Jets. Neighboring islands like Barbados and Trinidad already had runways of similar lengths, but democratic governments friendly to the United States controlled these.

The low level of security at the terminal surprised Scott. Cuban workers locked steel beams and laid bricks, while American medical students jogged along the incomplete runway.

He ran a couple of miles on the smooth dirt, looking for evidence that the airport could serve as a military airfield. The site had no parallel taxi ways, hardened aircraft hangers, signs of underground fuel tanks, or defensive surface-to-air missile platforms, basic infrastructures need to stage Soviet fighter bombers.

Armstrong's empty bravado about Soviet jets in Grenada had raised the neck hairs of White House and Pentagon military planners.

On the way home, Scott pulled off at Grand Anse Beach for a swim, but left before memories of his night there with Gillian began to stir his grief.

He planned to visit Mr. Farrow in Gouyave in the morning, and on his way back, to stop in on Sister Gertrude and Dr. Pilgrim to thank them for helping him escape to Trinidad. Maybe they would reveal more about Gillian in person, rather than by long distance phone calls. They might also tell him where to find Monica, now that Chinatown was gone. Scott couldn't think of anyone else he would rather have at his side when he visited Gillian's grave.

The seventeen-hour flying time from Honolulu finally caught up with Scott. Minutes after showering and crawling into bed, he fell asleep under an island-wide blackout, while a Cuban ship offloaded weapons a mile away.

It felt like moments later when Mommy shook him awake. He glanced at his watch in the glare of her flashlight.

Two o'clock in the morning.

"You have a visitor," she whispered.

CHAPTER
THIRTY-EIGHT

"**W**elcome home, comrade." Lennox's jeans and baggy military shirt hung on his thin frame in the candlelight.

"Man, good to see you." Scott embraced him. "You keep late hours, my friend."

Mommy returned from the kitchen and handed them each a beer. "Lennox is like a son. He worked hard to get Alicia to Cuba." She said goodnight and disappeared into her room.

"What can you tell me about Trini?" Scott gulped his Carib beer, remembering he'd not told Lennox that her real name was Gillian.

But Lennox probably knew nothing, and seemed more preoccupied with other concerns. His hands shook as he lit a cigarette and explained why he'd been recently sacked as an administrator with the ministry of health.

"They accused me of having petite bourgeois tendencies. The anti-Duncan clique enjoys their new cars and swimming pools, but if anyone else has an opinion, they're counters, targets for heavy manners. You're here at a bad time."

"Was there ever a good time? From day one of the revolution, I've had my letters opened and received threats. Why?"

Lennox dragged on the cigarette. "The *Revo* was built on paranoia. And now the people are paranoid about the *Revo*. They ask if the weaponry offloaded from Cuban ships in darkness are to protect, or control the people. Some at the top blame Duncan for the distrust, calling for leadership change to take the revolution on the path to scientific Leninism-Marxism."

"Armstrong, and Oliver?"

"They're planning something. Be careful."

"I'm just a visitor."

"It doesn't matter. Power has intoxicated a lot of people. Distrust is your best friend. Friends will be made to look like enemies, and enemies to look like friends."

A few minutes later, Lennox finished his beer and blew out the candle. "Best for me to leave in the dark. I can't stay in one place too long."

"How do I find you?"

"I'll find you. I might have some information about Gillian."

"Tell me now."

"Too soon. If you don't see me again, find Dr. Pilgrim."

"The old Dr. Pilgrim, or his daughter?"

Lennox hesitated. "Look for the female Dr. Pilgrim at the hospital. Her father teaches at the medical school. A U.S. Marine knocking doors there might raise suspicions. The female Dr. Pilgrim prescribes drugs for mental patients. Use Alicia as the reason to ask for her. Good luck."

Lennox embraced Scott and disappeared into the night.

Scott locked the door. Then a sharp realization jolted him.

How did Lennox know that Trini's real name was Gillian?

***

The next morning, on the way to Gouyave, Scott wondered if Lennox had learned of Trini's real name from Rodney and Oliver, or from health department death records. If records existed, why hadn't Trini's true identity as Gillian Calliste made public? The government newspaper on the nightstand at home still listed Trini among the victims of Gabbard's rule.

Maybe Lennox had discovered her identity because of investigations to prosecute Gabbard and Rabid for their crimes. But if so, why hadn't Scott been contacted, especially since Duncan knew that Scott witnessed Vincent's murder?

Maybe Lennox had more answers. Or the female Dr. Pilgrim.

A loud rally at Queens Park interrupted Scott's thoughts as he drove past. He could neither recognize the speaker on stage, nor distinguish the muffled words amidst the cheering.

He remembered Lennox's warnings, and continued on his way north to Gouyave.

When Mr. Farrow opened his door, Scott felt like he'd never left. They laughed and danced in each other's arms.

"Mr. Farrow, you don't look one day older."

"But you do, me boy." Mr. Farrow moved slower, but smile lines lit up his face. "Man, look at the muscles they put on your bones."

"I miss this." Scott gazed through the window at the sea bobbing fishing boats and chattering seagulls.

They talked, ate, drank, and laughed. And cried.

"I still think about her." Scott took down the picture from the ledge over the bed. Ruby looked more alive in the new glass frame Scott had mailed Mr. Farrow from North Carolina. Her soft smile and long braids had an uncanny resemblance to Gillian, probably the reason Daddy's hand shook when he saw Gillian's picture in Chinatown.

Scott dismissed any connection. After all, Danielle, halfway around the world, also reminded him of Gillian.

"I've waited a long time to give this to you." Mr. Farrow reached below his bed with surprising energy and pulled out a cardboard box containing a filled plastic bag. "Take this back to America with you and study it. Everything is here."

While Mr. Farrow sorted out papers in his bag and separated a cigar can from the stack, Scott turned up a little radio on the table.

A speaker addressed a cheering crowd. "Imperialism is among us to reverse our Glorious Revolution, but we're on the path of historical inevitability."

"That's Armstrong at the Queens Park." Mr. Farrow sat on the bed flipping through pages. "The Communist Doctor, they say."

In a not so veiled attack on Duncan, Armstrong criticized what he called a petite bourgeois conspiracy to roll back the revolution by cozying up to the United States. "We will never let the counter-revolutionaries turn back the gains of the struggle. If it's manners they want, then it's heavy manners they'll—"

A muffled explosion.

Screams.

Then the radio went dead.

"Damn," Scott said. "Sounded like a bomb."

"Quick." Mr. Farrow tied the bag in quick knots. "Take it. It's all about Fédon and your family."

"Why the hurry?"

"You friend Lennox warn me that if anything happens, they be looking for you."

Just then, heavy banging on the door.

Mr. Farrow pushed it open with his crutch. Several soldiers in green military uniform stood outside with AK-47 rifles.

Scott almost didn't recognize the soldier at the front.

"Scott McDonald, in the name of the People's Revolution, you are under arrest for counter revolutionary activities," Martin said.

"Man, I sorry," Martin whispered as he handcuffed Scott and led him to the back of a truck parked on the street.

"Get me the bag," Scott said.

Another soldier overheard him. "The only frigging bag you getting is a body bag, counter."

"Comrade Cunningham say bring all evidence," Martin said.

Martin retrieved the bag from Mr. Farrow and tossed it onto the front seat.

Scott studied the faces of the men sitting on the floor of the truck with him, all handcuffed behind their backs. Some bloodied. He recognized a few, but guards shut them up when they attempted to speak.

Martin drove while one soldier sat up front with him. Two others guarded the prisoners.

The well-orchestrated arrests had obviously started well before the bomb went off at the rally. On the way south toward St. George's, they made several more arrests. On the outskirts of the city, they stopped at a house surrounded by People's Revolutionary Army soldiers.

One of the soldiers approached the truck and spoke to Martin. "He refuse to surrender."

Just then, someone shouted from the house. "Okay. I'm coming out."

Scott twisted around to get a better view from the open-bed truck.

The house door opened and a man stepped out with his hands up. He'd barely made it into the yard when a barrage of AK-47 gunfire cut him down.

Lennox was probably dead before he hit the ground.

An hour later, they drove through the gates of Richmond Hill Prison. The guards separated Scott from the other prisoners, and walked him handcuffed down poorly lit hallways, through rusty gates, and into an office with a commanding view of the harbor.

A leather chair facing the window groaned when the occupant turned to face Scott.

Oliver had swollen into a bearded slob in ill-fitting uniform that stretched the buttonholes at his stomach. A Makarov pistol hung clumsily from a holster at his waist. He chewed on an unlit cigar.

"Well, well. A Gouyave man."

"What's your body count today, Comrade Cunningham?"

Oliver's eyes and lips lurked deep in his bearded face. "Still loaded with sarcasm, I see."

"Chief of National Security? What a joke. Sounds more like national insecurity, shooting a man with his hands up. You had Lennox executed, didn't you?"

"Armstrong escaped, but others were killed by an assassination attempt today. A capitalist bomb."

"Was that your best plan?"

"You made it easy. A Marine agent lands with an invalid passport, spies on our new airport, meets with a counter at two o'clock this morning, and speeds away from the park before the explosion. The case is bulletproof. Your choice, firing squad or the rope."

"Power has warped your brains."

"I knew you'd disgrace the McDonalds like your father did. He was just a drunken murderer. You're a paid Yankee murderer."

"You think you're clean because others do your bloody work? You murdered Lennox. You murdered Trini too. I heard it from Rabid's own rotten mouth. You sold her out to a butcher, you hypocritical snake!"

Oliver's lips quivered.

Scott continued. "If you put Gabbard and Rabid on trial, they'll name you. Is that why you stay up here with them? You made a pact with the devil, and now they have you by the balls, right Comrade Chief."

Oliver stormed around the desk and backhanded Scott across his face.

"You miserable coward!" Scott shouted. "Take these cuffs off so we can settle this man to man." Blood filled his mouth and his pulse pounded his temple. He spat in Oliver's face, and drove his knee into his groin.

Oliver grabbed himself, moaning.

The guard lurched at Scott with his rifle.

Scott stepped aside and, as the guard stumbled, Scott kicked him in the ribs, sending him reeling into Oliver. The two slammed into the desk and crashed to the floor.

Two other guards rushed through the door swinging clubs and overpowering Scott to the floor.

"Put him in the hole," Oliver yelled. "Let the two crabs kill each other."

They dragged Scott down two flights of steps and along a dingy hallway to a heavy door. They removed his cuffs, opened the door, and shoved him into a dark cell. It reeked of body odor and stale urine.

Locks clanged behind him.

A guttural voice crawled from the far corner. "Been waiting long time for you."

Scott lifted his hands and spread his feet in a defensive stance.

A gaunt man crouched out of the darkness. His voice cracked with a distant familiarity, but his pale skin, shaggy hair, and toothless gums still had no name. "I don't fight no more."

They faced each other in an uneasy silence.

"Junior Antoine," the man said finally.

Planass!

Scott grabbed him by the shirt, and slammed him into the wall. "I should break your fucking neck"

"Hate kill me long ago," Planass said. "Don't let it kill you too."

Scott's rage struggled with his growing pity for the delicate man who already looked and smelled like death. "What happened to Trini on independence night?"

"I don't know, I—"

He shook Planass against the wall, surprised at his featherweight and defenselessness. "The truth, dammit!"

"She try to shoot Rabid. He car all shot up. She drown trying to get away."

"Bull shit!"

"She run out of bullets. Rabid beat her up and throw her in the sea."

Scott swallowed hard. "Why did you try to kill me?"

"That was another me."

"Talk, dammit."

"Me mother tell me I have the McDonald curse. She died in hospital last month."

"I hope she didn't die like Mr. Welsh." Scott released him.

Planass slumped as if a weight tortured his shoulders. "I was eight years old."

"What the hell are you talking about?"

"They call me Junior then. He was drunk, break down we door like a mad bull."

"Who?"

"You daddy, Hector."

Planass explained that Daddy had shown up at their house in Belvidere searching for Pa after Ruby died in childbirth. When Junior's mother said she did not know Pa's whereabouts, Daddy, seventeen years-old at the time, grabbed young Junior by the neck and stuck the gun against his head, threatening to shoot him if she did not reveal Pa's whereabouts.

Just then, Junior's father walked into the house. In his drunken rage, Daddy told Junior's father that on the nights the man drove the banana truck to the port, Pa had been sleeping with his wife. Junior's father exploded. He beat Mrs. Antoine to near death and hung himself from a tree in front of Junior.

"All I think about for years was to make you father pay. In Gouyave, you look my age when you daddy did that to me. So I hold the gun to your head to make him see what it look like."

"How did Pa die?"

Planass pulled a soiled sheet of folded paper from under his mattress. "Me writing ain't no good, but it all here. I didn't trust to give it to you cousin."

"Too dark to read in here." Scott slipped it down his sock. "What does it say?"

"I never tell nobody this before. People say Hector kill he father, but I alone know. Your daddy find Pa hiding in the little house on Belvidere Estate."

Scott remembered the cottage on the estate that Claudette had shown him, the day he met Gillian.

Planass said he'd wandered around the estate in tears, traumatized by the night's events, believing that his mother was also dead, when he heard an argument between Daddy and Pa in the little house. Daddy stormed out the front door. Then a shot went off inside. Daddy rushed back in, leaving the door open and affording Planass a clear view into the house.

Pa sat motionless on a chair, a gun dangling in his hand, and the wall behind him splattered in red.

Daddy grabbed the gun from Pa's hand, and was on his knees screaming when Uncle Malcolm ran down from the big house and raced through the door. Uncle Malcolm attacked Daddy, seeing him with the gun and thinking that he'd shot Pa.

They fought on the bloody floor before Ma and Aunty Bridgette could pull them apart.

"There was blood everywhere," Planass said.

Just as Daddy had said that first night in Aunty Bridgette's house, *"He saw me holding the gun. There was blood everywhere."*

"Pa shoot heself. But the family believe you daddy did it," Planass said. "That secret was me revenge. But it poison me. You daddy never kill nobody."

Scott lay on the hard bed trying to comprehend the new compassion he felt for Planass, now in a deep sleep on the other side of the cell. A few minutes of lost temper, and Daddy had triggered a string of events that had ravaged lives and buried secrets for forty years. But if Mr. Farrow's papers contained more secrets about the McDonalds going back to Fédon, Scott might never know. Oliver now had the papers in his bloodstained hands.

Planass had expressed astonishing remorse for his deeds, including his attack on Monica. His life drained from his body in the tears he cried, until he fell asleep in complete exhaustion. Scott could not remember any other reaction he'd held for Planass except fear and anger, but twenty minutes of repentance had erased them.

Scott wondered if Rabid and Gabbard had any such remorse. Planass said they were segregated from the rest of the prisoners. He had not seen them in years. The rumors were that they lived and ate better than anyone else at the prison, which reaffirmed Scott's suspicions that Oliver owed them an allegiance he never owed Planass.

About an hour later, Planass sat up on his bed and stretched with a burst of energy. "My walk is soon."

"Oliver might be disappointed we didn't kill each other."

"You already have you scar from me. I was glad when you brother tell me you okay." He sighed. "Before me mother died, they take me to see she in hospital one last time. She tell me I was a bastard child."

A door slammed and footsteps echoed down the hallway.

"They coming for me," Planass said.

"We'll talk when you come back."

Planass smiled, his thin lips curled into his toothless mouth. "If I was you uncle, how would you call me?"

"Uncle Junior, I guess. Why?"

"I like that. I never had nobody call me Uncle Junior." Planass placed his hand on Scott's shoulder. "Me mother say Pa was me real father. You daddy is me half-brother."

Scott almost tripped over his words. "Then . . . you're Uncle Junior."

Planass smiled again, and for the first time Scott thought he saw a McDonald face peeking from behind the man's torment.

Keys clanked the door open.

Uncle Junior glanced at the guards and back at Scott. "Never hate you brother like I hated mine. You go end up like me, a walking dead."

The guards led him away for his daily walk.

A few minutes later, warning whistles and shouts erupted in the courtyard. A burst of gunfire followed.

Later Scott overheard guards say that the first time they had seen Planass smile was when he was hanging from the barbed wire fence—dead.

✱✱✱

Three days later, Scott gazed around at the half-dozen armed guards and then at Mr. Farrow's papers scattered across Oliver's desk.

"Is this the shit you and old man Farrow's been talking about all these years?" Oliver scooped up a stack of the papers, and fanned them. "What a pathetic joke you've become."

"That's my personal property," Scott said.

"Count your blessings. You escaped the firing squad. Your embassy in Barbados asked us to put you on a plane."

News of arrests and shootings on the island must have leaked out. Scott guessed that Lieutenant Baker and Colonel Blanchard had alerted the chain of command about his detainment.

"But this paper is going up in smoke," Oliver said.

"Destroy one page and I'll write every newspaper from New York to Port-of-Spain exposing you for the fraud you are." He closed his argument with a dig he knew Oliver despised. "And they'll believe me. After all, I *am* your cousin."

The chair groaned as Oliver leaned back and locked his fingers over his belly. "I should have tempted you with escape instead of Planass. Since you didn't kill each other, I gave him a little extra rope on his walk."

Planass must have already resigned himself to what he thought was a merciful end, just waiting to first offload his heavy conscience. Scott had given Planass the absolution to die in peace. But Oliver provided the lax security and bullets.

Scott leaned forward, his handcuffed hands on the desk. "I could rip your big head off your miserable body. You make me want to puke."

"Planass was occupying valuable real estate." Oliver chuckled dryly, his bearded face twitching. "It's long overdue. I need his cell for incoming tenants."

"Incoming tenants? Is that what you call former comrades?"

Scott's suspicions heightened. Duncan's trip to rebuild trust with the United States, coupled with his drift from Marxist-Leninist doctrines clearly threatened Oliver and Armstrong's thirst for power. A deliberate plan was in motion to overthrow Duncan. But had they also planned the assassination attempt at the park to justify the arrests of suspected counter revolutionaries?

Grenada was on the brink of draconian change, and Scott was helpless to stop it.

He slammed his hands on the desk. "Give me my goddamned papers so I can get out of here."

"Your embassy didn't say anything about personal property. The agreement is to get you on the first plane, with your signed promise never to return."

Oliver swept aside some of the pages and placed an official sheet along with a pen in front of Scott. "Sign here."

"Hell no. I'll sign it when I arrive in Barbados with every piece of paper on your desk."

"This pile of illegible shit really means something to you, eh? Maybe that's what you should stick to. Leave the running of the country to those better equipped to do so."

"You preach power to the people, but in practice you just use people to get power."

"You're fortunate I have more important business to attend to." Oliver turned to the guards. "Pack up this junk and get him out of here."

The guards packed each of Mr. Farrow's pages into the bag and removed Scott's handcuffs.

He swung the bag over his shoulder. "Best regards, Comrades."

"Here's your expired passport." Oliver removed a red stamp from his desk and slammed it on several pages of the passport. "It's non-renewable. You'll never set foot on this island again."

Scott fired one parting shot. "By the way, stop congratulating yourself about Planass. You killed your blood uncle. Just ask your parents. They knew, but were too self-righteous to admit it."

***

The Air Cubana plane pulled up in front of the terminal. Standing between two armed People's Revolutionary Army soldiers in the departure lounge of Pearls Airport, Scott gazed out as several people, a few in Grenada military uniforms, disembarked.

A photographer and another man in casual wear approached the plane.

A tall man emerged from the plane and stepped on to the tarmac.

Duncan looked like an aged shadow of the man Scott remembered. Skinnier and gray haired, he drooped as he scanned the empty terminal, probably expecting cheering supporters and a formal welcome after his trip to Washington D.C. For the benefit of the photographer, Duncan shook hands with the reception line made up only of fellow passengers.

When the small contingent moved toward the terminal, Scott recognized Rodney in full military regalia at Duncan's side. With so many years of bad blood between them, he strained to remember the last time he thought of Rodney as his brother.

Rodney broke from the group and marched up to Scott. His pronounced cheekbones, shadows ringing his deep eyes, and missing front tooth surprised Scott.

"I heard about your Richmond Hill stay." Rodney's voice was colder than Scott remembered. "Don't come back. You won't get a second chance."

Scott pointed to the pistol hanging from Rodney's waist. "Why don't you just do it now?"

Rodney turned and headed back to Duncan.

Duncan paused barely twenty feet away, and stared at Scott. The revolutionary fires that once lit Duncan's eyes and captivated Scott ten years earlier were gone. Instead, Duncan's eyes reflected the suffering of a man deceived by his own dream.

Mr. Farrow's words echoed in Scott's head. "Duncan might be on Fédon's revenge list too."

CHAPTER
THIRTY-NINE

Danielle met Scott at the Honolulu airport, in white sleeveless top, tight red shorts, and tennis shoes. She placed an orchid lei around his neck and kissed him. "Not much of a vacation, *oui?*"

He threw his luggage into the trunk of her red Mercedes-Benz 450SL and admired how her tanned legs and jeweled hands maneuvered the car in brisk traffic to a high-rise building overlooking Honolulu. They rode the elevator up to her thirty-sixth floor penthouse apartment, a gift from her Chinese grand-father who had made a bundle with Tahiti hotels. Richly decorated with potted palms, mirrors, and Mexican tiles, the apartment opened onto a balcony with sweeping views of Waikiki Beach and the Koolau Mountains.

After a delicious lunch of smoked-salmon salad and wine, Scott laid his silverware on the empty plate. "Thank you. You're a sweetheart."

"What's the surprise you called me about?"

He unzipped his luggage and stacked Mr. Farrow's papers on Danielle's table, glass top supported by dolphin sculptures.

"A gift from Mr. Farrow," he said. "Most of it is written in French, or Patois."

While Danielle reviewed the pages, Scott phoned Lieutenant Baker. "Thanks for bailing me out of prison. "

"No problem," Lieutenant Baker said. "Your sister called from New York with news of your arrest. I'll pass along your thanks to Colonel Blanchard. Hope you're in good hands."

"I am." He debriefed Lieutenant Baker on his observations in Grenada and hung up.

"This is priceless," Danielle said. "Some of these papers may be more than a hundred and fifty years old."

"Mr. Farrow hid them under his bed for over sixty years."

"This is a doctoral study by itself."

"Can you interpret it?"

"It's what I do every day." She smiled at him. "You must be tired. Get some rest while I organize it."

He showered, and collapsed on her feather mattress. He'd spent four days in Grenada, three of them in prison. His biggest regret was not getting to visit Gillian's burial site. But at least one major gap in his perplexing web of questions was resolved. When he'd called Daddy from Barbados to tell him about Planass' written statement, Daddy sobbed on the phone.

Now everyone knew the truth: Pa had committed suicide in disgrace over Ruby. Clearly, the incident had devastated the family. Maybe now Mr. Farrow's papers might reveal why the family had such an uncanny attraction to tragedy, going back to Fédon.

While one question was put to rest, another rose to take its place.

What information about Gillian did Lennox have before he died? Scott guessed that Dr. Pilgrim's daughter might have learned something from Gillian's autopsy records at the hospital. Calling her now would be risky and pointless. No one in Grenada today would dare divulge information by phone, especially about a murder covered up first by the Gabbard government, and now by Duncan's wobbling regime.

Grief welled up in Scott's eyes, and he drifted into dreams where his past and future danced together to Hawaiian music. Danielle became Gillian, and Gillian became Danielle. Lennox held their hands and led them onto a plane, waving goodbye.

Scott cried out, but only Danielle returned.

He awoke to her cuddled up to him in her bed, with wine-flavored kisses to his lips. "You were moaning in your sleep."

"I'm glad you didn't leave . . . "

She shook her hair free and rolled on top of him with her top off.

Later, lying next to him in bed and fingering his lips, Danielle said, "You called out her name."

He swallowed his embarrassment.

"I have something to show you." She sighed and rolled out of bed.

They showered and changed. She poured two glasses of red wine and insisted they keep them on the kitchen counter rather than on the same table with the neat stacks of Mr. Farrow's papers.

"I'll never forgive myself if these papers are damaged," she said. "Secrets, land deals, and history."

"I'm ready."

"The superstitions about Fédon probably came from his mother's roots." Danielle glanced over her notes on a yellow notepad. "Fédon's grandmother came from the Yoruba people, a proud African nation in areas of what is called Nigeria and Benin today. They have the highest rate of twin births in the world. Fédon's grandmother also had a twin sister. The Yoruba people believe that twins are born with supernatural powers to create health and happiness. But if their temperaments are disturbed, the twins' powers can result in disaster and death. When Fédon's grandmother was kidnapped into slavery and separated from her twin, they believed her powers turned vengeful, and might have carried down to Fédon."

"Go on."

Danielle tapped a pencil on her notepad. "Fédon himself was a plantation owner. But like other plantation owners, he also freed some of his slaves. Probably his own children with slave mothers."

She pointed to documents, signed by Fédon, giving freedom and money to several of his slaves: a mother with six children, two orphaned brothers, and a young girl crippled with polio.

"But we know he also had a bad temper. When his brother died fighting in the rebellion, Fédon had forty-eight of his prisoners executed, including the Governor and a twelve year-old boy. He made his wife and two daughters watch the entire episode. Maybe this started the beliefs that Fédon had inherited a vengeful soul, which still rode his white horse all over the island, hunting his enemies after he escaped."

"No one even knows how or if he escaped," Scott said.

"He did escape." She gingerly lifted a discolored page from the table. "Here it is, written with a quill pen, and dated October 1825 when he was about seventy years old. Some I haven't translated yet, but here are Fédon's own words."

She handed him the notepad with her handwriting in English.

He read it aloud. "*I pray the truth be told. My heart is burdened. When I dispatched the tyrant Governor Home and his Englishmen in front of my family, the day my dear brother was killed in battle, I lost my family as surely as the men crumbled in their bloody pile. The bond of trust, so strong in adversity, yet so vulnerable to betrayal.*

Consumed I was by the injustices of my enemies, I became them.

In a single moment of mercilessness, I lost all that was precious to me. My family's respect. The French lost faith in my ability to lead. The British doubled their resolve never to surrender to me. Seven-thousands of my followers died in the fight for Liberty, Equality, and Fraternity. God has seen fit that my escape be transformed into fear and superstition. I beseech that one day when circumstances are ripe, the people should know how I escaped General McDonald."

Scott stared at Danielle. "Damn. No one knew this. Where did he escape to?"

"I don't know yet, but it also seems Fédon had regrets in later years." She read haltingly. "*If there be but one lesson . . .my shattered life has taught me, whatever seeds you plant in your children today . . . will bear fruit in your grandchildren tomorrow.*"

"Mr. Farrow used to say that today's fruits come from yesterday's seeds. The McDonald curse, fruits blighted today from seeds planted on Mount Qua Qua. But what seeds?"

"General McDonald had a son on Mount Qua Qua, a young officer named Alan," she said. "Something happened up there that turned the general and his son into bitter enemies. The general won the war, but lost his family."

"Mr. Farrow's note is starting to make sense."

"What note?"

Scott told her about the note. *Fédon is dead, but Fédon is alive.* "Mr. Farrow's note was a warning. Whatever happened on Mount Qua Qua that day in 1796 is still alive today and preparing more havoc."

CHAPTER FORTY

Farrow gazed out his window, his thoughts so faint with years of malnourished hopes he could barely wrap his attention around the sound of the car rumbling into the yard next-door.

A car door slammed.

Old age played tricks with his mind again, sending a perfumed mist on hesitant footsteps across the empty carport toward his window.

The mirage drifted closer, with long black hair and smiling eyes. They became as clear as the day he'd first seen Jasmine. What a cruel game for the years to play on him.

"Mr. Farrow?"

Even though back then she'd called him Neil, she still spoke with the pillow softness that had long ago given his cold bones a warm place to rest.

His pulse raced. "Yes?"

He hoped his voice did not reveal his craving for the illusion to be real.

"I'm here from Trinidad," she said. "My grandmother is in the taxi waiting—"

"Your grandmother?"

"You knew her as Jasmine Bhola before—"

Somewhere deep in his abandoned soul, a light clicked on. His world must have jumped ahead a few minutes. He did not remember strapping on his wooden leg, or limping through the doorway and around the house to the yard next door.

An Indian woman stepped out of the car in a lemon-yellow silk sari.

He picked up his pace and melted into her warm embrace, her jingling earrings and bracelets sounding like wedding bells.

He kissed away her tears, and she, his.

***

Farrow gazed at Jasmine seated at his table, his memory stretching around the last sixty years. The day fate had taken away his goat, and delivered Jasmine still flowed vividly in his mind. But then came her pregnancy, and she was gone, shipped to Trinidad. Only a miracle could have returned her now, in the golden sunset of his life.

He handed her Ruby's picture. "Our daughter. She died having our grandbaby."

"So pretty." Jasmine's wrists clinked with Indian bangles.

He glanced at Jasmine's granddaughter seated next to her. "Just like you."

Her granddaughter smiled.

"I have a big family in Trinidad." Jasmine told Farrow that she'd borne three more children after her parents married her off to a Trinidad shop owner twice her age. Her husband had recently passed away, so sixty years and twelve grandchildren later she was back in Grenada to mend her first life. "I should have returned sooner."

"No regrets." He touched her lips with his finger. "You were married. You had a family. You would have lost them."

"Neil, there's something else you need to know."

"What?"

She held his hands. "I delivered two babies for you. Ruby had a twin sister."

***

The car inched through crowds of students, working people, and young men with rifles, in a massive turnout for Prime Minister Duncan, while Farrow sat on the back seat with Jasmine, her hand cradled in his. The radio had announced a week ago that Duncan was placed under house arrest by the Central Committee of the People's Revolutionary Government for attempting to surrender the revolution to American Imperialism. But the people had not fallen for it.

Two hours ago, they stormed the house where Duncan was held captive and rescued him. The crowd carried him up to the fort, named after his late father, and restored him as the only leader of the Grenada Revolution.

The fervor in the air felt like a gathering storm of human passions on a collision course with their government.

One poster in the crowd read, "Fédon's fighting spirit will guide us." Another said, "Fédon is among us."

Farrow detested the repeated attempts by Grenada's leaders to manipulate the Fédon mystique, by claiming him their spiritual ally. Farrow's distrust of political motivations had been nourished in the death trenches of World War I and hardened in the icy jails of Great Britain. It reinforced his tight-lipped protection of the Fédon truth— until he met an inquisitive eight year-old McDonald boy.

Now twenty years later Farrow understood why. Both he and Scott, by fate or chance, had been sentenced to walk two paths in life. One the reality everyone could see and touch, and the other a path tortured with questions, skepticism, and a quest for the pure truth.

What is, isn't. What was, wasn't.

Scott too would soon know the truth, if it weren't already too late.

The car stopped in front of the crowd choking the road to Fort Rupert.

The taxi driver sweated in the noon heat. "I can't go no more."

A hand slapped the roof of the car and an armed soldier peeked into the driver window. "Where you going?"

"To the hospital," the driver said.

"Who sick?"

Farrow recognized the soldier. "Martin, that you, me boy?"

Farrow had not seen him since Martin visited a couple months ago. Martin had come to apologize and explain that Comrade Oliver Cunningham ordered him to arrest Scott after learning of their longtime friendship.

"Mr. Farrow, what you doing in town?"

"Family business. Look like we pick a bad day."

"Nah, we could make it." Martin squeezed his way to the front of the car and sat on the hood with his rifle held above his head. "Make way for hospital traffic!"

The crowd opened up and the car rolled forward. They rounded the corner and drove past the headquarters at the base of the fort. Farrow almost did not recognize the man on the verandah waving at the crowds.

Duncan was all skin and bones.

Martin waved his rifle in the air and Duncan responded with a feeble salute.

They had barely passed the building when people began to scream and run.

Farrow turned around in his seat to view the commotion. Two armored cars, with machine gun turrets, metal windows, and rolling on eight sets of tires, pushed their way through the crowds and pulled to a stop facing the headquarters.

He held his breath, but not for long.

Gunshots. Then the lead armored car opened up with a deafening barrage, exploding a car in front of the headquarters, and raining shrapnel onto the taxi.

Screams.

"Go!" Martin shouted, lying on the hood of the car with his finger on the trigger of his rifle.

The driver stepped on the gas and the car lunged forward.

Farrow pulled Jasmine down on the seat and covered her with his body.

Machine-gun fire.

The rear windshield shattered into powdered glass. The car slammed into the hospital gate, and the horn blew steadily into the screaming frenzy.

Farrow glanced up. The driver sat motionless against the wheel, a jumble of gray and red plastered on the back of his head.

The windshield was gone and Martin was nowhere in sight. The hood where he was lying just seconds ago was covered with blood.

CHAPTER FORTY-ONE

"**S**taff Sergeant McDonald." The duty Corporal banged on Scott's open door.

Scott looked up from the platoon situation report he was completing at his desk. "Yes?"

"Lieutenant Baker wants to see you in his office ASAP!"

Scott dashed across the field to the headquarters building in the late afternoon.

"Grab a chair." Lieutenant Baker leaned forward at his desk and adjusted the dial on his short-wave radio. A Marine Corps emblem dominated the wall behind him, the eagle, globe, and anchor in gold against red matting. "Listen to this."

Scott pulled up a chair.

The radio crackled, and Oliver's voice filled the office. " . . . this is Comrade Cunningham, your Chief of Internal Security. We are under a national emergency. For your protection I have ordered a twenty-four hour curfew. Anyone found on the streets will be shot. Today is another glorious victory for socialism. Our People's Army acted heroically in stopping a plot to roll back the People's Revolution. These petite bourgeoisie conspirators and counter-revolutionaries planned to take away your free benefits like medical care, education, and housing. In the crossfire between our brave soldiers and the counters, several people accidentally died including Roger Duncan . . . "

***

"I just got off the phone with Mommy," Claudette said when Scott finally got past the busy tones around midnight New York time.

He'd thought of calling Mommy directly but decided against it. "Is it true? Duncan?"

"Yes. Alicia is safe on Richmond Hill. Mommy said Rodney came home, grabbed his uniform, and left without a word. She thinks he was reassigned to Pearls Airport. Daddy is also home, flew in after you told him about Planass. A lot of people died."

A tightening in Scott's stomach told him worse lay ahead.

"By the way," Claudette said. "Mr. Farrow and an old lady friend from Trinidad are staying with Mommy and Daddy. They were trapped at the hospital, but Dr. Pilgrim had an assistant drop them off at the house rather than risk the trip back to Gouyave."

"Was Mr. Farrow hurt too? Why were they at the hospital?"

"They were looking for a grave."

***

Under cloudy skies Scott stood at parade rest next to Lieutenant Baker in front of the platoon.

Colonel Blanchard barked somber words in the open field. "Marines, this morning two hundred and fifty of our brothers were slaughtered in their beds by Islamic terrorists in Lebanon. And a Marxist coup on the island of Grenada left many dead and a thousand American medical students in danger under a shoot-to-kill curfew. They could potentially be hostages."

The United States was still seething at the Iranians for taking fifty American Embassy staff hostage in Tehran in 1979, but Scott doubted the new Grenada government would do the same. It would amount to an open invitation for an American attack.

"Gentlemen," the colonel said. "In twenty four hours, we could be either in Beirut or in Grenada."

***

Scott chose his words carefully as he spoke to Danielle on the phone. "We're on alert. I can't say any more."

272

He doubted his platoon would be selected for a Grenada operation, given the proximity of other units on the East coast. But Lieutenant Baker had reminded him that their training on the Hawaiian terrain made them perfectly acclimated for a Grenada invasion.

"Please be careful." Danielle sighed. "I'll miss you."

"I'll miss you too."

In the weeks after returning from Grenada, he'd spent most of his liberty time with her, soaking up sun or walking the beach at night under Honolulu city lights, their desires fueled by wine. But afterward, he would leave her in bed to gaze out over the ocean and to sail his thoughts to Grenada.

She allowed him his distractions, turning her efforts to Mr. Farrow's papers, translating scribbles from French and Patois to English. He'd watched her organize the papers into stacks of plantation accounting, slave purchases and sales, and Fédon's notes, which she had bounded for protection. Her hard work paid off when she received university approval to use the papers as a primary source in her doctoral studies.

Her tight academic schedule kept the translation slow and tedious, but despite hearing that Scott might be leaving, a subdued excitement in her voice suggested that she'd uncovered new details.

"Anything new?" he asked.

"Remember that page I copied for you, about the slave master from Carriacou who moved his slaves to Trinidad in 1797?"

"Yes."

"The name Neil Jude *Fareau* was on the slave list." She spelled out the name. "The same name showed up three more times on other pages, for men born on different dates. It looked like a grandfather, father, and son, all with the same name. It sounds like the French version of Farrow."

"Interesting."

Just then, Lieutenant Baker stepped into the barracks office with an urgent expression on his face.

"I got to go now." Scott hung up the phone.

"Have the platoon fall out in formation," Lieutenant Baker said. "We got orders to link up with the 22nd Marine Amphibious Unit that just sailed from North Carolina. We're headed for Grenada."

CHAPTER FORTY-TWO

Farrow refused to wait any longer. Despite the McDonald's generous insistence that he and Jasmine remain sheltered in their Marryshow Lane house, the radio bombardment of invasion warnings fired the urgency to return to the hospital.

"You can't take her out there," Scott's mother, Gloria, said. "The shoot-to-kill curfew is still on."

Jasmine shifted in her chair. "If we have to go, it's best to do so before the invasion."

Their trip to the hospital five days ago still swirled in Farrow's mind. Machine guns spitting death, the taxi driver's head, explosions, screams, and hospital staff pulling Farrow and Jasmine from the bullet-riddled car. The injured and dying filled rooms and hallways and the air thickened with the nauseating odor of butchered flesh.

Duncan and other supporters had surrendered, but an hour later, another round of gunshots echoed over the hospital.

A few minutes later a woman sprinted into the hospital. "Oh God, they just executed Duncan and his ministers!"

Farrow and Jasmine roamed the halls in a daze, serving water, handing out bandages, and holding hands, until the young Dr. Pilgrim told them it was unsafe for them to remain. She made arrangements for them to spend the curfew night with the McDonalds on Marryshow Lane.

That first curfew night stretched into five. Now it was time to return to the hospital.

Hector, sober and alert, as Farrow had never seen him, walked in on the conversation around the dining room table. "I'll go with you, but we have to make a stop first."

They walked five minutes along the deserted road to a big house overlooking the harbor. Farrow held Jasmine's hand and waited at the bottom of the steps while Hector knocked on the door. Farrow wondered how his crude wooden leg looked next to the white concrete columns leading up to the door.

"Hector!" Oliver's father, Mr. Cunningham, opened the door with surprise plastered on his face. "I heard you're back in—"

"Cut the shit!" Hector snapped. "Call your son and have him send one of his patrols to take us to the hospital. Hurry, we don't have much time."

"Why? There's a curfew—"

"Call, or else we'll start walking. You don't want more blood on Oliver's hands, do you?"

"Now, wait a minute here."

Hector's sister, Hyacinth walked up to the door, her cologne scenting the air over the driveway. "I didn't know you'd returned."

"Ask your husband why he didn't pass along Bridgette's message," Hector shouted. "Or that I called from St. Croix a week ago to tell you about the letter from Planass."

Cunningham attempted to speak. "I can explain—"

"Then explain your cozy deals with Gabbard to get your hands on Belvidere Estate. Explain why you told your son I was a murderer. Explain why you raised him to despise my family. I know everything now. It's in writing. My conscience is clear today. But how are you and Oliver holding up?"

"I don't need to listen—"

Hector glanced at his watch. "Call now or we walk."

Cunningham turned to his wife. "Call Oliver and have him send a car."

Hector pointed his finger at Cunningham. "Tell him to move the patients from the Crazy House if he expects shooting on Richmond Hill. My daughter is also up there."

When the patrol car pulled up ten minutes later with two soldiers, Farrow squeezed into the back seat with Jasmine and Hector.

Only dogs and soldiers walked the city swept by guns and fear. The car drove past the headquarters building, the street and walls now washed clean of blood and flesh, a simpler task than erasing the images from Farrow mind.

He asked the soldiers if they knew Martin. The driver did, but had not seen him since the shootings.

"Mister," the passenger soldier said. "We don't have nothing to do with what happen on the fort. Armstrong kill we revolution."

"So why you still in uniform?" Farrow asked.

"They pull me out of bed before sun up, to defend the homeland against American invasion."

The driver stopped at the hospital entrance. "Fédon must be celebrating. I hear Duncan family was his enemy, like the McDonalds."

"Don't fool youself," the other soldier said. "You too could have their blood in your veins. Planass find out too late he had McDonald blood. Now he and Duncan dead. Nobody safe."

***

Farrow's empathy reached out to the young Dr. Pilgrim. She sat in bloodstained uniform on the hospital verandah bench, her sleeves rolled up to her elbows and the headscarf untidy around her head. Her eyes, probably puffy from fatigue and tears, hid behind dark sunglasses.

She mustered a smile. "Thanks for your help the other day."

"I haven't seen nothing like this since WWI," he said.

"It could get worse with an invasion," she said. "Or maybe without one. I don't know how many died. Duncan's body and others were taken away in trucks. Duncan's girlfriend, Beverly, was among them, pregnant. We lost twelve in emergency, schoolchildren and women. With the curfew, other wounded could be dying in their homes."

Hector walked up with Jasmine. She held a bouquet of flowers, and looked as lovely as Farrow remembered her the day they first met. Only now, her hair hung in long silver braids.

Farrow made the introductions.

"Nice to meet you, Mr. McDonald," Dr. Pilgrim said. "I know your family quite well."

"Your father is lucky to have such a gorgeous daughter follow in his footsteps," Hector said.

"I'm the lucky one," she said in a serious tone.

"How's he doing?"

"With Cuban doctors here, he'd cut back on his practice to teach at the medical school. But we've spent the last few days together in the emergency room."

"Should we look for her now?" Jasmine whispered to Farrow.

"Who are you looking for?" Dr. Pilgrim asked.

"We're trying to find our granddaughter's grave," Farrow said.

"The cemetery is on the other side. I'll show you."

"It's okay. They need you here."

"The walk will do me good. I have my walkie-talkie." Dr. Pilgrim pulled a black radio from her pocket. She led them down wooden stairs to a stone path overlooking the sea, meandering past the end of the hospital to a fenced-in gravesite perfumed by wild flowers. "What's your granddaughter's name?"

"We don't know."

Jasmine explained that she had given birth to twin daughters in 1923, but within days Jasmine's parents had them adopted by Grenadian families. Just before Jasmine's mother passed away, she revealed that the Fergusons in Gouyave had adopted one daughter, while the DeFreitas family in Grenville adopted the other. The Ferguson's adopted daughter Ruby, died in childbirth at seventeen.

"I traced the DeFreitas family to a nurse in Trinidad," Jasmine said. "She told me that my second daughter married a truck driver on Belvidere Estate. She died of TB, and was also buried in the Gouyave Anglican Church cemetery."

Dr. Pilgrim squeezed Jasmine's hand. "So is my mother. . . she also died of TB."

"The nurse in Trinidad said our granddaughter drowned on independence night, and was buried on these grounds."

"Oh my God!" Dr. Pilgrim dropped her radio and covered her mouth with her hands.

"Are you okay?"

Dr. Pilgrim's facial expression froze in jaw-dropping astonishment. She led Jasmine by her hand to a grave beneath a nearby tree. "That's it."

Jasmine stooped over the grave and placed the flowers on the plain stone inscribed *"Our dearly departed Trini."*

"But there's no one buried here," Dr. Pilgrim said.

***

Deep inside the prison, Gabbard sensed the paranoia clawing at those who had snatched power from Duncan just days ago. Gabbard had sweltered in his box for five years, even with the creature comforts he'd squeezed from Cunningham. The leather chair and polished desk, along with private visits from Snyder's daughter, reminded him of his past glory. But his gold-plated clock helped him count the hours before the changing tide returned him to power.

It surprised him though how quickly his prayers had been answered with such blazing finality. Vengeance was just one nail in his plan. He still had to calculate his next move, freedom from Richmond Hill Prison. Cunningham held that key.

Weeks after the revolution, Gabbard had attempted to convince the young imbecile that the best political solution was to exile him and Rabid to another country.

"Your imprisonment pleases the masses," Cunningham said.

"You don't please the masses." Gabbard scolded him. "You lead the masses."

One day Cunningham might be tempted to please the masses with Gabbard hanging from a rope.

As the months stretched into years, Gabbard wrote his own insurance policy: twelve pages of Cunningham's criminal double-dealings. Snyder's daughter smuggled the documents out of prison to an attorney's safe-deposit box in Piccadilly Square, London, with instructions that they be released only on Gabbard's untimely death.

Cunningham steamed when Gabbard handed him his own copy in the cell, but visited a few days ago, after he'd vented his fury, to point out crucial mistakes on the document.

Gabbard had been wrong that Cunningham's information to Rabid had led to Trini's death during the independence celebration.

But dead or alive, Trini no longer mattered. Gabbard was about to craft the most brilliant chapter in Grenada's history, once Cunningham released him and Rabid from Richmond Hill Prison.

***

Dr. Pilgrim had long lost count of the number of times she'd visited the grave and read the inscription *"Our dearly departed Trini."* But the time had finally come to liberate Trini from the façade that started the night Rabid left her for dead.

"This is an empty grave," she said to Jasmine.

A collision of bewilderment and disappointment burdened Jasmine's voice. "So where is she buried?"

In a moment bursting with exhilaration, Dr. Pilgrim helped Jasmine to her feet. "Trini didn't drown. Dr. Pilgrim was parked at the gas station that night. He pulled me barely alive from the harbor—"

"Who . . .I don't understand."

"Dr. Pilgrim and the nuns faked the burial to fool Rabid. Dr. Pilgrim is my adopted father." She pulled off her headscarf and removed her sunglasses. "Don't you see? I'm Trini, your granddaughter. My real name is Gillian."

Gillian dialed the number and waited for Oliver to answer. She almost dropped the phone when the darkness outside her window reverberated from first a screaming jet, and then the thundering response of anti-aircraft batteries on Richmond Hill.

"I am the lucky one," she had told Scott's father earlier. But nothing tonight promised that she would feel the same way tomorrow.

She recalled the times when luck rescued her. Like when Dr. Pilgrim parked his car at the darkened gas station overlooking Chinatown to view the independence fireworks, as the *Federal Palm* sailed out of the harbor with Scott. Rabid roared out from the blinding headlights, slapped away her empty pistol, and hammered her into unconsciousness with his knuckles. He dumped her limp body in the sea and sped off.

But Dr. Pilgrim, alerted by gunshots and screams, waded into the water and plucked her from certain death.

In the following months, he repaired her body while the nuns rebuilt her soul deep in the hidden chambers of the St. George's Roman Catholic Church.

Her secret survived the faked funeral, but Gabbard's despotic rule blocked any hope of escape to Trinidad. So Dr. Pilgrim forged her new identity among foreign students at the St. George's University Medical School.

Far removed from Chinatown, in a world of books and labs, she surrendered her passions to medical school, afraid that even a glance away from the pages might trigger the temptation to contact Scott. She ached for the chance to beg his forgiveness for not telling him the truth. But she feared that if he knew, he would return into Rabid's deadly clutches.

The decaying years of Gabbard's rule finally yielded to revolution and Gillian prepared to hear Scott's voice on the phone. Her new father, in discrete conversations with Scott's mother during hospital visits with Alicia, gleaned precious snippets on Scott's tours with the Marines. He'd gone from North Carolina to Japan, and as close as the American Naval base in Guantanamo Bay, Cuba.

In the days she waited for Scott's mother to return with a phone number, Gillian agonized over how to explain to him that not having him was the price she'd paid for loving him.

His price for loving her was a grief that should never have been.

But days after the revolution, Comrade Oliver Cunningham marched onto the island in Armstrong's shadow, and strangled her anticipation. Reports from Oliver's spies revealed that the plain intern with the head wrap and dark glasses at the hospital was the Chinatown slut he'd once loathed. The one he sold out to save his skin from Rabid in '74.

Maybe power had crushed the remainder of Oliver's pretentious scruples. Overnight he replaced his loathing for her with the same savage obsession that ran in Rabid's veins. Oliver's bearded pronouncements scratched indelible fears: Scott would die if he returned to Grenada.

He did return, and Lennox assured her of his safety the first night. But Lennox's death and Scott's brief imprisonment had taken such a toll that her hospital staff commented on her red eyes and sudden weight loss.

Now that an American invasion seemed certain, Gillian's fears gathered again like storm clouds. Even this phone call to Oliver ignited qualms in her stomach, like only Rabid once did.

"Comrade Cunningham speaking." Panicked shouts and clatter filled the background.

"It's me." She scraped from her voice every ounce of anxiety racing through her. "Thanks for the pass to have Monica drive the McDonalds and Mr. Farrow to Gouyave. I have one final request. We must remove the mental patients before—"

"Have you considered my proposal?"

"Comrade Cunningham, these patients are at risk." The gall Oliver had, asking her to marry him so he would stop the death threats against Scott.

"I hear his father visited you," he said.

"I called to talk about the patients."

"Gabbard knows about you." He chuckled. "But he promised he won't tell Rabid . . .yet. If Rabid gets his hands on you—"

"You're playing with fire."

"Lennox got himself killed, but Scott is alive only because of me."

"I am sure he's grateful," she said with undisguised sarcasm.

"The Yankees might use him in the invasion. He'd be a fool to do it. I'll have twenty assassins looking to take off his head."

The thought that Scott could return with an invasion burned into her temples. She'd already blamed herself for the rift between Rodney and Scott. Now they might be on opposing sides in a war.

She switched her attention from the rising agony to her immediate concern.

"Your guns are traumatizing the patients. If you transport them here, we can keep them safely in the nurses' hostel."

"Without the patients, the fort will become a tempting target. I will not roll out the red carpet for invading Yankees."

"Then let me talk to Armstrong."

"He's busy on the phone with our fraternal brothers at the U.N. and Non-Aligned Movement to block the American aggression. He has no time for hysterical doctors."

She slammed down the phone. If she could not move the patients to safety, then she would bring them tranquility. First, she had to make another call.

She dialed a phone number in Gouyave. "Hi, Bridgette, everybody arrived okay? Good. Yes, please put her on."

The giggling voice on the phone melted her tribulations. "Hi, Mom. The man with the wooden leg is going to tell me a bedtime story."

"His stories will help you sleep, sweetheart."

"Is he really my great-grandfather?"

"Yes Dawn, he is. Call him Papa."

Gillian wished that Rodney would be the one to tell Scott about Dawn.

It wouldn't be easy. But even during these treacherous days, it was the right thing to do.

***

Rodney took another swig from the bottle in the candle-lit room, the numbness from the last few days closing in around him. He'd passed out his final orders to his Pearls Airport soldiers. All there was left to do was wait. The rum burned his throat and settled in a pool of disgust on the floor of his stomach. He slammed the bottle on the table, rattling the Makarov pistol at his elbow.

His pistol, thousands of AK-47s, and a dozen armored personnel carriers across the island, were supposed to protect the masses. This was the reason he'd spent four years in the Guyana jungle and five years in the Army. The revolutionary benefits were for the people, those who toiled for bread and fish. It was what he'd always wanted for his own family on the nights Daddy was nowhere to be found. But in a moment of naked betrayal, the traitors turned the shield into weapons against the people.

But wouldn't the people think that their blood also stained his pistol? He reached for the bottle again.

"Don't drink no more," the woman across the table from him said.

"It's all I have left." The revolution was dead, and so were the people's dreams.

"Sorry it turned out like this for you and your brother."

"Maybe he was right all along. Only Fédon could explain this mess." He stared at the pistol. "He wants me dead. I should have done this a long time ago."

"You sure this is how you want to do it?"

"It's long overdue. If he lands with the Marines, find him before he finds me."

The woman sniffled.

He reached for the bottle. "Time to end this shit."

***

Colonel Blanchard wiped his sweaty bald head in the humid cabin aboard the amphibious assault ship, USS *Guam*, coasting twenty nautical miles off Grenada. "Our mission is to rescue a thousand American medical students and to restore freedom to the people. A few days ago Marxist thugs seized command of the island, executed half the government and shot dozens of civilians."

Scott wished the reality were as simple as this briefing to the platoon leaders.

The colonel turned to him. "Your knowledge of the island will help us save lives. But I understand how tough this must be for you."

How could the colonel possibly understand? Scott had become an imperialist mercenary, returning with American firepower to bury a revolution he once dreamed of.

 "The operational plan is to seize the entire island." The colonel pointed at the wall map. "Army Rangers and 82nd Airborne paratroopers will take the south, entering at Point Salines Airport in the southwest. We are the spearhead for the 22nd Marine Amphibious Unit's seizure of the north, entering here at Pearls Airport. An hour ago, Navy SEALs spotted heavily guarded Soviet and Cuban aircraft around the Pearls terminal. Any questions?"

Scott recalled the day he and Rodney gawked at the welcoming greenery and silver-sand beaches on the plane's approach to Pearls Airport. Now today Scott was attacking it, and Rodney defending it.

Coincidental?

"Colonel, is this a target?" Scott pointed to a red arrow on the southwestern quadrant of the island.

The colonel squinted at the map. "Yes, it's a target for Special Forces. Aerial reconnaissance identified it as a heavily defended military bunker."

"That's a mistake, sir. It's a mental hospital. We call it the Crazy House." The least Scott could do today was to use his knowledge of the island to minimize the loss of innocent lives, including his own sister, Alicia.

The colonel turned to an aide. "Ask Navy Intel to cross-check their info. We sure as hell don't want to be bombing hospitals." The colonel glanced around at the platoon leaders. "Gentlemen, this is not a cinch. We have bad weather, we're relying on tourist maps, we've lost a Navy SEAL team to the sea even before firing a shot, and delays may have already cost us the element of surprise."

Scott wondered if these were ominous signs of more disasters to come.

"Prepare your men," the colonel said. "We lift off in one hour."

An hour later, Scott climbed the ramp of the deafening helicopter. Razor-sharp misgivings slashed at his conscience in the predawn darkness. He had been trained in the Marines to obliterate America's enemies. Nameless, faceless enemies he didn't know.

Until today.

"You know why you're doing this, right?" Lieutenant Baker hollered over the roar of the helicopter's double-rotor blades.

"Too late for reasons, sir." Scott braced his rifle between his knees, buckled himself into the web seat, and adjusted the Ka-Bar combat knife sheathed at his waist.

Seeking relief from the dread saturating his thoughts, he reached into the leg pocket with his shaking fingers and fondled the soft handkerchief.

They had betrayed her. And now they had betrayed the Grenada people.

The moment for retribution was at hand.

Grenada's pain and Gillian's murder would not go unpunished.

It was obvious that Oliver was a key figure in Armstrong's coup, but was Rodney a member of that inner circle? How else had Rodney known about Scott's imprisonment at Richmond Hill Prison even before Duncan and his entourage landed at Pearls Airport?

Scott glanced around at his eighteen-man platoon strapped in along the helicopter's iron-ribbed belly. Their eyes stared out at him from black and green camouflaged faces, hands tightened around rifle stocks, and sweaty jungle fatigues soured the air. The vibrating fuselage rattled a 50-caliber machine gun straddled between Corporal Santana's boots.

The six Sea Knight and two Sea Cobra escort helicopters banked to the left, leaving the amphibious assault ship behind. The helicopters raced toward the island in attack formation, hauling Scott at a hundred knots across a tight-rope of memories. Between a future too treacherous to embrace and a past too painful to claim.

***

Gillian sped up the dark road, urging the car on with rapid gearshifts. The engine's screams deafened any comfort she felt that eight-year old Dawn was safe with the McDonalds, across the street from the Gouyave Anglican Church. She wished she'd contacted Rodney, at least to let him know that Dawn was safe, but all lines to Pearls Airport had been shut down as war closed in on the island.

Her thoughts choked on gunpowder smoke blowing into the car, probably from anti-aircraft guns now silent after a full night shooting at unseen planes. The terror probably sent her mental patients back ten years.

But worse was yet to come.

Clearly, the Americans were watching from the skies, waiting for the right moment to pounce on the Grenada Army. Armstrong and Oliver's reckless bravado and power-hungry ego had finally awakened the wrath of a sleeping tiger. Now, the Grenada people would pay the price.

She check-listed in her mind all that she'd done today in preparation for the inevitable. Earlier, she'd painted her car with white crosses and raced down to the medical school, knocking on every professor's door, searching labs and classrooms for bandages and antibiotics. Back at the hospital, she battled sleep-deprivation as she instructed nurses equally fatigued from the past week. She supervised rooming arrangements at the nurse's hostel, and inventoried the kitchen to ensure the staff and patients had enough food for a few days.

Satisfied there was nothing else to do but wait, she packed a bag of amitrip-tyline and barbiturates, and against the pleas of her staff, had raced out of the hospital gates to visit her mental patients at the Crazy House.

"Dammit!" Gillian's headlights lit up the intersection, blocked by a wall of sand bags, barbed wire, and oil drums. About a dozen soldiers stood guard behind heavy machine guns.

She slowed to a stop.

"Dr. Pilgrim?" A nervous soldier spotted a flashlight at her. "What you doing out here?"

"I have to get medicines to the mental patients."

"I dunno—"

"Should I call Comrade Cunningham?"

"That's okay. Drive slow and keep your lights low."

The soldiers rolled aside a couple of the oil drums and she squeezed the car by, driving slowly up the winding road into the mental home parking lot overlooking Richmond Hill Prison. She stepped out of the car into a cool breeze and gazed around the Fort Frederick hills in the graying morning. Clusters of soldiers murmured in defensive positions, some seated behind double-barreled anti-aircraft guns that stood out against the gray sky.

Guns, so close to her patients. A feeling of powerlessness overwhelmed her. She held the car door and wept.

"Dr. Pilgrim?" The white-clad hospital warden approached her. "I'm glad you came."

She grabbed her satchel and followed him to the back door, drying her tears with her sleeves. He unlocked the door and led her down dark hallways to the reception area.

In shock, she almost dropped her satchel.

Patients huddled on the floor under a dim bulb, holding pillows and each other, some moaning. The room reeked, shut tight behind locked doors and windows. Splattered human waste soiled the walls.

"Boom! Bang!" Alicia sat alone in a corner, her hands busy with her stainless steel knitting needle.

***

"Guard, tell Comrade Cunningham I need to speak to him right away," Gabbard shouted at his prison cell door.

He expected the Americans to invade, but they may not restore him to Mount Royal immediately, for fear of agitating the misguided revolutionary fervor that had overthrown him. He had to make it impossible for the

Americans to say no to him. They had to be convinced that he alone had the skills to command stability in Grenada, just as he'd convinced the British during his labor union riots of 1951. His pride soared as he remembered the British begging him to broadcast a call for an end to the chaos flaming across the island. His radio appeal brought overnight calm and earned him thirty years of power.

Today, he stood on the first rung of another power climb, and this was where young Oliver Cunningham would prove useful.

A salvo of anti-aircraft fire interrupted Gabbard's excitement, almost shutting out the sound of heavy keys clanking at the door. It groaned open and a bloated uniform filled the doorway. "You wanted to talk?"

"Comrade Cunningham. Thanks for coming at such a difficult time." Gabbard glanced at the clock and smiled. His plan was off to a speedy start.

He greeted Cunningham with a handshake and showed Cunningham to the leather chair with a docile wave.

Cunningham's ego swallowed the subservient gesture. He plopped into the chair and laced his fingers. "We're preparing for an imperialist invasion. The masses will never surrender their revolutionary benefits."

The lad saturated his vocal cords in communist gospel, but he did not fool Gabbard. The one thing Gabbard learned behind these bars was that political ideologies were convenient disguises, smoke-and-mirror tools to deceive the powerless. While communism dangled visions of free benefits with one hand, the system tightened chains around the people's necks with the other.

Gabbard did not care about methods, just the players. In this game of power, Gabbard was born to rule. Others, like Rabid and Cunningham, were born to serve. Rabid's value was his eagerness to please with the brute force he brought upon Gabbard's enemies. Cunningham's asset was the inflated self-importance he had inherited from his father, perfect for his role as a pawn.

Gabbard's pawns served him well over the years on the chessboard of his life; the smugglers at La Sagesse, a warning to lawbreakers; Snyder's daughter, for pleasure; Duncan's father, shot in the back to remind mobs that Gabbard, as the undisputed ruler of the island, held their lives in his hands.

Today would be Cunningham's day.

"Comrade Cunningham." Gabbard set the bait. "You stand at the cross-road of great opportunity."

"Yes?"

He first had to show Comrade Cunningham that a new day had dawned, with new rules. For Comrade Cunningham to be a victor rather than victim of the new game, he had to jump Armstrong's political ship. Abandoning one ship for another required a lifeboat. Gabbard would offer himself as Cunningham's lifeboat.

"If international pressure blocks the invasion, you win." Gabbard sat on his bed and crossed his legs. "But if the Americans invade, you can still win. I am the only legally elected head-of-state on the island, so the Americans will look to me to restore normalcy. I'll need a strong leader like you to help me."

Comrade Cunningham salivated at the scent of fresh power, pulling his beard as he gazed out the barred window.

Gabbard recalled the moment his blueprint to regain power had fallen into place. The guards had paused outside of his cell door a few days ago, whispering about Duncan's execution.

One guard said to another, "he died like his father, shot in the back. And Beverly Johnson carrying his unborn child, shot too."

"Me grandmother say Fédon getting revenge," another guard said. "Them McDonalds next."

"But nobody know who have McDonald blood. Look what happen to Planass."

At that moment the plan illuminated with a brilliance that reminded Gabbard of the night he'd switched on Gouyave's electricity. The night Rabid had run over some boy's dog.

Gabbard needed the Americans to beg him like the British had. But he needed a deciding event more compelling than the fires of 1951; and even more magnificent than the massacre on the fort. The follow-up jolt on the heels of Duncan's death had to sow fear that no Grenadian could escape.

Gabbard's most potent weapon of fear was Fédon, and the most fertile ground was in the people's veins. Gabbard intended to ignite the dread simmering just beneath the people's skin, that Fédon still traced his enemies' blood.

And no one knew for sure if they harbored but a single drop of cursed blood, enough to trigger Fédon's ravenous appetite for revenge.

He would launch his moment in Gouyave, Julien Fédon's hometown. In the Anglican Church, once set on fire by lightning. A sign, Gabbard's great-grandmother had said, of Fédon's displeasure that the people failed him.

Gabbard had already deciphered from careless conversations among the guards that McDonalds had been gathering in the house across the street from the Gouyave Anglican Church. The unsuspecting Cunningham would deliver the McDonald flock to the church in the middle of the invasion.

And what might a more powerful Fédon message be than *two generations* of Duncans being shot on a fort?

Of course, *three generations* of McDonalds going up in flames in a church!

The message would transcend words. Neither God nor the Americans could protect the people from the wrath of Fédon.

The people would sizzle from the hellfire of fear, distrust and blame they spat at each other. Only then would they beg him, the forgotten heir of the Fédon legacy, to return to power and relieve their desperation.

Cunningham rose from the chair and headed to the door, obviously still swimming in the delightful possibility of holding the number-two position under Gabbard. "I'll definitely consider your offer."

And Armstrong? Cunningham couldn't have two masters. If the Americans didn't get Armstrong first, Gabbard would serve him up to a vengeful mob, like the Italians did to Mussolini with meat hooks in World War II.

But one final detail still troubled Gabbard. His calculations assured him that with Cunningham, he might have two generations of McDonald blood in the church.

He needed a third generation McDonald.

The younger, the better.

***

Except for occasional jets screaming high overhead, the McDonald household in Gouyave waited in a night as still as the calm before a hurricane, but as tense as a stretched catapult. Farrow sat at the window in Bridgette's house, puffing his pipe and gazing in the darkness at the Anglican Church across the street. So much had changed in the past few days he barely had time to digest it all. But one thing for sure, Grenada was about to change from forces bearing down on the island from two directions, the future and the past.

The sound of soft feet gliding over the wooden floor and a whiff of floral perfume reached him before warm hands embraced his shoulders from behind.

"How's Dawn?" he asked.

"Sleeping soundly after your stories," Jasmine whispered. "But you haven't slept a wink."

"The Americans are coming. Scott too. I could feel it in me bones."

"I was reading more of your letters. I can't put them down. You've waited a long time."

"Some might say two hundred years. Everything changed since we found Gillian and Dawn."

"Yes," she said.

"Dawn changed the past. Gillian changed the future. But anything could go wrong now. It's all in Scott's hands, he just don't know it."

***

"Quickly," Gillian ordered the staff in the lobby of the mental hospital. "Open all the windows. Let's get these patients cleaned up and back to their rooms."

"They won't move," the warden said.

She opened up her satchel. "Pass these pills out, one per patient."

A patient marched up to her, handling a broomstick as if it were a rifle. "I'm a soldier," he said.

"Give him two pills," she said.

The staff hustled the medicated patients into their rooms and began to clean the walls. Gillian grabbed a bucket and headed outside to get water for mopping the floors.

Alicia stood at the door, still knitting. "This is for Dawn's doll."

"Thank you." Gillian hugged her and nodded at the warden. "I'll take her with me."

The fresh air fought back Gillian's growing exhaustion, and cleared her thoughts.

Just then, a loud voice went up over the hillside. "Here they come!"

In the distance over Point Salines, a column of planes flew low in the gray morning, discharging paratroopers. Long blasts of fire shot skywards and explosions shook the island.

On the horizon straight ahead, the first light of day flashed on four black helicopters racing toward Fort Frederick, spitting fire. The fort awoke with a deafening barrage.

Gillian dragged Alicia back into the building and slammed the door shut. The Crazy House shuddered from the bombardment outside and from her patients' deafening screams inside.

If Gillian died that instant, her last wish was for Rodney to tell Scott the truth.

Her little Dawn, safe in the house across the street from the Gouyave Anglican Church, was also a McDonald.

CHAPTER
FORTY-THREE

"Incoming," the crew chief yelled in Scott's helicopter.

Antiaircraft rounds cracked past as bright green tracers from Soviet ZU-23 guns floated skyward into the clouds like strings of Christmas lights. The escorting Cobras returned rocket fire and the door gunner sprayed his machine gun into the darkness below.

They sped over the shoreline and headed inland toward the outskirts of Pearls Airport.

Lieutenant Baker glanced at his watch and elbowed Scott. "Thirty seconds to touchdown."

The helicopter landed with a bounce and the tail ramp fell open. Tropical heat gushed in with the vibration of exploding Cobra rockets. AK-47 rounds pinged the helicopter.

"Let's go!" Scott and his Marines thundered down the ramp.

Scott and Lieutenant Baker charged across the field to seek cover behind a large tree. In the gray light, sporadic bursts of gunfire spat from isolated defensive positions, but quickly ended when the Marines returned fire.

The helicopters lifted off in fuel-scented clouds of leaves and dust. Scott signaled for the platoon to hold their positions and provide covering fire for the second wave of incoming Echo Company helicopters. Three 12.7 mm guns opened up from a nearby hill overlooking the runway. The Sea Cobra attack-helicopters made two firing passes over the Grenadian positions and the hill-side guns fell silent.

"This is almost too spooky," Lieutenant Baker said. "Where the hell's everyone?"

"Could be an ambush ahead." Scott signaled the platoon to move out.

Scott's platoon and an Echo Company platoon advanced toward the airfield along a road that snaked past sugarcane fields. Scott glanced up as a command and control UH-1 helicopter buzzed overhead, followed by two TOW helicopters with anti-tank missiles for close support.

When the control tower and terminal came into view, Lieutenant Baker pulled up alongside Scott. "What do you think, Staff?"

"A few weeks ago, there was a compound with barracks on the far side of the terminal." Scott glanced around, wondering if Rodney had set a welcoming trap for them. "I'll take Sergeant Jones and his squad with me to secure the tower, just in case we have snipers."

The lieutenant grabbed him by the shoulder. "Don't let this get personal. We need you alive. Santana and his squad will back you up."

Scott wondered who would pull the trigger first if he encountered Rodney. Scott trained his platoon, as he had been trained, to dispel emotions that interfere with efficient combat response. He shifted his mind into the focused zone that had steeled him since Parris Island.

With Santana's squad just behind him, he crept up the narrow road toward the light yellow airport terminal. Two planes sat on the runway facing the building: an *Air Cubana* and a Soviet *Aeroflot*. An empty red cigarette pack tumbled along the street. Terminal doors squeaked and banged in the strong breeze.

He inched his way to the main door and held it ajar with his rifle.

Loose papers blew across the floor of the lounge, past an AK-47 rifle standing against a couch piled with green uniforms.

He and Jones cleared the offices, Jones providing cover and Scott rushing in.

More abandoned AK-47s and uniforms.

They made their way up the stairs to the tower. No one.

Scott stepped out on to the landing and radioed the all clear to Lieutenant Baker.

"Let's get the barracks," Lieutenant Baker ordered.

The Echo Company platoon took up supporting positions while Scott led his platoon past the iron gates into a compound of low barracks. He led Santana's squad into the first building, while Harris took another into the second building. The rooms and offices looked deserted, except for discarded uniforms and occasional weapons.

Santana elbowed Scott and pointed down a hallway. A door cracked open and a broomstick protruded with a white t-shirt hanging like a flag.

"Could be a trap," Scott said.

The squad took up firing positions.

Scott called out. "Come out one at a time with your hands in the air."

About a dozen men filed out wearing the black hats worn by *Air Cubana* pilots and crew.

"Cubanos?" Scott asked.

"Si," one answered.

While the rest of the squad patted down and single-filed the Cubans out the door, Scott waved Santana over. "Let them know they're safe. Find out who they flew in from Cuba."

Scott led a search of the remaining barracks while Santana questioned the Cuban airmen.

Without a shot, the Marines occupied the deserted airport and set up defensive parameters as waves of helicopters from the USS *Guam* landed and discharged more Marines on the tarmac.

Scott and Jones headed across the compound to report to Lieutenant Baker, and as they stepped out of the doorway, a cow mooed in the field across from them.

Jones dropped to the ground and locked his rifle sights on the animal.

Scott chuckled. "Go easy, Marine."

"Damn! Scared the shit outa me," Jones said. "We ain't got cows running around in O'Hare Airport."

"You ain't in Chicago, son. Get used to it."

Lieutenant Baker marched up. "Anything?"

"Air Cubana pilots and crew with a white flag."

"Give them full POW rights. Share our water and meals with them until we're re-supplied." Lieutenant Baker pulled Scott aside. "Just got off the radio with the colonel. The Rangers and 82nd in Point Salines are facing stiff opposition from Grenadian and Cuban troops. Fort Frederick is still heavily defended, especially around the mental hospital. It's strange that all the resistance is in the south, and not here in the north."

"Any word about the patients in the mental hospital?" Scott still hadn't told Lieutenant Baker about Alicia.

"No, but there are antiaircraft fire around it."

"Please remind the colonel I was there recently. It was filled with mental patients. Nothing military about it."

"Will do, Staff. What's your assessment here?"

"I believe they staged the rifles and uniforms lying around to make us let down our guards," Scott said. "I think they're waiting in Grenville just south of here."

"The colonel wants us to join Echo and Fox companies in securing the town."

"We may be going house to house, fighting soldiers in civilian clothes. Could be nasty, sir."

"I'm meeting with the company commanders in a few minutes. I'll propose we lead the way in. Get the men ready."

"Aye-aye, sir."

Just then, Santana walked up. "Staff, the Cubans flew in a colonel with a team of advisors yesterday. Hand-picked by Castro himself. They're at the new airport, Point Salines."

"That explains the resistance in the south," Lieutenant Baker said. "Probably with orders from Castro to die fighting."

"One more thing," Santana said. "The pilots said that the Grenadian captain in charge of the barracks here spent last night passing out orders to his troops. They didn't understand all he was saying."

"Did they get his name?" Scott knew the answer before he heard it.

"Captain Rodney McDonald."

***

295

Scott was unprepared for what happened in Grenville. The colonel had approved Lieutenant Baker's plan for his platoon to spearhead the capture of the town, but had demanded that Scott take the number-five position behind Lieutenant Baker. The platoon would move in a staggered column formation to minimize the number of Marines in the kill zone but still close enough to remain a cohesive group in the event of an ambush.

The colonel had some harsh words for Lieutenant Baker after learning that Scott had led the search of the airport.

"Colonel Blanchard chewed my ass out." Lieutenant Baker spread out a laminated Navy map on the tarmac. "He said you wouldn't do him any good from a body bag. He needs your eyes and ears."

To allow them to move swiftly, Scott had the platoon store their heavy packs in the barracks and retain only weapons, ammo, water and medical supplies. They advanced two miles down the winding road under the scorching late morning sun without incident. Lieutenant Baker held the number-three position ahead of Scott on the left while Santana, the machine gunner, patrolled across the street and just up from Scott.

A grazing cow mooed and a few curious dogs barked. Cow dung soured the air.

At the edge of the town, in open windows of small wooden houses, curtains shifted slyly. Telephone and electric lines crisscrossed the skyline. Scott's senses locked onto every sound, every movement. Even his skin felt like it was watching, listening. His finger twitched on the trigger. Roosters crowed. Hens and yellow chicks scratched in dusty front yards.

A door creaked open and chills ran down Scott's neck.

He wheeled around with his M-16 rifle, but released the squeeze on the trigger when he noticed an old man with a cup in his hand. The man held the door with the other hand, cleared his throat, and spat into bushes on the side of his steps. He sat down in the open doorway and sipped from his cup in a steady gaze without any indication that he'd seen eighteen armed Marines patrolling past his front door.

Only then Scott realized that the man was blind.

A big woman with two children waved from their narrow front porch in the next house. "God Bless America!"

A couple applauded from another house. Then there were dozens applauding. Deeper into the town, hundreds more applauded. By the time the platoon reached the seashore at the end of the town, thousands of residents lined both sides of the road in a deafening roar of cheers. Many crowded second story verandahs overhanging the street. Some handed the Marines flowers, while others passed them bottled sweet drinks.

"Talk to me, McDonald." Lieutenant Baker looked nervous. "What the heck's going on?"

Relief found a foothold in Scott's voice. "You're a liberator, Lieutenant. The people are thanking you."

A woman dashed up to Lieutenant Baker and pinched his cheeks. "May God bless your mother's womb!"

***

A couple hours later, an Indian shopkeeper led Scott through a box-cluttered entrance to a black phone on the counter. "Sorry 'bout the mess. Today is the first day I open in five days since the shoot-to-kill curfew."

"Thank you, sir." Scott dialed Mommy's number that Claudette had given him. No answer. He tried again without success. He called Aunty Bridgette's house in Gouyave, but the lines stayed busy, even after several attempts. He wasn't sure what he would have said, except to try to get some assurance that everyone was okay. And maybe find out where Rodney and Oliver were.

But Scott sure as hell couldn't reveal that he was here on the island.

He offered the man a few dollars for using the phone, but the shopkeeper refused to accept any money.

"Allyu save we today," the man said.

Scott returned to the platoon's rest area and collapsed in the shade of a coconut tree along the Grenville seashore. Sweat poured down his face and soaked his fatigues to his back. He took a swig from his canteen and reveled in the afterglow of the warm reception they had received from the Grenville people. Any fear he'd had of being accosted with a sense of betrayal for invading his own country had long since evaporated in the sunny afternoon.

The grateful Grenville residents had turned in soldiers from the People's Revolutionary Army and led the Marines to weapons cached around the town.

None of the surrendering People's Revolutionary Army soldiers knew Rodney's whereabouts. He'd ordered them to return to their homes, saying he didn't want anyone dying for a dead revolution. Rodney had abandoned the airport without a shot.

Did that mean he had nothing to do with the events on the fort? For a fleeting moment Scott wondered if he'd been wrong in his judgments about Rodney.

One thing for sure, people were dying in the south, Grenadian, Cuban, and American soldiers, and most probably innocent civilians. Sadness flowed through him for the grief that lay ahead.

That's when it struck him that he was yet to fire his rifle.

Jones double-timed across the grassy knoll toward him. "Staff, there's a woman asking Fox Company Marines on the street if they know you."

Scott grabbed his rifle and followed Jones back to the street still congested with celebrating residents. Jones pointed out the woman and Scott recognized her immediately. She stood in a loose dress and slippers, her ample bosom and mangled hand just as he remembered.

"Monica," he called out.

She stared blankly for a moment, probably because his face was camouflaged behind sand and green paint. But then the doubting shadow drifted away from her face like clouds floating away from a full moon.

"Scott!" Her smile welcomed him home.

They embraced, and he kissed her on her moist cheek, letting his rifle hang off his shoulder. The last time they had seen each other was the night she'd driven Gillian and him to the Catholic Church to prepare for the boat trip to Trinidad.

She stepped back and cupped his face in her hands. "Just look at you."

He told her about his short-lived visit weeks earlier.

"I heard," she said.

"Planass was very remorseful for what he did to you."

"This stop hurting long ago." She lifted her scarred hand. "As long as my soul is at peace, I have no pain."

"What are you doing here in Grenville?"

She lowered her voice. "You must come with me."

It didn't surprise him that Monica would also want to lead them to People's Revolutionary Army soldiers or weapons.

"Let me get one of my squads," he said.

Fear darkened her eyes. "No, alone."

"Okay," he said. "I'll be right back."

Monica had already saved him twice. This was no time to doubt her.

Scott pulled Lieutenant Baker aside and explained his conversation with Monica. "This could be big."

"I'll have Jones and his squad tail you with a radio, just in case."

Scott slung his rifle over his shoulder and followed Monica away from the crowds, down a narrow alley with barking dogs and toward a small house on the waterfront.

He glanced back up the alley just in time to see Jones and his squad taking up positions. Scott removed his rifle from his shoulder and flipped the switch from safe to semi-automatic.

"You won't need that." She held his hand and led him up a short flight of steps, through a doorway, and into a dim muggy room. The scent of stale rum lingered in the air.

A frazzled man in People's Revolutionary Army uniform sat at the table. His unshaven face sagged and his bloodshot eyes smoldered in a lazy stare at a Makarov pistol in one hand and a bottle of rum in the other.

Scott tightened the grip on his rifle, and aimed. "Drop it."

"No!" Monica stepped between them with her hands up and her eyes watering. "No more blood."

"I didn't ask you here for a shootout." Rodney's voice came from behind Monica. "My pistol is only to ensure you don't take me back to your Marines."

Scott had waited a long time for this moment, but the revulsion he expected seemed to have run out of breath. Something had extinguished his rage. Maybe it was the compassion Rodney showed his troops, sending them home rather than having them die for a lost cause. Maybe it was the picture hanging in Mommy's living room wall of Rodney holding Dr. Pilgrim's little girl's hand, or seeing him now hopelessly defeated.

Scott's anger retreated.

Monica dragged a chair across the wooden floor and waved him over with her deformed hand. "Talk," she pleaded.

"Time for talking ended a long time ago." Scott sat with his rifle still pointed at Rodney and his finger on the trigger.

Rodney turned to Monica. "See how he hates my guts?"

"That surprises you?" Scott asked.

"Go ahead, John Wayne. End it all here and now." Rodney placed the pistol and the bottle on the table and lifted his hands. "You'll be doing me a favor."

Monica leaned toward Rodney. "Tell him what Mr. Farrow said."

Rodney took a swig from the bottle. "I might die today, but I can't go letting you hate me for nothing."

"For nothing?" Scott hammered his fist on the table. "You think Gillian was nothing?"

"She saved my life too. She gave me her place on the ship."

"And you repaid her by getting her killed? Oliver told Rabid who Gillian was. How did he know? You told Oliver, didn't you?"

"I told him you talked in your sleep about Trini and Gillian. Oliver remembered Gillian was Vincent's daughter from the time on Belvidere Estate. I didn't know he was going to blabber his big mouth to Rabid."

"Where is Oliver?"

"He's mine." Rodney picked up his pistol. "Armstrong took off on a Russian fishing trawler last night, probably halfway to Moscow by now. Oliver is running operations from Fort Frederick, with Gabbard and Rabid. While Oliver is ordering his troops to die fighting, he has other plans for himself. Gabbard believes he could get the Americans to restore him to power. He offered Oliver the Acting Prime Minister position."

"They're crazy!"

"Oliver offered me a promotion to join them. I can't wait to get my hands on that son-of-a-bitch."

"Tell him about Mr. Farrow," Monica said to Rodney.

"Is he okay?" Scott asked.

Monica shifted in her chair. "I drive Mr. Farrow and your parents to Gouyave last night. We talk long time. I have a car-pass, so Mr. Farrow asked me to find Rodney up here, and to look for you if you come with the Marines. I was lucky to find you."

"Mr. Farrow knew how much you hate me," Rodney said.

"Get to the point." Scott snapped.

"Daddy spent all his life a haunted man. Mr. Farrow didn't want you living with the McDonald curse over your head too."

"What the hell are you saying?"

"He knew if you killed me without knowing the truth, you would spend your life in worse misery than Daddy."

Scott waited.

"We didn't want you to return to Grenada," Rodney said. "Both Rabid and Oliver wanted you dead. You were lucky at Richmond Hill." Rodney took another drink. "We kept it a secret to keep you alive, to keep you away."

"Who's we? What secret?"

"Her name is Dawn." Rodney handed Scott a small copy of the promotion picture that Scott had seen hanging on Mommy's living room wall. "Mr. Farrow's great grand-daughter. He doesn't want her father to be what Daddy was to us."

"What does this have to do with me?"

"Dawn is your daughter," Rodney said.

Scott pushed back his chair. "Don't bullshit with me!"

"Gillian was pregnant before you left Grenada. She's alive."

"You've been drinking too goddamned much."

"It's true," Monica said. "Rodney was the best uncle Dawn could have. Gillian wanted him to tell you."

"Is this a sick joke?" Shockwaves ran through Scott.

"Trust me." Monica explained how Dr. Pilgrim had rescued Gillian. She also detailed how Mr. Farrow discovered that Gillian was the daughter of Ruby's twin sister, and therefore Mr. Farrow's granddaughter.

"It can't be!" He shook his head, wanting it to be true, but fearing that this surreal moment was another of his crazy dreams.

He had to see her to believe. The thought rippled through him, arousing starving desires to hear her mischievous laugh, to feel her moist lips on his, to be held captive in her presence. How could so many years of agony and grief turn out to be just a fabric of flawed reality in his mind?

Scott stood in a daze and walked around to Rodney. He lifted him by his shoulders and embraced the brother he'd damned, but never stopped needing since those days in Gouyave.

Years of misplaced rage poured out of their shaking bodies like a broken dam, one in People's Revolutionary Army uniform, and the other in U.S. Marine Corps uniform.

"Take me to Gillian." Scott said. "Where is she?"

"Fort Frederick, in the Crazy House."

∗∗∗

"Marines, we're going to Fort Frederick," Scott shouted to the platoon on the Pearls Airport tarmac over the scream of helicopters. The sign above him, erected by Fox Company Marines that morning, read *Marine Corps Air Base Douglas*, in honor of a Sergeant Major killed in his sleep days earlier in the Beirut Barracks bombing. "We'll accompany Golf Company. We'll be facing Soviet BTR-60 Armored Personnel Carriers, ZU-23 anti-aircraft guns, 82 mm mortars, and AK-47s."

Lieutenant Baker explained that the focus of the invasion had shifted to the south. Marines had already lost two pilots in a badly planned attack on the fort. Having lost the element of surprise, the pilots raced into a barrage of hell fire with the sun in their faces. The Governor General was trapped with a SEAL team in the official Government House, taking fire from all sides by People's Revolutionary Army soldiers with heavy machine guns and Soviet Armored Cars. The 82nd Airborne was pinned down in Point Salines, and another SEAL team had retreated from a plan to seize a communications terminal after a well-executed People's Revolutionary Army counter-attack in Beauséjour.

"Staff Sergeant McDonald just received reliable intelligence," Lieutenant Baker said. "Fort Frederick is the brain of the Grenada resistance under the command of a Soviet trained political officer named Comrade Cunningham. We will seize the command center and capture him alive, if possible."

"We have enough naval gunfire offshore to turn that fort into a parking lot," Scott said. "But there's a hospital and civilian houses outside the walls. The command post is underground, protected by solid stone walls two hundred years old. Our only option is boots on the ground. Our boots."

***

Gillian sat with fifteen patients on a backroom floor, the room darkened by mattresses stacked against the windows to protect against explosions. The barbiturates had calmed the patients and some even dozed during breaks in the firing, which started at sunrise, nine hours ago. The remaining patients occupied other rooms with hospital staff.

She had last peeked out about an hour ago, only to see a smoking helicopter nosedive into the harbor. The soldiers on Fort Frederick had put up a ferocious fight, and the helicopter attacks stopped.

She was debating whether to take advantage of this latest break in the fighting to offer assistance to any wounded on the fort when shooting broke out in the parking area.

"Put that down and get back in here now," the warden shouted.

Gillian pushed the mattress aside and stared out.

The patient who earlier had carried a broomstick now stood in the parking lot firing a rifle into the air.

Gillian raced out the doorway to the man. "Please, let me have that."

"I'm a soldier." He stopped firing. "This one is mine. Get your own." He pointed at other rifles scattered across the parking lot.

She looked around for soldiers to help her. Anti-aircraft guns sat abandoned around the hillsides pointing upward, their dual barrels still smoking. The door behind her pushed open and about a dozen patients raced onto the parking lot and grabbed rifles.

"Those are not ours," she shouted. "Leave them where they are."

They must not have heard her over the sound of a helicopter racing overhead. They turned their attention upward and blasted their rifles at the helicopter. The patients laughed and ran back into the building with the weapons.

Surely the Americans would now think that soldiers had overtaken the mental home. She gazed around once more, thinking maybe she should evacuate the patients. But where to, and how?

In the distance the afternoon sun glistened on the wings of two jets banking low on the horizon. They turned and roared toward Fort Frederick.

***

Scott's CH-46 helicopter veered right off the southern tip of Point Salines Airport and raced north toward Fort Frederick. The Marines strained to see the action at Point Salines through the portholes, but Scott's sights remained glued on the picture Rodney had given him.

The lieutenant returned from a cockpit radio briefing with the colonel and sat next to Scott. "Who are they?" He pointed at the picture.

Scott handed it to him, surprised at the pride that swelled in him. "My brother and my daughter."

"I didn't know you had a daughter."

"Just found out."

"And her mother?"

"She's in Fort Frederick, a doctor attending to the mental patients."

"Looks like they already evacuated the hospital." Lieutenant Baker handed him back the picture. "People's Revolutionary Army soldiers now occupy the compound. The colonel's last aerial reconnaissance reported that Grenadian soldiers in civilian clothes were shooting at our helicopters."

Just then, the crew chief hollered from up front. "Get ready to see some action starboard. Looks like our A-7 Corsairs flyboys from the USS *Independence* are going to take out Fort Frederick."

Scott caught sight of the jets as they sped inland. Bombs dropped, and the Crazy House disappeared in an exploding mushroom of smoke and dust.

The two-pronged helicopter landings on Fort Frederick started less than fifteen minutes after the bombing, the longest fifteen minutes in Scott's life. His helicopter raced through the smoke rising from the hospital and set down on flat terrain overlooking Fort Frederick, while Golf Company Marines roared in on other Sea Knight helicopters a hundred yards to the south to neutralize the prison and command center.

Scott and his platoon thundered down the ramp and spread out across a knoll covered with low shrubs. The Sea Knights immediately lifted and headed back to sea to wait in a circle pattern in case of an urgent evacuation order.

"Let Harris take point," Lieutenant Baker said to Scott. "Stay with me."

Scott suspected that Lieutenant Baker wanted to be the first to face Scott's rage if it turned out that patients were still in the hospital. They spread out and moved cautiously downhill toward the smoking rubble. Scott stayed with Lieutenant Baker and the radioman.

A black car sped off down the hill.

"Hold your fire," Scott shouted. "Could be civilians."

As they prepared to cross the street into parking area, a civilian jumped the wall and ran towards them holding his head. "You bomb the Crazy House!"

Scott called the man over. "Were patients in there?"

"What you think? It's a damn hospital."

Despair began to claw in his stomach. "But . . .but who were shooting at the helicopters?"

"Them crazy men that found guns lying around. Them soldiers gone long time. All you bomb a hospital." The man ran down the street bawling.

Scott bolted across the parking lot toward the smoking building. Several men lay contorted on the gravel surface next to strewn bricks and AK-47s. A bloodied leg, still wearing a slipper. A man without a face. Some people sat under trees holding their heads and sobbing. Half of the hospital's top floor was demolished and thick smoke spiraled out of windows.

Panic boiled in Scott's chest.

A gray-haired man in whites stumbled over to him. "You killed my patients."

"We thought the hospital was evacuated."

"It's too late for explanations. We need help to save people still in there."

Lieutenant Baker signaled the radioman. "We'll get all the help you need."

"Do you know if Dr. Pilgrim and Alicia are still in there?" Scott asked the man.

The man shook his head. "I don't know what happened to Alicia. But Dr. Pilgrim is gone."

Scott grabbed the man by the collar. "Gone . . . dead?"

"No. They took her away in a black Maxima a few minutes ago... with another girl covered in dust. Could be Alicia."

"Who took them?"

"Comrade Cunningham, with Gabbard and Rabid."

Scott listened to the colonel's cold voice on the radio. "Lieutenant, I want those men. Especially the number one target. I want that commie son-of-a-bitch to explain why we have a hospital without proper markings in a combat zone. Over."

"Ready to move, over."

"Is Staff with you? Over."

"Affirmative, over."

"Marine, you were right and I was wrong. There's nothing more I can say. Rescue on the way. Transport returning as we speak. Don't come back until you get them. Out."

CHAPTER
FORTY-FOUR

Gabbard studied the way Rabid sped around the corners with one hand controlling the wheel and a gun in the other. Rabid had not lost his driving skills even after five years in prison. A sure sign that Rabid had also not forgotten his most prized abilities: to follow Gabbard's every instruction without delay.

Explosions echoed in the city behind them.

"Boom," the McDonald girl said. "Bang."

"Shut her up." Rabid lifted his gun. "Or I will."

"Shhh." Dr. Pilgrim stroked the girl's head.

What a pity. Both beautiful, but disposable in the game of power.

Gabbard grinned at his genius. It had not surprised him when Comrade Cunningham led Gabbard and Rabid out of their prison cells to an underground communications center. With aircraft screaming overhead and rockets exploding around the fort, Cunningham embraced Gabbard's plan, especially when news came that Armstrong had fled the island and People's Revolutionary Army soldiers were deserting by the hundreds. Comrade Cunningham even agreed with Gabbard that they needed women in the car to pass like a family fleeing St. George's battles for the safe countryside.

But when Gabbard suggested that McDonald relatives might be their best guarantee into Gouyave, he had to contain his glee at Comrade Cunningham's immediate response. "We have one right here in the Crazy House, under Dr. Pilgrim's care."

Rabid flew into a rage when Oliver revealed that Dr. Pilgrim was actually Gillian, the Trini Rabid thought had been dead all these years. He was ready to ransack the hospital to find her, but roaring jets and the loudest explosions yet drew them up two flights of steps to a window.

The smoldering mental hospital almost dashed Gabbard's hopes.

But once again, manifest destiny intervened.

Cunningham sped them in his official car up the hill to the hospital. Rabid rammed the back door with his shoulders and rushed out a few minutes later dragging the two women covered in soot.

"Get your hands off me," Dr. Pilgrim yelled. "I have injured people in there."

Rabid growled. "Shut up before I take your head off this time."

"I want them alive," Gabbard shouted. "Let's go."

"What about the patients?" Dr. Pilgrim pleaded.

"Let the Americans save them."

They shoved the women into the car and raced off just as the helicopters landed.

So, while war raged to the south, Gabbard headed north to harvest fear in the hearts of the country people.

Gabbard glanced back at his passengers, Cunningham and the McDonald girl at the windows and Dr. Pilgrim in the middle. In a few hours Gabbard planned to tell her the reason she was forced to abandon her bombed hospital, but by then it would be too late.

She turned to Cunningham. "Whatever you're planning, it's not going to work."

"Don't try anything stupid." Rabid held the gun above his shoulder, even as he spun the car around the White Gun corner and headed toward the Government House.

"The Americans will put you right back in Richmond Hill Prison," she yelled.

"Shadup!" Rabid shouted.

"Enough." Cunningham elbowed her and stared ahead, tugging at his Castro-want-to-be beard.

"Take us to the General Hospital," Dr. Pilgrim said. "Alicia's behavior could be unpredictable if she doesn't get her medication soon."

Gabbard resisted the temptation to tell her that Alicia would no longer need any medication. A hint of a smile lifted one side of his face.

At the main gate to the Government House, smoke rose from two burnt-out armored cars. Several bodies lay in pools of blood on the roadside. A group of soldiers in prone positions fired into the house on the hill.

Rabid turned down Tempe to River Road and then right on to the western road toward Gouyave.

Explosions far to the south vibrated the car, but Alicia kept her sight on her knitting. "Boom. Bang."

"Hit the gas!" Gabbard said ten minutes later pointing out to sea at landing crafts racing into Grand Mal Bay from a huge ship offshore.

Rabid gunned the engine and the tires squealed as they sped north past the bay.

"Marines," Cunningham said.

Alicia slowly lifted her head from her knitting for the first time. "My brother is a Marine."

"You lucky you still have you brother." Rabid sniggered. "I shoot you dogs, I will shoot him too."

"Just drive." The last thing Gabbard needed was aggravation while he rehearsed the coming events.

All the pieces were in place. He had the three in the back seat and a houseful of McDonalds waiting in Gouyave across the street from the Anglican Church, including the final jewel to crown Gabbard's blueprint for power.

Cunningham had revealed that Dr. Pilgrim's eight-year-old daughter was also a McDonald.

Three generations.

How shocked Comrade Cunningham would be to learn that his own gull-ibility had betrayed him.

In less than two hours, under the cover of darkness he and Rabid would hustle the McDonalds, including Comrade Cunningham, at gunpoint into the church with the cans of gasoline in the car trunk. By dawn, Gouyave would awaken to the realization that a mysterious church fire had decimated the McDonald clan.

First the Duncans on a fort, and now the McDonalds in a church.

Who next had the tainted blood of Fédon's enemies? No one would feel safe, even in a fort or a church.

The panic would ricochet across the island, igniting blame and distrust, and like in 1951, he would stoke the fires. In the midst of mayhem, truth will flee, leaving the stage bare for Gabbard to proclaim himself the last remaining blood of Fédon, the chosen one to save the people from the fear boiling in their veins. The Americans would be forced to open the gates for Gabbard's grand entrance.

Even Fédon would have cowered at Gabbard's genius.

A helicopter roared overhead for a couple of miles, headed out to sea and turned north toward Gouyave.

Doubts scratched at Gabbard's confidence. He stopped smiling.

They passed Palmiste Beach and rounded Mabuya corner, to a full view of Gouyave. Gabbard's excitement revived for a second in his chest, but stuck in his throat at the sight ahead.

Dust rose around a helicopter in the middle of the park. Troops stampeded out the back, raced out of the gates, past a truck, and took up positions along the road.

"Marines!" Cunningham said.

"Pull off the road and squeeze past the truck," Gabbard ordered.

A Marine stepped into the street, waving a rifle.

"That's my brother," Alicia yelled.

"Run him over," Gabbard shouted.

"You shot my dog, now you want to kill my brother?"

"Shut her up!" Rabid stepped on the gas and the car sped toward the Marine.

The Marine jumped aside and the car sped past.

"Boom!" Alicia swung her fist and sank the stainless steel knitting needle deep into Rabid's neck. "Bang!"

Rabid's scream gurgled out of his mouth. He released the wheel and grabbed at his throat. His leg stiffened against the gas pedal and the car lunged forward.

Gabbard turned ahead just in time to see the back of the parked truck charging through the windshield at him.

CHAPTER FORTY-FIVE

Scott signaled for cover and eased his way through the brush toward the driver's side, his heart pounding. He glanced into the car trunk, flown open on impact. AK-47 rifles and gasoline cans. The crumpled front half of the car groaned under the weight of the truck. Steam hissed from the car engine block. A nauseating odor of blood and gasoline thickened the air.

He peeked into the car.

No movement. He recognized Rabid slumped over the wheel, his hairy arms dangling past his knees. A headless torso sat upright next to him, squashed between the truck and the passenger seat. Blood streamed from the neck.

Blood and debris covered Oliver in the back seat. He sat hunched over with Gabbard's bloodied head on his lap, its eyes opened wide, like camera lenses capturing the moment of death. Two girls sat next to Oliver, covered in soot, unrecognizable, and not moving.

Scott tugged at the back door, jammed solid. He rammed his breaching bar against it and the door swung free. Gabbard's head fell off Oliver's lap to the car floor with a thud. Oliver groaned and collapsed out the open doorway, his beard dripping red.

Scott gave the all clear. Two Marines rushed over and carried the unconscious Oliver over the embankment to the shade along the river, where the Navy Corpsman was setting up emergency gear.

Scott reached into car toward the girl slumped over in the middle, her face hidden by a headscarf.

She moaned.

His heart raced.

He lifted her out of the car and carried her toward the tree line, shouting at Jones. "Get the other girl."

She stirred and pulled off her headscarf.

He stared at her dusty face and stumbled to his knees under the tree.

Wanting to believe, but still resisting the urge to do so, he held her in his lap, took the headscarf from her hand, and wiped her face with it.

The glimmer in her eyes quickly spread into a smile across her face and full lips.

"It's me my love," Gillian said.

His military bearing took flight in a state of semi-consciousness as his lips met hers. Only when he inhaled her breath, warm with the life he'd craved on so many lonely nights, did he know for sure she was not his imagination. The grief dam broke and, in a moment of magical healing, washed away nine years of anguish. Her laughing cries electrified his soul and strummed musical strings in his heart. Afraid she would vanish from his life again he held her in a tight embrace, their bodies in a spasm of emotional release.

"Holy shit!" Lieutenant Baker hollered from where he stood with Sergeant Harris on the bed of the truck, tugging at a dark green tarp and exposing stacks of wooden boxes. "This truck is loaded with explosives. Staff Sergeant McDonald, get the others out before it blows."

Scott leapt to his feet.

"Hurry," Gillian whispered. "Alicia's in the car. Be careful."

He sprinted toward the car where Jones was tugging at Alicia's door. "She's my sister."

They forced open the door and helped her out.

"Bang." Alicia pointed her finger like a gun at Scott. "Now you have to buy me a new needle. Rabid took mine."

After Jones led her back to the tree, Scott kicked the car door to get Rabid's attention.

Even with his broken feet entangled among the floor pedals, the wheel crushing his chest, and the needle protruding from his bleeding neck, Rabid's snarl was unmistakable. "Gimme a fucking cigarette."

Scott pushed the muzzle of his rifle against Rabid's head. "How about a slug instead?"

Rabid rolled his eyes. "I shoulda finish you . . . when I had me chance."

"You blew your chance. When you were looking for me in '74, I was sleeping in Trini's bed. And the night you murdered Vincent in La Sagesse? I saw you from the trees next to the truck."

Rabid coughed, and blood sprayed on the wheel. He turned away, facing Gabbard's headless torso.

"Say hi to your boss," Scott said.

Lieutenant Baker walked up to the car. "What's the holdup?"

"He needs a cigarette."

Lieutenant Baker squinted at Scott. "Be straight with me, Staff."

"We hit the jackpot. The one missing the head was the old dictator. The driver was his secret police chief. He needs a smoke."

"What are you saying?"

"There's not much hope for him. If we try to save him, one spark and we're worm meat. I hate to refuse a dying man's wish for a cigarette."

"Let him have his wish." Lieutenant Baker turned and shouted. "Take cover. This shit could blow any second."

"Make sure the ladies are well covered." Scott grabbed a cigarette and lighter from Jones and waited until everyone was out of sight. He stuck the cigarette between Rabid's lips, and placed the lighter on the dashboard, where Rabid would have to stretch to reach it. "See you in hell."

Scott raced over the embankment to Gillian.

She sniffled. "Forgive me."

"For staying alive and giving me a daughter?" He kissed her. "I've never stopped loving you."

Her eyes seemed to reach out to him and he kissed her.

They embraced and waited. They'd both wished for Rabid's demise years ago. She'd almost gotten killed trying to shoot the henchman. Now that it looked like this was Rabid's final day, the moments ticked by slowly—too slowly.

"What's taking so long, Staff?" Jones asked.

Scott crawled up the embankment. No movement in the car.

Rabid should have gotten the lighter by now. There was no way he could have escaped the car. Maybe he died before he reached the lighter.

Santana chuckled. "Jones gave you a messed up lighter, Staff."

"If it's a light he needs, here it is." Scott aimed his rifle at the gasoline cans in the trunk of the car and squeezed the trigger for the first time that day.

A ball of yellow flame enveloped the car. Seconds later the truck erupted in a massive explosion that shook the ground where they lay, discharging a gush of warm air and debris over them.

Scott glanced around at everyone dusting off.

Everyone except Oliver. He was gone.

"Escaped prisoner!" Scott yelled. "Spread out. He's got to be close."

They trampled the brush along the riverbank and scanned the smoke-filled pasture.

Jones pointed toward Gouyave. "Maybe he escaped into that town."

"I hope not," Gillian said. "He has no friends there."

Thirty minutes after the search began Lieutenant Baker rushed up to Scott. "We have a situation on the road."

Scott pulled Jones aside. "You're responsible for the girls. If they get even a scratch, I'll kick your ass from Gouyave to Chicago. Understand?"

Jones grinned. "Aye aye, sir."

Scott raced after Lieutenant Baker past the burning wreckage and across the bridge to the road leading into the town. A crowd of about a hundred people, several with rifles, filled the street.

A Grenadian boy about sixteen years old marched up to Scott with an AK-47 rifle pointed in the air. He chewed a blade of grass in his mouth and spat on the road. "Hold it there, Yankee. We don't want no war in Gouyave. That's town people business."

Scott handed his helmet and rifle to one of the Marines standing next to him. "We're not here to hurt anyone. I'm a Gouyaveman too."

"No frigging Gouyaveman is Marine."

"I used to live next door to Mr. Farrow. McDonald is the name. I went to school in the fish market on the Lance with Martin."

Murmurs floated through the crowd. Another armed boy stepped forward. "*Bonjai*, you Captain McDonald brother?"

"Yes."

"Who side you on, anyway?"

"Yours. I don't want anyone here getting hurt."

Loud voices rose from the street behind the crowd.

"Coming through, coming through!" Martin squeezed his way to the front, a rifle in one arm, the other wrapped in white.

Scott embraced his friend.

Martin returned the hug. "Welcome home again, me friend."

"You okay?" Scott pointed at his arm.

"Just a scratch," Martin said. "Last time I saw you, you shoulder was shot up, and you looked like shit."

Scott shook his head. "I still look like shit, but now we have another problem here."

"How many times I go tell you don't do nothing without talking to me." He turned to the armed boys. "This is me . . .*my* friend. We don't need no guns. Leave them on the side and go home. *Revo* dead. War done."

"You came in good time."

"Always. We have somebody for you." Martin waved his rifle in the air.

The crowd parted and a few people from the back pushed forward, leading Oliver by a rope. He shuffled forward, barefoot and bareback, his belly hanging over his pants, and his arms tied behind his back.

"They already had the rope around his neck in the market. Rodney save he ass with this." Martin pulled a Makarov pistol from his waist and handed it to Scott. "He ask me to give it to you. He say he fighting days done."

Oliver growled. "This is not over."

"It's just beginning for you, Comrade," Scott said.

Later, Scott gazed up at the helicopter carrying Oliver to the USS *Guam*. It lifted above Cuthbert Peters Park and raced over the smoldering wreckage into the sunset. Maybe Oliver would receive justice he never granted others. Scott tried to feel empathy for his cousin, but all he had left were echoes of the bitter years between them, and the thought of the ultimate betrayal of the Grenada people's trust in their leaders.

People had died during the invasion too, most innocent. War had always been a tragedy, especially for civilians. He wondered how many more would have died without the American intervention. But actual deaths weighed heavier on the pages of history than unknown numbers of lives saved.

He hoped his fellow Marines and soldiers remembered the people's gratitude, even after those on ivory towers began to rewrite history with their pompous intellectual hindsight, a luxury no man on the battlefield could afford.

He returned his thoughts to Gillian, and the daughter he was yet to meet. The elation he felt for them looped with the fear, fatigue, and uncertainty of the past twelve hours. Martin had arranged a ride to get Gillian and Alicia to Aunty Bridgette's house, where Monica and Uncle Malcolm waited to take the household up to the safety of Belvidere Estate.

There was so much to talk to Gillian about, so many lost moments to make up for. With sporadic fighting continuing across the island, Scott had no idea how soon he would see her again.

He watched from the shore as Golf Company Marines rolled in with a column of armored amphibious vehicles after landing at Grand Mal Bay just north of St. George's. They left a platoon in Gouyave and continued north to Victoria without incident.

Just then, Lieutenant Baker walked up. "We have new orders." He explained that while ninety percent of the island had been secured, and the American students safely evacuated, the Army still faced fierce resistance around Point Salines Airport. The colonel wanted an observation post to call in remote fire on the southwestern quadrant of the island. "He thinks Mount Qua Qua is a good choice, but he wants your input."

"He's right. Even Fédon chose Mount Qua Qua back in 1795."

"He wants us in place by sunrise. What's the fastest way to get there?"

Scott could barely disguise his glee. "Through Belvidere Estate, of course."

"We need a truck," Scott said when Martin returned to the park to report that the family was on the way to Belvidere Estate.

"Truck? For what?"

"I can't tell you, my friend."

"Armstrong soldiers leave one on Back Street, but them Yankee Marines stopping everybody tonight. I climb through bush to get here."

"I'll get a squad and we'll come with you."

The moonlit walk through Gouyave revived recollections of Scott's boyhood days. People sat in doorways, most with welcoming words to the Marines.

Coal pot aromas spiced the air and waves crashed on the shore. Gouyave's past always seemed to be in a dance with its present. With electricity out, the people had dusted off their kerosene lamps. Yellow light waved in open windows, flickering on his memories of magical nights when *la diablesse* frightened drunks off precipices and when Mr. Farrow's stories tantalized Scott's imagination.

But while the secrets surrounding Planass, Ruby, and Pa had finally found a resting place in Scott's memory, one puzzle remained that only Mr. Farrow could explain.

Fédon is dead, but Fédon is alive.

They found the truck on Back Street and Scott gave Martin a farewell embrace. "Remind Rodney he's free as long as he is not armed or trying to reorganize his troops."

Scott drove back to the park, loaded up the platoon with their gear, and headed up the dark winding road to Belvidere. Thirty minutes later, they pulled up in front of the estate house.

The headlights lit up Mr. Farrow, seated on the verandah next to a woman with long silver hair.

Scott leaped from the truck and rushed up the steps. He embraced Mr. Farrow and shook the woman's hand.

"Gillian told me everything," Scott said. "You are her grandparents."

"Jasmine and I met sixty years ago," Mr. Farrow said. "She had twins for us. Gillian's mother and Ruby."

Jasmine smiled. "Actually we met sixty-two years ago."

Scott came to Mr. Farrow's rescue. "He's better at remembering older dates, like two-hundred years."

Just then Daddy and Mommy stepped onto the verandah, holding hands. The last time Scott had seen him was the day he'd left St. Croix for the Marines. At first Daddy stared at him in the lamp light with no recognition in his eyes. But when Mommy called out Scott's name, Daddy broke into a smile and the eight years that separated father and son vanished.

"You camping here?" Daddy asked after the hugs and tears.

"Just for a couple hours. The men need a little R&R before we leave. Where's Gillian and Dawn?"

"They're bathing," Mommy said. "They'll be down soon."

.The boisterous gathering on the verandah soon included Alicia, Aunty Bridgette, Uncle Malcolm, and two of his sons. The platoon dismounted from the truck and mingled on the steps. Scott had just finished introducing the family to the platoon when Gillian stepped on to the verandah with Dawn.

Scott's world came to attention.

Gillian wore a thin flowered dress that hugged the figure Scott had replayed in his dreams for all those years. Her curly hair shiny black, and cut just above her shoulders. Her smooth skin glazed deep ebony in the flaming *flambeau* light, and her eyes held an inviting twinkle.

Dawn, in matching pink sweater, pants and sandals, ran up to Scott, thick braids bouncing off her back.

"My name is Dawn." She smiled, revealing a missing front tooth. "You look like my Uncle Rodney. Are you my Daddy?"

Her words washed over him in a moment of pure joy.

"Yes." His lips trembled. "Forever."

"You need a bath," Dawn said.

Scott laughed. "Yes, I do, but it'll be worse when I return in a couple days." He hoisted her on to his shoulders and kissed Gillian.

Uncle Malcolm's wife peeked out. "Okay everyone, we have a war, but we still have a lot to be thankful for. Food and drinks inside for everyone."

Mr. Farrow limped up to Scott. "Tonight I will have answers for all your questions . . . and more."

CHAPTER FORTY-SIX

Mr. Farrow's pipe-smoke flavored the night air as torch flames from the *flambeau* licked at the star-drenched sky and reflected yellow on the bald crown of his head. He shared a bench with Jasmine, while everyone else sat where they could, on chairs, the banister, or the steps. Scott pulled up a chair next to Gillian after she'd put Dawn to bed. When Uncle Malcolm insisted that the platoon have a shot of rum for the occasion, Lieutenant Baker arranged for them to share a bottle of sherry instead, served in eighteen mini paper cups. He assigned a Marine from each of the squads to patrol the estate grounds, now peppered with flashing fireflies.

Monica had hinted that Rodney might show up too, so Scott instructed those on watch to look out for him. He could not imagine the turmoil Rodney, a People's Revolutionary Army captain, must have endured since Duncan's execution.

Mr. Farrow dragged on his pipe and gazed around at his audience. "Julien Fédon once owned this estate."

> *". . . conveying unto and to the use of the said Julien Fédon his Heirs and Assigns for ever a certain Coffee and Cocoa plantation Tract or parcel of Land in the parish of Saint John called Belvidere . . . by Admeasurement Four hundred and fifty Acres of Land...With the property came "the buildings thereon and eighty Slaves, Sixteen head of horned Cattle and five horses . . ."*

Mr. Farrow explained that Fédon was the *mulatto* son of a French father and a *negresse libre creole* mother, daughter of a Yoruba slave. As a French free-colored man, Fédon was allowed to own property and slaves in Grenada. His Belvidere Estate, one of the largest on the island, had about a hundred slaves, including others he brought from another estate he previously owned.

By 1783, Grenada had exchanged hands at least four times, the last time from French to British. The French angrily resisted British rule, complaining that even if the British landed first in 1609, it was French blood that succeeded in driving the indigenous Indians to their suicidal demise off Leapers Hill in Sauteurs. Whatever wealth Grenada returned to Great Britain, considerable during those years, it came from French plantation ownership and slave sweat.

Julien Fédon shared the French sentiment, even though he had signed the Declaration of Loyalty to Great Britain in 1790. By then, the French Revolution had begun to spread the ideals of liberty, equality, fraternity to Haiti. Many Haitian free-colored land and slave owners initially wanted equality, but not the abolition of slavery. In 1791, a Haitian slave rebellion led to burning, looting, and to the slaughter of many land owners, including some free-colored slave owners.

Mr. Farrow sucked on his pipe. "The French revolutionaries saw how effective slave revolts could be as a weapon."

The revolutionaries promised freedom to those who fought with them, first against the French whites who resisted the new ideals, and then against the British in Haiti.

On the retreat in Haiti, the British shifted their focus to Martinique, which they captured in 1794, much to the chagrin of the French revolutionaries.

Mr. Farrow gazed around at his audience. "Grenada was a ripe opportunity for the French to even the score."

The French population in Grenada had faced years of persecution under British rule, particularly along religious lines. The British whites in Grenada, in response to the repression they faced under French rule, seized French Catholic Church properties and even voided Catholic marriages, baptisms, and burials.

The slave population in Grenada, ever restive to seek freedom from the odious brutality of slavery, and French-leaning in their language and loyalties, proved the ideal weapon to strike at the British.

But, as the revolutionaries learned in Haiti, spontaneous slave rebellions from the field led to unpredictable and catastrophic consequences for human life and economic property. To be effective as a weapon, a slave rebellion had to be guided by a strong and charismatic leader committed to an overall military objective.

Mr. Farrow paused to relight his pipe. "That's where Julien Fédon came in."

"Did Fédon and the French agree to join forces?" Scott asked.

"Yes," Mr. Farrow said. "They supplied him with French soldiers, weapons, and a military rank, Commandant-General of the French Republican Forces. That's how he signed his name on the letter calling on the British in St. George's to surrender."

The rebellion started at midnight on March 2, 1795 with attacks on Gouyave and Grenville. Fédon led the Grenville attack, where British citizens were pulled from their homes and killed in the streets. Gouyave, more French than Grenville, was spared bloodshed that night.

Over seven thousand slaves, runaway maroons, mulattoes, and French settlers showed up on Belvidere Estate to join the rebellion. The estate became Fédon's main base and food supply.

"They killed ten cows a day to feed everybody," Mr. Farrow said.

Fédon took over the entire island except St. George's. He fortified a base two miles up the mountain and named it Fédon Camp, where stone walls still remained. But he built his headquarters another mile further up at the top of a mountain in the clouds. Mount Qua Qua.

The British put General Archibald McDonald in charge of crushing the rebellion. It lasted for almost a year and a half.

"It was brutal, on both sides." Mr. Farrow said.

Fédon captured the British Lieutenant-Governor, Ninian Home, and fifty others in Gouyave. But when Fédon's brother was killed during an attack by General McDonald and his soldiers, Fédon executed forty-eight of his prisoners, including two of General McDonald's cousins and a twelve-year-old boy.

"Fédon had a temper," Mr. Farrow said.

With one grief-driven decision in the throes of his brother's death, Fédon threw away his strongest bargaining chip, fueled his reputation for brutality, and reinforced General McDonald's resolve to never surrender.

"By the way," Mr. Farrow said to Scott. "Fédon's brother was killed on the same spot where your grandfather built his cottage behind this great house."

And, as Scott recalled from his conversation with Planass, the same place Pa had shot himself and the same cottage where Daddy and Uncle Malcolm had almost killed each other. *There was blood everywhere.* Scott recalled the night he first heard Daddy slur those words.

The executions also undermined French confidence in Fédon. They had sent a ship the previous day to take the prisoners to Guadalupe for safekeeping and to be used in eventual negotiations with General McDonald.

"The brutality also shocked Fédon's family," Mr. Farrow said. "He made his wife and daughters watch the killings."

The death of Fédon's brother and his executions of the British prisoners turned the fighting personal between Julien Fédon and General McDonald.

British hands were also stained with blood. Many rebellious slaves and French mulattoes were hanged by the British in the St. George's Market Square. Fourteen had their heads chopped off and stuck on poles as a warning to the rebels.

"Seven thousand died during the rebellion, from fighting, bulam fever, and starvation."

One out of every four Grenadians, Scott calculated silently.

Fédon used clever tactics to win a few significant battles across the island. He reversed the shoes on his horses to deceive the general and left rum for incoming British soldiers whenever the revolutionaries abandoned a post. French regular soldiers, increasingly weary of Fédon's fiery leadership style, fought their own battles against the British.

Mr. Farrow said that General McDonald studied Fédon's tactics and prepared his own. He landed reinforcements on Palmiste Beach and marched up to Belvidere. One night, the British left their campfires burning around Belvidere to deceive the revolutionaries into believing they were still encamped. But throughout the night, they slowly crawled forward and encircled Fédon Camp. By daybreak, it was captured.

Fédon escaped to Mount Qua Qua with some of his rebels. He ordered all his prisoners killed, then, rather than surrender to General McDonald, most of the rebels jumped off the mountain to their deaths.

"On reaching the camp an hour ago a most distressing spectacle awaited us: upwards of twenty prisoners, stripped, with their hands tied behind their backs, having but recently been murdered in the most barbarous manner. The wretches

held prisoner on this summit tonight will suffer the same fate to send a clear message across this island."

"This is where one war end and another start," Mr. Farrow said. "General McDonald had a son fighting at his side, a Captain. The general had promised his son that after the rebels surrender, no more bloodshed. But General McDonald also had a bad temper."

"Search patrol reporting back, sir," the captain reported.

"Come in, Captain. Did you find Fédon?"

"No, sir. He's not with the dead we found at the foot of the cliffs. He must still be up here among the prisoners."

"Let's find out." General McDonald stood and adjusted his red waistcoat, crossed at the chest with white leather belts. Gold epaulettes hung at the shoulders. His black top boots crunched on the dirt floor as he headed for the doorway. "Bring along one of those machetes. The sharpest you can find."

The captain hesitated.

"Let's go, Captain. This isn't over until we find Fédon."

The captain picked up a machete and followed the general into the misty twilight. Steady winds moaned through the trees. Beneath a nearby tree, about thirty rebel prisoners lay huddled in a pile of human misery. Loyal Black Rangers, barefooted Africans in red coats and blue trousers, stood guard holding muskets fixed with bayonets.

"Bring me that boy." The general pointed at a young rebel prisoner, no more than sixteen, dressed in a tattered pair of trousers, his hands bound at his back. Dried blood caked one side of his head and his sweaty black skin glistened in the light of flaming torches.

An African ranger walked over and prodded the young prisoner with his bayonet.

The boy struggled to his feet in obvious pain and limped ahead of the guard towards the general. He lowered his head and fixed his gaze on the general's boots.

The general barked. "Where is Fédon?"

The boy held his slumped posture in silence.

"Tell me where your leader is hiding, boy, and you're all free to be slaves again."

The boy looked up slowly and nodded at the remaining prisoners. "They go too, oui?"

"Yes," the general shouted. "All of you can go. But speak before I change my mind."

The boy glanced at the general and the captain with a meek grin. "You look father and son."

"I am losing my patience, boy."

"I tell you, and you promise we free go?"

The general stomped his boot and hissed. "Yes, that's what I said."

"Winds." The boy stared up in wide-eyed wonder at the cluster of swaying trees. "Winds…winds take Fédon. Fédon fly in wind."

"What in the name of King George is this savage mumbling about?"

"Sir," said the captain. "They've all been saying that. Something about Fédon disappearing in the winds."

"What African superstitious rubbish. I've heard enough. Off with his head, Captain."

"But you said—"

"Just do as you're ordered."

"But sir, must I act contrary to my passions?"

"Your only passions are to King and Country, son."

The guard slammed the butt of his musket on young rebel's back and knocked him to his knees in front of the general.

Tears streamed down the boy's cheeks. "You lie. Fédon punish all of you."

The general moved back three paces. "Off with his head, Captain, or you'll face a court martial."

The captain held the machete stiffly at his leg. "But Father, you—"

The boy stared up at the captain. "Fédon will pain you and all your kind many years. Winds come back with Fédon—"

"Captain," the general yelled. "This is your last chance. Off with his head, now!"

The captain stepped forward with a full swing of the machete. The boy's torso tumbled over in a spray of blood and the severed head rolled to a stop at the general's boots.

The captain's hands shook in their grip on the machete.

"Control your nerves, son. It's going to be a long night." The general turned to the colonel. "Pass this order down the ranks. By the powers granted me by His Excellency the Governor, anyone heard in superstitious utterances about Fédon and winds shall suffer the loss of their heads."

"Yes, sir." The colonel saluted and marched off.

General McDonald turned to the guard. "Bring me another prisoner!"

"They never found Fédon." Mr. Farrow puffed his pipe. "He vanished just like that. And stories started about his powers. I know Scott still remembered some."

Scott glanced around at the group. "Some believed he escaped by using African powers to swim under the island from Grand Étang Lake to Black Bay. As a boy I heard that he still used to ride the island on his white stallion. You could hear it and feel the wind as he rode by, but you could never see it."

"The stories spread by word of mouth," Mr. Farrow said. "*Sa key tan parlay lutte.*"

"What happened to the general and his son after Mount Qua Qua?" Gillian asked.

"They took over Belvidere Estate and ran it as a family," Mr. Farrow said. "The slaves heard a lot of drunken fights between them. But the worse didn't come for twelve more years."

Mr. Farrow explained that Fédon had a trusted rebel officer and friend named Jacque Chadeau, who also owned a plantation before the rebellion. He evaded capture until one of his women betrayed him in 1808. Still seething over Fédon's disappearance, General McDonald hanged Chadeau and left him to rot on his rope in Cherry Hill.

Two months later, the general received a letter from Cuba:

"Tyrant McDonald,

You take away my friend Chadeau. Today I take away your son. You sent him to find me on Mount Qua Qua. And find me he did.

He does not have the thirst for blood that you and I have. You had him take the head of one too many. For that, your son delivered me to freedom. I am free and alive. But your hell is just beginning.

Julien Fédon."

Lieutenant Baker spoke up for the first time. "The general's own son helped Fédon escape?"

"Yes." Mr. Farrow said that the general's son arranged to have a boat with a compass hidden in a secret location for him. Fédon made it to Carriacou, Trinidad, and finally to Cuba.

When the general confronted his son with the letter, the younger McDonald hanged himself from a tree in the old Fédon Camp. Soon, the general's wife left him and returned to England. He became a drunk and his other sons took over the estate. One night, the general was riding home alone, drunk, but only the horse made it back to the estate. They found him two days later on the river rocks below a bridge. Some people said Fédon's stallion scared the general's horse, which then threw him off to his death.

The general's remaining sons blamed each other for his death and fought bitterly over ownership of the estate. The infighting flourished and spread roots into following generations.

"Both Fédon and McDonald lost," Gillian said.

"Yes," Mr. Farrow said. "They lost everything they valued. Fédon died a lonely man in Cuba and the Fédon name vanished from the islands. General McDonald's descendants remained on the island, but they fought each other for two-hundred years."

"The McDonald curse?" Scott asked, finally understanding how the Mount Qua Qua events could have ricocheted pain and distrust down eight generations of McDonalds. "By the way Mr. Farrow, you never explained that note you sent me. *Fédon is dead, but Fédon is alive.*"

"Fédon the man is dead, but Fédon the lesson is always alive. The lesson of trust. Broken trust comes in many disguises. Inhumanity, like slavery, is broken trust. Dishonor between men and in families is broken trust. It leads to rebellions, wars, and divided families."

"Why didn't you just tell me all this before?"

"Some lessons are learned better when you feel them, than when you hear them."

"So how does one stop this cycle from affecting future generations?" Lieutenant Baker asked.

Mr. Farrow drew on his pipe and turned to Lieutenant Baker. "Truth and forgiveness, me boy. Forgiveness heals the forgiver. Truth unburdens the forgiven. The one causing the pain tell the truth with repentance. The one feeling the pain must forgive. What happened on Fort George last week could start another two-hundred years of agony, unless they bring both truth and forgiveness to the table."

Scott reached into his pocket and pulled a folded page that Danielle had given him in Hawaii. "Do you know who Marryshow Lane was named after?"

"It is the English spelling of a French *Creole* named Maricheau." Mr. Farrow spelled out the French spelling. "In those days, many people changed their French names to English-spelling names."

"Like Farrow?" Scott handed the page to Mr. Farrow. "This is a copy from the papers you gave me. Fédon says here that he and his family were taken to Trinidad from Carriacou, smuggled aboard the ship as slaves, their skin darkened by charcoal soot. The slave master was a Frenchman named Fareau."

"Yes. Fareau." Mr. Farrow spelled the letters. "His slaves took his name."

"Your family became Fareaus too. But when your grandfather moved to Grenada he changed it to Farrow to sound English, right?"

"Yes. The British hated everything French. My grandfather changed his name to Farrow and returned with the hidden papers written in French. He got a job as a janitor at the courthouse and found more papers that he copied by hand. His own son, my dying father, spent his last shilling to visit me in jail in England to tell me where to find the papers."

"Where did he hide the papers?" Scott asked.

"Under the floor in the Gouyave Anglican Church. That was twenty years after lightning burned it down. He said lightning rarely strike the same place twice. And the British will never look for anything French in their own church. He was right."

"Clever," said Lieutenant Baker.

"My father said never show nobody the papers until the time was right. To only pass it to a son. I never had a son, and I was just a one-legged dishonored soldier. No one would believe me. So I needed somebody I could trust."

Mr. Farrow turned to face Scott in the light. "I trusted you since that day you and your daddy came to my window. You was the trusted son I never had."

Scott tried to find words to thank Mr. Farrow, but he knew his silent smile carried more weight than words to the old man.

Scott cleared his throat. "Your father's first and middle names was also Neil Jude, just like yours. And so were the first sons in your family, going back to 1812. Why?"

"Take the first two letters from Jude, and the backward spelling of Neil. *Ju* plus *lien* is *Julien*. To remind us to deliver the Julien Fédon papers when the time was right."

"Whose idea was that?"

"My great great-grandfather."

"And who was your great great-grandfather?"

"Julien Fédon."

Two hours later, the platoon geared up under the starry sky for the climb to Mount Qua Qua. Scott held Gillian as they stood on the steps watching the moonrise over the mountain ridge. "Today is the luckiest day of my life," he said.

She kissed him. "My heart feels like a butterfly flapping its wings for the first time."

Just then, Dawn pushed open the door rubbing her eyes and trailing a blanket. She ran up to Gillian. "I can't sleep, Mommy."

"Daddy has to go," Gillian said. "Say goodbye."

She turned up big sad eyes at Scott. "Where are you going?"

"For a long walk with my friends," Scott said. "But I'll be back."

Dawn stared at the platoon. "Are they going to take a shower too when they get back? I could spray them with the water hose."

Scott laughed "Listen up, Marines! How many of you would like to have this young lady hose you down when we return?"

Every hand shot up, followed by cheers.

"Especially Jones," Santana said.

"Great," Scott said to Dawn. "You have a job when I get back."

"Promise?"

"I promise," he said.

She patted the tip of his nose with her index finger. "I love you."

"I love you too."

"Okay, back to bed." Gillian took Dawn by her hand.

Scott kissed them both and watched them disappear into the house.

The all-powerful revengeful Fédon that lived in the people's superstitions would never have given them Dawn, a flower of Bhola, McDonald, and Fédon petals.

Mr. Farrow placed his hand on Scott's shoulder. "So what next?"

Scott tugged at his uniform. "My enlistment ends in a few months. It's time I come home. I have the best family and grand-father-in law to come back to."

Mr. Farrow laughed. "But you not married."

"I asked tonight, she said yes. We have a request."

"Yes?"

"When she walks into the church, she wants her name to be Gillian Fédon."

"A McDonald marrying a Fédon." Mr. Farrow shook Scott's hand. "Now we learned the lessons of our fore parents, it's time we unshackle the burdens and pains they passed us."

"Yes, we have our own to carry." Scott strapped on his gear and checked his rifle. "Okay Marines, let's roll."

Lieutenant Baker asked him to take the point position since he'd climbed Mount Qua Qua before. Scott led the way around the back of the house, past the old cottage where Pa had spent his last night in guilt-ridden torture, and where Fédon's brother had died almost two-hundred years ago.

Just then, a figure in a white t-shirt and jeans stepped out of the shadows and into the moonlight sprinkling through the trees.

Scott signaled a halt. "Dawn was asking for her Uncle Rodney."

"She won't have to look far." Rodney's deep-set eyes stared without blinking in the gray light. "Quite a story Mr. Farrow had."

"Where were you?"

He tugged at the lobe of his bad ear. "Close enough to hear."

Scott wondered how Rodney had evaded the Marine guards. "Yeah, quite a story. And lessons too."

"Maybe we should find Martin and do some fishing before you leave the island."

"If you cook your favorite fish broth," Scott said.

"We have a deal. Take good care of yourself. And your men too."

Just then a cool wind blew through the trees. Scott shut his eyes and took a deep breath.

After two-hundred years of enmity, betrayal, and fear, the bloodlines of Belvidere finally flowed as one.

ABOUT THE AUTHOR

Dunbar Campbell is a writer, public speaker, director of a research group, and a former U.S. Marine.

His earliest writing skills were honed in danger when, as a teen-aged student activist growing up during turbulent years on the Caribbean island of Grenada, he contributed to and distributed antigovernment newspapers in support of a revolutionary movement. When secret police brutally crushed the organization, Campbell migrated to the United States and enlisted in the U.S. Marines.

The revolutionary group eventually reorganized under the leadership of Maurice Bishop and overthrew the government in the 1979 revolution. Another violent coup in 1983 led to Prime Minister Bishop's execution and the U.S. invasion of Grenada.

Among Grenada documents the U.S. military seized and stored at the National Archives is a passionate letter of congratulations to Prime Minister Bishop, written four years earlier and mailed from halfway around the world in Hawaii. It was signed *Dunbar Campbell, U.S. Marines.*

Campbell is a certified scuba diver and runs an occasional marathon. He has a bachelor's degree in political science/economics and a master's degree in economics.

He channels into his writings the dangers, secrets, and intrigues that shaped his life.

Made in the USA
San Bernardino, CA
03 April 2015